New Year's Through the Looking Glass

THE LOOKING GLASS SERIES
BOOK ONE

J.G. SAUER

New Year's Through the Looking Glass Copyright 2018 © Joni Sauer-Folger

Cover art by Dar Albert at Wicked Smart Designs

Map Design by Diane Kreider

Published by Oliver-Heber Books

0 9 8 7 6 5 4 3 2 1

Acknowledgments

As always, thanks to my CP, Liz Lipperman for her friendship, encouragement, and tough love when I need it. You stick with me through thick and thin, and I love you, my friend. A huge shout out goes to my long-time buddy, Natalie Bellissimo for challenging me, supporting me, and for your enthusiasm (even though this isn't your genre), and of course, your eagle-eyed editing skills. A very special thanks to Melissa Jenck, my fantasy barometer. I'm not sure this story would've been the same without you, pal! And finally, to my outstanding beta-readers: Melissa Jenck, Val 'Valine' Braun, Georga Dorsey, Diane 'Temptress #3' Cross, Cara Mico, and Roberta Bettis—Love you guys sooooo much and couldn't do it without you...

Map

CANTILEY MNT RANGE
ARCTIC OCEAN
NORTHERN WASTELANDS
THE UNWELCOMING RISE
WILLOW GLEN WOOD
WESTERN SEA
EASTERN GLADE
N
E
W
S
ROSELAND WOOD
TARKINGTON FOREST
EASTERN BARRENS
LARKSPUR MEADOW
ROSELAND
CHESHIRE WOOD
WYSTERIA
SOUTHERN OCEAN HORN
REALM of ARTEMYSIA
COURTS
EVENING
KALEB'S CABIN
TWILIGHT
WHITE PALACE
STARLIGHT
RED PALACE
DAYLIGHT
DAWN
TEMPLE OF ORACLES
WINTER
SPRING
AUTUMN
SUMMER

One

Realm of Artemysia
Mid-December

Outside the enormous, arched stone windows of the passageway, the pristine snow fell silently, covering the palace courtyards and surrounding landscape in an enchanting haze of white. The holiday season had descended on the Kingdom of Wysteria, but the tall, handsome man dressed in royal garb of black and gold paid it no mind as he strode with purpose toward his mother's chambers, his dark gaze intent, his mind on the meeting he'd just left.

Prince Graydon Edward Christian Hartford was a dutiful son, and when the White Queen summoned, he would always answer the call, but her timing could have been better.

The security wards protecting the kingdom and the subjects therein had been ... faltering in recent months. There was little concern at first, as the occurrences seemed random enough—like the flickering of electricity during a storm in that other earthly realm. But when it was discovered—a bit too late for Gray's liking —that the wards were being systematically tested by an outside intruder, security had been beefed up immediately and the magick of the wards increased, strengthened. But the heart of the matter was that someone was looking for a way around them—or to sabotage them in order to cross into Wysteria without detection.

And there was no doubt in Gray's mind who that somebody was, that the attempted violation was at the behest of Wysteria's enemy—King Aramond of Roseland.

Aramond had been the consort of Gray's aunt, Queen Renata —better known as the terrible Red Queen—prior to her death, and had taken the throne by force upon her passing. He'd been on a mission to destroy Wysteria since that time, blaming Gray's mother, Queen Beatrice, for being handed a defeat in war, as well as her sister's descent into madness, and ultimately, death. This had not been the first sly attack on Wysteria—and it wouldn't be the last.

The heated discussion between his myriad of counsellors, Horace Solkolov—Wysteria's Minister of Defense, and Field Marshal Alexi Tovin—Gray's first in command had been brewing for several months, since they'd first discovered the attacks on the protective wards. It had finally come to a boil this afternoon when word had reached them of an actual breach.

"I don't think that we should go off the deep end here," one of the queen's advisors had suggested. "After all, this was a small incursion, and quite brief. No one was injured."

"You can't be serious," Alexi had growled, the very tips of his pointed elven ears growing red with his annoyance. "There were no injuries ... this time. But if we don't act, and act quickly, mark my words, the next time there will be."

The advisor had scoffed at the notion. "We don't know that for certain. The wards are strong and have been reinforced after this latest incident."

The warrior's face had been grim when he'd replied in a dangerously quiet voice, "Make no mistake, these incursions will only escalate from here. This is Aramond's insidious work, and he won't stop until he either conquers or destroys this kingdom."

That was the one thought which kept Gray up at night. He

agreed with Alexi wholeheartedly—and not out of any sort of loyalty. The Elven commander may have been Gray's oldest friend and close as any sibling, but he'd earned the title he now carried and was a trusted ally. He was as shrewd and discerning as they came, a fierce warrior. And he was right. Something had to be done to protect the people of Wysteria from the threat Aramond posed.

When the queen's page had interrupted the heated exchange with the summons, Gray had tasked the group with coming up with plausible options in his absence to correct the security of the wards and stem the growing hostilities with Aramond's forces to the west. He feared that any brief opening in a remote area of the kingdom was all it would take to compromise them entirely. Knowing Aramond's cruelty, and his hatred for the White Queen, the results would be devastating ... and deadly.

Putting those terrible thoughts aside, Gray had headed toward the royal suite. The people of Wysteria had enjoyed peace and prosperity for over a century. But now that tranquility was at risk, and he knew war must be averted at all cost. They were running out of time and options.

"My Lord! My Lord! A moment, please."

Displeasure rose in Gray's chest. He knew that whiny, fawning voice as well as his own. And as he came to an abrupt halt in the covered passageway, Finnious Richter—one of his mother's most odious advisors—nearly crashed into him in his haste.

"A thousand pardons, Highness. But might I have a brief word?"

The advisor's lips peeled back in what Gray was sure was the man's idea of a smile. It missed the mark by an incredible distance. Gray had always found Richter unpleasant, even as a youth. There was just something about the man that made his skin crawl.

"What is it?" Gray blew out a plumb of frosty air and answered more sharply than he'd meant. "I'm on my way to speak with the Queen and have little time for chit-chat."

The advisor waved a hand in the air. "Oh no, I would never

waste your valuable time in such a manner, especially now, when trials of the past seem to loom once again. Most dire, indeed."

"And yet you ramble on and do just that. Get to the point, man, I'm in a hurry." Gray took another deep breath, his mother's constant plea for patience playing over and over in his mind. "What is it you wish to say that is important enough for me to hear before answering the Queen's summons?" he demanded with more tolerance than he felt.

"Again, apologies, my prince." The man gave a slight bow. "I would only ask that you speak with the Queen again about retrieving the Scepter of Fire ... from wherever she's hidden it, that is. With the recent attempts to breach our wards in an obvious effort to invade our lands, it is more vital now than ever that we use its powers to nullify this threat."

"You're one of the Queen's advisors, aren't you? Why don't you take it up with Her Majesty personally?"

Why try to use me, you pathetic twerp?

"I am, indeed, Highness, but you ... you are her only son." The man's rheumy eyes glittered with craftiness. "Would it not hold more import coming from you? Besides, the Queen is the only one who knows the location of the scepter. If—Oracles protect us—she became unexpectedly incapacitated in some way, we would surely be lost and at the mercy of King Aramond. Is it not better, safer to retrieve it now?"

"And as an advisor, do you hold so little sway with the Queen that you would need me to intervene on your behalf?" Gray countered.

He watched the barb hit home, as was his intent. Richter's eyes narrowed and his lips pressed together in a hard line. A moment later, the angry look vanished to be replaced by another simpering smile. "Of course, it is my station to advise the Queen, yes, but is it not your *duty*—as heir to the throne—to make the difficult choices required to protect the kingdom and its subjects? You, my prince, must find a way to retrieve the scepter before it is too late."

Fury flooded Gray's veins as he took two menacing steps toward the man, to which Richter hastily stepped back a pace. "You *dare* to counsel me on my *duty*?" he asked, his voice deadly quiet.

Richter's face went pasty white in a heartbeat. "N-no, my Lord!" he stuttered. "Never. I only meant—"

"You overstep your bounds, *advisor*." Gray leaned in, speaking in an ominous tone. "I shall endeavor to forget your misstep, but let me make this perfectly clear for you. As long as my mother has breath in her body, if and when difficult choices are to be made for the protection of this kingdom and its subjects, they will be Her Majesty's choices to make ... and hers alone. Furthermore, I would think twice—were I you—before attempting to circumvent your sovereign Queen in this way in the future. I won't be as pleasant the next time, of that I can assure you. Are we crystal clear on these points?"

Richter cleared his throat and his Adam's apple bobbed several times as he began to back away in a semi-bow. "Of course, Your Grace. Of course. I meant no disrespect."

Before the man could grovel more pathetically—or before Gray did the little weasel bodily harm—he turned on his heel and strode away.

TEN MINUTES AFTER THE UNPLEASANT ENCOUNTER, Gray entered his mother's suite of rooms and found the Queen staring out of the vast windows in her private library, a pensive look on her face.

"The message you sent sounded urgent," he said by way of greeting. "I was in the middle of a briefing."

Queen Beatrice turned then, and Gray was struck, as he so often was, by his mother's beauty and youthful countenance. The Queen had reigned for over two centuries, but looked no more than mid-sixties. Though silver lavishly painted her once dark brown hair, her complexion was smooth and rosy, her eyes

—the color of fine cocoa, so much like his own—still clear and bright.

"Has something else happened? You look … troubled."

The Queen gave a brief nod, then tilted her head and made a show of studying him. "I think perhaps that I could say the same of you. That scowl you're wearing speaks volumes. Is it in place because my summons interrupted your meeting?"

Gray scrubbed his hands over his face and then blew out an agitated breath. "No. Richter waylaid me in the passageway outside the briefing chamber." Sighing, he shook his head. "I fail to see why you keep that smarmy toad on as advisor."

His mother smiled. "Finnious has served this court for over a century—only two others have been with me longer."

"God, he's just detestable, and I gotta say, I don't trust him any farther than I can see him. I don't know how you can."

"And who—may I ask—said that I trust him?" Beatrice countered with a raised eyebrow.

"Well, if you don't trust him, then why keep him in such an important position? I mean, seriously, Mother. There's something devious about the man, a cunning that lives behind his eyes that I can't stomach. He's always given me the creeps, and somehow, now more than ever."

The Queen shrugged. "Perhaps his cunning is what makes him useful to me. He has had some … inventive ideas over the years. Besides, there are eight advisors in my court, so the others keep him in line—for the most part." Moving to the sofa, she sat and patted the seat next to her. "Now, come and sit. We'll compare miseries. You can start by telling me what Richter said that upset you so."

Gray sank down next to his mother and leaned forward. "He wanted me to intervene with you on the subject of the Scepter of Fire. It's his view that it should be retrieved immediately."

"Oh, my love, that's hardly a secret. Why should that upset you? He's been harping on that particular subject for months."

"Yes, but it was the way that he asked. It felt … underhanded, as if he was going behind your back. He said that since you were the only one who knew the scepter's location, we would be in dire straits if something unforeseen should happen to you."

"Did he now?" the Queen murmured.

"He insinuated that I should learn its location and retrieve the scepter myself before it was too late."

"Well, he was obviously fishing for information, which I've shared with few. And since I'm not the only one who knows where the scepter is hidden, he was wrong on that count."

"Someone else knows its location?"

"Mmm, there are two others, but don't worry—I trust them both implicitly. The scepter has been hidden for a very long time, and will stay where it is until I deem it to be retrieved. Finnious Richter cannot change that fact."

"Well, that's a relief."

"What else did my advisor have to say?"

"He told me it was my *duty* as heir to the throne to make the difficult choices to protect the kingdom. He's got a steel pair on him, that one. Anyway, I didn't like his implications, and I'm afraid I wasn't patient or kind in my response."

"And what *was* your response, my darling?"

"I told the little cretin that when difficult choices arose for the protection of this kingdom, they would be yours to make." Gray smiled. "And I made it perfectly clear that I didn't appreciate his counsel on what *he* thought my duties should be."

The Queen laughed out loud at that. "I dare say, I would've loved to have been privy to that exchange."

She smiled at Gryphon, her royal chamber elf, as he quietly placed a steaming pot of tea on the low table in front of them. "Thank you, Gryphon. That will be all."

As the elf bowed and left the room, Beatrice grew pensive and poured them both a cup of tea. "Unfortunately," she began as she handed him his cup. "I find that I must agree with the *little cretin*, as you call him, as Richter is correct on one point. I am increasingly worried about this business with the wards. If they fail us, we will be vulnerable. We could have Aramond's troops on our doorstep without notice."

"I agree. That thought has been hovering at the back of my mind."

The Queen nodded. "Therefore, after much deliberation—and a lengthy discussion with all three Oracles—I've decided that retrieving the Scepter of Fire is, at this juncture, our best option."

"Okay ..." Gray responded slowly and studied her over the rim of his cup. There was something else coming, he was sure of it. He waited for the other shoe to drop.

"We must protect our borders at all cost."

"Also agreed."

"Should Aramond gain a foothold, war would certainly follow—a war that could be devastating to both kingdoms." She put up a hand when he would've spoken. "And before you start in with me, let me say that I have the utmost confidence in Alexi. Your closest friend has become a most formidable field commander for my armies. But I must first consider the innocent people of Wysteria, as well as Roseland, and how war would affect them. Aramond would show no mercy—you know that—to us or his own people."

"That's true. He's as mad as Aunt Renata ever was. Probably worse."

His mother's shoulders seemed to droop at her sister's name, and she sighed. The lines on her beautiful face seemed suddenly more pronounced to Gray, her burden more obvious.

"It saddens me that you didn't know your aunt. Hatred and madness had claimed her long before you were old enough to understand ... after that wretched war, which took so much from all, had come and gone. How I wish you could have known the young princess she once was." She waved a hand in the air. "Oh, I know that you've heard the stories. Renata was always spoiled and willful, but she was beautiful even as a child. When she was young, there was ... a sweetness about her. She could charm you with a look."

The wistful smile she gave him was gone in a moment. "I'm not certain just when that began to change, but it did. And as we grew into young women, she became increasingly obsessed with inheriting the throne. Being the oldest, she was first in line and expected to one day rule over all of Artemysia."

Gray nodded. He had heard the stories over the years, and it was hard to listen as sorrow and melancholy colored his mother's voice, her grief still palpable after so long ... for a sibling lost.

Queen Beatrice cleared her throat and tried to regain her smile. "Our mother was a benevolent and extraordinarily clever queen. And while she loved her daughters as only a mother can, her love for her people and their well-being was always foremost in her mind."

"So she made the decision to divide the realm into two kingdoms."

His mother picked up her tea cup and raised it to her lips. Gray watched her hands tremble ever so slightly as she did so. "Yes. She consulted the Oracles and made a very hard choice, but one she felt was best for the realm. And the Oracles agreed."

"So she gave Roseland to Aunt Renata and bequeathed Wysteria to you."

The queen stared toward the far window, as if seeing it all again. "I think that Renata was lost to us before that moment, but she never recovered from what she saw as betrayal, a theft of her birthright."

Gray took the cup from her and set it aside, then took his mother's hands in his as he read the deep sadness behind her eyes. "You continue to punish yourself for something that was out of your control, and it breaks my heart. It was the Queen Mother's right, and you're not responsible for Aunt Renata's failings."

Queen Beatrice shook her head. "Perhaps not, but I mourn for what could have ... should have been. Our kingdoms should have jointly prospered and enjoyed a peaceful coexistence—which is what our mother had hoped for when she split the realm. But my sister allowed selfishness and hatred to destroy that vision of a bright future for the entire realm of Artemysia."

"But you've carried on that vision here in Wysteria, given so much for your kingdom. You lead with compassion and grace, and your people love you. I think the Queen Mother would be very proud of what you've accomplished here."

The queen raised a hand to his face. "You are a great joy to me, Graydon. The one true soul that I can always count on is you."

Gray smiled. "That's what I'm here for."

"I see so much of your father in you. It is a comfort to me."

The queen rose then and crossed to one of the bookshelves, choosing a ragged tome from the volumes there. As she ran her hands lovingly over the tattered cover, another thoughtful smile on her face, he realized that the volume was familiar to him, a favorite from his childhood. A story of a young girl's adventure in a wonderland of magick, danger, and fantastic characters—a story based on Artemysia but written by human hands in another realm.

"And because I can always count on you, my son," she turned and pursed her lips. "It's one of the reasons that I'm charging you and Alexi with the retrieval of the scepter."

He blinked at her. "I beg your pardon?"

"Don't look so surprised," Queen Beatrice said with a chuckle. "My people may love me, as you say, but there are few in my court who I would trust with a task of this magnitude. And you, my darling, along with your closest, most trusted friend, are perfectly suited to the job."

"But why me and Alexi? Why not send the two who know the scepter's location? You said you trust them implicitly, right?"

"Ah, yes. But Hamish is now too old. He would have a difficult time blending in and retrieving the scepter from its place of safe keeping. You two, on the other hand, will have no such problem. As I said, you both have experience in this area."

Gray frowned. "Mother, you're talking in circles. What experience? Where is the scepter hidden?"

The queen's smile was just a touch mischievous. "Why, where you received your college education—in the kingdom of New York City, of course. It has been cared for by old, old friends of the family."

"Are you serious?" Gray asked in a stunned voice. "If you've entrusted the scepter to friends in another dimension, then why not just contact this family and ask them to return it to us?"

"Unfortunately, it's not that simple. As you know, the humans of that land age differently, and through the years the history of the scepter has become ... muddled, lost, just another jeweled trinket on a shelf. The more recent generations of the family have no idea what the scepter is and no understanding of its incredible power."

Queen Beatrice again ran a hand over the cover of the book. "Up to this moment, that situation has suited me. Once Hamish relinquished his post in that realm and opted to return home, another good friend of yours was given the task of keeping a close watch on the scepter ... in case circumstances ever arose when we would need its power and protection again. Since he'd already chosen to live in that realm, it was a good fit for us both."

"Another friend? Which friend are you—" The answer came to him before his question was fully formed and his mouth dropped open. "*Valian?* You're talking about Alexi's cousin Valian Winchester?"

Queen Beatrice laughed out loud and her eyes glittered with amusement. "You've always been such a bright child. Yes, Valian. And I must say, I'm hoping he can keep you and Alexi in line." She sobered then and became laser focused. "He can get you close, Gray, but you'll need to use every bit of caution and ingenuity—not to mention your abundant charm—to reclaim the Scepter of Fire." She held out the ragged volume she'd pulled from the shelf. "Do you remember this story?"

Wild thoughts and more questions swirled through Gray's mind, but he nodded. "Of course. The story of Wonderland. What does that have to do with any of this?"

She gestured with the book. "The original 'Alice.' She followed the 'Hatter' to Wysteria, Graydon. After that battle so long ago, she went back to her home with a jeweled scepter to hide and a story to tell."

Gray began to rise, but sank back down in stunned confusion. "Are you telling me that the story is real?"

Queen Beatrice chuckled. "Some. Not all. A clever little weaver was our Alice. It is her descendant who possesses the scepter—the great-granddaughter of her great-granddaughter."

"*Seriously*?" Gray burst into laughter. "The mystical number of three, too?"

"Indeed." His mother nodded with a grin. "The great-granddaughter of the original Alice's great-granddaughter ... and the mystical number of three," she repeated. "All three Oracles found this fascinating as well." She sobered then. "But this mission will not be easy, my son, and time is of the essence. I'd like you and Alexi to leave as soon as possible. So prepare."

Two

"For the love of God, keep your pants on," Alyssa Montague muttered, as her cell phone buzzed with another text message, the fourth in the last twenty minutes.

She was running late. So, what was new? She'd been trying to get out of the gallery for over half an hour, but the staff had been so busy with last minute sales that she felt guilty leaving—especially to meet her best friend Isabella for holiday drinks and to finalize plans for her upcoming New Year's Eve party. She might own the gallery which carried the Montague name, but she wasn't about to leave her staff to get slammed.

Especially on Christmas Eve.

Smiling, Alyssa handed the last customer his receipt just as her gallery manager, Lenore came out of the backroom with the blown glass vase he'd purchased wrapped up and ready to go. "Have a wonderful holiday, Mr. Marks. Hope your wife enjoys the vase."

The man chuckled. "Oh, I have no doubt of that, Alyssa. You

know very well that Edith's been ogling this piece for months. Just about drove me crazy with all the hinting. I waited as long as I could to collect it so I wouldn't have to worry about her finding it before Christmas. She can be tenacious."

"Aw," Lenore heaved a sigh and leaned on the counter. "That's so sweet. Wish I had someone to surprise me with goodies. I'm lucky if my husband remembers what day it is, let alone what holiday."

Mr. Marks chuckled. "Well, you girls have a merry Christmas. And, Alyssa, tell your father to work on his golf swing. I'll be ready to trounce him again directly after the first of the year."

"Will do. And give my best to Mrs. Marks."

He gave a wave and headed for the door with his wife's present tucked under his arm just as Alyssa's cell phone began to ring. "Oh man! It's Isabella. I'm late. She's gonna be so pissed."

Lenore shook her head. "Didn't I tell you several times? You should've just gone. We could've handled that last rush."

Alyssa shrugged. "Hey, Izzy," she said into the phone. "Look, I know I'm really late, but I'll be there in fifteen minutes."

"Don't bother," Isabella Christensen said from the doorway. "I'm here, you big dork. I waited outside your building for close to half an hour—in the freezing cold, I might add—before realizing that you were never going to acknowledge my texts, let alone show up."

"Geez, I'm so sorry, but we got really busy right when I was about to leave. I meant to text you back, but I got caught up."

Lenore smirked. "Don't let her off the hook on our account, Isabella. I told her repeatedly to take off, but she wouldn't leave."

"I wanted to make sure you guys were covered," Alyssa insisted. "Besides, it's Christmas Eve and everyone should be going home to their families, not stuck here while I'm off enjoying myself."

"Oh, for the love of God, Aly," Isabella groused. "You're the boss, idiot. And one of the perks of ownership is that you get to hire people to work here so that you *can* go off and enjoy yourself.

Besides, if you were that worried about it, you could've just closed early, you know. Again, another perk of calling the shots."

"Yeah, yeah. So you keep telling me." Alyssa shook her head. "Not my style and you know it. Anyway, we can go now, but I suppose we've probably missed our dinner reservation."

"We most certainly have not. Because I am your BFF, I know exactly how you are. You're never on time for anything—always late for a very important date."

Alyssa sighed. "Ha, ha. You're so funny. You're killing me here." It was yet another reference to her family history. That she was a direct descendent of the original Alice that prompted Charles Dodgson—better known as Lewis Carroll—to write his Wonderland tale was a constant source of amusement for Isabella. For Alyssa, it was just old and stale.

"The point is that since I do know you so well, I added an hour to the time we'd set to meet. And we can just make it if you'll move your ass."

Lenore laughed out loud and nudged Alyssa. "She's definitely got your number, pal. Now, get out of here. Candy and I will lock up."

Alyssa slipped on her winter coat and tugged a knit cap on over her long blonde hair. "Okay, okay. We're going."

Heading out to the street, they walked to the corner and caught a cab to the upper west side and arrived at Alberto's, Isabella's favorite restaurant, with ten minutes to spare. Though the place was packed, they were lucky and got seated almost immediately.

Once the wine was poured and they'd given their food orders, Isabella leaned forward, her bright green eyes sparkling with excitement. "So ... I have some interesting news."

"Yeah? About the party?"

Isabella ran an event planning business called Party Poppers. And though her business had really seemed to take off over the past year, one of the benefits of their friendship was that she'd made time to plan and execute Alyssa's first New Year's Eve party.

And that meant Alyssa didn't have to do much but show up—a plus, to her mind.

"Uh... no." Isabella rolled her eyes and shoved a lock of curly red hair behind her ear. "This is *personal* interesting news, but I suppose it is sort of related ... in a round-about way. I got a call today from Antonia Roth, of Roth Business News. She wants to do an article on Party Poppers in their January edition. Can you believe that?"

"Oh my gosh, Izzy! That's fabulous. It'll be great publicity for Poppers. And I bet you get a ton of new business from it, not that you need any more. You've had a stellar year as it is doing something you love to do."

"True. But then we both have—you with the gallery and me with Poppers. You love art and I love parties." Isabella laughed and wagged a finger in the air. "But it's been a long road getting here—for both of us. We've had our struggles."

"Lord, you can say that again. My folks were pretty skeptical when I wanted to open my own gallery, but they've been so supportive. And now that we're beginning to see daylight, I'm just so grateful to Lenore and the rest of my team for sticking with me."

"I know. My staff, they've worked so hard and do such an amazing job. They deserve this kind of recognition. This opportunity with Roth Business News is very prestigious. They may even want pictures from an event or two, which means I'll need to make sure we get some good shots at your party."

Alyssa held up her wine glass. "Well, then here's to us."

They'd no more than clinked glasses and each took a sip of wine before Alyssa's cell phone rang again. She dug it out of her purse, saw the number on the screen, and abruptly ignored the call.

"What was that about?"

Alyssa made a sour face. "Brad."

"Brad Scarborough?" Isabella set down her glass and raised

her eyebrows. "Oh ... my ... God. I thought you were going to kick him to the curb. You're still seeing him?"

"Oh, hell no!" Taking a hasty sip of wine, Alyssa looked away, but she could *feel* Isabella's glacial stare. "Okay, I've been trying to disentangle myself for over a month, but *man*, he's dug in and as stubborn as a New York cockroach. Just when I think I've finally gotten through to him, he pops up somewhere out of the blue, and I've got to deal with him all over again."

Isabella shook her head, the look on her face speaking volumes. "Lame," was all she said.

"I *know*! And God help me, my parents just love him. I guess because he *seems* like a good choice. He comes from the right family, belongs to the right clubs, blah, blah, blah. It would be baffling if I hadn't watched him suck up to them on more than one occasion when we were dating. He always seems to show up at just the right moment."

"Wow. Aly, the guy is such a douche." Isabella made a vomit gesture.

"You're telling me? I don't know what I was thinking going out with him in the first place."

"Yeah, well, at least you came to your senses pretty quick. Though I really thought your folks, especially Lidia, were better judges of character. You need to cut that tie before the 'what if's' set in."

"What do you mean?"

"You know ... *what if*—God forbid—the creep gets it into that tiny pea brain of his that he wants something more? Something permanent... like perhaps even marriage."

"Eeeuuw." Alyssa gave her friend a horrified look. "Now you're just being mean."

"That's my job as your best friend. Somebody has to keep you in line. I know you ... you don't like to hurt people's feelings, which is probably why he keeps showing up and calling when you think he's finally taken the hint. I mean, really, pal. This guy is starting to feel a bit stalker-ish."

"Yeah well, don't pop a gasket, but he's already been invited to Christmas dinner with my folks."

"*What?* Why on earth would you do that?"

"*I* didn't. My mom did a few weeks ago. It was actually the last time I had dinner with them here in the city. Brad just *happened* to be having dinner at the same restaurant with a couple of his buddies."

"Uh-huh. And do you think that was just a coincidence?"

"Of course not. But there's really no way to prove it, is there? Anyway, he not-so-subtlety dropped by our table for a brief chat. He gives Lidia the puppy dog eyes and tells her that his parents are going to be in London for the holidays ... '*whaa-whaa-whaa, oh poor pitiful me, all alone on Christmas*' ... laid it on pretty thick. So mom told him to come out to the house with me. What was I gonna do? Blurt out that I'd rather he didn't?"

"Hell, yes! Without question." Isabella shook her head. "Well, at least he won't be at the New Year's gig."

Alyssa closed her eyes and started to count. She barely made it to five.

"Are you friggin' *kidding* me?" Isabella exclaimed. "Is Lidia responsible for that as well?"

Alyssa leaned in. "Tone it down, would you? People are staring. And yes, actually. Same dinner, same conversation. I kid you not, she was like a roller coaster out of control. I just kept thinking 'Mom, please *stop!*'"

"Jesus, Mary, and Joseph."

"I know, right?" Alyssa pulled a bread stick out of the basket on the table and swirled the end in the dish of olive oil. "Like I said, for some reason they like him, especially Lidia. Personally, I think she likes all of his fawning."

"God, that's so not right. Parents. But we digress. Are you telling me that you're willing to ruin your own party—which is going to be epic, mind you—by having Brad the stalker by your side all night long just because you don't want to disappoint your folks or ruin *his* holiday season? Because that's just so sweet it makes my jaw ache."

"Bite me," Alyssa said with a sugary smile before taking a crunchy bite of the bread stick she held.

"Seriously. What kind of pinheadery is that?"

"*Izzy!*"

"*Aly!*" Isabella selected a bread stick of her own and pointed at Alyssa with it. "Truth sucks, doesn't it?"

"Geez, stop, already. Can we just talk about something besides Brad Scarborough, please? Really, anything else will be fine."

But before Isabella could respond, another phone began to ring. This time it was Isabella's.

Glancing at the screen, Isabella's eyes widened. "I'm sorry, Aly, but I have to take this. I'll be right back."

As Isabella rushed out to take the call, Alyssa couldn't stop thinking about what her friend had said. She hadn't dated Brad that long, and they'd never been exclusive—well, it hadn't been exclusive on her part—but the notion that he might be thinking along the line of something more permanent was disturbing and had never crossed her mind ... until now.

"Thanks, Izz, for putting *that* in my head," she muttered into her wine glass. Well she'd just have to do something about it—put an end to any further action on his part once and for all. Isabella was probably right. She did hate to hurt people's feelings, but this situation had gone on long enough. She and Brad were about to get some clarity.

Surprisingly, Isabella was only gone for a few minutes before she re-appeared with a dazzling smile and a wicked look in her emerald eyes, and Alyssa put unpleasant thoughts of Brad Scarborough out of her mind for the time being.

"So, what's that look about?" she asked as Isabella sat back down. "You look like a cat that's just been given a whole jug of cream ... or ate several juicy canaries ... I can't decide."

"Okay, first of all... gross ... and second of all, you would not be wrong."

"Well, spill already."

"More very interesting news, and this time it is about the party. Specifically, about the guest list." Isabella's grin widened.

"Izzy, I hope you haven't gone crazy. Last time we spoke, the invitation list was already topping a hundred and fifty. My townhouse is spacious, but I'd rather it wasn't wall-to-wall people."

Isabella took a sip of her wine. "Look, you wanted this to be the event of the season, right? And that's what it's going to be. Trust me, this is what I do. Besides, a portion of the hundred and fifty won't show up anyway. There are always those that send their regrets because they're out of town or going to another event, so that will hone it down some. No, that call was from a very special acquaintance who asked if there was room for a few more on the list."

Alyssa frowned. "That's it? You're nearly giddy over a few more invitations?"

"Well, I'm nearly giddy because of *who* the invitations are for. As it turns out, we're talking about royalty."

Alyssa blinked and paused with her wine glass halfway to her lips. "I beg your pardon? Did you say... *royalty*?"

Isabella sat back and nodded. "I did indeed ... and a prince no less."

Alyssa rolled her eyes. "Please. What prince would want to come to my little New Year's soirée?"

"Hey! This 'soirée' is going to be a spectacular *bash*, and don't you forget it."

Alyssa ignored Isabella's offended tone. "You're pulling my chain, right? This is some kind of weird joke, isn't it?"

"Not even a little bit, girlfriend."

Alyssa shook her head and sighed, but gave Isabella a skeptical look. "Okay. I'll bite. Where's this prince from, exactly?"

Isabella waved her hand in the air. "Oh, I don't know. Some place I've never heard of, but still. A friggin' prince, Aly. This event is gonna be my crowning achievement... so far, that is. We are definitely going to get some photos for the Roth article with this one."

"You're actually serious."

"Oh yeah."

"Are you sure this is even real? I mean, my family rubs shoulders with some hoity-toity families in the city from time to time, but royalty? Who is this friend that called?"

The waiter arrived with their food, and Isabella waited until he walked away before leaning in and speaking in a low voice. "Listen, the call was from Valian Winchester ... *the* Valian Winchester."

"What? The fantasy author? How the hell do you know him?"

Isabella actually preened a bit. "I have many facets, my friend."

"Whatever." Alyssa raised an eyebrow. "Seriously, how do you know him? And well enough for him to have your phone number?"

"Oh, please. I was doing this garden party for a client in the Hamptons a couple years ago. Fantasy theme, elves and fairies, that sort of thing." Isabella frowned. "Very odd event. Hand to God, some of it is still muddled and hazy in my mind. The whole thing had a really weird vibe to it—still weird now when I think about it—but that's a story for another time. Anyway, he was hawking his latest book, and we struck up a conversation. We spent a couple of hours chatting about books and favorite authors —that part is very clear. He's an interesting man, and *very* attractive." She shook her head, her fiery curls bouncing from side to side. "Anyway, like I said, we're more like special acquaintances than friends."

"And why am I just hearing about this now?"

Isabella picked up her napkin and sent Aly a frustrated look. "Would you please focus? The point is that this is real, Aly, believe me."

She dropped her napkin across her lap and then paused with

another frown. "Wait, you're in, right? Please say you're in... because royalty? At one of my events? This could really punch up bookings, not to mention my prices."

Alyssa laughed out loud. "Leave it to you, my friend. Always thinking about the bottom line." She wiggled her eyebrows. "But to get to say that I've hosted royalty in my home... a prince, no less? Don't be stupid. Of course I'm in."

"Outstanding! Now let's eat and then go back to your place so I can give you the run-down. This needs to be executed perfectly, now more than ever ... and I mean right down to the last detail."

"Hey, I thought you said that I wouldn't have to do anything, that you had it all worked out."

"Geez, don't be such a baby. After all, it is your party. Besides, we're a little over a week out and the heavy lifting is already done ... for the most part. Anyway, I just want to get your approval on a few last minute things. It'll be fun."

IT WAS AFTER MIDNIGHT BY THE TIME ISABELLA TOOK her event books and left, and Alyssa was feeling pretty overwhelmed. She'd been in the townhouse for almost two years and this would be her first major shindig. Isabella seemed to have everything well in hand, but Alyssa's head was swimming with all the details.

To add annoyance to her anxiety, Brad had called a few times over the evening, leaving a variety of messages with enough fodder for Isabella's continued grief. The last call came on her cell phone just after Isabella walked out the door.

Alyssa debated picking up, but since he'd already been invited for Christmas dinner at her parents', she finally answered.

"Hey, Brad."

"Jesus, Aly, where the hell have you been?"

She was so taken aback by his strident tone that it took her a moment to answer. "What do you mean, where've I been?"

"Well, I've been calling all evening."

"I know. I'm sorry I haven't gotten back to you, but I was having dinner with Isabella."

"Uh-huh. Dinner. Until after midnight? Really?"

His dubious tone had her pausing with her mouth open. "I beg your pardon?"

"Well, you obviously knew I'd called. And since we're having dinner with your folks tomorrow, I guess I thought you'd be considerate enough to either pick up or call me back so that we could coordinate our drive to Connecticut."

His angry tone raised her own heated attitude. "Considerate? Is that what you just said? Because I gotta tell you, I don't find it in any way considerate that you orchestrated getting yourself invited to Christmas dinner when I've made it clear—numerous times, I might add—that I didn't want to see you anymore."

"What are you talking about? I didn't orchestrate anything. Your mother invited me, remember?"

"Yes. I sat right there and watched the whole charade. I should have put a stop to it then and there, but didn't want to embarrass you by explaining to my parents how inappropriate the invitation was in the first place. But then, silly me, I thought *you'd* be considerate enough to refuse the invitation."

There was a brief pause on the other end of the line, then a heavy sigh. "I'm sorry you feel that way, Aly."

She rubbed the spot between her eyes where a headache was starting to pound. "Oh, and please don't make it sound like this is a surprise, Brad. Or that you're the injured party here. If you'll recall, we've had a few different versions of this conversation over the last couple of months alone. I don't want to be unkind, but I'm just really hoping that this is the last time."

"I understand." There was another pause, before Brad cleared his throat on the other end of the line. When he finally spoke again, it was with anger and derision. "And I was hoping that you might come to your senses and change your mind. In any case, I suppose you think that I should skip Christmas dinner tomorrow."

"Yes, I think that would be best, don't you? I mean, it would just be uncomfortable for both of us."

"Whatever. Give your mom and dad my regrets and wish them a Merry Christmas for me," he sneered.

"Oh, I will. Believe me."

Alyssa hung up the phone with a mixture of anger and guilt. She really hated getting played, which is exactly what he'd been trying to do over the last few weeks, but it was hard to kick someone on Christmas Eve, no matter how much they deserved it.

Christmas dinner was going to start off with a bang when she arrived without her date, but she'd worry about that later.

Shaking her head, she went to hunt up some aspirin for the throbbing in her head.

Three

Gray hadn't set foot in the human dimension for close to fifteen years, and the first thing he saw as he followed Alexi through the old portal in the heart of the great park at the center of the New York realm was Valian Winchester. Alexi and Valian could have been brothers with their pale skin and long silvery hair. Valian's ice-blue eyes twinkled with mischief as he immediately dropped to one knee, seemingly oblivious to the snow in which he knelt.

"My prince," he murmured as he dipped his head in courtly fashion. "You grace us with your attendance in this humble New York realm. We are grateful for your royal presence."

"Oh, for the love of the Oracles ..." Gray rolled his eyes. "Get up, fool. You're not funny."

Alexi snickered, and then did a poor job of covering his mirth at Gray's sidelong scowl.

"You two are so completely pathetic." Gray shook his head. The three of them had mostly grown up together, and the cousins had constantly teased Gray with his title. Truth be told, they were closer to Gray than any sibling could be, but annoying all the same.

A wicked grin split Valian's handsome face, and he laughed out loud. Standing, he brushed the snow from his slacks before grasping Gray's outstretched arm at the wrist, pulling him in for a bear hug and pounding him on the back. "You've been gone way too long, brother," he said, and then turned to give his cousin the same treatment. "It's damn good to see you both. I just wish it was under better circumstances."

"Agreed," Gray replied. "I assume Alexi has filled you in on the latest news."

Valian nodded. "Sounds like Aramond is on the warpath … yet again. You'd think that he would've learned after the last time —or should I say *times*—that he got his ass handed to him."

Even with the wards, Aramond had attempted to invade on several occasions since the Great War, but had been soundly turned away each time. Valian had previously fought with Wysteria's armies before taking a post in the New York realm.

Alexi snorted. "One would think he'd get it, but the old fart is so full of hate, greed, and madness that it seems he can think of nothing else but Wysteria's destruction. But I gotta say, this latest is a very different tactic, Val."

"Sounds like."

"Alexi and I have talked about this, and I hate to think it, but we both feel there might be someone helping Aramond from inside the Wysterian realm."

"Inside? You mean a traitor? That is a disturbing thought." Valian's brows drew together as he scanned the area. "However, let's take this discussion back to my loft. There are nosy eyes and ears everywhere, and this part of the park isn't as safe as it once was."

"Out of shape, cousin? Afraid for your well-being, perhaps?" Alexi teased.

"Keep it up, and I'll show you what shape I'm in. Considering that I hunt here when I'm bored, I know this area well and fear nothing. And though I'm not sure anyone would really notice in the Village or even around SoHo, you'll want to glamour those ears of yours while you're in this realm, especially here in the oldest area of the park. There's a band of rogue trolls who have territory not far from here and consider Elven ears a delicacy."

Alexi wrinkled his nose and then chuckled, but Gray watched him glance around, a wary look on his face. "Anxious to show off your digs in SoHo, then is it?"

Valian spread his arms wide and gave his cousin a look of mock surprise. "Me? A show off? Come, cousin. I'm just a simple writer of words. My humble abode is nothing compared to the White Palace to which you're surely accustomed."

Alexi laughed out loud at that. "A simple writer of words. Yeah, right! What bullshit."

Gray shook his head. "If you two are finished acting like smitten love birds, can we take this conversation somewhere else? I'd like to discuss the possibility of war in a more private and secure location. I also want to hear what the situation is regarding the scepter."

"The latter is going to take some time, but I have a plan in motion." Valian grinned and gave another courtly bow. "But as always, your wish, Sire, is my command."

"Yeah, yeah. Bite me."

With as bark of laughter, Valian took Gray's left arm with Alexi taking his right, and the Elven warriors faded them from the park altogether.

VALIAN'S SoHo LOFT WAS HUGE EVEN BY NEW YORK standards—airy and spacious, with floor to ceiling windows along one wall and a completely open floor plan.

"I can see why you made the decision to stay in this realm, Val," Alexi said with a wink, as he strolled around the main expanse of the loft. "At least you moved to a much more desirable area. This is quite the step up from that studio off of Fourteenth Street that you had a decade ago."

"Ain't nothin' wrong with Fourteenth Street, buddy. I have

great memories of that studio. But since my books have done so well, and with a couple of them making the leap into films, I've done alright."

"What?" Alexi turned with a surprised look. "Movies? When did that happen and why am I just finding out now?"

Valian shrugged. "I don't know. Maybe because you haven't visited this realm for about a decade and a half?"

"Did you get comps for the openings?"

Valian's smile was a bit evil and his crystalline-blue eyes—so like Alexi's—twinkled. "I did, yes. Two of the premiers were in L.A."

"Well, shit. You could've sent me a message."

"Could've ... didn't," Valian replied in a bored tone.

"God, you're such an ass," Alexi said with a shake of his head.

Valian only laughed. "And your point would be...?"

"No point. You just answered the question of why I haven't visited, you old, tired *writer of words*."

"Old?" Almost before Alexi had finished his sentence, Valian was on him, moving at the lightning speed of an Elven warrior and wrestling him to the floor.

Amused, Gray hiked himself up onto the kitchen island, more to get out of harm's way than anything. A wave of nostalgia rolled through him as he watched the cousins roll around bitching and punching and kicking. He figured it wouldn't be long before one of them put an end to the brawl. And he found that he wasn't wrong, when moments later the sound of ripping material brought them both up short.

"You *sonofabitch*! See what you've done?" Alexi complained. "You've ripped the shoulder of my favorite jacket."

"Aw, poor baby," Valian replied in a simpering tone. "But since the collar of my shirt is almost torn off on one side, I'd say we're even."

But Alexi wasn't ready to give up. "I'm pretty sure my jacket cost a hellova lot more than that lame shirt you're wearing."

Valian's mouth dropped open. "Lame? Is that what you just said?"

"You heard me."

Before the whole wrestling match could begin again, Gray decided to put an end to it. "Again, you two are beyond pathetic." He rarely used his considerable magick these days, but waving a hand in Alexi's direction, he repaired the rip in his jacket's shoulder, then turned and did the same for Valian's collar. "There. Are you idiots happy now? Can we get back to the issues at hand? Like where the scepter is located and how we're going to retrieve it."

After examining his collar, Valian smirked at Gray. "Wow. I thought you'd sworn off using magick, though I'm happy to see you haven't lost touch with your roots altogether."

"Please. I never said I was swearing off magick. It's part of my heritage. I just don't really need to use it these days. *Anyway* ... the scepter?"

Valian waved a hand in the air. "Oh, that's all set. We have a soirée to attend at the end of the week."

"I beg your pardon? We're going to a party?" Gray frowned at his friend. "Exactly how is that going to help in getting our hands on the scepter?"

"Well, probably because the soirée is being held at the scepter's location." Valian paused and glanced at his cousin with a shit-eating grin. "But first ..."

"Huh-uh. No ..." Gray shook his head and held up a finger in warning. "I mean it. *No!*"

Alexi nodded and chuckled. "Oh, yeah."

Gray barely had time to defend himself, as both cousins pounced.

THE WEEK FOLLOWING CHRISTMAS SAW A BIT OF A slowdown in sales at the gallery, but that was to be expected. The

Montague Gallery was becoming known for its exclusive art and blown glass, most of which carried a substantial price tag. Alyssa spent most of the week with paperwork, getting together tax information for her accountant, and doing an audit of art on hand. The gallery would host a gala for a watercolor artist in February, so there were preparations to begin for that, as well.

With business resuming as usual, the week seemed to fly by, and New Year's was suddenly knocking at the door. She hadn't heard a peep from Brad since their final phone conversation, so maybe she'd finally gotten through to him. And even Christmas dinner with her parents hadn't been the uncomfortable affair that she'd feared. Though her choice had been met with a bit of bewilderment, her parents had been surprisingly supportive of her decision. It left Alyssa to wonder how she'd so misinterpreted their feelings about Brad in the first place. Altogether, it was a relief and a load off of her mind.

Isabella and her team descended on the townhouse at the crack of nine a.m. on the thirty-first like a horde of locust to begin the process of transforming Alyssa's home into a fantasy of gold and silver. A good-sized bar was placed in one corner of the dining room, and the fifteen foot dining room table would hold an extensive buffet of delights by early evening. A plethora of small tables and chairs had been set up in the parlor giving guests a place to sit and eat if they wished, and the catering staff would also circulate with trays.

Alyssa pitched in where she could—answering questions about placement and flow where it was needed—but Isabella's team was like a well-oiled machine, and she mostly tried to stay out of their way. The party was to kick off at seven p.m., so at just after five, she headed up to her room to bathe and dress for the evening. Isabella had brought her party clothes with her, so she'd used one of the spare rooms to change and came into the master suite as Alyssa was finishing her makeup.

"God, I *love* that dress, Aly. It's flawless, and you look stunning in it. It really makes your baby blues pop, too."

Alyssa looked down at the shimmering silver cocktail dress she'd purchased expressly for the evening. It was like a perfect little black dress … only in a sparkle of silver. She'd fallen in love with it herself the moment she'd set eyes on it.

"Fairly screams New Year's Eve, doesn't it?"

"At the top of its lungs, baby," Isabella said with a laugh.

"Well, after tonight, you can borrow it anytime you like."

"I don't think so. With this bright red mop on my head, it wouldn't do much for me. That's why I always go for the gold." She did a quick spin in her backless gold-trimmed, black sheath.

"Very sexy, pal."

Isabella pursed her lips and gave Alyssa the once-over, from her sleek golden chignon to the silver pumps on the floor next to the chair. "Seriously, Aly, your royal guest won't be able to keep his eyes off of you."

Alyssa snorted. "And who says that's a good thing? You haven't seen him. He could be a hundred years old and homely as a goat, or married … or gay. You don't even know what country he comes from, remember?" She waved away the whole idea. "Besides, he probably won't even show up."

Isabella's bright green eyes narrowed. "Why do you have to suck the joy out of everything?"

"Because I'm pragmatic, that's why. I would rather be prepared for the worst and be pleasantly surprised than have high expectations and be sorely disappointed."

Shaking her head, Isabella chuckled. "You're *such* a romantic … and completely hopeless. Now shake a leg, girlfriend. It's thirty minutes to showtime."

Alyssa grinned and slipped on her sparkly silver heels. After doing a final check in the mirror, she followed Isabella downstairs.

And as she descended, she was stunned by the transformation. She couldn't help it. She'd watched Isabella's team during set-up and had an idea of what was planned, but the final version took her breath away. With her home decked out in finery, everywhere she looked seemed to gleam like stardust. From the decorations to the Party Popper's staff, who were crisp and neat in their black and gold uniforms, everything was perfect.

"Oh my gosh, Izzy!" Turning, she grabbed Isabella up in a tight hug. "I wanted my first shindig to be something special, and this is beyond words. It's spectacular."

Isabella leaned back and shrugged. "It's what I do—wait. What am I saying? Of course it's spectacular. I'm spectacular."

Alyssa laughed out loud. "Yes. Yes you are. And I can't thank you enough."

"Yeah, tell me that again when you get my bill, pal. Now, come on. I want to get in a few photos before the great masses arrive. Let's get a couple of you in that incredible dress over by the fireplace... maybe with a champagne flute in your hand?"

As Isabella's photographer clicked away with his camera and the minutes ticked by, Alyssa's nerves began to fray. Her personal fear was that no one would show, or worse, just a handful would attend and the night would be a huge disappointment. But within the hour, people began to arrive, with her mom and dad the first ones through the door at exactly seven. Her mother spent a good ten minutes gushing over Isabella's work.

"Oh, this is just lovely, Isabella. You really do have a special gift when it comes to planning a splashy affair."

"Thanks, Mrs. M. My pop always said that if you could find a job that you loved to do, it wouldn't be work. Turns out, he was right."

"Well, I know that Isaac and Marie are very proud of what you've accomplished. Are they coming tonight?"

Isabella laughed. "Sure, they'll be along. But you know my parents. They're never on time for anything. It's a continual source of frustration, but what are you gonna do? They're mine."

Lidia turned and gave Alyssa a considering look. "Hmm, yes, I know exactly how that goes."

Alyssa rolled her eyes. "Don't start, Mom."

"What? I didn't say a word."

"Yes, but you're thinking really loud. Oh, look. Delia Good-fellow just came in. I'll be right back," she replied and escaped to the foyer.

By eight forty-five, the party was really jumping, and Alyssa's earlier worries had evaporated. Unfortunately, just when she was beginning to relax and enjoy herself, bad news arrived in the front hall.

Isabella rushed over to her where she was chatting with friends by the fireplace and whispered, "For the love of *God*, Aly."

"I know. I see him."

"What the hell is Creepy-McCreeperson doing here?"

Alyssa watched Brad Scarborough hand his coat to a staff member and lean in to listen to whatever his gorgeous Amazon of a date was saying. "Well, Brad was invited at one point, remember?"

Isabella swore viciously under her breath and pulled her to the side. "Sure, but most people—after getting dumped—would have the decency not to show up. I will not have this event marred by that idiot making trouble. My bartender, Terry used to be a bouncer down in the Village. I could have him throw Brad out—discreetly."

"No. I don't want a scene, and it would be just like him to make one." Alyssa felt annoyance rise when Brad looked over at her and grinned. She shook her head as the couple made their way across the room. "He's not here to cause trouble. He came to make me uncomfortable. But it's not going to work. As long as he behaves, I can ignore him. But the minute he doesn't, Terry can have at him."

"Good evening, Alyssa, Isabella. Great party. Looks like it's in full swing with a good turnout."

Alyssa gave the man a thousand-watt smile. "Hey, Brad. Thanks for coming. Isabella has really outdone herself, hasn't she?"

Brad completely ignored Isabella and plunged ahead. "This is

Kasandra Delacourt. Her plans for New Year's got messed up, and since I was suddenly without a date, she agreed to come with me. You don't mind, do you?"

"No, of course not." She could feel Isabella's disgust, but her smile never faltered as she turned to Ms. Delacourt. "I'm sorry that your plans fell through, but happy Brad could rectify that." Tilting her head, Alyssa studied the woman. There was something about her that seemed a bit off, but she couldn't put her finger on it. "Kasandra, have we met before? You look really familiar."

Before the woman could answer on her own, Brad stepped in. "Kasandra's a top model. She was on the cover of *Art World* last month."

"Oh my gosh! Yes. I remember now. That was a very innovative cover."

Kasandra shrugged and flashed a beguiling smile. "I just show up and stand where they tell me to stand."

"Oh, come on, Kasandra," Brad grinned. "They don't hire just anyone, right? I bet you beat out a whole bunch of other models for that gig."

Though Kasandra sent him an incredibly sensual look that had him practically mesmerized, Alyssa got the feeling that the woman wasn't any more enamored with Brad than she'd been. In any case, Brad Scarborough was no longer her business, and she'd spent enough time making small talk for the jackass's benefit. "Well, I hope you both have a good time. The champagne is flowing and hors d'oeuvres are circulating, so enjoy."

Brad gave her another broad grin, and he and Kasandra melted into the crowd.

"Well, that left a bad taste in my mouth."

Isabella made a disgusted face. "Yeah, and I think I need a shower, as I've now got 'creepy' all over me from just standing in such close proximity. But since that won't happen for a while, let's get another drink."

"Excellent suggestion. Looks like your prince is a no show." Alyssa sighed and made a face. "And we get Brad Scarborough instead. But it's a good turnout, so I guess one can't have everything, right? "

Isabella linked her arm through Alyssa's and winked. "You never know, my friend. It ain't over until it's over. Now, come on. Those drinks aren't going to make themselves."

Four

As the limo double parked in front of the residence, Gray studied Alyssa Montague's lovely, old brownstone while Valian gave the driver instructions for a later pick-up. Gray had enjoyed the time he'd spent in this city and was fond of its architecture. Here, beneath the coating of dirt and grime that the metropolitan area had collected over the years, the European influence could still be seen—more stone and mortar than the newer steel and glass predominant on the west coast. He preferred the old over the new, partially because of the history the timeworn architecture conveyed, but mostly because it reminded him of home.

"Ready?" Valian asked, pulling him out of his musings.

Gray glanced at his watch. It was almost eleven. Hopefully the party would be in full swing, giving them good cover for what they were about to do. Taking a cleansing breath, he gave Valian a short nod. "I'm as ready as I'm ever going to be. I'm anxious to get this done and be back in Wysteria with the scepter in hand before anyone's the wiser."

"Agreed. I'll admit that I'm a little anxious myself," Alexi muttered with a roll of his shoulders. "Having the threat of sabotage and possible treason hanging over our heads, I know I'll be looking closely at every face I see until we have the damn thing in our possession and can portal home."

"Well then, let's get to it," Valian replied. "If all goes to plan, it shouldn't take but an hour or so to get it done. And if we time it right, the chaos of midnight and the revelry to follow will be a perfect distraction. We can all be gone before the crowd begins to thin out. So, good luck, my brothers."

They got out of the limo when the driver came around and opened the door, then climbed the steps to the entrance with Valian in the lead. He rang the bell, and they didn't have long to wait before a tall, thin woman in a Party Poppers uniform greeted them and invited them into the festive atmosphere.

"May I take your coats, gentlemen?" she asked with a welcoming smile.

"That would be grand." Valian gave her a brilliant smile. Removing his gloves and stuffing them into a pocket, he doffed his coat and handed it over. "And could you do us a favor, love? Find Isabella Christensen and let her know that Valian Winchester and party have finally arrived."

The woman's eyes lit up at his name. "Oh, of course, Mr. Winchester! Ms. Christensen has been expecting you."

"Better late than never—isn't that the phrase?"

"Oh, no worries, but she did leave specific instructions. If you'll just follow me."

"Absolutely. Lead on." Valian exchanged glances with Alexi and his grin widened.

Gray chuckled as Alexi rolled his eyes but fell in line to bring up the rear as the three of them followed her up the stairs to the second floor. She stopped at the first door she came to, and after opening it, gestured them inside. "If you'll make yourselves comfortable here for a few moments, I'll find Ms. Christensen and Ms. Montague and send them right up. Would you like a beverage while you wait?"

"Champagne would be lovely," Valian said and then turned to Gray.

He shook his head. "I'm fine, thank you."

"Lager for me, if you've got it," Alexi chimed in as he handed her his coat.

"Of course. I'll just go and find Ms. Christensen. Someone will be right up with your drinks."

As she closed the door behind her, Gray turned and perused the spacious room. It was a library or study with elaborate floor to ceiling bookshelves on two of the four walls, each filled to capacity with books. An ornately carved, wooden desk graced the far end of the room with a large almost industrial-looking hutch tucked in behind it. A sitting area took up the opposite wall with a settee, two wing chairs, and a coffee table.

"It appears the descendant is an avid reader," Valian said as he stepped up beside Gray and scanned the shelves to their right. "And of many different genres, it seems, though she appears to be particularly fond of fantasy, adventure, and romance. Oh, and look, Alexi. Here's *my* latest release."

Alexi made a face. "Jesus, could you be any more full of yourself? You know, just because she has a room full of books doesn't mean that she actually reads them. Remember Aunt Dorcas? She collected hundreds of books but couldn't read a word."

Gray smiled, and Valian laughed out loud.

"Lord, I'd forgotten that about her," Valian conceded. "Nonetheless, though I've never met the descendant, I'll wager fifty Wysterian gold pieces that she's read at least half of what's here."

Alexi put a hand over his heart. "Bless the Oracles, you're such a sucker. I'll take your money, cousin. It's a bet."

Gray shook his head as the two clasped hands to seal the deal just as the door opened and a staff member brought in a tray with their drinks.

As the cousins each picked up their drink of choice, Gray watched the waiter leave and then took a breath around the apprehension that had taken up residence in his chest.

"What's the matter, Gray?" Valian asked with his glass halfway to his mouth. "You've got that look."

"What look?"

"The look that says something isn't quite right, but you can't put your finger on what that something is," Alexi answered, then grinned and gestured with his beer glass. "Of course, it could just be gas or constipation."

Gray shot him a vulgar hand sign, and then glanced back at the bookshelf where his eye went right to the Lewis Carroll tome.

"Quit worrying, Gray. It's a solid plan," Valian murmured. "At least it's as good as it's gonna get without actually breaking and entering."

Alexi snickered. "Yeah, all you have to do is be your charming self. Oh, wait … maybe you or I should do that part, Val, considering."

When Gray glared at him, Alexi put up a hand. "I'm just trying to break up the tension. Dude, you have got to relax. You're never gonna get her to take you to the scepter with a scowl on your face."

"He may be annoying, Gray, but he's right. You look like you're waiting for the plan to unravel any second."

"That's because I am, damn it. Something does feel off, has since we walked in the front door. Don't either of you feel it?" When neither cousin replied, he continued with a sigh. "But there's nothing to be done about it now. We just have to keep our eyes and ears open and play it out, roll with whatever happens. So, we stick to the plan."

"Right." Valian took another sip of his champagne. "As soon as the niceties are handled, I'll take care of Isabella, Alexi will stand guard, and you'll charm the socks off of the descendant and get her to tell you where the scepter is being stored."

Gray was aware that both Valian and Alexi were waiting for his response, but his attention had been snagged by the hutch at the back of the room. "I'm not sure it's going to be all that difficult."

"Really? That certain of your charm, are you?" Alexi asked as Gray started toward the hutch.

"Well, I can be a charming beast when I put my mind to it." Gray shot a grin over his shoulder. "But that's not exactly what I was getting at. Come have a look at this."

The two men stepped up beside him and they all three stared at the top shelf of the hutch where the Scepter of Fire sparkled like a magnificent cluster of stars captured for their personal delight. Just a foot long and covered with glittering jewels, the golden scepter was close enough to reach out and touch, if it wasn't for the thick glass of the cabinet.

Indeed, Alexi reached out a hand to do just that, but Gray stopped him. "If I'm not mistaken, this cabinet may look fairly innocuous, but it's actually a high-tech security hutch, locked and equipped with a very effective security alarm."

Alexi scoffed. "Please. Elven magick will make quick work of that. I can have the scepter out in a few seconds with no one the wiser."

"Yes, but then how do we explain its absence when the ladies arrive?" Valian asked.

"So we take it and fade," Alexi replied with a shrug.

"That would be fine for you, dickhead. You don't live in this realm, do you?" Valian frowned at his cousin. "You'll not leave me holding the bag."

Gray put up a hand when Alexi would have argued. "Valian's right. Again, we follow the plan and wait for an opportune time."

"And if one doesn't present itself?" Alexi asked. "What then?"

Turning to give his Field Marshal a hard stare, Gray repeated, "Like I said before, we follow the plan"

Alexi put up his hands in surrender. "Okay, okay. Your call."

Looking back at the scepter, Gray blew out a breath. "Besides, I'm curious about the descendant. I want to at least meet her before we grab the scepter and disappear."

Valian snorted and looked toward the door. "Then we should move away from this hutch, and you'll need to put on a charming face, because my superior Elven hearing says you're about to get your chance. There are footsteps coming up the stairs right now."

The three of them stepped away from the cabinet, and moments later, the door opened and two women entered the room.

"Valian!" The woman in the lead gushed as she glided across the room and kissed both of his cheeks. "It's good to see you again."

"And you as well, Isabella."

Isabella Christensen was a vision in black and gold, with luminous green eyes and bright red curls that brushed her shoulders. However, it was the woman who'd accompanied her into the room who caught and held Gray's attention from the moment they'd entered.

Tall, svelte, and sheathed in a shimmer of silver, with golden hair swept up in an elegant fashion and the bluest eyes he'd ever seen. Quite simply, Alyssa Montague took his breath away. But as Valian began to make introductions, Gray tore his attention from the descendant to give Isabella a charming smile.

"Prince Graydon, may I introduce Isabella Christensen and Alyssa Montague. Ladies, I give you Graydon Edward Christian Hartford, Crown Prince of Wysteria, realm of Artemysia."

Both women executed small curtsies and beamed at him.

"It's an honor to have you in my home, Your Highness," Alyssa said.

"Thank you, Ms. Montague, but the honor is mine."

"Are you enjoying your stay in New York?"

"I'd say that it's been average up to now." Gray grinned at her. "But it does seem to be looking up."

Their eyes caught and held, and she gave him a coy smile. In the awkward silence that followed, Valian stepped into the gap. "Alyssa owns the Montague Art Gallery here in Manhattan, Your Grace, which I would highly recommend visiting before you head home."

"I'll make a note of it."

"And Isabella owns Party Poppers, through which she plans and executes events of all kinds." He turned to Alexi then, almost as an afterthought, added, "Oh, and ladies, let me also introduce Field Marshal Alexi Tovin. He'll be acting as Prince Graydon's bodyguard while he's in New York City."

"Welcome to you, too, Field Marshal," Isabella murmured.

"Thank you." Alexi dipped his head and gave her a cocky grin, his eyes alighting with interest. "And it's Alexi, please."

Gray watched the interaction between the two with curiosity. He thought he could almost feel the sexual energy climb a notch as the two sized each other up, but then Isabella answered Alexi's grin with a reserved nod. If he wasn't mistaken, there was a kind of reluctant attraction on both ends from the moment their eyes met.

And then Isabella fired off the first volley in a slightly aloof tone. "So, what exactly does a field marshal do? I mean, do you have other duties besides guarding the prince? That is, if you don't mind me asking, *Alexi*."

Gray thought her tone had just the right combination of disinterest and allure, and he watched his friend bristle a bit, though the smile didn't leave his face and his tone was pleasant enough.

"Oh, I have many other duties, *Isabella*. I actually have command of the queen's vast armies."

Isabella tilted her head and made a show of studying him. "Huh," was all she said.

"And do you have other duties besides ... what is it? Party planning? If you don't mind *me* asking?"

Gray hid his smile. It felt a tad like watching the mating ritual of fifth-graders, punching at each other to show they were in 'like'. But then she muttered, "Yes, I do," before abruptly dismissing Alexi. Turning to Valian with a brilliant smile, she purred, "Valian, now that the introductions are out of the way, do you want to head downstairs and check out the party? It's been a while, and I'd love to catch up with you."

"I would like that very much, Isabella." Valian grinned at Alexi and then gave Gray a meaningful look. "I know the prince would like to have a chat with Ms. Montague about a private matter before exploring the festivities, so why don't we give them that time."

"Um, I guess that would be alright." Isabella glanced at her friend. "Aly?"

"I'm sorry, I don't understand." Alyssa blinked and glanced at Gray with a blank look. "No disrespect, Your Highness, but what kind of private matter could we have to discuss?"

Gray gave her a reassuring smile. "As it turns out, our families have a distant connection."

"I beg your pardon? Connection? As in us being related in some way?"

"Oh, no, nothing like that." Gray chuckled. "At least, not that I know of. It concerns a bit of history that our families share. When I found that I was going to be in your city for New Year's, I asked Valian to contact you. I hope you don't mind."

Alyssa recovered quickly, but there was a touch of uncertainty in her eyes. "No, not at all. It's just surprising, to put it mildly."

"Okay, obviously you two have some things to talk through, so if that's all settled, I guess we'll go down and do some mingling while you two discuss family business." Isabella threw a casual look in Alexi's direction. "And what about you, *Alexi*? Will you join us downstairs?"

"No, ma'am," he replied with a sardonic look. "I'll need to hang out in the hallway and do my 'body guarding' thing. But thanks for thinking of me."

Gray watched the fleeting disappointment flicker across her face to immediately be replaced by a studied indifference.

"That's a shame, but then, I guess duty calls." Turning to Valian, she raised her eyebrows. "Shall we?"

Valian shot another triumphant grin in Alexi's direction before nodding and offering her his arm. "We shall."

Alexi's gaze followed her as she and Valian disappeared into the hallway, before he turned and gave Gray a stiff bow. "I'll be just outside the door should you need me, Your Grace. It was a pleasure to meet you, Ms. Montague."

With that, he exited the room, closing the door behind him.

And Gray was left alone with the descendant.

❧

ALYSSA WASN'T CERTAIN JUST WHAT TO MAKE OF THE prince's request. What kind of 'history' could their families possibly share? Not that her family boasted of such things, but surely she would've heard of a connection with royalty long before this. Her mind reeled with possibilities, each with its own fantastic quality.

"I suppose I should apologize. I can see that I've thrown you with this," the prince began. "I didn't mean to spring it on you in quite this way. I should have had Valian give more pertinent information when he contacted Ms. Christensen about the invitation."

Alyssa studied him a moment. He was extremely attractive, probably one of the most handsome men she'd ever met face-to-face, which was kind of ironic, in a fairy tale sort of way—a handsome prince and all that. Tall, dark, and gorgeous seemed to fit him to a tee. Everything about him spoke of sensual grace, an ease that said he was comfortable in his own skin. Yet, there was also something vitally dangerous about him, something secretive and voracious in those warm, chocolate-colored eyes that didn't exactly scare her, but made her long for a bit more distance between them or at least that they weren't so alone. And wasn't that a ridiculous thought, given that there was a houseful of guests just one floor beneath their feet?

"Ms. Montague?"

She blinked and shook the disturbing thoughts away, made a conscious effort not to step back, to put that distance in place even as something deep inside her yearned to move closer. "I'm sorry, Your Grace. This is just kind of surreal, you know? I don't understand why I've never heard of you or your family before now."

The prince tilted his head and smiled, his eyes shining with empathy—and something else she couldn't quite identify. "I can appreciate that. I've only recently learned of the connection myself. And since I'll be leaving for home tomorrow, I wanted to at least meet you before then. When Valian told me about your gala, it seemed like the only opportunity I was going to get."

"I see. So, then what is this history between our families that you mentioned, Your Highness?"

"Your Highness? Your Grace? Please, call me Gray." His voice held a familiar tone that had her pulse picking up speed and a shiver skittering along her skin.

She looked at him from beneath her lashes and tried to remember to breathe. "Alright. Tell me how we're connected, Gray."

He grinned at her then, and she swore she could feel the warmth of it all the way to her toes. As hard as she tried, she couldn't help grinning back at him. Then she reminded herself not to allow his title and the circumstances to cloud her thoughts, that she didn't really know this man.

When it was clear that she wasn't going to speak again, he laughed out loud. "You have a very expressive face, Ms. Montague."

"Alyssa," she said before she could stop herself.

He stared into her eyes, and his smile faltered. "You have a very expressive face ... Alyssa," he whispered, and she felt it again, the pull, the almost elemental need to move toward him, be closer. He seemed to feel it, too, because he leaned in, began to close the gap between them. And then he blinked and the feeling dissipated.

He straightened, then cleared his throat. "Anyway, to the reason I wanted to meet you. Again, I should apologize for making you feel like this was some kind of deep mystery. It's really not." He narrowed his eyes and gave her an intent look.

"History and family heritage are very important in my realm. I like to investigate whenever I run across something about either of them that I don't already know, no matter how small. As I was preparing for this trip, I was apprised of something that I'd never heard before."

Alyssa swallowed. "And what was that?"

"Do you know much about your ancestors, Alyssa?"

"Some. I know my family is originally from England ... that my great-great grandmother married and moved to America in the early nineteen-hundreds."

"Well, long before that time, I found that one of your maternal ancestors assisted my family during a time of great trial. You could say that in a way it turned the tide on what could have been a disastrous situation. Anyway, your family was considered a close ally for quite some time. It's only over the last few generations that history seems to have been forgotten."

"That's amazing." Alyssa shook her head, and then gasped as a thought struck her. "Oh my gosh! You should meet my parents —" The minute the words were out of her mouth, she felt the blush heat up her face, and she watched the knowing smile ease across his handsome features. "Oh, no. No, no, I didn't mean it like that ... I-I only meant that my mother is downstairs, and if this is history on my maternal side of the family ... well, I mean, she should hear this story as well, right?"

Clamping her mouth shut so as not to make matters worse, she closed her eyes and prayed for the floor to open up and swallow her whole. When she opened them again, Gray had stepped closer to her, so close that she could smell his woodsy cologne, feel the heat from his body.

"As much as I would like that, I don't think it's a good idea right now," he murmured, and she felt her breath back up in her chest as she watched his eyes dip to her lips, linger there.

And suddenly she was struggling to hold onto her thoughts. What had she wanted to do? Something about her mother, wasn't it? No, what she really wanted to do was to press her lips against his. Then he looked into her eyes and it was all she could do not to beg.

There was a distant blast of noise from downstairs—horns and music and shouts. It seemed that midnight had arrived.

Gray leaned down, his lips a mere breath away from hers. "Happy New Year, Alyssa Montague."

Then he was kissing her, and every thought completely dissolved. There was only him and his lips on hers. She couldn't breathe, couldn't think. Sensations came too fast, one overlapping the next. It was like nothing she'd ever experienced.

In the next moment, he lifted his head and stared down into her eyes, and a bewildered look crossed his face. "I probably shouldn't have done that."

Alyssa looked up at him and laughed softly. "Hey, a kiss from a real live prince at midnight? I can cross that right off my bucket list."

"I'm sorry ... I—" Whatever he was going to say was lost when there was an abrupt knock at the door and they jumped apart like felons just before a grinning Alexi opened the door and Isabella slipped past him into the room.

"I hope we're not interrupting," Isabella said with a half-smile and a quick look back at Alexi. "But your Field Marshal here would like a word, Your Highness. And Aly, your parents are about to leave. You want to come down and say goodbye?"

"Oh, yes. Tell them I'll be right down." As Isabella nodded and left the room, Alyssa looked back to Gray. "This shouldn't take long, and then we can finish our discussion."

"Of course. Take your time. " The prince reached out and took her hand, lifting it briefly to his lips. "I'm very glad to have met you, Alyssa."

She paused at his words. They were imparted pleasantly enough, yet seemed somehow so final. "I am, too, Gray. I'll be back in a flash."

Then she turned and headed downstairs.

Five

G ray smiled at Alyssa as she left the room, guilt raising its ugly head for what he was about to do. Crossing to the cabinet at the back of the room, he stared at the scepter through the thick, security glass as Alexi joined him.

"I doubt we have much time, so we should probably grab the scepter and go," the Elven warrior said as he came into the room. When Gray didn't answer, Alexi put a hand on his shoulder. "Gray?"

"I heard you." He glanced toward the doorway. "It's just that …"

"Just that what?"

Gray met Alexi's gaze. "It seems a little like a betrayal, you know? To just grab the scepter and fade."

Alexi sighed. "How can it be a betrayal when she doesn't know its history—what it is or why she has it? She only knows that it's been handed down in her family for generations. Dude, to her it's just a relic on a shelf. She'll never even miss it." Alexi waved a hand over the coded lock on the door to the cabinet, and after a soft click, the door swung open. "And if we go now, she won't know who took it, probably won't even realize it's gone for weeks. Then, when she does ... well, she'll more than likely just think it was stolen and wonder when it could've happened."

Reaching into the cabinet, Gray gently retrieved the scepter, could sense its sleeping power even as he took it into his hands. "It's not just that."

Frowning, Alexi held out the velvet sleeve they'd brought with them to carry the scepter back to Wysteria. "What is it then?"

Gray paused as he looked down at the potent artifact he held. "It was different than I thought it would be—meeting her, talking to her, the descendant of the original Alice." He shook his head. "She's interesting, attractive, nice ... and trusting. I guess I thought it would be easy because I didn't know her. Stealing from her, I mean."

"Come on, Gray. We're not stealing from her or her family. It never belonged to them in the first place."

"Don't be a dick, Alexi. That's not the point." Gray snapped, and then shook his head again. "Look, you know what I mean. Can't you put your pragmatic Elven warrior aside for one damn minute and see it from her point of view?"

Alexi blinked. "Uh ... no. I won't be a dick if you won't be an idiot. I *am* a pragmatic elven warrior, an Elven warrior who's sworn to serve the White Queen, and whose loyalties are to the Wysterian Empire."

When Gray continued to stare at him with a raised brow, Alexi relented with a grunt and a sigh. "Okay, yes. I get what you're saying. And does it bother me? Maybe a little, but it makes no difference, does it? Wysteria needs the Scepter of Fire now. It has to be returned to where it belongs, and you know it. It's the right thing to do, and our kingdom's safety depends on it." Alexi took a breath and rolled his shoulders. "Besides, what else can we do? Explain the situation to her? Just how do you think she'd take that?"

Gray sighed. "She'd think we were both lunatics."

Alexi gave a brief nod. "Exactly. We do this any other way and it gets really muddy."

"I know," Gray said as he slipped the artifact into the velvety confines of the bag. "Look, I realize this is important for the kingdom. I'm just saying that though it may be the right thing to do, it sure doesn't *feel* that way right now. I mean, her parents are right downstairs. She wanted me to meet them, if you can believe that, tell her mother the story I'd told her."

"For the love of the Oracles, you didn't tell her why we were here, did you?"

"Okay, seriously? Now who's being an idiot? Of course I didn't. I just told her that one of her ancestors on her mother's side had assisted my family during a difficult time."

Alexi snorted. "Yeah, that's an understatement."

Gray gave him a bland look. "The point is, she wanted me to repeat the story for her mother. I literally had to use magick to suppress the notion so that she wouldn't drag me down to meet her parents. And then ..."

"Then what?"

"Nothing." Gray sighed.

"But you handled it, right?"

Pulling the ties together and sliding the bag under his arm, Gray frowned. "I suppose."

"Well, then where's the problem?"

Other than that brief, incredible kiss that we shared?

He'd lost himself for a moment when he'd all but had Alyssa in his arms. He could still feel the softness of her lips, the taste of her on his own. He'd meant to use magick to distract her, but had ended up using it to protect himself. He couldn't explain how she'd made him feel and found he was reluctant to discuss it with Alexi. "I guess there isn't a problem," he finally answered.

Alexi threw his arms out to his sides. "Okay then, what exactly are we waiting for? Put it away and don't make this personal. Valian has probably already slipped out like we'd planned, and we need to do the same before she comes back."

"You're right." Gray held out his arm to Alexi. "Which means we'd probably better go before I think too hard on it and change my mind, right?"

The Elven warrior grinned, and tilting his head, his icy-blue eyes twinkled. "So, with your royal blood and family history of magick, remind me again how it is that you've never learned to fade?"

When Gray just glared at him, Alexi burst into laughter. Grabbing Gray by the arm, they were gone in a blink.

ALYSSA GLANCED AT HER WATCH. TWELVE THIRTY-FIVE in the morning and the exodus of guests was already beginning. She'd said goodbye to her parents first, then Isabella's parents, and then a handful of friends, before finally turning the duty over to Isabella and hurrying back upstairs as fast as her four-inch pumps would allow.

She'd only been gone for about fifteen or twenty minutes, but when she stepped into her office she was slightly baffled to see that the prince and his bodyguard were nowhere to be seen. Since she'd been in the foyer with a clear view of the staircase, she knew they hadn't come downstairs.

However, the room was not empty. Kasandra Delacourt was perusing the cabinet of heirlooms at one end of the room, while Brad sat on the sofa staring off into space, mouth open, a vacant look on his face.

"Kasandra? What are you and Brad doing up here? And when did you two come upstairs. I've been in the foyer for the last half an hour and I didn't see you come up here." When the woman didn't acknowledge her, she tried again, an uneasy feeling beginning to blossom in her chest. "Kasandra? Most of the other guests are beginning to leave or have gone already."

The super model slowly turned then, shifting her startling green eyes in Alyssa's direction.

And her unease grew.

"I was hoping to get to it first," she said, her voice soft and lilting. "But I was too late. They've already gone and have taken it with them."

"Hoping to get to what first?" Alyssa asked slowly, but her attention was on Brad. He didn't look right, didn't give any indication that there were others in the room with him. And there was an almost hollow look on his face, as if there was nothing at all behind his eyes. "Brad? Are you okay?"

"He's fine," Kasandra assured her. She tilted her head and came toward Alyssa while she studied Brad as if he were some kind of curiosity. "He's just ... unavailable right now."

"What do you mean 'unavailable'?" Alyssa frowned. She'd never known Brad to dabble in drugs, so this was something new to her. "He doesn't look fine, Kasandra. Is he on something? Some kind of drug?"

Kasandra's chuckle was low and almost sensual. "I suppose you could say that. He's enchanted, Alyssa."

"Enchanted ... right." She had no idea what the hell Kasandra was talking about, but she didn't care for the crazy vibe that seemed to be pouring off the woman.

I think there's something wrong with both of you.

"So, would you like me to call a cab for the two of you?"

"That won't be necessary. Transportation is not a problem."

Alyssa studied Brad for a moment more before glancing around the room. "Um, Kasandra? Where did Prince Graydon and his bodyguard get off to?"

The model gave her a patient look. "I told you. They took the artifact and left."

Alyssa shook her head. "I've been in the foyer for the last twenty minutes, and I didn't see them leave. So, unless they flew out of a window, that can't be right."

"Maybe they did fly away ... or simply *faded*." The woman actually giggled.

"Okaaay," Alyssa answered slowly. "Why don't we just let that go for the moment? So, tell me what *artifact* you're talking about."

The woman gestured toward the heirloom cabinet. "The Scepter of Fire, of course."

"The what?" Blinking, Alyssa glanced toward the hutch and then back at the model. "Kasandra, you're not making any sense. Are you sure you're feeling okay?"

And what drugs are you *on?*

"Oh, I'm not on any drugs," Kasandra said, as if she'd read Alyssa's mind, then she chuckled again, and this time a touch of fear made its way down Alyssa's spine.

"It's ironic, though, don't you think?" the woman asked. "A powerful artifact like the scepter hidden in this mortal realm for decades. It's been resting right here in this ordinary cabinet, and you had no idea what you were hiding. Just a trinket on a shelf."

From where she was standing Alyssa could see that one of the family heirlooms was gone from the top shelf of the security hutch. She hurried around her desk to the cabinet and tried the door. It was armed with the lock secure, the alarm light still lit. Who could have possibly taken the heirloom, and how on earth did they get into the hutch without the alarm blaring? She was the only one with the combination and the alarm code.

Kasandra took a slow step toward her then, and another, almost like a jungle cat stalking its prey. Alyssa frowned and moved around her desk in the opposite direction. Inexplicably, she felt a sort of panic begin to rise at the back of her throat, as the woman followed her around the desk. For some reason, the closer Kasandra got, the stronger the feeling became. She wanted to move farther but couldn't seem to get her feet to work fast enough as she backed toward the sitting area. Adding to her anxiety, she was fast becoming light-headed, finding it difficult to draw a good breath, as if the air in the room had gotten thinner and she was lacking the appropriate oxygen.

"Yes, you're a bit smitten with him. I can see that now,"

Kasandra murmured and ran a long, slender finger down Alyssa's cheek.

"What ... are you ... talking about?" Alyssa replied, her voice sounding out of breath, even to her own ears.

"Prince Graydon. You're quite taken with him."

"I'm ... not. I've only just met him."

"Ah, but sometimes that's all it takes. Like speaks to like, as they say," Kasandra crooned tenderly. "I find the human heart a strange creature, and often it reacts swiftly to a twin beat. I've seen it happen on many occasions."

Alyssa was having a really hard time following the conversation. It was something about the prince, but her head was filled with a soft humming, foggy. And languid warmth was seeping into her limbs.

As the woman took Alyssa's face in her hands and looked deeply into her eyes, Alyssa could literally *feel* that lazy warmth spread through her veins like honey.

"But the point is," Kasandra continued. "The prince and his warrior stole your scepter, Alyssa. Don't you want to find them?"

Alyssa wheezed in a breath, and then finally found the strength to take that step back, but with her head swimming, she was no longer sure why it was so imperative. "What's ... what's happening here?"

"If you want to retrieve your property, Alyssa, I can help you. I can take you to the portal, if you'd like." Kasandra tilted her head, and Alyssa felt an incredible sense of well-being pour over her. "All you need do is ask, child. If we hurry, we may be able to catch them. Wouldn't you like that?"

Suddenly Alyssa wanted that very much. "Yes ... yes, where did they go?"

"No worries. I'll show you. Brad and I will accompany you to the portal," Kasandra said, and Alyssa was vaguely aware of Brad rising and coming toward them. Then the woman beckoned to her. "Take my hand, Alyssa. And we'll fly."

But Alyssa's attention was snagged by Kasandra's

outstretched fingers. They were fascinating. Long, incredibly long and ... leaf green? An insistent voice at the back of her mind seemed to shout *'back away, back away, back away.'* But it was so distant, and she watched as her own fingers involuntarily reached out to take hold of those long, green digits.

And then they did fly, or so it seemed. Her office dissolved and a wind blew all around them. A brilliant swirl of colors assaulted her eyes, and she had the oddest sense of weightlessness.

I'm dreaming this, she thought with a giggle. *But what an interesting and lovely dream. Like something out of a fairy tale.*

Moments later, everything came to a halt, and she struggled to get a hold of her equilibrium and make sense of what she saw. The three of them stood in what looked to be a forest or a park.

And though she had no recollection of voicing her thoughts, Kasandra answered them. "Yes, that's right. The old park in the heart of the city. Here lies the earliest portal in the New York realm. It will take you to Artemysia, where you will find your prince, if you are worthy, that is. Are you worthy, do you think? I am so hoping that you are. Otherwise, the fun will be over too soon."

Alyssa shook her head, the frigid night air clearing away some of the fog. She was still in her party garb without a coat, and her teeth began to chatter. What the hell was going on? They were in Central Park? And how on earth had they gotten here?

"Is this ... am I dreaming?" she asked no one in particular. Then she started to giggle again, couldn't help herself, really, as the whole thing suddenly seemed absurd. "I can feel the cold, smell the greenery, but this can't be real, right?"

"It can be anything you'd like it to be."

Kasandra pulled her close and waved a hand toward the nearby copse of trees. "I know it's a bit confusing, but all will become clear when you step through the portal. It's just there. Can you see it?"

And suddenly she did see it—a lovely whirlpool of light and air that distorted the surrounding trees and bushes. Again, it was enchanted, like something out of a storybook, and her mind reeled. What would she find on the other side of that light?

"What do you wish to find on the other side, Alyssa?" Kasandra asked again and gave another wave.

And just like that, Alyssa found she was wearing a warm fur coat, and though she was grateful for it, was baffled about how it came to be. Of course, this had to be a dream. There was no other explanation, though it was one of the most realistic dreams that she'd ever experienced. She stared at the swirling light. "Is it safe?"

"Of course it's safe—again, if you are worthy. *Are* you worthy, Alyssa?" Giving her a gentle push toward the eddy, Kasandra smiled. "Shall we find out? It's the doorway to Artemysia. A few short steps and you're there. Go. *Fly.*"

Close, so close she could feel the pull of the vortex, but she stopped just short of going through. Fear rose in her mind. Suddenly she wasn't certain that she wanted to find out if she was worthy or not, or what was on the other side of the spinning light. It felt almost *alien* up close, strange and a bit scary, like a rip in the fabric of time and space. Looking back at Kasandra, Brad standing slack-jawed at her side, she faltered.

"Go ahead, Alyssa," Kasandra urged. "Don't be afraid, be fearless. Step into your adventure and *soar.*"

Turning back to the churning turbulence, Alyssa reached out a hand, felt the sucking motion, yet still hesitated. This had become the strangest night in her memory. She had no explanation for any of it. But then, looking at the churning colors, she wondered what she had to lose? She was dreaming after all, so nothing, it seemed.

With that last thought, she stepped into the swirl of the portal.

Six

Well, this is a bit of a quandary, Valian thought as he watched Isabella say goodbye to a few more guests. Just what the hell was he supposed to do now? The crowd was dwindling at an alarming speed, and he was now left with a plot gone sideways.

The idea had been for him to slip out unnoticed shortly after midnight, with Gray and Alexi grabbing the scepter and fading back to the portal at an opportune moment. He could have then told Isabella later that Gray had been called back to Artemysia on royal business, and they'd had to leave quickly.

Unfortunately, though he'd begun a casual trek toward the foyer over an hour ago with that specific intent in mind, he'd been waylaid over and over again. And just when his goal was finally in sight, Isabella had popped up in front of him, and she'd dragged him into the foyer to meet her parents as they were leaving.

Thus, he'd ended up drafted into the 'farewell' brigade and stuck between Isabella and Alyssa a mere twenty feet from the front door, watching guest after guest depart yet unable to do so himself. Since he'd been the one to arrange the invitation and had brought Gray and Alexi with him, he couldn't very well leave without them.

He glanced up at the top of the staircase with trepidation. Alyssa had come down to say goodbye to her parents and had spent twenty minutes or so thanking a few guests for coming before turning the duty over to Isabella and heading back upstairs. He was pretty sure the guys had snatched the scepter and faded the minute she'd left the room but now almost hoped they hadn't. He had no clue how he was going to explain their absence after Alyssa left them upstairs, only to find them gone when she'd returned a short while later.

Awkward, very awkward—especially when both women had been within clear view of the front door during that time frame.

And just when he thought the situation couldn't get any worse, Kasandra Delacourt appeared at the top of the stairs, and Valian's evening went a little farther down the rabbit hole.

She gave him her sweetest High Fae smile as she descended, and he had a feeling that something really bad must have happened upstairs. With a faerie in the mix, especially High Fae, it never boded well.

"Kasandra," he said as she neared the bottom of the stairs. "I didn't know you were here this evening."

"That's funny. I saw you through the crowd several times."

"And apparently avoided me."

Kasandra made a pouty face. "Valian Winchester, that's a terrible thing to say. Why would I want to avoid a charming elf like you?"

He cringed and gave a sidelong glance toward Isabella but to his relief, saw that she'd walked a young couple to the door and was out of ear-shot.

"Why, indeed?" he asked, turning back to Kasandra. "How do you know Alyssa?"

"Oh, I don't. I'd never met her until tonight. But she seems to be a lovely young woman ... for a human." She gestured to the man who'd followed her down the staircase, a human male who'd clearly been enchanted. "Brad here used to date Alyssa. Isn't that right, my pet?" The man took her outstretched hand

and gazed adorningly at her. "He was kind enough to let me tag along."

Valian's bad feeling moved right up to dreadful. Leaning in, he kept his voice low. "What have you done, Kasandra? I know you're not here just for the canapés."

The faerie tilted her head, and her eyes were vivid, green fire. "You don't play fair, Valian," she replied in a quiet voice. "But then, elves never do. Naughty, very naughty. I really wanted to join the fun upstairs, but unfortunately, I was just a smidgen too late. For the first part ... that is."

"Uh-huh. I'm gonna assume that means Gray and Alexi are gone."

"Mmm. They did get away with the prize, but I got a little fun in afterward ... with our lovely hostess."

"What do you mean? Why hasn't Alyssa come back down yet? I'll only ask you once more. What have you done? Where is she, Kasandra?"

Before she could answer, Isabella interrupted them. "Where's who?"

Kasandra gave him another evil grin. "Valian was just wondering where Alyssa's gotten off to. I was about to tell him that the last time I saw her, she was looking for her prince. I just gave her some ... direction."

"Okaaaay," Isabella said slowly. "So, are you and Brad heading out?"

Kasandra nodded. "We are. I do need my beauty sleep." She leaned in and spoke in a conspiratorial whisper. "You know, everyone thinks super models are party animals, but the truth is, I prefer a quiet evening with a good book. I'm really into fantasy and adventure." She smirked at Valian and then turned back to Isabella. "You did a spectacular job with the party, Isabella."

"Thanks. I'm glad you enjoyed it."

"Oh, I did. It was *very* entertaining. I'll definitely think of you the next time I'm in need of an event planner." The woman guided Brad to the door and then looked back over her shoulder at them. Good luck with the puzzle … and the clean-up, Valian. It was such fun to see you again. Ta-ta."

The moment the door closed, Isabella turned to him. "That is a very strange woman."

"Oh, you have no idea, love."

"Not sure she deserves to be hounded by Brad Scarborough, but then, different strokes, right?" Isabella narrowed her eyes. "How, exactly, do you know her?"

"It's a long story." Glancing at the top of the staircase again, he shook his head. "And one we don't have time for. Right now we need to go up and check on Alyssa."

"What? Why? She and the prince probably just got caught up in conversation. I mean, did you see the way he looked at her? He was absolutely infatuated. And you didn't hear it from me, but I think there was some New Year's smoochin' going on up there. They looked pretty guilty when I walked into the room." She wiggled her eyebrows. "Besides, I need to man the door. There are still quite a few folks left."

Valian's internal alarm was beginning to peal. Something was definitely off, and the fact that Kasandra was here—and cryptic about what she'd been up to—told him he wasn't going to like whatever she'd done.

Snapping his fingers at one of Isabella's staff members, he instructed the woman to take over at the door before grabbing an outraged Isabella by the arm and ushering her toward the stair-case. But before he could haul her upstairs with him, she balked, and the look on her face, as well as the way she jerked her arm from his grasp and slapped her hands on her hips, told him she didn't appreciate it.

"Listen up, pal. You don't get to manhandle me and order my staff around like this. I don't care how pretty you are."

Valian laughed out loud in spite of the situation. "Why, Isabella Christensen, you think I'm pretty?"

Isabella shrugged and examined her fingernails. "Maybe. Don't let it go to your head." His amusement faded when she looked up at him, and he saw the worry in her eyes. "Now, why are you so intent on me checking up on Aly? What's going on, Valian?"

"Perhaps nothing, but I'd feel much better if you'd just come with me upstairs and have a look."

She crossed her arms and stared at him for a moment, and he thought she might give him more grief. But then she nodded. "Alright. I'll go up with you, but just remember, I'm nobody's lackey. You get me, mister?"

Valian tried not to smile, though with her diminutive size combined with that regal attitude, it was almost impossible. "I do, indeed, love."

With another nod, Isabella turned and started up the stairs. Valian followed her with a mixture of dread and resignation. He felt certain that Gray and Alexi were long gone. So, if that was the case, why hadn't Alyssa returned? The only explanation was faerie mischief. And that could include all manner of terrible options.

They made their way to Alyssa's office, and when Isabella preceded him into the room, he stopped dead in the doorway. He could smell the magick, almost taste it before he'd even crossed the threshold.

Faerie magick.

God damn it!

"Okay. Where is she, Valian?" Isabella blurted, after scanning the room. "Where have they taken her?"

"I beg your pardon?" He frowned at her. "Where did *who* take her?"

"The prince and his bodyguard."

"You think Prince Graydon and Alexi took her somewhere? I can assure you, that isn't the case."

"Oh really? Well, they were the only ones up here, and now they're all gone."

Valian shook his head. "No, Isabella. They weren't the only ones up there."

Her eyes widened as his meaning became clear. "Kasandra and

Brad? Are you kidding me? You're telling me that you think Kasandra and Brad did something to Aly? How? And when? We just saw them leave."

"I'm not telling you anything, Isabella. Other than the fact that I know neither the prince nor Alexi would've had a part in anything underhanded."

Isabella put a hand on his arm as he started to pass. "I don't understand what's happening here, Valian. Are you sure this wasn't something to do with the prince?"

Valian gave a surprised bark of laughter before he could contain himself. "I think you've been reading far too many political thrillers. However, having said that, I suppose it's possible that Artemysia politics could be involved in some way." Valian ran a hand over her hair and gave her what he hoped was a reassuring smile. "But let's not borrow trouble by jumping to conclusions just yet. Okay?"

Crossing to the security hutch, he could see that the scepter was gone, so Gray and Alexi must have been successful. He gave the room a brief but thorough scan. However, he found nothing else of interest, not one clue as to what had transpired. So if Gray and Alexi had taken the scepter and faded back to the portal, where had Alyssa gone? Surely they wouldn't have taken her with them. For what purpose? Even if she would've caught them in the act, either man could have handled that situation with a bit of magick.

Then it hit him. What had Kasandra said?

'... the last time I saw her, she was looking for her prince. I just gave her some ... direction.'

What if Kasandra had sent Alyssa to the portal? That would explain the taint of faerie magick in the room, but how would Alyssa have known how to navigate it? Kasandra didn't have enough time to take Alyssa to Wysteria herself and get back to the townhouse in time to be seen leaving, and definitely not with an enchanted human in tow.

But if she'd only taken Alyssa to the portal and sent her

through alone, Alyssa could have ended up anywhere in Artemysia that Kasandra had desired to send her. And *that* was a very disturbing thought. Kasandra was High Fae, originally from Roseland's Evening Court. And faeries from her court weren't known for their benevolent assistance.

One thing was certain, he needed to get back to Wysteria and make sure Gray and Alexi had gotten safely home with the scepter, and then figure out what had happened to Alyssa. Because it was a sure bet that the White Queen would *not* be amused if they'd lost her.

Isabella was watching him with unrestrained impatience, and he was really at a loss as to how to explain what he felt certain had happened. He could use magick, fog her memories again. He'd done it once before when they'd first met at an immortal party she'd catered, but that wouldn't really solve anything now. And what if Alyssa was lost in Artemysia for an indefinite amount of time? It was a very slippery slope. But could he make Isabella understand without sounding insane? Maybe it *would* be best to alter her memory.

"So?" Isabella began, her eyes wide and searching. "You know what's happened here, don't you?"

Before he could answer or decide what course of action to take, a staff member entered the room and cleared his throat. "Um, Isabella, sorry to interrupt, but we've started packing up. There are only a few guests left, and they're getting ready to leave as well. Do you want me to find Ms. Montague and get the paperwork signed?"

Isabella shook her head. "No, that won't be necessary, Terry. I'll handle the paperwork with Aly myself." She gave Valian a meaningful look. "Mr. Winchester and I need to *clarify* a few things regarding Prince Graydon and then we'll be right down."

"You got it."

The minute the man left the room, Isabella repeated her question. "You *do* know what's happened to Aly, don't you? Tell me what's going on."

He was between a rock and a very hard place. If he altered her memory, which would allow him to leave without any issues, what then if Alyssa didn't return from wherever she'd gone? And if he did choose to tell Isabella something, what exactly should it be? A concocted story? Partial truth?

"Valian?"

Taking hold of her arm again, he guided her out of the room keeping a tight grip as they descended the stairs to the foyer.

"Valian? Talk to me. Please. I'm scared."

"I know you are, love." He turned and ran a hand over his face. "And yes, I do have an idea, but Isabella, I really can't give you an explanation you'll understand or probably even accept."

She crossed her arms and frowned at him. "Can't or won't?"

He mirrored her stance and then leaned in. "Look, it's not that I don't want to explain, it's that I know you won't believe me … no matter how thoroughly I do it."

"Try," she said with a narrowed look.

Valian glanced toward the living room where Party Poppers staffers were in the process of packing up the event before shaking his head. "Not here. No prying eyes or ears."

"Please. Look around. I'm pretty sure the last few guests departed while we were upstairs. All that's left in the house is my staff."

"Huh-uh. I won't get into it here. And I can't wait around for you to close up the house. Time is a luxury that we don't have, so I'm afraid an explanation is going to have to wait."

When he turned toward the door, she grabbed his arm. "I don't have to be here to close up the house, and you're not going anywhere without me, pal."

He looked down at her hand on his arm and then up into her impossibly green eyes where her determination was evident. "Isabella—"

"I mean it, Valian. Just give me time to get the staff squared away. Then I can go wherever you want."

Taking her with him was a terrible idea, no question, and

would involve explaining so much more than he was prepared to reveal. And what if they didn't find Alyssa in his home world? That would be disastrous. Then again, what if they did? Maybe it would be best to have a familiar face along to soothe Alyssa, to help her–understand what was happening? They could always alter both women's memories after the ordeal was over. It would be messier but possible.

Making an executive decision, he gestured to her cocktail dress and pumps and grinned. "I hope you have something else to change into, because what you're wearing, though exquisite, is not really suitable for the journey we'll need to make."

She answered his grin with one of her own. "I happen to have more *suitable* attire upstairs."

"Good. Get them and bring them with you. We'll need to drop by my loft before we go. You can change there while I try to prepare you for the unbelievable." He made a show of looking at his Rolex. "You have ten minutes. I'd get moving if I were you."

She rolled her eyes at him, but hurried up the stairs to collect her things. A few minutes later she was back downstairs with a bag, her suitcase of a purse, and a wool overcoat. "Give me two minutes to give the keys to Terry with a bit of instruction, and then we can jet."

He looked at his watch again. "It seems that you have four of your ten minutes left. Looks like you're right on schedule."

"Ha-ha. You're just so funny."

He watched her go with a smile on his face. She was holding up rather well, considering the scenarios that were no doubt running around in her head. Come to that, he was fairly surprised at himself, as he was seriously contemplating telling her the whole, unvarnished truth ... well, at least a goodly portion of it. It would be interesting to see how she processed the information.

Moments later, she was back and slipping into her coat. Grabbing her purse from the foyer table and the bag from the floor, she gave him a saccharin smile. "I'm ready. Where to? And do you have a car waiting?"

He took the bag out of her grasp, and then held the door open for her to step out into the frigid night. "We're going to my loft, and we won't be needing a car."

She turned to him before going down the steps to the sidewalk. "Um, Valian, you do realize it's almost two in the morning and freezing out here, right?"

"Yep, but it won't matter for long." He took her arm as they descended the stairs.

"Why? Because we'll freeze to death walking and then won't care?"

"Now who's being funny?" As they started up the sidewalk crossing into a dark patch between the townhouses, he added, "Take a breath, love. And hold on tight."

With that, they disappeared from the street, reappearing moments later in the middle of his living room.

Valian glanced down at her face to gauge her reaction so far. What he found was promising.

She looked up at him with a mixture of shock and wonder, though she was having a bit of trouble finding her words. "What the … did we just … how did you …"

Walking to the sofa, a tad wobbly on her four inch pumps, she dropped down and blinked several times.

He followed and hunched down in front of her. "Isabella? Are you alright?"

She gazed into his eyes, opening and closing her mouth several times before saying, "Did that really just happen?"

"Yes, I'm afraid this is all quite real. I told you it would be difficult to explain and fairly unbelievable. Fading, what we just did to get from the townhouse to my loft, is just the first, small step into my world. Are you sure you want to go any farther?"

She surprised him again by taking a deep breath and nodding.

"Alright, then. But we don't have much time. So, why don't you change your clothes, and I'll tell you what I can."

She nodded again, and picking up her bag, followed him to one of the spare bedrooms.

When he went to shut the door behind her, she grabbed a hold from the other side. "Huh-uh. Since I'm not dreaming or hallucinating, and since we don't have a lot of time, leave it cracked and start explaining. I have a feeling things are only going to get more bizarre from here on out, and I hate getting blind-sided. I want to know as much as possible before we head out."

"Fair enough," he said through the door. "Then I guess I should start with my home world."

"Your *home world*? What does that mean?"

"Well, I'm not actually from… here."

He heard her snort from behind the door. "What? Like you're an alien?"

Valian sighed but continued. "Not exactly. I'm Artemysian."

"Artemysian? Like, you're from the same country as Prince Graydon?"

"Yes, sort of. Artemysia is divided into two kingdoms, Isabella. Wysteria and Roseland. Gray, Alexi, and I are from Wysteria. However, Artemysia isn't exactly a country in this realm."

The crack in the door widened, and Isabella's face appeared. "In this *realm*?"

"Yes. Artemysia actually lies in … another dimension, love. It's a place of incredible wonder, where magick flows in abundance. But it can also hold great danger, especially to the unaware."

"Uh-huh. Another dimension." She clearly wasn't buying it and her eyes narrowed before her face disappeared behind the door again. "And you think that's where we'll find Aly, in this other dimension?"

"I really hope not, but I'm afraid it's likely."

"So, what kind of danger would that pose to her, if that's where she is?"

In for a penny, in for a pound.

Closing his eyes, he plunged ahead. "Well, there are elves and trolls, faeries, all manner of magickal beings, really. Some are benevolent, some... uh ... not so much. That's one of the reasons finding Kasandra at the party was disturbing."

"Why is that?"

"Kasandra is High Fae from Roseland's Evening Court."

Isabella's face appeared in the door crack again. "What the hell is 'High Fae'? I assume from your tone that's not a good thing?"

"Think of High Fae as the upper class of fair folk. They're much more powerful than lesser faeries and can be unpredictable. Being High Fae is not necessarily a bad thing, but faeries from Roseland's Evening Court are not known for being kind or helpful. They're more like dangerously mischievous."

"And Kasandra is one of those? Figures," she muttered before disappearing around the door again. "And what about the prince and Alexi? Are they magical beings, too?"

"Gray comes from a magickal family, but he's human."

"And Alexi? You two seem pretty tight."

"Alexi is actually my cousin." He took a deep breath. "He's from a clan of Elven warriors who've served the White Queen for generations."

"Elven? As in *elves*, like in Lord of the Rings? Like, with long silver hair and pointy ears?"

Valian sighed and ran a hand over his face. "Sort of."

"So then why didn't Alexi look like that?"

"Because his Elven features were disguised. Anyway, our realm is full of unrest right now, Isabella. It's one of the reasons that Gray and Alexi were here, to retrieve the Scepter of Fire from the descendant—Alyssa."

"Excuse me?" The door flew open at that, and Isabella stepped into the hallway.

She'd finished changing, and he scanned her new outfit. The designer jeans; thick, cream-colored sweater; and leather riding boots, though very stylish, would also be a much better choice for the journey ahead than her cocktail dress and heels.

"Scepter of Fire? Descendant? Are you saying that Aly is somehow mixed up in this absurdly farfetched story?"

Valian scrubbed his hands over his face. They were running out of time, and he had a few things of his own to get together before they could head to the portal—like collecting his weapons. He wasn't about to portal to Wysteria without some kind of protection for them both. Just in case.

Turning, he spoke over his shoulder as he headed for the living room. "The scepter is a powerful artifact that must be returned to Wysteria to help avoid a costly war. Alyssa's ancestors have been the custodians of the scepter for generations, going back to the original Alice. So, yes, she's very much mixed up in this, whether she knows it or not."

"The original Alice?" Isabella choked out a laugh. "You've got to be joking. You're not talking about Wonderland's Alice, right? The child's story connected to Aly's family? That's fiction, Valian."

"Yeah, not so much a fictional story as an embellishment of some actual events."

"So, you're saying that Aly's ancestor was the original Alice?"

"Yes."

"And you, Gray, and Alexi were at the party tonight to steal her family's scepter?"

He turned to her with another sigh. "Isabella, Alyssa's family has safeguarded it through the generations, but it was never theirs. It belongs in Wysteria."

She waved a hand in the air. "Okay, so you were there to take it back. But ..." She looked up at him from beneath her lashes. "Was that the only reason you called me? To wrangle invitations for the three of you just to get access to the scepter?"

"Isabella—"

"It doesn't matter." She shook her head. "You said that there are others here from your world. That fantasy-themed party my company worked in the Hamptons? The one where we first met? Were those people from Artemysia?"

Valian went to the weapons cabinet and pulled out his favorite sword and a couple of daggers, placing them on the kitchen island next to his backpack. "Many of them, yes. There is a good-sized community of us in and around New York City."

She nodded toward the weaponry. "Expecting trouble, are you? Perhaps anticipating a sword fight?"

"Charming. Look, because the kingdom is on the brink of war, it's unpredictable and dangerous. We're portaling in through a very old tunnel, one that is rarely used these days, but I don't know how safe even that is. I'm not about to be unprepared, especially with a guest in tow."

"Spoken like a seasoned veteran," she said with a twinkle in her eye before a calculating look crossed her face. "So, if Alexi is an *Elven warrior*, and you two are cousins, does that mean you're an Elven warrior as well?"

He'd hoped to avoid this part, but loved the way her mind connected the dots, even if she didn't believe a word of it. He gave her a direct look. "Yes it does, but we really don't have time to get—"

"Show me." Isabella grinned, and the sheer joy in her eyes nearly took his breath away. "I mean, I assume—like Alexi—that you're disguised or your features are magically hidden or something, too. I want to see what you really look like."

Or if I'm making shit up, he thought and couldn't help but smile. "It's called glamouring, love. And it goes something like this."

Closing his eyes for a moment, he dropped the glamour that he'd worn so long in the New York realm that it was like a second skin. When he opened his eyes, she had a look of stunned wonder on her face that was magnificent to behold. It had been a very long time since a female had looked at him—the real him—in that way. It was sort of intoxicating.

"That's like something out of a fairy tale," she breathed. Standing, she came to him then, took in his long silver hair, the pointed tips of his ears. "Your eyes are even different. And here I thought you were just another pretty face. But you're beautiful,

Valian. How can you stand to cover your true self day in and day out?"

Valian cleared his throat. She'd surprised him yet again. "We live much longer than humans. Some of our kind can live for centuries, so those of us who've chosen to live among you must glamour ourselves. It's just the way it is. I've lived in this city for a very long time, from your perspective, so I guess it's become second nature."

Reaching out a hand, she placed it gently to his cheek. "I think I like you this way better ... if that's possible."

He wanted desperately in that moment to turn his head and press his lips to the palm of her hand, wanted to feel her in his arms, but a voice in the back of his mind told him that would be a mistake, and one he may never be able to rectify. It took every ounce of strength he had to take a step back from her, and he watched the light of joy and longing fade from her eyes as she dropped her hand to her side.

"I'm sorry, but we really do need to go. We've lost too much time as it is."

She nodded and awkwardly glanced around the room. "Um, so what happens now?"

He took her by the arm and smiled. "Now we fly."

And then they did.

Seven

G ray and Alexi came through the portal just a mile or so from Wysteria's northern palace gates. It was still several hours until dawn, and Gray was anxious to get their precious cargo back to the safety of the White Palace as quickly as possible. To that end, both he and Alexi drew their weapons the moment they stepped from the portal, and he settled the straps of the bag holding the scepter over his right shoulder to keep it clear of his sword arm. With the breaches they'd suffered in the perimeter wards over recent weeks, they could no longer take the security of the kingdom for granted. And taking chances with the Scepter of Fire—the one object that could ensure that safety —was not an option.

Gray would have loved to have faded from the portal to the palace, but when the breaches were first discovered, one of the earliest precautions to be put into place was a spell to restrict fading within a mile perimeter of the palace walls. So, he and Alexi would have to get to the palace on foot. And if the border wards had been breached again while they'd been in the New York realm, they wouldn't know that until it was too late. Accordingly, they'd agreed to move quickly and keep a steady eye on their surroundings until they were safely inside the palace walls.

"So, do you want to talk about it?" Alexi asked when they had walked for a few minutes in silence.

Gray glanced in his direction. "Talk about what?"

Alexi's chuckle was low and suggestive. "About what else happened between you and Alyssa tonight?"

A self-conscious twinge rose at the back of Gray's mind. "What *else* happened? I don't know what you mean."

"Uh-huh." Alexi grinned as he dropped the glamour he'd taken on for the New York realm. "How about whatever it was that you didn't want to tell me before?"

As Alexi's words sank in, Gray stopped walking and stared at the man with his mouth open. "Are you kidding me? You were listening in on our conversation?"

Alexi laughed out loud and gestured to one of his pointed ears. "Hello? Elven hearing here, remember? Of course I was eavesdropping. Why wouldn't I." The man held up a hand, stemming what would've become a string of obscenities. "And before you freak out and start calling me names, I was acting as bodyguard, remember."

"Yeah, right. That's your excuse?"

"Oh, hell no! I was listening in because I could." Alexi chuckled again. "Besides, just after the New Year's commotion began, I heard you wish her a Happy New Year. Then it got really quiet in there. I'm a pretty sharp guy, and I know the New York realm and their customs as well as you do. I put two and two together."

Gray snorted and started walking again. "It was highly inappropriate."

"What was?" Alexi asked as he fell into step beside him. "My listening in? Or you kissing her? You did kiss her, right?"

"Maybe."

"Did she kiss you back?"

His friend's amusement was like salt in a fresh wound. "For the love of the Oracles, Alexi."

"Come on, buddy. Inquiring minds want to know."

"You know, I could say the same." Gray stopped again and turned with a frustrated look.

Alexi blinked at him. "What are you talking about? I didn't kiss anyone tonight."

Gray gave a bark of laughter. "Maybe not, but there were definitely sparks flying between you and Isabella Christensen."

"Don't be ridiculous," Alexi replied, but even in the darkness, Gray could see that he was uncomfortable and probably blushing before he turned and abruptly started walking again. "We barely said a handful of words to each other."

"Yeah, well, in this case, it wasn't so much the quantity as the quality of those words, believe me. It was like watching some weird, brief mating ritual."

"What the hell are you talking about? The quality? *So, what exactly does a field marshal do?*" he mimicked in an unattractive imitation of Isabella, then made a face. "I'm telling you, that woman is too hoity-toity and condescending for her own good."

Gray laughed again. "You know, you can bitch and deny all you want, but it only proves my point. Besides, I swear the sexual tension in the room jumped about ten notches the minute you two looked at each other, even though it looked like you were about to go a few rounds in a ring. Must have pissed you off when she left with Valian."

"That's absurd. Why would it piss me off?" Shaking his head, Alexi stopped and pointed a finger at Gray. "And why in the hell are we talking about me? I'm not the one who kissed the girl."

"Skill, my friend. Deflective skills."

"Oh brother. Pathetic."

Before Gray could respond, Alexi's head whipped around, and he stared off to the right of the path they were on.

"Alexi?"

The Elven warrior put up a hand for silence. "We've got company. About forty or fifty yards back. Stealthy, but not stealthy enough. Definitely too silent for trolls, but elves, maybe fae? We need to move. Now!"

They turned in unison and began to run. This was exactly what Gray had feared—being ambushed before they could get to the palace with the scepter. He hadn't known from whom the threat would come or where it would take place, but the feeling that someone would make a play for the scepter before they could secure it had been strong.

About now, he was really regretting the fade-restricting spell that had been placed around the palace proper. "Larkspur Meadow is not too far," he said as he scanned the darkness in front of them. "We'll be exposed and vulnerable there until we can get to the other side."

"*If* we can get to the other side. I say we need to get off this path. We'll have a better chance with cover of some kind. If we stay on this course, we'll have no choice. We'd be forced out into the open meadow. We get surrounded there, and we're in deep shit."

"On the other hand, if we can get to the other side of the meadow, we'll have plenty of cover in Cheshire Wood. Then it's a straight shot to the palace."

"Again, if we can get to Cheshire Wood."

"Ever the optimist." Gray laughed. "Where's your sense of adventure, Alexi?"

The warrior grunted. "Oh, I'm all for adventure, and I'll take odds on you and me any day, but I'd rather not take chances with the scepter hanging in the balance."

"Amen, brother. But looks like we're gonna have to play the hand we've been dealt. So, off the path or through the meadow?"

Before Alexi could answer, a disembodied voice from behind them asked the same question. "Yes, Field Marshall. Off the path or through the meadow?"

Alexi and Gray came to a halt at the same time and flipped around so that they were back-to-back, each facing sideways in the path, fine Elven steel swords held at the ready. Behind them, several figures stepped out onto the trail.

And Gray saw that Alexi had been correct.

Definitely faeries. From what he could tell, not High Fae, thank the Oracles, but still ... Even lesser faeries could be extremely dangerous, especially in large numbers. By his count, there were only ten or twelve on the trail behind them. Ten or twelve that they could see in the moonlight. But how many were hidden in the trees?

Then there were night calls from the meadow up ahead, and Gray's blood ran cold. No telling how many they would face there. It seemed as though they were indeed surrounded.

Then another figure stepped out into the moonlight, and Gray realized that he knew that silhouette. Righteous fury exploded within him as he recognized the man. "Well, well. Advisor Richter," he drawled in a deceptively pleasant voice. "Now what in the world would you be doing out on this lonely path in the middle of the night? Accompanied by a group of faeries, no less. What do you think about that, Alexi?"

The Field Marshal's smile was grim. "Maybe the queen's advisor came to escort us home and has enlisted the assistance of these lovely lesser faeries for good measure."

Gray's tone was pleasant, almost playful. "Is that the case, Advisor? Or did you have something else in mind?"

Richter came a few steps closer, careful, Gray noted, not to get too far from the armed faeries at his back. "You always were an impudent boy, and you've only become more so as a man. Arrogant, spoiled. And yet the White Queen has coddled you, given you everything."

"Ouch. Alexi, did you hear? I don't think Advisor Richter likes me much?"

"Doesn't sound that way, does it?"

"Advisor, you wound me. I had no idea that you felt this way." He gave a casual shrug. "Of course, I've always thought of you as an odious, sniveling, self-serving, gasbag with no real purpose. In other words, a waste of space and oxygen. So, I guess the sentiment is mutual."

Richter grimaced. "I have eagerly awaited this moment for some time now."

"And what moment would that be? The moment when you could boldly show your true and traitorous colors? The moment when I contemplate running you through with my sword to save the queen's court the time and effort of hanging you in the palace plaza? Or maybe the moment when I snap your neck with my bare hands for your treachery?"

Richter shook his head. "King Aramond will have this entire realm in due time once he has the Scepter of Fire. The king has vowed to reward me handsomely for delivering it to him."

"Over my dead body."

The advisor cackled with obvious glee. "That was my first and most fervent thought."

"You would betray your own people—sell your blackened soul—on the promises of a mad man?" Alexi's silvery eyes glowed with white-hot fire, and he spat on the ground at his feet. "It will be an honor to rid this kingdom of your foul stench, Richter."

"Enough talk," one of the lesser faeries shouted, stepping in front of the advisor. "You can hand over the scepter now, or we'll take it from you. It's your choice."

Alexi smiled evilly. "Well, come on then, faerie. Step up. You can be the first to die by my sword."

The lesser faerie smirked. "It would be my pleasure to take that sword *and* the scepter, from your cold, dead hands, elf."

Then all hell broke loose.

At first, there weren't as many faeries as Gray had feared—maybe a few dozen—but definitely more than he would have liked. Yet soon they seemed to be coming from all directions, and as fast as he and Alexi could strike them down, they were replaced by more.

It had been too long since he'd used his magick, and he found his aim, his strength, all a bit sloppy. Both Alexi and Valian had urged him to practice time and again, to hone his skills, but he hadn't listened. Now, in the heat of battle when it was really needed, he wished he had.

He lost track of Richter after the first few minutes, and then it was all he could do to hold onto his focus and keep fighting. His shoulders began to sing with fatigue and the sweat poured from him, but he and Alexi kept swinging, ducking, pivoting, and charging. They fought with magick and steel, but Gray soon realized that they were rapidly being overwhelmed by sheer numbers.

Spinning to strike at a faerie to his left, he caught movement on his right out of the corner of his eye. He began to pivot, tried to block the blow that was coming, but in his exhaustion, was just too damn slow. Pain exploded in his right shoulder as the fae blade cut deep into his flesh.

The hilt of his sword was slick and covered in blood—both his and countless others—but he managed to wield it at the last minute, cutting down the faerie before he could land another more fatal blow. But the move cost him, and he staggered backward, nearly going to his knees. His right arm was throbbing now and covered in warm, red blood. And it was getting worse, as his head swam and his vision blurred. He reached for the scepter, but found that it was no longer hanging over his shoulder.

It was gone.

Frantically looking around, he realized that the dwindling horde of faeries was beginning to retreat.

And that was when he saw Alexi get hit from behind and go down.

"*No!*" he roared, and felt a flash of energy burst from his chest along with the cry. He watched every faerie within a thirty yard radius literally explode; their lifeless remains dropping like bloody sacks, before his vision grayed and his world faded to black.

"OKAY, THIS IS REALLY GROSS," ISABELLA COMPLAINED for the third time in less than ten minutes, as she swept the light of her flashlight back and forth from side to side in the tunnel. "Are you sure this is absolutely necessary? I mean, there could be rabid bats or rats or a myriad of other nasty things down here."

Valian had portaled them to Wysteria using an ancient, mostly forgotten underground entrance on the southwest side underneath the palace itself. From the moment that they'd stepped out of the swirling vortex of the portal, Isabella had been quite unimpressed with the vine-covered, packed-dirt tunnel. Of course, it didn't matter how many times he'd insisted that since they didn't know which portals had been compromised, this old tunnel was probably their safest bet.

"Seriously, Valian, are you sure you even know where you're going?"

He rolled his shoulders, praying for patience. "Isabella ... love, I was born and raised in this realm. You didn't even know of its existence until a couple of hours ago. I find the fact that you're questioning my directional skills in my home world quite insulting."

"Please." She stopped and swung her flashlight up to his face, nearly blinding him. "Don't be so sensitive. It's just that we've been walking for an hour, and we don't seem to be getting anywhere." She whipped the light from side to side again, and then back to his face. "There's only more dirt."

Raising an eyebrow, he gently re-directed her light from his face to his watch. "Darling, we've been walking for precisely seventeen minutes since we left the portal. And the door to the lower level of the palace should be around the next corner or two."

She heaved a sigh. "Okay. If you say so, but I'm going to have serious doubts about those 'directional skills' if we get around that next couple of bends and there's just more dirt."

"Duly noted."

They continued walking in silence for a few moments before Isabella spoke up. "So, how long have you been living in New York, and why did you leave Wysteria in the first place."

Valian sighed. "I've been living in New York City for a little over five decades."

"*Fifty years?* How is that even possible?"

"As I said before, we age differently in this realm, and with my Elven ancestry, I'll live for a very long time."

"Okay. So why New York?"

"Many years ago, after the war ended, the Scepter of Fire was sent to your world, to England with the original Alice for safe-keeping. A sentinel was then put in place to keep tabs on it and the family protecting it, in case it was ever needed again. When the scepter was moved to New York City with the marriage of one of Alyssa's ancestors in the early seventies, the request was made by the sentinel guarding it to come home."

"And that's when you moved to New York?"

"No. I'd already been there for a few years at that point, going back to my own realm only occasionally. I'd lived in a couple other realms before that, then Europe, Asia. War had left a bad taste in my mouth. I'd needed a change, at least for a while. Anyway, I took over the sentinel's position at the request of the queen. Since I was already living in New York, it seemed like a simple task."

Isabella's flashlight began moving from side-to-side again before she turned to him with a snide tone. "Um, Valian, we've rounded several corners since you said 'the next corner or two.' Exactly when are we going to get to this palace of yours?"

As they rounded yet another bend, Valian had a bad moment when it looked like just another corridor with the same dirt walls. But then, fortunately for his sanity, he located the door he'd been seeking. "See? It's right here. What did I tell you? Now stand back. I don't know if anyone's been through here in a while or what kind of security is in place on the other side."

Placing his palm on the security plate above the handle, they heard a soft click before the door swung open into a well-lit corridor.

But before he could step through, a magick fire stick was

shoved into his face and a rough voice said, "Move slowly into the light of the corridor and state your business here."

Valian did as he was told, and since he hadn't re-glamoured after leaving the New York realm, he gave the guard a pointed look. "I'm here on the Queen's business, of course."

"Oh, by the Oracles!" the man gasped. "Chancellor Winchester? Is that you?"

"It is. And you are?"

"It's James, James Hoyden." The guard narrowed his eyes. "What are you doing down here in these old tunnels, sir?"

Isabella stepped into the corridor behind Valian and pinched his arm. "*Chancellor* Winchester? Are you kidding me? You tell me details about this place, about Aly's family history, even the damn Scepter of Fire, but you leave out the part where you're a friggin' *Chancellor*?"

"And who is this with you, sir?" the man asked warily, giving Isabella the once-over. "With the breaches and various security issues we've had recently—especially here in the palace tunnels—I'm afraid I'm going to need your confirmation."

"Understood. Will this do?" Pulling out his ancient pocket watch, he plugged the end of the fob into the security verification port next to the entrance, placing his hand on the port's palm plate. Within seconds, Valian's security photo miraculously appeared on the stone wall above it confirming his identity."

"That'll do it," James said with a nod. "Sorry, but gotta follow protocol, especially now with the problems we've been having with the security wards. Out in the province, it's not monitored, but here in the palace ..."

"Of course. Well done, James."

The man eyed Isabella again. "And is this a guest of the Queen's court, sir?"

Valian turned, and tilting his head, considered Isabella for a moment. "Oh, don't worry about her, James. She's with me." He gave Isabella a final warning glance before turning back to the guard. Not that he thought it would remotely curtail any further outbursts or inappropriate questions, but it was a shot. "Look, James, I need to speak with Queen Beatrice and Prince Graydon immediately. I have important information they must be made aware of as soon as possible."

"Understood, sir. Unfortunately, I don't think the prince is back from his trip yet. I know he left the palace a day or two ago. 'Course, I've been on tunnel duty rotation over the last week, so he might have returned and I just haven't heard. And at this time of the morning, well, the queen is probably still asleep in her chambers." James eyed Isabella one last time and then bobbed his head. "You want me to escort you the rest of the way? Or can you make it on your own?"

"Thank you, James, but I wouldn't want to take you away from your duties. I can get us there."

"Very well, sir. And may I say it's good to see you again, Chancellor."

"Good to be seen, James." Valian waved a hand in the air and started off down the corridor, as the man secured the door behind them. "Come along, Isabella."

He heard her huff of feigned outrage but smiled to himself and kept walking.

"Okay, explain something for me," she demanded after a few moments. "How is it that you can be Chancellor here and not live in this realm?"

"I've pretty much been Chancellor in name only since I've been living in New York. Alexi has taken on my day-to-day responsibilities as well as his own duties as Field Marshal for too many years to count."

"Yet that man back there knew you immediately. What am I missing?"

"Well, I *am* still Chancellor, Isabella. Think of your own country. You know who your president is and would recognize him if you ran into him in an unexpected place, right?"

"I guess."

"So, it's not a huge surprise that a soldier in the field would recognize me. And I do come home from time to time."

"But you still had to do the confirmation thing with the port deal?"

Valian stopped and turned to her. "Isabella, this is a magickal realm. You've seen how I glamour myself to fit into your world. James may have recognized my face, but he was quite right to ask for confirmation with the *port deal* to make certain that it was really me. It's just a security protocol that's necessary in this realm, especially inside the palace proper."

"Wow. What a pain in the ass."

Valian laughed out loud and started walking again. "Indeed it is, love. Indeed it is."

Within another ten minutes they were in the Field Marshal's outer office where the officer on duty confirmed that Alexi and Gray had not returned.

"That's incredibly disturbing, Staff Sargent, as they should've been here hours ago." Valian paced the office and brooded. "They left for home at least two hours before we did."

"I'm sorry, Chancellor. I don't know what to tell you."

Valian turned and pinned the man with a stare, his voice was velvet steel. "Well, then let *me* tell *you*. I want a patrol sent out to every portal within a mile radius of this palace. I want each area thoroughly searched. And I want the prince and Field Marshal Tovin found. Do I make myself clear?"

"Yes, sir. Crystal."

"I'll be in my chambers. You will inform me the minute they've been returned to the palace."

"Understood."

Valian frowned when the man merely stood there. "Well? What are you waiting for? Move it."

The man left the room in a hurry then, and Isabella giggled from the divan where she was currently lounging. "Wow, you are one scary guy, Chancellor Winchester. I had no idea."

Valian sighed. "Yeah, well, don't get too excited about it. Like I said, I'm pretty much a figurehead at this point."

"And yet people jump the minute you walk into a room. Interesting."

He watched her yawn so wide he was afraid her jaw might snap. "Come on, wise-ass," he said with a shake of his head. "Let's find you a place to get some sleep for a few hours."

Like a grumpy, overly-tired child, she made a face and began to whine. "I'm fine. I want to know what happened to Aly and the prince and Alexi. I can wait up for them to be found."

"Please. The sun should be up within an hour or two. You're about half asleep on your feet now. You can take the second bedroom in my chambers. And I'll wake you if there's any news."

She stared up at him with a mutinous look. "You promise?"

"Yes, love. I promise."

"Okay, then." She stood up on shaky legs and preceded him out the door, but not before she turned back and raised her eyebrows. "Your chambers?"

He sighed and shook his head again. "Keep moving, sister."

Eight

After yawning for the hundredth time, Isabella's eyes watered with her fatigue as she followed Valian out of the Field Marshal's office and along the richly appointed hallways of the palace. She had been up for close to twenty-four hours, but as tired as she was, couldn't help gawking at the surrounding grandeur. It was like something out of a magazine. She mused that it could be called *Palace Living* or *Royal Style* or some such silly name. The thought made her chuckle.

Up ahead, Valian glanced over his shoulder. "What's so funny?"

"Oh, nothing. Well, nothing beside the fact that I'm traipsing down a grand corridor of a fairy tale palace in a world that as of yesterday I didn't know existed." She shrugged. "But don't mind me. I'm just tired and everything seems pretty comical to me at the moment."

"That's understandable, love. I suppose it is a lot to take in."

Understatement of the year, handsome, she thought.

As she followed him, she continued to marvel at the decor. There definitely *was* a lot to take in. Ornate side chairs flanked a thin hallway table here, tall golden vases filled with some kind of dried plumes on each side of a doorway there. When they passed a full suit of armor, polished to a mirrored shine, she just shook her head.

All sorts of the most amazing artwork dotted the smooth stone walls, and hanging every twenty or thirty feet along the corridor were gigantic, vibrant tapestries depicting all manner of creatures. The landscapes they illustrated were of such beauty that it made you want to step right into them and frolic within the scenes depicted. Who knew? From everything she'd seen so far, that could be entirely possible.

She couldn't help but think that if Aly was here to see it all, she'd be in hog heaven. That thought made her incredibly sad, and she wondered again what had become of her friend.

In any case, this had definitely been the strangest night of her entire life, and while she could tell herself that perhaps it was all just an elaborate dream ... it really wasn't. It was all too real. The attractive man ahead of her in the corridor—no, elf, she mentally corrected herself—had re-entered her life in the most peculiar of ways. He'd introduced her to a world that she'd never dreamed existed, turning her own sedate reality upside-down in the process. And though she was more than a bit terrified inside, there was also an element of childlike wonder and anticipation mixed in.

Climbing yet another wide staircase and traversing several more passages, Isabella finally cleared her throat. "Um, Valian, are you sure you remember where your chambers are located?"

He spared her another glance over his shoulder. "Is this your version of 'are we there yet, dad'?"

"Ha-ha. Such a comedian. You should try your hand at stand-up in the Village when we get back to New York." Warming to her needling, she expounded. "It could be quite a lucrative side business for you. I mean, I know that you're a renowned fantasy author and all, but you could supplement your income and your reputation with a career in comedy in the evenings."

She heard his deep rumbling of laughter. "I'll keep that in mind. Perhaps you could act as my agent."

"Of course, you'd have to remember a litany of jokes, and if you can't remember where your chambers are, memory could be an issue."

She was so engrossed in their inane banter that when he stopped abruptly at the next doorway, she almost ran into him. He turned to her with a smirk. "Oh, ye of little faith," he said as he opened the door and gestured her inside.

"Just checking." Tilting her head, she gave him a sleepy smile as she slipped past him into the room. And what an amazing room it was. "Well, well. Chancellor Winchester, what have we here?"

A short foyer opened up onto a huge sitting room with leaded windows fourteen feet high along the far wall that would no doubt flood the chamber with light during the day. The focal point of the room was the massive stone fireplace where a crackling fire burned brightly, sending out its warmth into the space. Eyeing it, Isabella felt certain a small vehicle would fit comfortably inside its enormous belly.

The behemoth was surrounded by a sitting area consisting of a large, comfortable-looking sofa upholstered in a dark burgundy textile, and two well-worn leather wing chairs in a russet tone. The thick, luxurious carpets covering the stone floors added to the manly feel of the room with their intense colors of forest green, claret, and chocolate brown.

Isabella turned to find him leaning against the foyer wall watching her as she took it all in. "What? No entertainment center?" she asked. "Where's the fifty-two inch wide-screen TV? Where's the DVD player? How can you hope to pick up chicks in this place without music and ambiance?"

A sexy smile played around his lips as he pushed away from the wall and sauntered toward her. "I figure the palace has all the ambiance it needs. Besides, I told you, I'm rarely here. Well, that and I keep all my best accoutrements for 'picking up chicks' at the New York loft, remember?"

"Hmm, that's odd. I didn't notice." Running a finger along

the slender table behind the sofa, she turned and held it up to scrutiny. "Rarely here and yet nary a single speck of dust to be found. Did you have the place cleaned before we got here? Or does the cleaning lady come in once a week whether the Chancellor is in residence or not?"

Valian heaved a sigh and shook his head. "Are you enjoying yourself?"

Isabella's throaty laugh filled the room. "I am. Very much, thank you."

"So glad I can provide you with amusement on your first trip to Wysteria."

Wandering past an elegant dining table and chairs, she crossed to the other side of the room and the soaring windows with their graceful leaded panes. Looking out, she found a lit courtyard below with a fountain surrounded by gardens that she was sure would be beautiful and fragrant in spring.

"Some digs you got here, Chancellor."

"They'll do in a pinch, but I think we'll save the rest of the tour for later. Right now you should get some rest. The spare bedroom is just through here." Nodding his head toward the hallway behind him and to the right, he turned and started in that direction.

Following him down another short corridor, she simply lost her breath when she entered the room. "Dear God, Valian. If this is the spare, I can't imagine what your master bedroom looks like," she exclaimed as she skirted the gigantic four-poster bed near the windows. Looking up, she caught his narrowed glance. "Oh, take a breath, Nellie. That wasn't a come-on."

Hefting herself up onto the lush, mile-high mattress, she bounced in place a few times, then flopped onto her back and turned her head to look at him. "But Jesus, Mary, and Joseph, this is incredible. I can't imagine why you'd want to leave all this behind to live in a loft in New York City."

Valian waved a hand toward the smaller version of the sitting room fireplace and had flames springing to life. "I do believe I told you why."

"Yeah, yeah. The war and all. You needed a change. I remember." She glanced at the fire now burning cheerfully behind the grate. "Neat trick, by the way. Where did you learn to do that? Or is it a talent you were born with?"

Rolling his eyes, he gestured to the tasseled cord next to the bed and deftly changed the subject. "If you need anything, just ring. I'll wake you when Alexi and Gray are located and returned to the palace."

She stopped him as he turned to go. "Wait! Could you ... could you just stay with me for a little while?"

"Isabella ..."

When he hesitated, she hurried on. "Look, I don't sleep well in strange places, never have. And this definitely fits that category. Please? Just talk to me for a few minutes, would you? Just until I fall asleep?"

She scooted farther back on the bed and laid her head down onto the fluffy pillows as he came over and drew the thick, feather quilt from the end of the bed over her body.

"What would you like to talk about, then?" he asked.

Patting the bed, she turned on her side to face him as he sank down next to her. "Tell me a story."

When he simply raised an eyebrow, she made a face. "Don't be a goof. I don't know. Tell me what it was like growing up in this realm, before the war. Do you have siblings?"

The wary look in his eyes faded away to be replaced by simple joy, and an easy smile spread across his striking face. "I do, yes. A brother and two sisters."

"Younger or older?"

He gave her a comically stern look. "I'm the elder son of my family."

She giggled again, then yawned and snuggled down a little farther under the quilt. "I bet they drove you crazy when you were young, you being so serious and unyielding."

His mouth dropped open. "Me? Serious and unyielding?" He laughed softly then. "They drove me mad incessantly. But they finally grew out of their antics, and we got along fine after that."

"Where are they now? Do they live here in Wysteria?"

Though his smile dimmed a bit, the love in his eyes continued to glow. "My sisters Kali and Amra both live in this realm—in the northeast on my family's land. My brother Garrik was killed in the Great War, as were both of my parents."

She gasped and reached out, taking his hand. "Oh, Valian, I'm so sorry."

"It was a long time ago, love." He rubbed the back of her hand with his thumb. "They fought valiantly and died with honor. That's all one can ask in times of conflict."

"Still, you must miss them terribly."

"I do, yes. At times. But though they may be gone from the realm of the living, they're still with me." He raised their linked hands to his chest, and she could feel his strong heartbeat beneath his ribcage. "Here."

The look in his ice-blue eyes was her undoing, and she felt her own heart melt just a little. They'd known each other for such a very short time, but she suddenly wondered what it would be like to be loved by this Elven male who inspired such a range of emotion in her. He could be kind and gentle, yet she'd had glimpses of the rugged strength beneath the surface. He and his strange new world fascinated her in ways that she'd never experienced before. What must it be like to straddle two such completely different worlds? To make a home in both to suit you so perfectly.

Taking a deep breath, she sighed and heard the tremor in her own voice. "Can you tell me about them? What they were like?"

Her heart melted just a little more when he began to speak, and his smile grew warm with his recount. "My mother was an ethereal creature—beautiful and caring, nurturing but she never coddled. She was a fierce warrior in her own right. She gave me my first bow and quiver of arrows, and taught me how to use them."

"Really?" Isabella yawned again and felt her eyelids growing heavier. "Do you look like her?"

"I do, yes. I have my father's build but her eyes and hair color. She and Alexi's mother were sisters. That's why Alexi and I look so much alike."

"Mmm. I didn't notice." She could feel herself starting to drift, but struggled against it.

"That's because Alexi and I were both glamoured in the New York realm. If you saw him without his glamour, you'd be amazed at our resemblance."

"You did say you were close. What was he like as a boy?"

"I guess we're as close as cousins can be. I think he took Garrik's place in my mind decades ago." Valian suddenly laughed out loud. It was a rich, rolling sound and warmed her from the inside out. "As a boy, Alexi followed us around like a scrawny little puppy. He was very annoying—still is at times."

"You can say that again," she replied with a dreamy smile. "He comes across as an arrogant ass, but I sensed something more beneath all his swagger."

"Yes. He does seem that way on occasion, but mostly with good reason. He wears it like a shield, but he's dependable. A good man."

"Elf."

Valian winked. "Elf, indeed."

"And your father was an Elven warrior as well?"

Through eyes half-closed, she watched the pride alight in his gaze. "He was. Venali Winchester was a force unto himself. He was revered by many with the exception of his enemies, of which there were quite a few. But I believe that he was respected even by them."

The need to shut her eyes, even for a moment, was overwhelming, and she yielded to the urge. With their fingers still entwined, she pulled him closer as she murmured the burning question hovering at the back of her mind. "Valian, will you stay here in Wysteria when this conflict is over? When this world is safe again? Or will you come home to New York?"

She heard his voice as if from afar. "I'm not sure, Isabella. I've made my home in the New York realm for five decades, but if the queen asks me to stay, I will."

As he gently tugged his hand from hers, she sighed and reached out for him. "No. Don't go. Stay with me a little longer." Her mind was fuzzy with sleep, and she wasn't certain if she was talking about the here and now, or coming home to New York when all was said and done.

"Isabella, you're exhausted. Sleep now, love." She felt the brief press of his lips to the top of her head. "I'll be right in the next room and will wake you when Alexi and Gray are found."

"And Aly, too?"

"And Aly, too."

She heard him step away, but it was hazy, and she was fading. "Valian?"

"Yes?"

"Thank you for bringing me here with you to help find Aly."

There was a long pause before he answered. "You're welcome, love. Now sleep."

She barely heard the door snick shut before slumber took her under.

Nine

Once the turbulence and swirls of color diminished, Alyssa stepped out of the portal, stumbling on her four-inch heels and flailing her arms to regain her balance. She nearly went to her knees in the light snow but managed to keep her feet by grabbing hold of a nearby sapling and hanging on for dear life.

For the love of God, where the hell have I landed?

She was still quite dizzy, but now that the fog in her head was beginning to clear, she was fast coming to the uneasy conclusion that perhaps she wasn't dreaming after all. Because if this was a dream, it was an incredibly substantial and realistic one. On top of that, several things were becoming apparent.

First, it was freezing cold, and she had no recollection of ever having a dream in which she could literally see her breath. Shivering, she pulled the warmth of the fur coat a little tighter around her neck and shoulders and tried to stop her teeth from chattering.

The air *smelled* differently in this place, as well. She didn't know how else to explain it and couldn't exactly put a finger on how it was different. It just was. The scent of moist earth, the fragrant aroma of pine and cedar—these were all familiar. She was reminded of a phrase her grandmother sometimes used as winter set in. *Smells like snow, Aly.* She'd never understood what that had meant or how her grandmother could smell snow coming, but it was starting to make more sense to her now. However, there was a fuller texture woven over and through those comforting scents, a richness that was both foreign and familiar at once. It was almost mesmerizing.

Another issue—it was also much darker here, darker than it should be. There were no streetlights, and the moonlight filtered by the thick undergrowth and tall trees outlined against the night sky, gave her pause. She'd never been afraid of the dark that she could remember, but again, this darkness was quite different. It definitely had a heavier quality to it and seemed somehow more vibrant.

But the thing that bothered her the most? It was way too quiet—eerily so—without even the familiar and soothing sounds of traffic in the distance to quiet her nerves.

And then to make matters worse, she almost went down again when she took a step toward the path and the heel on one of her expensive pumps sank into the thick undergrowth, snagging it. She struggled with it for a moment, and when she tried to pull it out, the damn heel snapped right off.

"Are you kidding me?" She let out an exasperated growl. "Well, isn't that just friggin' awesome. I have no idea where I am, it's freezing cold with a good inch of snow on the ground, and now I get to hobble along on a broken shoe."

"Well, you could break the heel off of the other shoe. Then at least they would be even."

The voice held an almost musical tone, and Alyssa whipped around toward the sound but could see nothing through the strange darkness and restricted light of the moon. "Who said that?"

The answering giggles seemed to come from everywhere at once before twin smoke-like streams rippled their way through the trees toward her. She watched in amazement, the dreamlike feeling returning, when both streams began to solidify into slender silhouettes, and then into pale, silvery beings.

Small and child-like, with creamy white skin that sparkled in the meager moonlight, both creatures wore exquisite lace gowns —so complex and delicate—and iridescent, silver slippers. Their hair, white as the snow around them, was worn long and softly curled and entwined with what Alyssa initially thought were strips of the same lace, but on closer examination looked more like strands of ice crystals rather than fabric of any kind.

However, the strangest thing about these creatures was their eyes—shiny black and fathomless with no detectable irises.

What the hell is happening?

Alyssa swallowed hard and took a step back. This was all becoming way too real, way too fast.

"She's not from here, is she, Ligia?" one of the creatures asked the other.

"Don't be silly, Drifa. Just look how she's dressed." The second creature studied Alyssa with curiosity and clucked her tongue. "So very inappropriate. And while she is a human, I'd say, no, definitely not from this realm."

Alyssa took a few more hobbling steps away from these apparitions, only to have them follow, hovering several feet off the ground. "What are you two?" she whispered.

One of the creatures pursed her lips, her head moving bird-like this way and that. "We are frost pixies of the Roseland burrow. I am Ligia, and this is Drifa. What is your name, human?"

"Um, my name?" She looked around in bewilderment and wiggled her now freezing toes inside her shoes.

"Yes, your name. You do have one, don't you?" Ligia asked again with a curious bob of her head.

Alyssa swallowed again and tried to calm the pounding of her heart inside her chest. So far these pixie creatures didn't seem dangerous ... but then, what did she know? They had black eyes and were hovering around in mid-air, for God's sake. "My name is Alyssa. So, exactly where am I?"

Ligia smiled. "You are here, because you are no place else."

Drifa tilted her head and blinked those strange black eyes. "Wherever you go, there you are."

"What?" Alyssa frowned. "You're talking gibberish. That makes no sense at all."

"Of course it does. It makes perfect sense," Ligia replied. "It's logical, correct."

Alyssa sighed. "Look, do me a favor. No riddles or inane questions, okay? That's nothing but annoying." She gestured around the area. "Just tell me where *here* is?"

"Where do you wish it to be?" Ligia asked.

In her frustration, Alyssa lost her fear for a moment, and slapping her hands on her hips, glared at the pixie. "For crying out loud, what did I just say?" When both diminutive beings continued to watch her with those black-eyed, bird-like stares, she hobbled around in a circle, muttering to herself. "I am so not in New York anymore. And this is definitely not Central Park."

"Is this where you are from? This Central Park?" Drifa asked. "We are unfamiliar with that realm." She turned to Ligia. "We must query Isolde. She may know."

"Indeed."

"Okay, hold on." Alyssa put up a hand. "This is my dream, right? So at the risk of my head exploding from exasperation, I'll ask you again. Where are we?"

"Do you think you are dreaming? Truly?" Drifa asked. "Does this happen to you often?"

Ligia pursed her lips again. "Don't be silly, Drifa. Are we not here and conversing with her? I think it may be a human figure of speech, is it not?" Turning to Alyssa, the pixie blinked several times as if waiting for an answer.

Swallowing her frustration, Alyssa took a deep breath. "Let's just stick to the topic at hand, shall we? What *realm* have I landed in?"

"What realm? Well, why did you not ask that in the first place?" Drifa gave her a blank look.

Alyssa tried desperately not to scream. "Dear God, would you please just answer the question?"

"This is the realm of Artemysia, of course. Is this what you wish to know?" Ligia asked. "It is indeed strange that you do not know where you are."

"Yeah, let's just skip past that. Is there a town or city nearby? Somewhere that I can warm up, thaw my toes? And another thing, do you know Prince Graydon Hartford?"

The two pixies looked at each other, and then Ligia finally nodded. "We do know of Prince Graydon, yes."

"Okay, now we're getting somewhere." Alyssa breathed a sigh of relief. If she could just get to wherever he was located, maybe he could explain a few things for her—like these peculiar creatures, for one. "Do you think you could point me in the prince's direction? Like, does he have a house or palace nearby?"

Drifa pointed toward the path in one direction. "There is a village a short flight from here with a palace not far from there. Can you fade or fly? If not, it will take you much longer to walk there."

Alyssa narrowed her eyes. "Define 'longer'."

"It depends on how quickly you walk." Drifa's head bobbed. "Isn't that right, Ligia?"

"Indeed. Quite right." The other pixie turned to Alyssa. "And with a broken shoe you'll be hampered, so it may take even longer."

Alyssa scoffed. "Yeah, that's super helpful, thank you."

"You are welcome."

Letting out another growl, Alyssa threw her hands in the air. "That's it. I think we're done here. Thank you for your meager help, but I'll just be on my way."

"Don't you think she should come back to the burrow with us, Ligia?" Drifa asked with a sly look. "Perhaps we could give her food and drink, find her something better to wear on her feet."

"That is an excellent idea, Drifa. Would you like that, human? I promise we shall have such fun."

Ligia smiled at Alyssa, but it didn't give her the warm, cozy feeling she thought was probably intended. It seemed somehow on the sinister side.

"Again, my name is Alyssa, not *human*." Taking a few uneven steps backward on the path, she shook her head. "And I think I'll pass this time around. See, I don't have much time and really should be getting to the palace. But thanks for the offer."

Though her smile didn't alter, the look on Ligia's face hardened slightly and both pixies hovered closer. "It seems a bit hasty to refuse such a generous offer, don't you think, Drifa?"

"Indeed," the other pixie agreed. "Especially when she is obviously in need of assistance. I think you are correct, Ligia. It is quite rude to reject such an offer."

Alyssa hobbled backward a few more paces. "Look, I don't mean to be rude, and your offer *is* extremely generous, but I'm afraid that I must still decline."

"An exceptionally wise decision, I'd say," a deep, male voice said from the tree line behind her.

The two pixie's faces filled with fear, and they immediately retreated several yards. Turning, she found a tall, beautiful man with long, fiery-red hair and brilliant green eyes watching her closely. He wore leather pants tucked into knee-high boots and an armored chest plate over a thick, long-sleeved shirt. He carried a small pack over one shoulder and a lethal-looking bow over the other with a quiver of arrows strapped to his back. When he turned to glower at the pixies, Alyssa's pulse picked up speed when she noted his pointed ears poking through his long hair.

Are there any normal human beings in this crazy place?

"What mischief are you two about?" this new arrival asked of Drifa and Ligia.

"No mischief at all, Lord Niall," Ligia stammered. "We were only offering assistance to this human."

"Indeed?" His deep, baritone voice was pleasant enough, yet

held a note of menace, and Alyssa suddenly felt caught between this imposing male and the scary, hovering pixies.

Drifa scrambled to Ligia's side. "Yes, my Lord. Her name is Alyssa, and she is looking for Prince Graydon. She seems to have lost her way, and of course, is dressed inappropriately for the weather. We only thought to give her sustenance, and perhaps some guidance."

Niall's green eyes glittered dangerously, and he nodded as if he approved. "That is very considerate of you both. I don't suppose you gave any thought to having some fun with an unaware human, now did you?"

The pixies both shook their heads like marionettes and answered in unison. "No, Lord Niall, never."

The warrior gave another brief nod. "That is good to hear, as the king would be very displeased to know that frost pixies in his realm were interfering in his business."

"The king?" Drifa and Ligia drifted back a few more yards, and Ligia shook her head again. "We had no idea she would be involved in the king's business. Truly."

Alyssa felt a chill of fear skittle down her spine as Niall spared her a look and a savage grin before turning back to the pixies. "I will recount to the king how helpful you both have been in this matter. Now, off you go. And not a word of this encounter to anyone, do you hear?"

The pixies both nodded vigorously before dissolving into twin rivulets of silvery mist and vanishing through the trees, leaving Alyssa alone with the beautiful-yet somewhat frightening male. He stared at her for a long moment with an inscrutable look on his face until she began to fidget and felt compelled to speak.

"Uh, thank you for that." Clearing her throat, she continued. "I was beginning to feel a little threatened by those two."

But I'm not so sure I'm any better off with you, she thought.

"Mmm." Niall came toward her with the grace of a lion scenting its prey, and her heart pounded faster in her chest. "Frost pixies aren't usually dangerous but can be hazardous in the mischief they perpetrate. Going back to their burrow, eating or drinking anything while there, would have been a bad idea. Their magick is insidious, and you'd have likely been stuck there for days, weeks, perhaps longer. Though I would imagine once enthralled by their spells, you probably wouldn't have cared."

What the hell kind of place is *this?*

Alyssa's mouth dropped open. "Then I guess I should be grateful that you showed up when you did. So, thank you. I don't have that kind of time to spare. I need to get home soon."

"You're welcome. Glad to be of service."

"So, um, are you a pixie as well? You seemed to know those two quite well."

"Am I a pixie?" Niall went perfectly still for a moment before his deep laughter rang out in the still of the forest and raised the hackles on the back of Alyssa's neck.

"No, I am no pixie."

"Well, I'm glad I could amuse you with my ignorance," Alyssa replied in an offended tone.

"You really aren't from this world, are you?" The amusement in his voice was replaced by a more interested tone—which was something she felt certain would be disastrous to encourage—and he came a few steps closer.

Alyssa had to steel herself not to retreat from him. "I'm sorry, but no, I'm definitely *not* from here."

Niall seemed to ignore her insulted tone, and grinning, held up a hand. "No apology necessary. I'm a faerie. High Fae, in fact. I suppose it was rude of me not to introduce myself." He gave her an exaggerated bow. "I am Niall, High Lord of the Roseland Twilight Court."

Seriously? First pixies and now faeries? What next?

"Okaaay. So, you're really a faerie?"

The warrior laughed again, and it annoyed her that he was finding such amusement at her expense. "I am, but enough about me. Drifa said that you're looking for Prince Graydon? Is this correct?"

"Yes, it is." She probably answered a bit too quickly, but she really wanted to find the prince and get back home to where things weren't so confusing and peculiar.

Or at least be done with the nightmare, if that's what this is.

"He attended my New Year's Eve party tonight but left abruptly with one of my family's artifacts. I came to retrieve it. I was on my way to find him and do just that when my shoe broke, and that's when those two strange little beings showed up."

"Ah. And where did this party take place, may I inquire?"

"New York City. Do you know of it?"

"I do, indeed. I happen to have been there not too long ago." The relief Alyssa felt at his acknowledgement quickly became edged with a hint of fear when Niall turned to her with a dangerous smile. "So ... you would be Alice, then? Correct?"

"Alice?" Alyssa shook her head. "No. No, my name is Alyssa Montague."

That smile lazily eased across his handsome face, and Alyssa bristled at the intimate tone he used when he spoke. "That's interesting, as you look very much like Alice."

"I don't know what that even means, and I don't know any Alice."

"Ah, well. Perhaps it is my mistake." His grin widened, and he winked.

She ignored his bizarre behavior, and tilting her head, gave him a considering look. "You told those pixie creatures that I was involved in the king's business. What did you mean by that? And what king? Prince Graydon's father?"

Again, Niall chuckled. "No, but they are related ... after a fashion. And since you're on your way to the palace, would you allow me to escort you? I'm certain that the king will want to meet you, and because you can't fade or fly, I can have us there in a blink. That is, unless you'd rather walk with your broken shoe."

Alyssa looked around the stark forest for a moment. His answers hadn't given her much to go on, nor a very comfortable feeling. Plus, she really wasn't sure that she should trust this High

Lord after what he'd told her about the pixies. Going with him could be equally as dangerous. She could end up stuck in *his* court instead and never get to the palace to find the prince. On the other hand, did she really have another choice? The way things had gone so far, she could stumble onto something far worse on her own.

However, if Niall worked for the king, and the prince was somehow related to the king, perhaps she should go with him. Speaking to the monarch could be the fastest way to retrieve her family's heirloom and get back home. And that was, after all, her end goal.

The engaging smile was still on Niall's face as he patiently waited for her to make up her mind. Taking a deep breath, she let it out in a foggy gust and nodded. "Alright. I'll go with you, but no funny business, you get me? Right to the palace. I need to recover my property and get home before daylight. Understood?"

The High Lord gave her another regal bow, but the look on his face did not inspire confidence. "Certainly. You have my word. I'll take you directly to the king. On that you can count." He held out his muscled arm for her to take. "Shall we?"

With much trepidation and her heart beating out of control, she took his arm.

And they disappeared—as he'd said—in a blink.

Ten

Gray came awake gradually with the frigid pre-dawn temperatures seeping through his jacket like the icy hand of death, chilling him right to the bone. He was stiff and disoriented, momentarily uncertain of where he was or what had happened to him. It took great effort, but he finally managed to roll to his left and pry open his eyes. The move left him gasping and gritting his teeth when his right shoulder exploded in pain, blurring his vision. After a moment or two the pain ebbed some, leaving behind a mind-numbing throb. But as his sight began to clear, the scene in his immediate field of vision had his throat closing up and his heart nearly stopping.

Alexi, highlighted by moon glow, lay pale, still, and covered in blood not twenty yards away, and those last horrible moments of the battle came back to Gray in a devastating rush. The vision of Alexi being struck down flashed across his mind in ugly, vivid detail.

No, no, no, no ...

Holding his throbbing limb, Gray struggled into a sitting position, but then had to pause as a wave of dizziness washed over him with such strength that it threatened to send him under again. Glancing down at his shoulder, the sleeve of his jacket soaked and wet with blood, he knew immediately that he'd lost more of the precious fluid than he'd realized.

Once he caught his breath, bit by bit he fought his way to his knees and then unsteadily to his feet, before doing a wobbly kind of stagger toward his friend, all the while terrified of what he would find. Dropping down next to Alexi, his vision blurred a bit again as another punishing wave of agony poured through him. But he took several deep breaths and willed himself to ignore the pain while frantically searching for Alexi's pulse. Panic-stricken when at first he couldn't locate a beat, the breath whooshed out of him in one long, vaporous gust when he finally found a weak, erratic rhythm and realized that, though Alexi's breathing was shallow, he *was* still breathing.

"Hold on, Alexi. I'm going to fix this and get you home. You have my word." Although Gray wasn't quite certain how he was going to accomplish that weighty task with his right arm hanging almost useless at his side and his pitiful magick skills fairly depleted, he had to try. Alexi wasn't just his friend or Field Marshal for the kingdom's armies. Despite the fact that they may not be kin by blood, they were family.

Damned if he'd let him die out here in the cold.

Rubbing his hands together to generate some heat, he tried to focus on his healing powers rather than the excruciating pain radiating through his shoulder like molten lava. As with the rest of his magick arsenal, he hadn't used his curative skills in too long to remember, either. He wasn't even certain he'd be able to produce the energy required to even partially heal Alexi, but if he could at least get him up and moving, they just might make it back to the White Palace where they could get the help they so desperately needed.

He sent up a prayer to the Oracles as he opened Alexi's jacket and underlying shirt, placing his palms directly onto his injured friend's chest. Closing his eyes, he began to concentrate on Alexi's wounds, but it didn't take long to find that there was too much damage, much more than he would be capable of healing in his current state. He'd have to focus on patching up what he could, which meant doing his best to stabilize the deep stab wound to Alexi's abdomen as well as the gash at the back of his head. By the looks of the blood-soaked clothing, he was amazed that Alexi was still breathing, that he hadn't bled out long before Gray had regained consciousness. Alexi's normally pale Elven skin was ashen. It was sobering and spoke to just how dire the situation really was.

Shoving his morbid thoughts aside, Gray concentrated on sending as much healing energy as he could to the worst of Alexi's injuries. Precious minutes ticked by, and yet there seemed to be no change. Just when he was afraid that his ministries were for naught, Alexi groaned and his eyelids began to flutter. Gray felt the tension in his own chest ease slightly.

"Alexi? Can you hear me?"

The Elven warrior coughed, licking his dry, cracked lips. "Did we win?" he asked in a barely audible voice.

"Well, I'd love to say yes, but I don't think what happened here could be construed as a win, no matter how I'd spin it." Gray heaved a sigh of relief. His friend wasn't out of the woods by any means, but at least he was awake and talking. "And unfortunately for us, they got away with the scepter. It's probably in Richter's hands by now."

Alexi opened his eyes to slits and whispered a vulgar expletive. "I'm gonna take that traitorous piece of shit apart limb by limb the next time I set eyes on him."

"Right there with you, pal. But hey, the good news is that we're both alive, right?"

"I suppose that depends."

"On what?"

Alexi had another brief coughing fit, and Gray felt his panic begin to rise again when this time his friend expelled a small amount of blood. "On how long that sentence remains true. I'm cold, Gray, so damned cold. I can hardly feel my fingers. I don't think that bodes well, you know what I mean?"

"Just hang on. I'll try to do a little more, and then we'll get you back to the palace. You're going to be fine."

But Gray knew exactly what Alexi meant. Valian may have been the only one of them to have actually fought in the Great War so many years ago, but they'd all seen the devastation, the horrific death that came with conflict. They'd all witnessed the ruin war could bring.

The two of them had spent their fair share of time on the battlefield and in bloody border skirmishes. The lesser faerie uprising a decade earlier had been exceedingly vicious and had dragged out for several years. The Scion revolt three years before that had taken place out in the goblin sector had been relatively short-lived but brutal. And King Aramond had periodically tested the wards over the decades since his ultimate defeat, sending raiding parties that had to be repelled. But through it all, through every battle, every engagement, they'd emerged beaten up and battle-weary but whole. This night's event was different, was as close to death as he or Alexi had ever come.

"Just hold on, Alexi," he repeated. "I'm gonna fix you. I promise."

"How many times have both Val and I counselled you to practice your damn skills?" Grimacing, Alexi took a rattling breath, and his voice sounded feeble when he continued. "You'd better figure this out, slacker, because if I die out here in the middle of nowhere, I'm coming back to haunt you. And Valian will beat your pathetic ass into dust."

"Yeah, yeah. Shut up and let me work, wouldja? You elves are all alike. Even on your last leg its bitch, bitch, bitch."

Alexi laughed, but then his laughter morphed into another coughing attack, which produced more blood and sounded pretty bad to Gray.

"Last leg, for sure. I'm thinking if you're gonna do something, you'd better hurry," Alexi said once the coughing subsided, and all humor fled from his voice. "I mean it, old friend. Doesn't feel like this is going to end well."

"Stop it. You're not gonna die. Not if I have anything to say about it." Gray again rubbed his palms together for a few moments, encouraged by the white-hot power that surged between them, and then placed them back onto Alexi's chest. "Okay, hang on to your ass."

With that, he closed his eyes gathering as much energy as he had left. With every ounce of his being and an enormous mental blast, he sent healing power surging into his friend's damaged body like an electrical charge.

Alexi jerked once, twice, and arched his back as if he had indeed been electrocuted. His eyes moved rapidly back and forth beneath his lids, and then he finally dropped back down, going limp and deathly still.

"Alexi?" Gray panicked again when he realized his friend wasn't breathing. Fumbling for a pulse, his own heart just about stopped when Alexi suddenly gasped and his eyes popped open. And he had no time to react when his friend jackknifed up, cracking his forehead with Gray's and about knocking them both unconscious.

"Oouuch!" Alexi groaned, flopping down and rubbing his forehead.

Gray saw stars for a minute as he held a hand to his head. "For the love of all that's holy, Alexi, are you trying to crack my skull open? That's gonna leave a mark."

"Don't be such a whiny-baby. Besides, I probably now have a concussion to go with everything else." Alexi groaned again and squinted up at Gray. "What the hell *was* that, anyway? It felt like you friggin' fused my damn insides."

"Sorry." Gray gave him a sheepish look and shook his head. "I was just trying to send you as much energy as I could. I guess I over-compensated."

"You think?"

"I was afraid that I'd lost you for a minute there, brother. That is, before you cold-cocked me."

"Serves you right, idiot."

Relief rolled over him, and Gray laughed out loud before another wave of pain shot through his shoulder, doubling him over.

"Gray?" Alexi's voice held a note of concern, and he reached out a hand. "Are you okay?"

Breathing in through his nose, Gray did what he could to ignore the excruciating pain and the terrible burning sensation that was beginning to spread down his arm. This felt worse than cleaved flesh. But he didn't want to think about that right now. If they could just get back to the palace, he was certain both he and Alexi could be healed. Then together they would hunt down and retrieve the scepter and make Richter pay for his treachery.

"Gray?"

Alexi's worried tone brought him back to the situation at hand, and he smiled with more confidence than he felt. "Please. You know it would require a lot more than a lesser faerie to take me down. What I want to know is how you feel?"

"Like I've been in a battle ... and been stabbed, bashed in the head, and electrocuted. In that order."

Gray rolled his eyes. "So dramatic. But do you feel any better, moron? I tried to heal as much as I could, but I'm not strong enough to finish it."

"I think I may live, if that's what you mean, which I wasn't altogether certain of a few minutes ago."

"Do you think it's enough? Can you move or at least stand? My right arm is in pretty bad shape and there's no way I can carry you, but if you can stand, you can lean on me. Since nobody knows where we are, we're gonna have to get ourselves back or die out here alone."

"Well, fuck that," Alexi muttered and held out a hand. Gray grabbed it and helped him into a sitting position. "I'm not dying so close to home, and neither are you. I either expire in my own bed or not at all, so I guess we're gonna have to do this thing. But let me assure you, the way I feel, it's gonna take some time, so we'd better get started."

Gray nodded. He was still light-headed with what he assumed was blood loss but managed to get to his feet before helping Alexi to his.

"You sure you're okay?" Alexi asked as he flung an arm around Gray's shoulder. "You're generating some pretty awesome heat, my friend. I can feel it right through your jacket. You sure you don't have a fever?"

"Don't worry about me, mother. I'm fine. Can we just get a move on?"

"If you're waiting on me, you're backing up, buddy."

Like two battered and broken warriors, they clung to each other and started hobbling in the direction of home. They made it as far as the edge of the forest before pausing at the expanse of Larkspur Meadow between them and Cheshire Wood.

"Do you think it's clear?" Alexi asked, his voice tense. "You know we're finished if they've left anyone behind. I'm unsteady on my feet and probably couldn't lift my sword, let alone wield it. You're in rough shape, as well."

"Only one way to find out." Gray shook his head to clear his vision but only succeeded in increasing his vertigo. "I have a feeling they're probably gone. They came for the scepter. It was that bastard Richter's endgame. In any event, they got what they came for, so we can only hope no one was left behind to lay in wait in case we survived."

"Such a comforting thought when you put it that way." Alexi took a deep breath and let it out slowly. "Are you ready for this?"

"As I'll ever be. I'd rather not think too hard on it, if it's all the same to you."

"Okay then. Fast and furious it is, brother."

At Gray's nod, they started forward into the open meadow as quickly as their wounds would allow, each keeping an eye out for any movement that might suggest unwanted company. Gray felt exposed and vulnerable with the moon tracking their progress like a giant spotlight as they traversed the first half of the meadow. With his head spinning, it felt like trying to run hip-deep in water with Cheshire Wood continually moving just a little farther out of reach with each step they took.

"Well, that was a bit nerve-wracking," Alexi said when they finally crossed into the cover of the tree line on the other side and could breathe a momentary sigh of relief.

"Just a bit. But we still have to get through The Wood."

They staggered on for another quarter mile before Gray's vision began to waiver again. When he stumbled for the third time, Alexi made him stop.

"There's a fallen tree over there. Let's sit for a minute or two, Gray."

"Not a good idea. We need to keep moving. We're still too far out, and we don't know if the wards are compromised. Getting back to the palace has to be our priority."

"Agreed. Look, you're not telling me anything I don't know. But dude, you're looking worse by the minute. And if I don't catch my breath, I may not make it much farther, either." Alexi gave Gray's jacket sleeve a weak tug. "Just a quick rest stop and then we'll get moving again. Come on."

Gray finally relented, and they lurched their way over to the log and collapsed on top of it side by side. He had to steel himself against the pain and dizziness, but after a moment the wave passed and his vision cleared somewhat.

"Do you really think the wards are completely down?" Alexi asked in the silence.

"I don't know. They may not be down all the way, but the fact that Richter had so many lesser faeries from Roseland with him doesn't give me much confidence that they're still solidly in place, either."

"I know." Alexi was silent for a moment before chuckling under his breath. "Fucking faeries. They never fight fair, but we did a pretty good job of kicking their asses ... for the most part."

"And yet, here the two of you sit, looking the worse for wear and quite forlorn," a melodious voice said, taking Gray and Alexi by surprise. "Seems like a pretty bold statement, considering."

Gray examined the brush and trees around them, and with effort, pulled out his sword. That's all they needed to end a perfectly shitty evening—another confrontation. Alexi was right. At this point they'd both be worthless in another fight, but no one else had to know that. "Who's there?" he shouted with more bravado than he felt. "Show yourself."

Farther up the path to their right, yellow eyes flashed and appeared to hover in mid-air before a large, dark feline shape materialized. As it moved through a patch of moonlight, Gray could just make out the shadowy black leopard before it morphed into a swarthy man dressed in black leather from head to toe.

"Now, what would the Wysterian crown prince and his trusty sidekick be doing in my Wood before the rise of the sun, I wonder?"

"Halifax!" Alexi blew out a tense breath. "You friggin' devil cat. What the hell is wrong with you? You about gave me a heart attack?"

The shifter chuckled and came closer. "I would think that would be the least of your worries, by the look of you."

"Yeah, well, you keep sneaking up on people like that, and it's a good way to lose that prized tail of yours to a startled warrior's sword ... or worse."

The dark-skinned man rubbed his jaw and gave Alexi a speculative look. "Mmm, normally I might agree with you, elf. But as you know, I am equipped with a goodly portion of speed, being part cat and all. Therefore, that warrior would have to catch me first, wouldn't he? No mean feat." Halifax shrugged. "And the fact that neither of you has even attempted to stand tells me I've nothing to worry about where you are concerned. Had a skirmish with some lesser faeries, did we?"

"You're such an ass," Alexi grumbled. "If you knew about it, where were you during the 'skirmish?' We could've used your help."

Halifax looked down his nose at Alexi. "So like an elf to point fingers and assume the worst. For your information, I'd been summoned to the palace and only returned to The Wood as the faeries were—and I shall use this term very loosely—*retreating*."

"Oh, don't play as if you'd have jumped in had you been here. You would've hung back and watched from a safe distance."

"Perhaps," Halifax replied with a faint smile. "But then, the confrontation didn't take place in my Wood, did it? So, not my circus, not my monkeys."

Alexi let out a frustrated growl, but before he could get spooled up, Gray cut in. "Who called you to the palace, Halifax? And for what purpose?"

Halifax turned to Gray with a defensive look and crossed his arms. "So, I'm a liar now? Is it so inconceivable that my presence would be requested?"

"Yes," Alexi smirked.

"Shut up, Alexi." Gray took a deep breath and let it out slowly. He worked to focus on the conversation, though it was becoming increasingly difficult to concentrate over the buzzing in his head. "I'm not calling you a liar, Halifax, and no, it's not inconceivable. I'm simply asking how it came about. I know you don't like to leave Cheshire Wood. Did the queen send for you?"

The man pursed his lips and narrowed his eyes, as if trying to decide if Gray was mocking him or not. Finally, he shook his head. "It wasn't the queen, although she was in attendance when I arrived. The Chancellor is here, got in a little over an hour ago. He sent the request."

"Valian's here?" Alexi's mouth dropped open and he turned to Gray. "But he was going to stay in the New York realm, make sure nothing blew up there."

"Mmm, yes. About that." Halifax tapped a finger against his lips. "It is my understanding that things there went a bit awry, shall we say. He showed up with a human in tow, which I found interesting."

"*What?*" Gray jumped up, and then staggered as his whole world spun and he saw double of everything. "What human?"

"How should I know? You all look alike to me. Some random

female, perhaps? Anyway, the Chancellor was visibly concerned when he found that you and the Field Marshal had not returned from wherever you'd been, which I'm assuming now was the New York realm. He was quite... *insistent* that you should be found immediately, and he instructed the Field Marshal's staff sergeant to send out search parties. The poor man was still on pins and needles when I left to search my Wood. And, oh lucky me, here you are."

"But what about the human female?" Gray took a step toward the double Halifax and suddenly had the sensation of weightlessness. Then he was falling.

"Gray!" he heard Alexi shout in a faraway tone.

It was very much like a slow-motion movie with voices all talking at once, echoing and distorted as if they were underwater.

"Here they are!"

"Get the carrier over here ..."

"The prince is gravely ill. We must get him back to the palace!"

Too many voices to keep track of ...

Then Gray felt himself being lifted and Alexi's face filled his vision. "Hang on, Gray. No dying out here in the cold, remember? Help has arrived. We'll be home shortly."

"Alexi?" Gray tried to speak, but there was nothing but the ringing in his ears. So dry, his mouth was so terribly dry.

Alyssa ...

It was his last coherent thought faded away.

Eleven

"What do you mean you don't know where she is?" Isabella shouted. "Wasn't she with Alexi and the prince?"

Both Alexi and Gray had been located and returned to the palace over an hour ago, and Alyssa hadn't been with them. Valian and the rest of the royal court had been on pins and needles ever since. He'd waited to wake Isabella until ten minutes ago in the effort to get as much information as possible, which hadn't been much. Now she was freaking out after being told that her friend was still missing.

Unfortunately, though he was undeniably concerned for Alyssa's whereabouts and well-being, Valian had more pressing issues on his mind. Gray had partially healed Alexi's more massive wounds in the field, but he was still in pretty bad shape. However, the prince's condition was much more dire. Gray had been brought in unconscious and gravely ill, and the healers were still working to save his life. The queen hadn't yet returned from the hospital wing, and Valian was trying not to dwell on the possible outcome. And though he understood her panic, Isabella wasn't making it easy.

"Isabella, I know you're upset—"

"*Upset?* You're damn right I'm upset. My friend is missing, for God's sake. And you have no idea where she is or if she's okay. You don't even know if she's actually in this realm. The only reason I came here with you is because you told me Aly had gone with Alexi and the prince."

"I most certainly did not." Valian crossed his arms and tried to hold onto his temper, but his tone was stern. "What I told you is that neither Alexi nor the prince would've had anything to do with Alyssa's disappearance, but that I was afraid she *might* be here. If you'll recall, you were the one who insisted on coming with me, which I allowed against my better judgment, I might add."

"Okay, okay, you're right." Isabella blew out a frustrated breath and put up a hand. "I'm sorry. I'm tired and just so worried about her. Did you ask either of them if they'd seen her?"

"Unfortunately, we weren't able to get much information." Valian ran a shaky hand through his hair. "The prince was unconscious when they brought him in. He's in serious condition, Isabella."

"Oh my God! He's going to be okay, isn't he?"

"The healers are doing everything they can."

Isabella came to him and tenderly put a hand on his arm. "And Alexi? Valian, is your cousin all right?"

Valian sighed, and seeing the anxious look in her eyes, worked to keep the fear from his voice. "Alexi was in pretty bad shape as well, but he's strong."

Alexi wasn't his only living relative, but one of the few connections to family he had left. And though they'd rarely spent time together over the last decade, Valian was terrified at losing him. He'd tried to put that thought out of his mind. It would do no good to dwell on the 'what ifs'. Still, it was difficult to do.

"It seems that Gray had healed a portion of Alexi's more serious injuries in the field, but they had to put him under to work on the worst of his wounds." Valian shook his head. "He's not out of the woods by any means."

"Okay then. We stay positive." She gave him a gentle shake. "Right?"

"Yes, of course. But that's why we don't have much to go on where Alyssa is concerned and won't have until one of them is awake again, which could be hours from now."

"So, we really don't know, do we? I mean, it's possible that she was with them and got separated. She could be out there ... alone. Shouldn't we be looking for her while we wait? I mean, as opposed to doing nothing?"

Valian glanced at Halifax, who'd opted to wait for news before heading back to Cheshire Wood and was lounging in a wing chair by the window. "You found them. Did you see any evidence of the woman being with them at one time?"

"I wasn't there for the skirmish, mind you. The faeries had departed by the time I arrived." The shifter shook his head. "But the only human in attendance when I stumbled upon them was the prince, though he did seem interested that you'd brought a human with you from the other realm." Halifax nonchalantly studied his fingernails for a moment before looking up with a sly smile. "That said, I suppose your Alice could have been taken along with the scepter during the fight. I have no way of knowing that. However, if she was taken, I'm certain King Aramond would be positively giddy at the prospect of seeing her again."

Isabella whirled toward him and pointed a finger in his direction, her eyes flashing. "Look, you, her name is Alyssa not Alice. And exactly who are you, anyway?"

Halifax stood then—as graceful as any cat—and crossed to her where he gave her an elegant, exaggerated bow. "My name is Halifax, Milady," he murmured in a deep, baritone voice.

Isabella blinked several times and jumped back as the shifter changed from man to black leopard and back again in quick succession. He studied the dumbfounded look on her face and then grinned. "But you may know me from diminutive Alice's story as the Cheshire Wood cat."

Valian worked to keep the smile off his face as Isabella goggled, her mouth opening and closing in her shock.

"Are you kidding me?" she finally blurted. Turning to Valian, she broke into astonished laughter. "Seriously? The Cheshire Cat?"

Shrugging, Valian chuckled along with her. "I told you the story was more of an embellishment of actual events ... and people."

Halifax returned to the window and slipped into his chair with a satisfied look on his face. "I must tell you, I was skeptical of the child at first, but in the end, quite pleased with the way she portrayed me. She caught all my amusing attributes in the most delightful way."

"You do realize that the child you speak of didn't actually write the story, don't you, cat?" Gryphon, the queen's royal chamber elf said as he brought refreshments into the room and placed the tray on a side table. "However, I dare say that the way she embellished the details she gave to the author was a bit much ... especially with some of the *minor* characters." He looked up at Halifax with a meaningful stare while he poured Isabella a cup of tea.

Halifax sat forward. "Just what do you mean by that, elf? Are you calling me a minor character? I don't recall even a mention of a royal chamber rat in the story."

"That's because she made me an actual griffin in the tale—part lion, part eagle. In mythology, griffins were thought to be king of all creatures. Powerful, dignified, and majestic."

Halifax made a rude noise. "Powerful, dignified, and majestic, indeed."

Gryphon smiled serenely. "Better that than a grinning buffoon of a disappearing cat." With that, the chamber elf slipped quietly—and Valian thought, quite majestically—from the room, leaving Halifax staring after him with his mouth hanging open.

"Why, that little gutter snipe," he muttered. "I'd have him for dinner, but it would put me in bad graces with the queen."

Valian chuckled. "Yes, Her Majesty is incredibly fond of Gryphon. And trust me when I say that he's keenly aware of that fact, so I would tread lightly where he's concerned."

Halifax made a disgruntled face, the dark skin crinkling around his golden eyes as they narrowed. "This is exactly why I rarely leave my Wood these days. I find the favoritism at any court so distasteful and unjust."

"Wait just a minute." Isabella set her cup and saucer down on the table with a clatter, drawing their attention. She turned to Halifax. "Did I hear you correctly earlier? Did you say the scepter was taken during the battle?"

Halifax blinked and glanced at Valian. "Would you like to handle that query?"

Valian sighed, the light-hearted tone of the room evaporating as quickly as it had arrived. "Yes, Isabella. You heard him correctly. Gray and Alexi were ambushed with the specific goal of stealing the scepter."

"How do you know that it was actually taken?"

"Because Alexi was conscious when they were brought in. It's the first thing he said to me."

"But who would've done that? You said the scepter was needed to prevent another war. Are you saying your enemies now have it in their possession?"

Valian sank down on the settee opposite Halifax, the gravity of the situation weighing heavily on him. "I'm afraid that's probably the case or soon will be. Gray and Alexi were ambushed by a large horde of lesser faeries from the Roseland kingdom. King Aramond will stop at nothing to gain control of the scepter's power, to remove any protection it would provide for Wysteria."

"How on earth would this king have known that they had the scepter with them or where to set up the attack? Are Wysteria's protections down completely?"

Valian shook his head. "We don't know yet if the wards are down entirely or were only disrupted long enough for Roseland forces to enter the perimeter. I have troops scouring the borders as we speak looking for openings or weakened spots. As for how our enemies knew who had the scepter and where to look? Alexi provided that information as well." He ran a hand over his face and paused before continuing, his next sentence hard for him to comprehend let alone say out loud. However, a regal voice did it for him, letting him off that particular hook.

"One of my oldest advisor's committed treason," the queen said from the doorway. "That's how our enemies got through our security and knew where to lie in wait."

"Your Majesty," Valian murmured as he and Halifax both rose, bowing deeply before their queen.

Queen Beatrice nodded to each in turn. "Halifax, we've had our differences in the past, but I am extremely grateful to you for finding my son and the Field Marshal and returning them to us."

"No thanks or gratitude required, my Queen." The shifter bowed again. "Duty and honor. And yes, we may have our differences from time to time, but I pray you never doubt my loyalty."

Valian stepped forward, searching her weary face. "Is there word on the prince's condition, Your Majesty?"

She smiled and nodded. "The faerie poison used was unusual, but the healers have finally countered it. Graydon is not awake yet, but they've assured me that he will completely recover." She glanced at Halifax. "They also told me that it was a close thing. Had you not found him when you did, it could have ended much differently. So you have my gratitude whether you want it or not."

Halifax said nothing but simply nodded.

"And I know you're worried about your cousin, Chancellor. So let me assuage your fears as well. Alexi is sore but recovering nicely—and is very vocal. I suggest you go and see him."

Valian felt the weight of his fear for Alexi lighten at her words, and he grinned. "I had no doubt of my cousin's resilience, Majesty. I can only imagine how *vocal* he is right now. I shall visit him as soon as possible. I'm sure he also has more to tell regarding the ambush."

"I'm sorry, but speaking of the ambush, shouldn't we be out

looking for Alyssa?" Isabella broke in. "I mean, it's great that Alexi and the prince are going to live and all, but my friend is still out there. She's alone in a very strange world. What if she's been captured along with the scepter?"

The queen turned with a surprised and curious look. "And who would you be, dear?"

"My apologies, Majesty," Valian interjected. "Let me present Isabella Christensen. Alyssa Montague is her best friend, and Isabella came back with me from the New York realm with the hope of finding her."

Queen Beatrice looked confused. "But why? What would the descendant be doing here in Wysteria?"

"I'd meant to speak with you in private shortly after we arrived, but things took a turn when I found that Alexi and the prince were missing. Alyssa disappeared from the New Year's party we attended around the same time that I presumed Alexi and Gray had taken the scepter and returned home."

"Disappeared, you say? This is very unsettling." The queen frowned and walked to the window. After a moment she turned. "So you are of a mind that she accompanied them to Wysteria? For what purpose?"

Valian shook his head. "We don't know what actually transpired, but I can think of no logical reason for them to bring her here with them. However, more disturbing is the fact that the last person to speak with Alyssa before she disappeared was Kasandra Delacourt."

Queen Beatrice's eyes narrowed at the name. "High Fae from Roseland, one of Queen Mabry's lieutenants. I see. Then you think it was the faerie who had a hand in the descendant's disappearance."

Valian related the gist of his conversation with Kasandra after finding her at the gala. "Most troubling was what Kasandra said just before she left the party. Her exact words were 'the last time I saw her, she was looking for her prince. I just gave her some direction'."

"Wait— You never told me that part," Isabella said, pointing an accusing finger.

Valian rolled his eyes. "I told you what I could in the time we had. While I couldn't be certain that Alyssa hadn't actually left with Gray and Alexi, my gut told me the faerie was somehow involved." He turned to the queen. "So, yes, I do think Kasandra's at the root of it, and the implications are worrying, to say the least."

"Mmm, yes," Queen Beatrice agreed. She paced back and forth in front of the window, and Valian could almost hear the thoughts turning in her head.

But before the queen could relay those thoughts, Isabella let out a frustrated growl. "For those of us in the cheap seats who have no idea what's going on—and that would obviously be just me—what, pray tell, are the implications you're talking about?"

Valian shook his head again. "I'm sorry, Isabella. The problem is that Kasandra is from Roseland's Evening Court. That's King Aramond's realm."

Finally, the queen stopped her pacing, and the look she gave Isabella was grim. "What Valian is trying to say is that if this High Fae was the one to send Alyssa through the portal, it's a fair bet she wouldn't have been sent to Wysteria."

"You mean she's probably in Roseland?" Isabella looked distraught when she realized what the queen was suggesting.

Queen Beatrice nodded. "While we obviously don't know that for certain, it would be my best guess."

"Roseland is under King Aramond's control, right? I know he's kind of your sworn enemy, and all, but why is that, anyway? Was Roseland part of the war?"

Valian and the queen exchanged glances, and he could see the sorrow flare briefly in her eyes before she held up her hand. "It's all right, Chancellor. She's here now and deserves to know the truth." Turning to Isabella, the queen gestured toward the settee that Valian had vacated. "Come and sit with me. I will give you a brief explanation of our history."

"Alright," Isabella replied cautiously but followed the queen and sat. "Does this have to do with Aly's ancestor, the original Alice?"

Queen Beatrice tilted her head and smiled. "Indirectly, I suppose. You see, my mother, Oracles rest her soul, reigned over all of Artemysia once upon a time, and as she grew older, wanted to make certain her kingdom would go on and prosper after she was gone. My older sister Renata was in line to succeed, but as time wore on it became apparent to my mother that she wasn't quite up to the challenge of managing an entire kingdom."

The queen glanced out the window to her left—the sadness in her demeanor increasing—and Valian's heart went out to her. So much loss for one woman to bear.

"Anyway," she continued. "Her solution was to divide the realm into two separate yet connected kingdoms."

Isabella nodded. "Wysteria and Roseland. She gave you each a kingdom."

"Yes, that's correct. Though it was my mother's right as queen, I'm sure you can well imagine how unhappy Renata was with the arrangement. As the oldest child, she'd expected to be crowned at some point, but not to share that crown with me."

Isabella leaned forward, completely engrossed in the story. "She was jealous of you?"

"I'm not so sure that was the case in the beginning. I think it was more that she felt betrayed, robbed of her birthright. But as time wore on, the perceived wound festered and grew into jealousy, yes. She became more and more paranoid and treated her subjects harshly."

Isabella gasped. "Renata is the Red Queen from the book, right? The one that's always shouting 'off with their head?'" At the stricken expression on the queen's face, Isabella looked horrified. "Oh, God! I'm so sorry. I didn't mean to offend you."

"No, no, it's fine." The queen waved away her concern. "It was a long time ago, but you are correct. Renata is the Red Queen portrayed in the story of little Alice and her Wonderland."

"What happened to your sister? How did Aramond become king?"

"Our two kingdoms went to war." The queen sighed. "By that time, my sister was beyond reason—quite mad, I'm afraid. The Oracles felt she was unfit to rule and gave Wysteria the Scepter of Fire to repel her armies and create the wards that protect our borders. It was a defeat from which Renata was unable to recover. She sank deeper into her madness which ultimately led to her death."

"Is that when Aramond took over?"

The queen nodded. "As the queen's consort, he took my sister's kingdom by force and has ruled since that time. He blames Wysteria, and specifically me, for Renata's death, and he's been searching for the scepter for decades."

Isabella grew still and then her eyes went big and round with her panic. "We have to find Alyssa. Right now!" When no one reacted, she leapt to her feet. "Don't you see? Alice helped you fight your war and safely hid your scepter from Aramond. What do you suppose they would do to Alyssa, Alice's descendant, should they find her first?"

There was a dreadful pause before the queen nodded slowly. "Your point is well taken." She drew herself up in regal fashion and squared her shoulders. "Chancellor, go and speak with Field Marshal Tovin. Find out for certain if Alyssa was with them or not. If I'm going to send a search party into harm's way, I want to know every detail possible."

"Of course, Majesty." Valian gave a slight bow, and grabbing Isabella's arm started for the door. "Get a move on, Halifax. You're coming as well."

The cat grumbled but followed them out of the room.

Twelve

Though Alyssa was reserving judgment for now, the High Lord of Roseland's Twilight Court seemed to be a man—or faerie—of his word. Niall indeed had them inside the palace gates almost before she could blink, just as he said he would. This strange world that she'd literally stumbled into was going to take some getting used to. People traveled so quickly here and in such outlandish fashion.

Once her head had stopped spinning, they'd proceeded into the palace itself. And while Niall left her to speak with the guards in the vestibule, Alyssa took the time to peruse the palace interior while she waited. It definitely wasn't as stately as she'd anticipated it to be. In fact, if the long hallway before her was any indication of the rest of the castle, it seemed to be in a bit of disrepair.

She figured it took a large staff and huge effort to keep a palace of this size tidy and up to snuff, and at first glance it didn't seem so bad, but the closer one looked, the more inconsistencies were noticed. Like how the huge tapestries adorning the walls of the massive hallway were frayed here and there and sadly faded. The artwork—her specialty—was lackluster and coated with what looked like years of dirt and grime. Even the guard's uniforms were dull and worn. The overall effect was a tad shabby, but then who was she to judge?

Perhaps Artemysia had fallen on hard times and had never fully recovered. It was possible that they lacked the means needed for maintenance of such a massive structure. She'd visited more castles in Europe then she cared to count that had dealt with the same issues. Many historically wealthy families had been forced to sell their properties or turn them into businesses such as hotels or museums. Old castles like this one were costly to sustain.

Before she could ponder the subject longer, Niall rejoined her. Tilting his head, he gave her a knowing look. "You look a bit disappointed. Not everything you thought it would be?" he asked, as if reading her thoughts.

Not knowing how closely Niall was aligned with Prince Graydon or the king, she chose her words carefully. If his court was located somewhere in this kingdom, the last thing she wanted to do was insult him in any way. "I wouldn't exactly say I'm disappointed. I love old architecture, and I know how expensive it can be to maintain."

The High Lord laughed out loud. "Very diplomatically put, Alice."

"Alyssa. My name is Alyssa, remember?"

"Of course. My apologies," he replied with evident amusement before glancing around the vestibule. "But as you've probably surmised, King Aramond has little interest in maintaining this place. His focus lies in … other areas."

"I see," she replied, though she really didn't. But as she studied him, another thought occurred to her. "You said before that you were High Lord of the Roseland Twilight Court. Is your court under King Aramond's jurisdiction?"

The congenial smile on Niall's face didn't so much fade as become a touch brittle. "The Twilight Court lies within Roseland's northern borders, yes, but be assured, it is under no one's jurisdiction but my own. The human king has no authority in my court or within the boundaries of any faerie lands."

The tone he used sent a chill skittering down her spine. She'd obviously stepped into a touchy area and looked to smooth over any errors she may have inadvertently made. "I'm sorry. I meant no offense. It's just that when you were talking to those pixies you seemed to insinuate that you worked for the king, so I assumed—"

"Not a good idea." Niall's eyes narrowed and the brittle smile on his face evaporated completely. "Since you are not from this realm, let me give you a bit of advice, *Alyssa*. Assumptions can be perilous. Fidelities are made and broken in this realm with acute regularity. It will serve you well never to presume anything while you're here, as everyone with whom you come into contact will have their own agendas and goals."

Including you?

The menace in his warning—for it certainly was a warning— and the tone he'd used gave her pause. Just because he'd kept to his word and brought her to the palace, didn't mean he was an ally. He was correct; making assumptions in this strange place could be very dangerous, especially where he was concerned. She'd do well to remember her earlier trepidation about this faerie and his intent.

"Understood." She cleared her throat and tried a different tack. "You said your court was within the northern border. Is that nearby? It's hard to tell distance with the way we traveled to get here."

Niall shook his head. "The Twilight Court is much farther north. If you were traveling by horse, it would be more than a day's ride." He glanced down at her broken shoe. "Of course, walking would take much longer."

"Very funny. So, if the forest where you found me isn't part of your territory, which presumably it isn't, what were you doing there?"

"If you have no perception of distance, what makes you think it isn't within my lands?"

When she simply stared at him and waited him out, he gave

her an inscrutable look. "What I was doing in Roseland Wood would be my business."

"Uh-huh."

And none of mine, right? she thought.

"So, do you have a palace in your Twilight Court as well?"

"Would it disappoint you if I said no?"

"What? No, not at all. I just … well, you said you were a High Lord. I'm not sure what that means. Is High Lord like being monarch or ruler of your court?"

Though his demeanor didn't change all that much, he suddenly appeared quite imposing. The air around him seemed to charge with mystery and more than a touch of danger. "Hmm … ruler? Many would tell you so. In the Twilight Court, my word is law and governs all, so I suppose you could say that being High Lord is like being king."

"I can't even imagine how daunting that must be." Alyssa shook her head. "I would think it's a weighty obligation, to make decisions for the good of your court, to be responsible for the well-being of your people."

His bark of laughter was devoid of humor. "One would think. However, not all High Lords are burdened with the sense of honor or duty you would suggest."

"Are you?"

He went still for a moment and studied her intently. "Ruling is a nebulous thing," he said carefully. "Sometimes ideals like honor and duty are a hindrance one can't afford."

Before she could press him on the subject further, one of the guards he'd spoken to earlier came over and took him aside. Though Alyssa strained to hear their conversation, they spoke in such low tones that she could make out none of their discussion. The next thing she knew, Niall was taking her arm in a vise-like grip and pulling her with him along the lengthy corridor.

"Hey! What are you doing?" she sputtered.

"You said you wanted to meet the king. It seems he now has a free moment."

She tried to jerk free of his grasp without success. "Yes, but that doesn't mean you can manhandle me like a rag doll. I'm perfectly capable of getting there under my own steam."

"Of that I have no doubt." He chuckled but refused to release her arm.

At the end of the corridor, two guards were stationed on either side of enormous wooden doors intricately carved with all manner of creatures. Alyssa would've loved to study the carvings more thoroughly, but as she and Niall approached, the guards pushed the doors open, taking her attention away from the artwork as the interior of the chamber came into view.

This was obviously the king's throne room. It was huge, with stone pillars two to three feet in circumference lining the way to the raised dais and holding up a ceiling painted with garish scenes of battling armies. Marble stairs ringed the platform upon which sat King Aramond on his ornate throne surrounded by soldiers in armored breast plates holding long, lethal-looking spears. It was like something out of the middle ages, and Alyssa suddenly felt incredibly small and vulnerable. What had she been thinking, coming here?

The king himself was a large, barrel-chested man with a hard yet striking face. His lavish golden crown sat atop his head of short, gray hair like a glittering beacon. He exuded a raw kind of power, but it was his eyes that sent a ripple of alarm through Alyssa. They held no emotion, no warmth in their piercing black depths as they passed over her with disinterest.

"Lord Niall." The king's booming gravelly voice held a hint of derision as he turned to the High Lord. "What is the meaning of this? It's not even dawn, yet you demand an audience. What would bring you down from the north to my kingdom at such an early hour? And who is this human you've brought with you?"

"King Aramond." Niall gave the king the briefest of nods. "I realize the hour is early for you humans, and for that, I do apologize. As for this woman, I found her wandering in the forest, and you'll never guess who she was looking for."

"What are you playing at, faerie? What care would I have in who this woman was seeking?"

"I would think you would be very interested to know that she was looking for Prince Graydon."

The king immediately sat forward, his dark, penetrating gaze sweeping over Alyssa again. "Graydon, you say? Why was she seeking that lowly whelp?"

Niall smiled and waved away the king's question. "Oh, we'll get to that soon enough. But first, I'd like to address something that may be related."

His tone was pleasant enough, yet Alyssa got the feeling that Niall did not like this king and perhaps had an agenda of his own, as he'd alluded to earlier. His next question may have been posed in the same agreeable fashion, but there was a definite edge to his words.

"It has come to my attention that you may have located a certain artifact and have set a plan in motion to acquire it. Is this true?"

"What I do in my kingdom and any plans I make do not concern you, *High Lord*." The king's response—though hostile and full of contempt—was tinged with unease, which Alyssa found interesting.

Niall laughed out loud and wagged a finger at the king. "Ah, but that's not quite accurate, now is it? I have it on good authority that the prince returned from the human realm with the Scepter of Fire."

"Wait. Are you talking about my family's artif—" Before she could get out the rest of her question, Niall raised a hand in her direction, and her words simply evaporated. She grabbed at her throat, trying desperately to communicate, but try as she might, she couldn't get out a word.

Niall went on speaking to the king as if she wasn't struggling in silence beside him. "I'm sure you understand that if you intend to wage war against Wysteria by stealing and then utilizing the Scepter of Fire, it very much concerns me, as it will most of the other fae queens and High Lords in Roseland."

The king tried to look nonchalant, but in Alyssa's opinion, was doing a poor job of it. "The Fair Folk have nothing to fear from me. My quarrel is not with you but with Wysteria's White Queen." The king's voice began to rise, taking on an agitated quality. "She drove my Renata—her own sister, mind you—into madness and death, and then had that heinous human child use the scepter against my army before I could extract my revenge. Beatrice may have hidden the scepter, but once I have it, I will destroy both her and her kingdom. My vengeance will be absolute, and the Red Queen will at last be avenged!"

Alyssa was horrified by what she was hearing. Obviously, the man was crazy as a loon, and she'd stepped into the middle of it, thanks to Niall.

Amazingly, the High Lord looked unfazed by the king's outburst. "I have no interest in your human feuds. My apprehension comes when—and if, for I do have my doubts—you manage to use the scepter and best the White Queen. What would prevent you from turning the scepter's power on the fae realm?"

Aramond struggled to get himself under control. Leaning back, he took a deep breath and once again appeared calm and regal. "Then join me in my pursuit. Bring your warriors to fight alongside my armies. With the scepter, we can reunite the kingdoms and enjoy prosperity again, the fae courts included."

The High Lord tilted his head as if considering the king's proposal. "And what of the courts that decline your fine offer?" he finally asked.

"Again, my quarrel is not with them. They are free to decide on their own, as are you. But I will say this, those who join me will inherit much. Those who don't ... will take their chances."

Say no, say no! This guy is insane.

Though Alyssa still couldn't speak, she prayed that Niall would refuse the king's proposal, but before he could give his reply, the doors of the chamber burst open. A group of warriors covered in mud, and in some cases what looked to be blood, entered the room led by a wizened old man carrying a velvet bag.

"Why, Finnious Richter, one of the White Queen's oldest advisors," Niall said with a grim smile as the group approached the dais. "What an unfortunate turn of events for Wysteria. And attended by fae warriors from the Evening Court, no less." He turned to the king. "I suppose this means that Queen Mabry has made her choice and agreed to join your festivities."

"The Queen of the Evening Court was one of the first," The king replied with obvious satisfaction before turning to Richter. "So? Was it as Mabry said?"

Richter bowed low before holding up the velvet bag he carried. "Just so, my King. It was a fierce battle, but the prince and his field marshal were exactly where she said we would find them. Unfortunately, many of her warriors were lost, and as I hurried away with the prize when it was finally brought to me, I can't be certain if they were able to dispatch the prince properly. However, as per your wishes, the scepter was liberated."

"Excellent! Bring it to me at once," the king demanded. "I must see it, hold it, and feel its power."

The advisor ascended the platform and pulled the scepter from the confines of the velvet bag.

No! It's not yours. Alyssa tried to scream, but was still unable to utter a sound. When she attempted to rush toward the dais, Niall's powers easily held her in place with a shuttered look.

"It's magnificent," the king exclaimed, his dark eyes gleaming with anticipation and madness. But his maniacal smile began to fade within moments of handling the scepter. "But here, what's wrong with it? I feel nothing, Richter. Why can I not feel its power? Are you certain this is the Scepter of Fire?"

"Of course it is, Majesty. I would recognize it anywhere. It was taken from Prince Graydon by one of the fae warriors during the fight." The advisor turned to the faeries that had accompanied him into the chamber. "Tell him," he demanded. But before any of the warriors could respond, the advisor's gaze fell on Alyssa, and his mouth dropped open. Pointing a gnarled finger in her direction, he shouted, "You!"

The king glanced at the advisor. "What's the matter with you, Richter?"

"You have her, Majesty. All the pieces are falling into place."

"What are you babbling about? I have who?"

The old man smiled at Alyssa then, and she felt panic rise, though she didn't quite know why. What did the old man mean, and why was he pointing at her? She was stunned when he finally answered. "Alice, my King. You have Alice *and* the scepter. Victory is assured."

She shrieked in her head, *my name is Alyssa!* But of course, no one heard her.

"Alice? *The* Alice?" Aramond rose slowly from his throne, and his shadowy gaze seemed full of malice as he zeroed in on her. "You can't be serious. She was but a child, and that was long ago."

"Yes, Sire. She is definitely older, but do you not see the resemblance?"

Alyssa was filled with dread as the king descended the stairs to where she stood. He took hold of her jaw and turned her face this way and that. Then he turned to Niall. "If this is Alice, why did you not say so?"

Niall shrugged. "She says she's not Alice." With a wave of his hand, he released her from the hold he'd applied. "Tell him, *Alyssa.*"

She cleared her throat and swallowed. "It's true. My name isn't Alice. It's Alyssa Montague. And I've never been here before. You have the wrong person."

Richter stepped forward. "Absurd. One only has to look at you to see the truth," he hissed. "And besides, did Prince Graydon not retrieve the scepter from you on this very night?"

Alyssa's frightened gaze slipped to the scepter in the king's hand, and she felt the noose tightening around her. "Okay, yes, that is my family's heirloom, and it did disappear from my home tonight. But other than that, I don't know what you're talking about. I'm not who you think I am—"

"See!" Richter crowed. "She admits it, Majesty. She colluded with the White Queen to hide the scepter in the human realm all these years."

"No. That's not true!"

Taking her by the wrist, the king pressed her hand to the scepter.

And nothing happened.

"You are purposely holding its power from me. Well, it won't save you. Tell me how to wield its power, and I might be inclined to spare your life," Aramond demanded. "Otherwise, as my dear Renata used to say, it will be off with your head, little Alice."

"I told you, my name isn't Alice!" she screamed. "And I don't know what you're talking about."

The king sighed. "That is quite the shame, but have it your way. Maybe some time in the dungeon will soften your resolve. Take her away."

As the guards dragged her toward the door she heard the king say, "You best make your decision quickly, High Lord. Now that I have the scepter and the human to wield it, there's no time to waste."

As Alyssa glanced back, Niall turned and their eyes met for a moment. In that brief instant, she realized that he'd used her, perhaps had meant to all along. Was regret what she saw in his beautiful green eyes, or something more ominous? Then he was gone in a flurry of starlight, and she was hauled out into the corridor and down several flights of stairs into the bowels of the palace.

The deeper they went, the worse the smell became. The lower levels were dark and dank with only odd flickering torches on the walls to light the way. There were wet patches here and there that she didn't even want to consider, and the smell of urine was prevalent, making her gag. Pitiful moans and whimpers emanated from some of the cells as they passed. It was surreal and terrifying—

something out of a nightmare—and she couldn't quite believe it was happening.

As they approached the final cell in the corridor, the guard in the lead opened the door wide and motioned her inside. When she cringed away and refused to enter, the guard behind her shoved her through the door. Unable to keep her balance, she stumbled over her broken shoe and went down hard on the filthy stone floor, scraping her bare knees and the palms of her hands.

"Wait!" she cried as the guard slammed the door to the cell, locking her in. Her next plea died in her throat as they retreated and she heard the evil snicker as Finnious Richter came into view.

"I've waited a very long time for this moment," he said with obvious glee. "At last, young Alice, you will reap what you've sown. Like King Aramond, I lost the love of my life when you wielded the scepter all those years ago. Now, if you don't give the king what he wants, I'm going to have the pleasure of seeing you beheaded. We will both have our revenge."

Glaring at him, she slowly shook her head. "You're all completely insane. I don't know you or what you're even talking about. No matter what your delusion may be, my name is Alyssa. And like I said, I've never been here before, so you've got the wrong person."

"We'll see." The old man chuckled again. "Yes, we'll see soon enough." With that, he strolled off into the darkness, leaving her in the dreadful cell with the hopeless cries echoing in the shadows as her only company.

Thirteen

"The descendant is here?" Alexi's face paled. He tried to sit up in bed, but with a slight wince, put a hand to his side and laid back. "Are you sure?"

"Of course we're sure," Isabella snapped. She threw up her hands in exasperation. "She disappeared right after she went back upstairs to talk to the prince."

"Isabella, you're not helping," Valian said in a quiet tone, giving her a quelling look that, surprisingly, she heeded.

This was not starting out well. The healers had patched up the worst of Alexi's wounds—those injuries that Gray had been unable to tackle—but even though Elven metabolism allowed for accelerated healing, he was still far from a hundred percent.

"Alexi, are you saying that Alyssa didn't accompany you and Gray back to Wysteria?"

"What?" Alexi's mouth dropped open. "Of course not! Why would we bring her here? That was never the intent, and you know it, Val."

Valian nodded. "I suspected as much, but we needed to be certain."

"Alyssa knows nothing of this world. Bringing her here would've been irresponsible, not to mention dangerous." Alexi threw a meaningful glance in Isabella's direction. "And just how did this one get here?"

"*This one* has a name, thank you," Isabella said in a haughty tone. "And if you must know, I came with Valian."

"I beg your pardon?"

When Alexi turned to him for explanation, Valian felt a pang of guilt but simply shrugged. "Events unraveled and went downhill very quickly. There was little time to quibble, so I had to make a decision on the fly. The problem is that Alyssa is missing, Alexi. And I'm worried about her well-being." He went on to describe Kasandra Delacourt's appearance and her cryptic remarks, as well as the steps he and Isabella had taken after the faerie had left the party.

"So you think the High Fae sent Alyssa through the portal after we left?"

"That's my theory. I could feel the faerie magick in Alyssa's study the minute we entered. It's the only thing that makes sense. And if Alyssa is alone in this realm, we're going to need Isabella if we find her."

"*When* we find her," Isabella corrected him.

"May not have been the wisest choice, but I get it." Alexi nodded. "A familiar face."

"Alyssa is my friend," she said, her emotions riding high in her tone. "Learning that this world existed, coming here and seeing it firsthand has been really scary and confusing. And I had Valian to at least give me a quick rundown. But Aly's out there all by herself, Alexi. She's got to be freaking out. We have to find her."

"Okay, okay, you're right." Alexi ran a hand over his face and took a deep breath. "I'm sorry, Isabella. I didn't mean to be insensitive. I know how scared you must be for her." He turned to Valian. "Look, we grabbed the scepter and faded almost the minute Alyssa left the room, just like we'd planned. We used the northern portal, which in hindsight was probably a mistake, considering the issues we'd been having with the wards. We ended up being caught with our pants down by Richter and what seemed like about a thousand Roseland fae warriors, so it was a good thing Alyssa wasn't with us."

"Agreed. That could've been disastrous. I've sent out patrols to check the borders. We need to know if the wards are only out in certain areas or down completely."

"Yeah, Gray and I wondered about the state of the wards, especially with the horde of Roseland faeries we ran into, so if they're down, we need to get them back up and running as soon as possible."

"Either way, we need to start preparing for the worst. If Richter has the scepter, it's only a matter of time before he turns it over to Aramond, if he hasn't already. An attack could be eminent and hold dire consequences if Aramond figures out how to use it."

"That's a chilling thought. He'd like nothing better than to destroy Wysteria using the very artifact that kept him from his goal during the Great War. But there's another concern we should think about with regards to Alyssa," Alexi said, and the look he sent Valian spoke volumes. "If Kasandra had a hand in her disappearance, you know she would never have sent her here."

"That was my thought as well." Valian's face was grim. "The queen wants to send a search party into Roseland. If Kasandra did send Alyssa through the portal, that's where she'll be."

Alexi whistled through his teeth. "That's a dicey proposition at best, Val. I mean, where do we start the search? Roseland is as large as Wysteria in size, and you know that they guard their borders aggressively. Taking a cadre of soldiers into the territory would be a bad idea, so we'd need to keep it small and move fast to avoid detection."

"Who's *we*, Field Marshal?" Halifax had been lounging against the wall next to the infirmary door, but now stepped forward, a curious look on his face. "Surely you're not thinking of joining this insane undertaking. You're obviously in no condition to get out of bed, let alone lead a search into enemy terrain. You'd only be a liability."

"Says the weak-kneed cat who doesn't like to get his hands dirty." Alexi smirked. "I don't hear you volunteering. Besides, I'm an Elven warrior, remember? We heal very quickly. You have no idea what I'm capable of." Alexi looked to Valian, and his smirk slowly dissolved. "By the Oracles, Val, you can't seriously think to do this without me."

Valian sighed. "Alexi, you know there's no warrior I would rather have by my side than you, but I'm afraid that Halifax has a point. Time is running out, and Elven healing aside, I'm not certain that you're in any shape to participate. It's only been a few hours ago that you were gravely injured."

Alexi gaped at him. "Are you kidding me? You'd take the cat and leave me here to cool my heels?"

Halifax chuckled. "Well, I may not like to 'get my hands dirty' with crazy stunts like this, but I most definitely am the best choice when it comes to stealth. I don't enjoy the fight, but I do delight in the intrigue."

"Oh, for fuck's sake." Alexi rolled his eyes before turning back to Valian. "Come on, Val. You know I can do this. And with Gray out of commission, you need me with you."

"I'm going, too," Isabella chimed in.

All three males turned to her in unison.

"Have you lost your mind?" Alexi blurted before Valian could respond. "Absolutely not! Have you not been following the conversation? This mission is going to be extremely dangerous, even for us."

"Alexi is right." Valian put up a hand before Isabella could argue. "You will stay here in the palace until we return. And that's not negotiable, Isabella."

"But Alyssa is *my* friend. You'll need me with you when you find her. You said so yourself," Isabella cried. "I won't be treated like a pathetic child waiting for the *menfolk* to save the day."

"Isabella, nobody's treating you like a child." Valian shook his head and stood firm. "Like Alexi said, Roseland is an immense kingdom with numerous portals. Kasandra could have sent Alyssa to any one of them, so we've no idea where to even start looking. You can't imagine how dangerous this is going to be. We'll likely be dodging Roseland forces, may be required to defend ourselves at any point, and you have no combat training."

"Chancellor Winchester is correct, child," Queen Beatrice said from the doorway. As they all turned toward her, she swept into the room with regal grace, taking Isabella by the hand. "And I will not allow you to accompany them on this search."

"But I can—"

The queen cut her off with a look and shook her head. "No. You can't. I know you're worried about your friend, but you have little understanding of this realm and would only be a hindrance in a very perilous situation. This is not something you're equipped to handle, no matter what you may think to the contrary."

Queen Beatrice moved to Alexi's side. "And what of you, Field Marshal? How are you faring?"

"I'm healing quickly, Majesty. I will be ready to go when the time comes. You have my word."

"Alexi—" Valian began but his cousin shut him down.

"I'm going, Val." Alexi glared at Halifax. "If for no other reason than to make sure the black cat doesn't get you into trouble."

Valian sighed but left it at that. Alexi could be stubborn as an old goblin's mule, and the time for dickering had passed. "Alright. But don't make me sorry I consented to this." Turning to the queen, he asked the question on everyone's mind. "How is the prince, Majesty? Has his condition improved?"

The queen gave him a weary smile. "That is what I came to tell you. Graydon is weak, but on the mend. He was awake briefly, and is now sleeping comfortably. It was touch and go for a while, but my son is from strong, magickal lineage. Although the faerie poison used was particularly toxic, the healers were able to isolate it in time to save his life." She went to Halifax and placed a hand on his shoulder. "I'm told that another hour and there would've been no hope, so let me again tell you how grateful I am that you found them both when you did."

Valian pressed his lips together to keep from chuckling when Halifax actually blushed at the compliment. It was so out of character for the cantankerous shifter.

The Cheshire Wood cat bowed low, his golden eyes shining with reverence. "And I will again tell you that it was my honor, Majesty. But you are most certainly welcome."

The queen smiled and then looked to Valian. "Chancellor, High Lord Finvar and several of his warriors have arrived from his northern court, and he's offering assistance for whatever you plan. They're in the briefing chamber. I know you must keep your force small for this mission, but I thought perhaps his offer would be welcomed."

"It would, indeed, Highness."

"The High Lord of Wysteria's Winter Court is here?" Halifax asked. "I'd say that will even the odds a bit."

The queen took a deep breath and addressed Alexi. "Now, if you are up to the task, as you say you are, then I would suggest you get yourself dressed. We shall adjourn to the briefing room to discuss strategy with Lord Finvar. Join us there as soon as you can."

"Majesty, I know that I consented, but I'm still not certain that Alexi is well enough to accompany us," Valian spoke up. "It is a relevant concern."

"Val—" Alexi began but the queen silenced him with a glance.

Turning to Valian, there was a question in her warm, brown eyes as she tilted her head and gave him a considering look. "There was a time long ago when I had the same concerns for you, Chancellor. Do you recall what you said to me then?"

Valian frowned. "With all due respect, Highness, that was a much different situation."

"Mmm, and remind me what words you used to convince me that you were fit to lead?"

The room went silent as he cleared his throat and met the

queen's gaze. Those words, spoken so long ago, were etched into the fiber of his being. "'I will never stop nor give way while there is breath in my body and fire in my heart. For queen and country I fight until death.' Those were my words. But this is not the same, my Queen. Then we were in the midst of war."

Queen Beatrice raised a delicate eyebrow. "Are we not on that brink as we speak? If Aramond has the scepter and can learn to wield it, will we not have to defend ourselves and our people to our last breath?" Turning back to Alexi, she narrowed her eyes and pinned him with her steely gaze. "And you Field Marshal. You say you're up to this task?"

"Yes, Majesty. I won't let you down."

The queen gave a short nod. "See that you don't. Now ready yourself and meet us in the briefing chamber."

TWENTY MINUTES LATER, ALEXI ENTERED THE BRIEFING chamber. He'd donned his Elven leathers complete with breast plate stamped with the Wysterian crest, as well as arm and leg guards. As an Elven warrior, he looked the picture of health, and one would never suspect that he'd been at death's door only a handful of hours ago. Valian would keep an eye on him, all the same.

Surveying the assembled group, he took a quick mental inventory. Besides Alexi and Halifax, the High Lord of the Winter Court would assuredly be a strong addition to their undertaking, for Finvar was no stranger to war. Standing just over six feet, his powerful build was encased in fighting leathers beneath a long vest of rich, white fur. Ice-blue eyes set in a lean, pale face exuded strength and wisdom from centuries of rule. His shoulder-length, steel-gray hair was braided elaborately on either side of his head. And the warriors he'd brought with him looked equally fit and up to the challenge.

"Alright, let's get this party started." Valian began to lay out his plan, such as it was. "Since we have no idea where to begin, I suggest we start by revisiting the area where Alexi and the prince were ambushed here in Wysteria, see what clues we can dig up there before heading across the border. Alexi says Alyssa wasn't with them, so I doubt there will be any sign, but we'll keep a watchful eye anyway."

"But the scepter is the objective, is it not?" Finvar asked. "It must be found at all costs."

"True. But we'll be looking for both," Alexi replied with a glance toward a nervous Isabella. "Alyssa is the descendant. For her to fall into Aramond's hands would be equally as bad. As a child, her ancestor was the one to wield the scepter in the first place. We don't know what part she plays in this, so we can't lose sight of that fact."

Finvar gave a short nod. "Understood."

Valian pointed to an area on the map he'd spread out on the table. "We cross here and look for the northeastern portal first. Kasandra is from Roseland's Evening Court which lies further to the west. I'm thinking that's where she would've sent Alyssa, but of course, that's a crap shoot."

Finvar narrowed his eyes and shrugged. "It is a logical assumption."

"However, anything is possible where High Fae are concerned." Halifax snorted, then leisurely glanced over at Finvar. "Present company excluded, of course."

Finvar grunted, and several of his warriors glared, but Halifax only gave them a cheesy grin.

Valian shook his head at the cat's audacity, but wrapped up the conversation. "Well, gentlemen, there's not much else to discuss, as this mission will be fast and loose, so I suggest we get moving."

As the meeting broke up and the group began to prepare, Valian stepped over to Isabella. "I can see you're anxious, but stay calm and try not to worry. We'll be back before you know it, hopefully with Alyssa in tow."

"I hate that I have to stay here and stew, but I'll be fine as long as you all come back safe and sound." She blew out a breath and there was a silent plea in her eyes as she continued. "Find her, Valian. And then get your ass back here. You get me, mister?"

Valian chuckled. "I do indeed, love."

They left the palace as dawn was peeping over the horizon with Valian leading Alexi, Halifax, Finvar, and the small crew of armed fae warriors through Cheshire Wood toward the Roseland border. The mood was tense, especially when Finvar had confirmed their deepest fear—the security wards were completely down along most of the western perimeter. It was certainly unwelcome news, but Valian had already suspected as much.

"My guess is that would be Richter's doing as well, the treasonous bastard," Alexi growled, slightly out of breath. "I can't wait to get my hands on that turd and mess him up."

Noting Alexi's shortness of breath, Valian made a mental note to keep a vigilant eye on his cousin. "Believe me, you aren't the only one." He was also looking forward to that moment. There would be no mercy for the advisor when all was said and done. Richter had betrayed his queen, his people, and Valian would make certain that the man was dealt with harshly for his treachery. "But let's keep our focus on the task at hand, shall we?"

They began their search in Tarkington Forest where the ambush had taken place. Halifax morphed into his black leopard persona and ranged around the expanse hoping to pick up on something that would suggest that Alyssa may have been in the area, though Valian was convinced it was a long-shot. They were still inside Wysteria's borders, and his gut told him Alyssa's disappearance was Kasandra's doing, which meant Roseland was where they'd find her, if they found her at all. It would be like looking for a needle in a haystack—an impossible feat, considering the sheer size of the kingdom and the fact that they had no idea where to begin their search.

Halifax did detect Richter's scent just outside of the battle site as Valian had hoped, so the group followed it to the west and across the border into Roseland Wood. Here the snow was several inches deep with a fresh layer covering any tracks they may have found, making it difficult for Halifax to track further by scent.

Instead of fading, the group continued on foot another forty minutes to where the northeastern portal was located, in case there were clues to find, but because of the dense undergrowth and fresh layer of snow, nothing else materialized.

However, that all changed when they got to the portal and found their first real lead.

"There's a broken branch on this sapling, and the underbrush is a bit crushed," Halifax said. Now in the form of a man, he walked around the area sniffing the air before crouching down to inspect the snow-covered ground more closely.

Finvar glanced over his shoulder and sneered. "There are many beasts in these woods that could have done that damage ... including felines, cat."

"Ah, yes, High Lord. But I don't know of any of my brethren —or beasties, for that matter—who take easily to wearing high-heeled shoes." He pulled his hand out of the undergrowth and held up the spikey four inch heel of a shoe.

Alexi went over and took it from him, then turned to Valian. "This has got to be from one of those stilts Alyssa had on last night. I remember wondering how a person could walk in those things."

Valian narrowed his eyes. "That's a good bet. And I don't know of anyone in this realm who wears those kinds of heels. Finvar?"

"No. Not to my knowledge. And by the Oracles, why would they? It would be most uncomfortable." The High Lord made a face and then shook his head. "Humans."

"I wondered if you would come," a languid voice said from the tree line. "I dare say, it took you long enough."

The entire group drew their weapons and turned toward the sound of the voice.

"Who's there?" Finvar demanded to know. "Show yourself."

"Who are *you*?" the voice countered with a snicker.

"Pilliar?" Halifax stepped closer. "Is that you?"

A tall, excruciatingly slim wood sprite with pale green skin and an elongated neck stepped out from behind the tree that had completely hidden his body. He raised a long, thin smoking pipe to his lips and puffed several times—the fragrant smoke billowing around his head—before answering, "And who else would it be, may I ask?"

"Gentlemen, you may put away your weapons." Halifax chuckled and swept his arm toward the sprite. "Let me introduce you to Kaleb Pilliar."

Kaleb gave a lazy nod toward the group. "I know Halifax quite well, and the Chancellor and the Field Marshal by sight. But who are the rest of you?"

Valian stepped forward and gestured to Finvar. "This is Finvar, High Lor—"

"Ah yes," Kaleb interrupted. "The High Lord of Wysteria's Winter Court. I recognize him now. Welcome to Roseland, one and all. I assume you're here because of the recent hubbub?"

"Which 'hubbub' are you talking about, Kaleb?" Alexi asked.

The sprite puffed a few more times and blew out a stream of sickly yellow smoke. "It is dangerous to discuss these matters here. The trees have ears, you know. My humble abode is just over that rise. Come with me, and I will tell you all I've seen and heard."

Valian glanced at Halifax. Though annoying at times, he knew the cat was loyal to the queen and wouldn't put them in harm's way if he could help it. But Valian was not so certain about Kaleb Pilliar. It was a calculated risk if they wanted the information he seemed to have, a risk he was willing to take ... with caution.

He looked at Alexi, who adjusted his crossbow on his shoulder and raised an eyebrow, and then Finvar, who merely shrugged. "Alright, then. We'll go with you, as long as Halifax will vouch for you."

"Absolutely."

"Excellent. Then you take the lead. We'll be right behind you."

The cat gave him a curious look, but complied.

Kaleb's house was a small, haphazard affair tucked back into the trees. Off to one side was a large garden filled with leafy green lettuce plants and huge, multi-colored mushrooms, both of which seemed impervious to the snow that dusted them.

After instructing his warriors to stand guard outside, Finvar, Valian, Alexi, and Halifax followed the sprite inside. They all sat down next to the small fireplace in a living area that was spotlessly clean and toasty warm.

"I'd offer you tea or cider, but I know how most elves feel about accepting food or drink from Fair Folk, especially in their homes," Kaleb said.

"Its fine, Kaleb," Valian replied. "Just tell us what you know. We're in a bit of a hurry."

"Oh, I do not think so. You need go no further, you see, because you're very late. Too late, in fact, for either hubbub."

Alexi frowned. "What do you mean?"

Kaleb smiled sadly. "Well, if you seek the scepter, that horde of faeries from Queen Mabry's Evening Court came through the forest hours ago with that wrinkled, old man. They've taken the scepter to King Aramond."

Though the news was expected, Valian had held out a sliver of hope that they'd be able to find the scepter and recover it before Aramond got his hands on it.

"And the other hubbub?" Halifax asked.

"Ah, yes. That of the human female that came through the portal." The sprite nodded sagely.

"You've seen Alyssa?" asked Alexi.

Kaleb's smile was a bit dreamy. "She was quite lovely, though dressed inappropriately for the weather. And she did have a broken shoe."

Halifax huffed out an agitated breath. "Please try to focus, Kaleb. What happened to her? Where did she go?"

The sprite puffed on his pipe some more—Valian thought, just to be contrary—but finally sighed and continued. "Well, at first, Ligia and Drifa tried to get her to come back to their burrow, but she didn't want to go, which was very smart, if you ask me."

"Ligia and Drifa?" Halifax asked. "Those daft frost pixie twins?"

Kaleb nodded. "They were just about to get mean about it, too. You know how frost pixies can be when they want you to do something you don't want to do."

"Yes, yes, get on with it, man," Halifax urged. "So, she didn't go with them?"

"No. Lord Niall saved the day ... for once."

"The High Lord of the Twilight Court?" Finvar glowered. "His court is much farther north. He has no authority here. What was he doing so far from home?"

Kaleb tilted his head on his long neck and smiled. "I'm sure I don't know. I stayed hidden during the encounter." He leaned forward. "To be honest, Lord Niall scares me a bit. He has a temper and can be quite unpleasant when provoked," he finished in a conspiratorial whisper before sitting back. "Anyway, he shooed the twins away and introduced himself in very courtly fashion. He also said that she looked very much like Alice."

"Like Alice?" Valian exchanged looks with Alexi. What was Niall playing at here?

"Yes," Kaleb replied. "But she told him her name was Alyssa and that she knew no Alice."

"But what happened to her?" Alexi demanded. "Did Niall take her?"

Kaleb poked at the bowl of his pipe with the end of a wooden match and frowned. "Well, she seemed to be looking for the prince and wanted to be taken to the palace. Because she could never have walked to the palace with a broken shoe, Lord Niall offered to take her."

"Let me guess," Alexi said with a disgusted look. "He took her to the Red Palace."

"Well, that was her problem, you see. She didn't stipulate to which palace she wished to be taken." Kaleb clucked his tongue and shook his head in sorrow. "Very unfortunate. Very unfortunate, indeed. And as you know, the king is not a very nice human." The sprite shuddered. "I hate to think of what will become of her. I've heard she's been taken to the dungeon. Such an abysmal place."

Valian exchanged looks with Alexi again, and then Halifax, who held up a finger. "I have a notion, Chancellor. May I?"

"It depends what you have in mind." Running a hand over his face, Valian nodded. "But by all means, be my guest."

Halifax pulled his chair closer to Kaleb's and grinned. "Kaleb, my friend. How would you like to help us in a quest to rescue a damsel in distress?"

Fourteen

Graydon awoke in stages, gradually becoming conscious of his surroundings. His thoughts were hazy and fragmented as he sifted through them in an effort to determine where he was and what had happened to him.

He immediately recognized the strong scent of antiseptic, which brought to mind the hospital wing. The next thing he noticed confirmed his suspicion. His body felt thick and ached all over, yet somehow seemed hollow at the same time. It was the oddest sensation, as if someone had scooped out his innards with a trowel. His limbs were incredibly heavy. And he was thirsty, devastatingly parched, so much so that he could hear the dry click his throat made when he swallowed. His eyes were as gritty as sandpaper behind lids that seemed glued in place.

Struggling to open his eyes to slits, he saw that his assumption had been correct. He was indeed in a hospital bed. As he took inventory of his state, he was relieved to discover that though he may hurt everywhere, he was still in one piece.

Attempting to lift an arm, he sucked in a breath as the pain intensified in his shoulder with the effort. When he turned his head, he saw that his right shoulder was encased in a pristine white bandage, and memories of why came flooding back to him.

He and Alexi had been ambushed as they'd returned from the New York realm with the scepter.

Alexi!

Panic spread through him when he recalled watching his friend being struck down before he himself had lost consciousness. But try as he might, Gray couldn't remember anything that had happened after that. How had he made it back to the palace? Had they both been rescued? Was Alexi here somewhere, too? Or was he ... No, he wouldn't let himself even finish that thought.

"Ah, I see you're finally awake, Highness," Gryphon, the queen's diminutive chamber elf said as he came into the room carrying a small tray. "Her Majesty sent me to check on you and report back. I've brought a bowl of warm millet porridge and hot spiced tea in case I found you awake and hungry."

Gray cleared his throat, but his voice sounded rusty even to his own ears when his spoke. "No, thank you, Gryphon. But I wouldn't turn down a gallon or two of water."

The elf set the platter on a side table and then poured a large glass of clear, fresh water. Gray tried not to whimper as Gryphon raised the bed and then handed him the glass of salvation. Taking it in both hands, he told himself not to guzzle, but his thirst was so overwhelming in that moment that he did just that.

"I would have another, Gryphon," he said after drinking the entire glassful in several huge gulps. "Please."

"Of course, Sire." The elf took the glass and refilled it. "But you really should eat something. You've been gravely ill and need to regain your strength," he said as he handed the water to Gray.

This time Gray made himself drink more slowly. "I will. I just feel like all the fluid has been drained from my body." It was then that he noticed the IV stand next to the bed holding a bag of clear liquid dripping into the tube attached to his right hand. How had he not noticed that?

Gryphon's eyes followed Gray's to the IV stand. "The bag contains a combination of electrolytes, amino acids, nutrients, and other restorative elements to speed your recovery. But it won't take the place of a belly full of food. I would again urge you to at least have a few spoonfuls of the porridge."

"I will in a bit. How long have I been out?"

"Just over thirty-six hours, Sire.

"*A day and a half?*" Gray's mouth dropped open. "I've been unconscious for a day and a half? Are you joking?"

Gryphon tilted his head and looked confused. "Not at all? I would never jest about something like that."

Gray sighed. "I know that, Gryphon. I'm sorry. I just had no idea that I'd been so incapacitated from my injuries. And my mind seems to be in a jumble."

"Oh, it wasn't your shoulder wound that did the deed, Sire. It was the poison from the fae's sword that nearly took you from us, which is probably why you're a bit confused. The Cheshire Wood cat was the one to find you and the Field Marshal in the wee hours of the morning almost two days ago. And none too soon, I might add."

"I see." Gray swallowed then and asked the question shouting in his mind to be answered, though he was terrified of the response he would get. "And what of Alexi? He was gravely injured in the battle as well. Was he also brought to the palace?"

The elf looked surprised. "Do you not remember, Sire? You partially healed the Field Marshal in the Wood before being found. You saved his life."

"I did?" Gray blinked down at the elf. "No. I don't remember that at all. Truly? Alexi's going to recover?"

Gryphon nodded. "He has already, for the most part. He was even well enough to go on the mission into Roseland within hours of your rescue."

"Mission into Roseland? Why on earth would they go there? Were they in search of the scepter? It was lost during the battle. We need to locate it before it finds its way into Aramond's hands."

"I'm afraid it's too late for that, my Lord." The chamber elf's look became shuttered. "But it is not my place to speak of such things. Chancellor Winchester can explain it all to you."

"Valian is here in Wysteria? When did he get here?"

"The Chancellor arrived only hours before you were found. He was the one to initiate a search for you and the Field Marshal." Gryphon placed the salver of porridge and tea on a bed tray and set it over Gray's lap. "But enough talk of that. Eat as much as you can, and I will search out the Chancellor and send him to you at once."

Before Gray could object or query him further, the elf was out the door, quite spry and stealthy for his age and diminutive size. He was left with a plethora of questions and a bowl of unappetizing gruel in front of him. After taking a few bites, he settled for the lukewarm tea and what was left of his water.

Fortunately, he didn't have to wait long for Valian's arrival. The Chancellor followed the queen into the room ten minutes later, accompanied by Alexi, and to Gray's great surprise, Isabella Christensen.

"Graydon. How do you feel, my darling?" Queen Beatrice asked as she smoothed the hair off of his forehead.

"Checking my temperature, Mother?" He asked with a chuckle.

"Am I that obvious?" The queen countered with humor in her voice, but the strain in her eyes told him how worried she'd been.

"I'm sore and can't seem to pour enough water down my gullet, but I'm actually feeling much better than I did even twenty minutes ago. So, don't you worry. I think I'm gonna live."

The queen frowned and the humor in her voice fled. "Do not even joke that way. You were very close to death when you were found." Her eyes suddenly glistened with tears as she put her trembling fingers to her lips. "I was so frightened," she whispered.

"Hey, hey. No tears. I'm going to be fine, remember?"

She nodded and took a deep breath. "I know. Just think of them as tears of relief." Wiping her eyes, she shook her head and leaned down to kiss his cheek. "I only came to see for myself that you were awake. I have some other matters to attend to at the moment, so I will leave you with these two vagabonds. They can bring you up to speed on recent events." She turned and swept toward the door. "And eat your porridge," she commanded as she shut the door behind her.

Gray glared down at the offending gruel on the tray. "Not in this lifetime, no matter how hungry I get."

"That's terribly unkind, Gray," Alexi said with a smirk. "Gryphon probably slaved over that mess."

"Then you eat it."

Alexi laughed out loud. "I'll pass. Thanks."

Gray put out his hand and Alexi took it immediately. "It's good to see you up and around, brother. I thought the worst when I saw you drop."

"Hey, it'll take more than a horde of Roseland faeries to take me down for long." But then Alexi grew sober. "If it hadn't been for you, I would've died out there."

"Gryphon said that I partially healed you, but I don't remember anything after I passed out. The last thing I recall was seeing you drop."

Valian stepped forward. "That's probably due to the poison that ravaged your system. Let's hope events come back to you at some point once you've fully healed."

"You can say that again. I don't like the blank spots in my memory," Gray said. "In the meantime, fill me in on what I've missed. I'm told we have Halifax to thank for our rescue."

Alexi rolled his eyes at that. "Please. Don't get me started. It doesn't take much to have him prancing around like a peacock, and he's already been lavished with praise by the queen."

Gray laughed, and then winced as his shoulder began to throb. "Now who's being unkind, not to mention ungrateful?"

"Whatever."

Gray's attention turned to Isabella, who'd been observing from across the room. "I notice we have a visitor, gentlemen. Anyone care to explain?"

Valian ran a hand through his hair. "I'm to blame for that," he said with a sheepish grin.

"Don't talk about me like I'm not in the room," Isabella said stepping forward. "You know that makes me crazy. Besides, coming here was my choice, remember? Finding Aly is my priority here."

Gray frowned. "What do you mean, 'finding Aly?'"

Valian cleared his throat. "Alyssa Montague is missing, Gray."

"*What*?" Gray nearly choked on his tea. "How? When?"

"Not long after we left with the scepter, evidently," Alexi replied. "It seems Kasandra Delacourt sent Alyssa through the portal, probably within minutes after we faded."

"Kasandra Delacourt? Mabry's lieutenant was at Alyssa's New Year's Eve party? How did we not know that?"

Valian pulled up a chair and sat. Gray noted the strained looked around his friend's eyes. "Val?"

"She's as cunning as they come," Valian replied in a tone laced with contempt. "I think she was very careful to avoid being seen. She definitely saw us and knew we were in the house."

"How do you know it was her or that she sent Alyssa into this realm?"

"Because I saw her with my own eyes, Gray. She came downstairs just a few minutes after Alyssa had gone back up." Valian explained the conversation he'd had with the faerie before she'd left the party. "I had a bad feeling about the whole thing, so Isabella and I immediately went to check, but Alyssa was already gone."

Gray blew out an anxious breath. "So when you went into Roseland you weren't just looking for the scepter. You were looking for Alyssa as well?"

"Yes." Valian frowned. "Who told you about our trip across the border?"

"Gryphon mentioned it when I asked about Alexi."

Alexi made a face. "That little weasel needs to be more discrete," he muttered.

"I doubt he's told anyone else. He's pretty tight-lipped. Besides, I am the crown prince." Gray may have been joking, but like Valian, he was having some bad feelings of his own. Since Alyssa wasn't with them now, it stood to reason that they hadn't located her. And there'd been no mention of the scepter as yet. "What did this mission into enemy territory turn up? Anything?"

Alexi and Valian exchanged looks, and Gray could tell that the news wouldn't be good. Valian finally spoke up. "We found the heel off of one of Alyssa's shoes in Roseland Wood very near the northeastern portal."

"Okay." He glanced at Isabella whose pale face and continued silence spoke volumes. "And?"

Valian sighed. "And then we ran into Kaleb Pilliar."

Gray frowned. "Kaleb Pilliar? Who the hell is that?"

"He's a very chatty wood sprite who lives about half a mile from the portal. He had lots of pertinent information for us."

"For the love of the Oracles," Gray shouted. "It's like pulling a bone from a dog's mouth with you two. Just tell me, already."

Valian cleared his throat and folded his arms over his chest. "Mr. Pilliar actually saw what happened to both the scepter and to Alyssa. The scepter was taken to Aramond. We were far too late to intercept it. He'd witnessed Richter and the fae warriors pass through the area long before we arrived. And then he'd heard through his sources that it was already in the king's possession."

"That's certainly not good news," Gray murmured. With Aramond in control of the scepter, if he learned how to wield it, he could destroy Wysteria and kill them all. He took a deep breath and set that thought aside for the time being. "And Alyssa? You said this wood sprite saw what happened to her as well?"

Alexi nodded. He glanced back at Isabella before answering, a sympathetic look passing over his face. "It seems she was accosted by a pair of frost pixies, but the High Lord of Roseland's Twilight Court intervened."

"Niall? What was he doing in that area? Isn't his court a considerable distance from there?"

Valian nodded. "It is, indeed. Makes one wonder what he was up to so far from home, but that's another puzzle, and unless I miss my guess, it'll be revealed eventually."

"Yeah, we'll stick a pin in that for later," Gray replied, but his mind was already turning over possible implications. Niall was a wily one with a fierce army of warriors under his control. By all accounts, the High Lord ruled his court with compassion and strength and was much revered by his people. But he was incredibly secretive and unpredictable. From what Gray knew, most of the other High Lords in Roseland were leery of him and gave him a wide berth. And he was well known in the Wysterian courts as well, his twin being the Queen of Wysteria's Twilight Court.

"In any case, his motives would definitely be suspect here," Valian continued.

"How so? You said he intervened with the frost pixies."

"Yes, that's true, but Kaleb Pilliar told us Alyssa was looking for you, Gray," Alexi said with a grim look. "She'd asked the pixies for directions to the palace. So when Niall shooed the pixies away, he offered to take her there ... to speak to the 'king.'"

"Sonofabitch! He took her to the Red Palace." Gray's stomach, devoid of food, roiled at the thought. The Scepter of Fire in Aramond's hands was bad enough, but the thought of Alyssa at his mercy was terrifying. And it was all happening because they'd invaded her life to retrieve the hidden artifact.

Valian leaned forward with his elbows on his knees. "The next thing Kaleb knew, they'd faded. But yes, he did hear Niall say that he would take her to the king straight away."

The Chancellor glanced at Alexi, who nodded.

"What?" Gray demanded. "There's something else. Spit it out."

Valian looked up at him then, and the expression in his eyes had Gray's stomach doing another sickly spin. "Kaleb said he'd heard Niall say that she 'looked very much like Alice'. He also told us his spies have verified that Aramond has locked Alyssa up in the dungeon."

"Gray, this isn't your fault. I can see it in your eyes. You're already blaming yourself." Alexi shook his head. "This is Richter's doing. Never forget that. If he wouldn't have betrayed his queen, betrayed his people, we would have the scepter and Alyssa would be safe at home right now."

Gray ran a hand over his face. "But we have to face facts, Alexi. We don't have the scepter. And if Aramond has locked her in the dungeon, Alyssa is in grave danger."

Valian leaned back and smiled for the first time during the conversation. "Well, that may be, but we have a plan to hopefully rectify the situation."

Gray narrowed his eyes. "What scheming have you two been doing now? I will remind you that your previous venture is what got us into this mess."

"Oh, I'd hear them out, Your Highness," Isabella cut in, and the look she gave him was crafty. "I think you'll be very glad you did."

Valian laughed out loud. "Though I'd love to take credit, this isn't our scheme, Gray. No, no. The Cheshire Wood cat has come up with an excellent idea that I think just might work. And Kaleb Pilliar is going to help."

Fifteen

The dampness of Alyssa's cell, coupled with the cold stone bench—the only furnishing in the tiny area—made it nearly impossible to actually sleep. With the dungeon hidden underground beneath the castle, it lacked windows of any kind, adding to her disorientation and giving her no indication of time.

When she'd first come to this place, she'd assumed she was having some kind of lingering, post-New Year's revelry-infused dream. But it quickly became apparent that this nightmare was all too real.

And now it seemed that her sleep deprivation would continue, as a mad clanging of metal-on-metal startled Alyssa out of the dozing state she'd finally been able to achieve.

Moaning, she pulled the fur coat Kasandra Delacourt had given her closer around her body and squeezed her eyes shut tight, praying that the perpetrator would simply give up and go away. But her prayers went unanswered as the ruckus only grew louder and more obnoxious.

"Rise and shine, Alice," the guard's sing-song voice called above the din.

On top of everything else she'd endured, this was something that was beginning to work her very last nerve. Almost everyone she'd met appeared to believe that she was a character out of the classic child's tale associated with her family. They all seemed to be having the same delusion, and no amount of arguing to the contrary had made a dent in that notion. Along the same lines, the maniacal king now holding her hostage had her family's heirloom that Prince Graydon had taken from her brownstone office during her New Year's Eve party. The lunatic monarch believed it to be some sort of enchanted scepter, which would be laughable if he wasn't so unhinged.

"For the thousandth time, my name isn't Alice," she finally muttered. Cracking one eye, she glared at the guard.

The man only shrugged. "I don't care if you call yourself the March Hare. The king wants to see you, so make it snappy."

Rising up on an elbow, she shook her head and scowled. "Exactly how many times do I have to break it to that vile man that I can't tell him what I don't know? He's got the wrong damn person. I don't know what power he thinks that heirloom has, but I don't have the slightest idea how to turn it on or operate it. And it doesn't matter how long or how frequently he grills me about it, the answer is always going to be the same."

This was the fourth occasion—in what seemed like days— that King Aramond had sent someone to drag her up to his throne room in order to demand answers about the so-called scepter. Each visit had ended in the same manner—with her insisting that she had no idea what he was talking about, and him threating to chop off her head.

The guard gave her an evil grin. "Oh, I think this may be the last chat you two have. He's running out of patience, you know."

"*He's* running out of patience? Really?" She knew it was an inappropriate response, but she was obviously loopy with exhaustion and couldn't help the slightly hysterical giggle that bubbled out of her throat before she could stop it. "Trust me, I zipped past 'out of patience' quite a while ago."

"Perhaps this is the visit when he'll make good on his promise and relieve you of your head if you don't give him what he wants."

Her laughter dried up in an instant, to be replaced by a sudden righteous anger that flared in her chest. "You know what? I've been held in this disgusting cell against my will for what seems like forever. I've been insulted, manhandled, fed meager portions of hideous gruel, and treated like an animal. My arms and legs are bruised and scraped beyond reason, and I'm beginning to smell like a sewer. At this point, I couldn't care less what your idiot of a king wants."

Alyssa sat up but held her bare feet off the nasty floor of the cell. The king had taken her silver pumps from her during their second tête-à-tête, laughing uproariously as he'd given the expensive—albeit broken—heels to a confused servant who'd brought him a goblet of wine. Her feet were now freezing and filthy, as were her legs up to her knees. She really didn't want to think about the foul muck she'd been forced to slog through during the ensuing trips to the throne room and back.

At this point, she wasn't sure that she cared about any of it anymore. She obviously didn't want to die in this ghastly place, especially in such a horrific way, but her outlook had grown increasingly bleak with everything she'd been forced to endure.

She blamed Niall for getting her into this mess in the first place, for hoodwinking her into trusting him, and she took it out on the guard. "Look, you ass-wipe, I'm hungry, smelly, and so tired that I'm surprised I remember my own name. So, if your king's gonna lop off my head, I wish he'd just get on with it, already."

"Enough complaining," the guard shouted and wrenched opened the cell door. It was apparent he didn't like being yelled at.

He seized her by the arm the minute she'd left the cell, probably fearing that she'd make another run for it. She could have told him that he had nothing to worry about on that score. She'd already made one ill-fated attempt when they'd come to fetch her the second time, but in four-inch heels—one of which had already been broken—she hadn't gotten far. With her lovely chignon destroyed and her hair hanging in clumps around her face, she'd nearly been tackled, scraping her already raw hands and knees on the stone floor as she'd stumbled and fallen.

Now she lurched along beside him as he dragged her through the reeking corridor and up the endless flight of stairs toward the throne room.

When they entered, the king was lounging on his throne in much the same way he'd been each time before, with the exception of his apparel, which gave her pause. Instead of his normal royal garb, Aramond was now dressed in battle gear. Wrist and shin guards covered his legs and forearms, while a golden breast plate glinted beneath a blood-red, thigh-length vest. Fear coated her throat at the sight of the gigantic sword sheathed in an ornate scabbard hanging on a stand next to his throne. Had the guard been right? Would this be the last time she faced the king? That sword was probably capable of severing her head with ease.

Aramond's deep rumble of laughter scraped along her already frayed nerves and garnered her attention. "Well, I must say, you're looking a bit worse for wear, Alice. Not sleeping well?"

She desperately wanted to scream at him in frustration and disgust, call him every contemptible name in the book. But she glared her hatred at him instead, determined not to let him see the terror mounting within her.

This was another lesson she'd learned after mouthing off during their third meeting. He'd threatened to fill her mouth with horse manure from the stables then and there, had gone so far as to have one of the guards bring a bucket filled with the stuff into the chamber. She glanced nervously at the fresh bucket that sat on the step between them now and figured he was baiting her. While he may not intend to cut off her head during this chat, the manure thing was very doable, and she wasn't about to take the chance that he'd actually carry out this latest threat with little provocation.

Aramond was obviously enjoying himself. Casually leaning back, he followed her glance and then gave her a knowing grin. "Nothing to say this time around? Cheshire Cat got your tongue? I can see the words you wish to hurl at me in your eyes, little Alice."

Though it just about choked her, she held to her silence, noting that his grin slowly vanished at her refusal to speak.

"I don't know why you carry on with this ridiculous stubborn streak," he growled. "It will get you nowhere but back in your cell to await the guillotine. Do you really wish to die? Tell me what I want to know, and I may spare you."

It was a lie, and they both knew it. Even if she could tell him how to power the scepter, the moment she complied, her use would be at an end. She pressed her lips together in a hard line and remained mute.

The king sighed and waved a hand in the air. "Have it your way, you foolish girl. At any rate, it makes no difference now. Within the hour I will take the scepter and mount my attack on Wysteria. I will finally destroy that kingdom and everyone in it with the very instrument the White Queen used on my army so many years ago."

"Then you don't need me, do you?" Alyssa shrugged and smiled sweetly. "You should let me go."

"Let you—" After a moment his rolling laughter filled the chamber. He rubbed his chin and eyed her thoroughly. "Yes, very amusing. However, you do make a good point. Though I must say, not in your favor. You see, I've always held to the notion that those who aren't with me are against me. Therefore, if you refuse to help me in my endeavor, what good are you?"

Crossing her arms, she narrowed her eyes. "And what about those here in your own kingdom that refuse to fight with you?" she countered. "You told Niall that he and the other faerie courts were free to choose but would take their chances should they decline. Does your *notion* hold true for them as well?"

The king stood then, looking handsome and regal in his

finery. He took the scabbard from the stand next to the throne and fastened it in place at his waist. When he finally looked down at her, his eyes burned with malice. "They will join my ranks and fight with me, or they will perish once my quest is finished. I will reunite Artemysia into one kingdom under my rule and then rid the realm of all who oppose me."

A chill ran down Alyssa's spine at how calm and sure his answer had been. Had Niall made his choice as well? Of course he had. Why wouldn't he join this madman in destroying an entire kingdom? He was just as crazy as Aramond. And she'd trusted him. She should've known better.

Her blood ran cold at her next thought. And what of Prince Graydon? Did he know what was coming for Wysteria? She had no idea how far away his kingdom was or how long it would take to get there, but someone had to warn them before they were all massacred. Could anyone make it there in time? And who was there to go? There was certainly nothing she could do. Her heart sank at the hopelessness of the situation.

Descending the dais steps, Aramond stopped in front of her, and though the guard held her in place, she flinched away as the king ran a finger down her cheek. "But not to worry, little Alice. Soon none of it will be your concern. When I return victorious, we will have quite the spectacle in the palace courtyard when I have your pretty head detached from your body. Get some rest. For you will need your strength."

With a royal wave of his hand, the sentry pulled her aside as the king swept past. She felt completely powerless as she watched Aramond stride from the chamber followed by a half dozen of his personal soldiers. Her guard snickered as he hauled her along after them.

Dark thoughts raced through her mind as they descended into the bowels of the palace for the last time. Once back in the depths of the dungeon, the guard shoved her into the cell, locking it securely behind her.

Leaning close, he leered at her through the bars. "Don't look so downhearted. Maybe I'll come back and give you a little ... *comfort* tonight after my supper." He wiggled his eyebrows at her.

Though terror churned in her stomach like bile at his repulsive suggestion and panic rose up the back of her throat, she swallowed it down and refused to let him see her fear or her weakness. Instead, she looked pointedly at his crotch, and then tilting her head, gave him a pitying smile. "Oh, you poor thing. Seriously? Is that what you call it? That's truly unfortunate."

Though the remark would ultimately make no difference—or perhaps make matters worse—she felt her spirits lift a bit at the confusion on his face.

"What do you mea—?

"Because I gotta tell you, if that's the case, I really don't know how much comfort it would be, do you? But no matter, I do believe I'll pass."

His confused look disappeared and was replaced with a scowl when he realized what she was inferring. "Go ahead and laugh, you pathetic little bitch. We'll see who's laughing when your head is on the block. And I'm gonna make sure to be front and center for the occasion." Without another word, he turned on his heel and strode off into the gloom of the corridor.

Alyssa stood very still listening to his footsteps retreat until nothing was left but silence. She should have felt relief at his departure, but her moment of triumph winked out like a fire being dowsed with a bucket of water, leaving nothing but the embers of fear simmering in her belly at his words.

We'll see who's laughing when your head is on the block.

The very real possibility that she was going to die a hideous death in this place washed over her, taking root and digging in. As the trembling began, she sat down hard on the stone bench when her legs simply refused to hold her upright.

The faces of family and friends paraded through her mind like a bittersweet slide show. Though her parents may not have missed her yet, Izzy would sound the alarm. But what good would it do? No one knew where she was or would ever know what happened to her when she died in this realm.

Tears sprang to her eyes, and her breath came in short gasps until she hung her head between her knees just to keep from passing out.

"Get a grip, Aly, and think!" she said aloud. "Nobody's coming to save you, so somehow you're gonna have to do it yourself."

"Perhaps I can be of assistance?"

The voice was so close that Alyssa's heart just about stopped. Raising her head, she uttered a shriek and scrambled back against the wall. Standing before her was a tall, thin girl with pale green skin and deep lavender eyes. The golden hair flowing around her shoulders was braided haphazardly and shimmered with magickal iridescence even in the meager light of the cell. But the most interesting thing about her was the delicate translucent wings protruding from her back.

"Wh-who are you?" Alyssa asked in a whisper.

"I sense your fear," the lovely creature said. "But you have no reason to be afraid. My name is Violet, and I was sent to retrieve you."

"Sent by whom?" Glancing over at the cell door—which was still closed—Alyssa frowned. "And how did you get in here?"

Violet smiled. "My cousin Kaleb sent me. And gaining entrance to this cell was no special feat."

The next moment, Violet seemed to burst into nothing but glittering dust, only to reappear fully formed *outside* the cell door. "You see? Cake and pie."

Alyssa gaped at her and then shook her head. "I don't know what that means, but okay. So, are you a faerie?"

Violet tilted her head and gave Alyssa a curious look. "I am a pixie, which is a type of faerie, yes."

"I see. Well, unfortunately, if you came to break me out, I

hope you have a key, because I can't disappear like you obviously can."

"But you do wish to leave, do you not?"

"Oh, hell yeah!" Alyssa's excitement at the prospect of escape momentarily lost its charm when the memory of her earlier encounter with the frost pixies came to mind. Niall had warned her against trusting them at the time, and Violet had just admitted she was a pixie as well. Yet the High Lord himself had betrayed her by delivering her to the king. Did she dare trust this lovely creature? Did she have a choice? "Okay, I mean, yes, I do want to leave this place behind, but what's your help going to cost me?"

Violet giggled. It was a musical sound like wind chimes in a soft breeze. "Do not be silly. There is no cost for my assistance, I assure you. My cousin sent me on behalf of the White Queen of Wysteria."

"Uh-huh. And how do I know you're telling me the truth? This could be just an elaborate ruse to lull me into a trap of some kind. I've had dealings with pixies before."

The pixie's smile slipped from her face, and she grew serious. "Ah, yes, Ligia and Drifa, the frost pixies. Kaleb told me about their interference. But it is not possible for faeries to tell an untruth," she murmured. "I was tasked with helping you, so you truly have nothing to fear from me. Do you wish to leave or not?"

"Well, sure, but we're then back to the no key issue. How are you going to get me out of this cell?"

"Cake and pie," the pixie repeated, and her impish smile returned. "It's true that I don't have a key, but I know where to find one." She turned and motioned to someone out of sight in the corridor.

Alyssa's eyes went wide when the guard she'd insulted earlier came into view, and she could tell from where she sat that he wasn't quite right. There was a goofy smile on his face, and his eyes were at half-mast. He lumbered toward Violet like a man in a daze, and the pixie leaned in close to whisper in his ear. The next thing Alyssa knew, he was opening her cell door.

"Good Lord, how did you make him do that?"

Violet stroked the man's hair and then tenderly ran the back of her hand along his cheek. "Just a bit of sparkle dust and a suggestion. But we should hurry if we're going to go. The changing of the guard will be upon us soon." With another whisper, Violet ushered the enchanted guard into the cell. "Sit and sleep," she added.

Alyssa grinned as the man did exactly as he was told. "Wow! That would be a *killer* skill to have where I come from. I don't suppose you could teach me how to do that."

Violet shook her head. "Come. Let's leave this terrible place."

"I'm all for that, but hang on a minute." Crossing to the sleeping guard, she took measure of his feet. She was going to need shoes if they were going to make progress once outside the palace. *If* they made it out of the palace, she amended. "Can you help me remove his boots? I won't make it very far with bare feet, especially if we have any distance to cover."

"Would it not be faster if he did it himself?" Violet suggested. "Wake and remove your boots, fine sir."

Alyssa laughed out loud as the man complied, then nearly purred with satisfaction as she slipped her frozen foot into the toasty interior of the first boot. They were probably all kinds of nasty inside, but her feet were already filthy and at least now they would be warm. She pulled on the other boot and tied the laces of both snugly. Standing, she took a few tentative steps. The boots were a bit large, but not too ungainly, so they'd do in a pinch.

Once Violet had commanded the guard to sleep again, she turned to Alyssa. "Can we go now?"

Alyssa nodded and started out of the cell, but a sudden thought had her turning back again. "Wait. One more thing."

Returning to the sleeping guard, she retrieved the key from his hand and locked the door behind her as she exited. Slipping the key into the pocket of her fur coat, she followed Violet down the dank hallway.

I'd give money to see that guy's face when he finds out that he's locked in without a key, she thought with a snicker.

Picking up their pace, they'd cautiously climbed the first flight of stairs when another thought occurred to Alyssa. "I don't suppose you could just sprinkle me with your glitter dust and transport me out of here, could you? Because that would be fantastic, not to mention really convenient," Alyssa whispered when they got to the next landing.

Violet shook her head. "I'm sorry. My magick doesn't work that way. But I know a secret passage on this next level. It's a circuitous route but will keep us concealed. It leads to a little-known exit at the back of the palace."

"I'd rather not run into any armed guards, so concealed is a good thing. Now that I'm out of that cell, I don't want to get caught again."

Following the pixie to the next floor, Alyssa was surprised by the lack of activity. On the other trips to the throne room, the palace had seemed to be alive with movement. But there was little of that now. No other guards, no sentries, and they'd yet to see even the odd servant during their progression. Where was everyone? Not that she was complaining, but still. It gave her the willies, and she said as much.

"Though there are sentinels about, it is fortunate for us that the palace was left with minimal staffing," Violet said. "The king and his army march on Wysteria as we speak."

Alyssa stopped in her tracks mid-flight. "Oh my God! That's right. He's going to attack. Violet, we have to warn them."

"No, no. Not to worry," Violet said as she stepped to the wall at the next landing. Flipping back the edge of the tapestry hanging there, the pixie pressed her hand against a stone in the wall and a panel large enough to accommodate a body slid open. "Wysteria has prepared. Now, come along," she added as she slipped through the opening into the shadows beyond.

Warily, Alyssa followed, and once inside, the pixie pressed another stone along the interior wall, sliding the panel closed behind them, and leaving them in utter darkness. "Wow, I hope you can see where we're going, because I can't see my hand in front of my face."

With a sudden flurry, Violet's sparkling dust lit up the air of the passageway and faerie lights began to glow along the walls. "Is that better?" she asked.

"Yes, much, thank you." Alyssa blinked in surprise. "So, what did you mean when you said Wysteria has prepared?" she asked as they began walking single-file along the slim corridor. "Did they know the king was going to attack?"

"Yes. Kaleb told them what he'd seen and heard after the lesser fae ambushed the prince and his field marshal."

"I see," Alyssa replied absently before the pixie's words hit home. "Wait, what? Prince Graydon and Alexi were attacked? When? Are they okay?"

"They both survived the attack, yes," Violet answered over her shoulder. "Chancellor Winchester sent soldiers to rescue them."

"Chancellor Winchester?" Alyssa put a hand on Violet's arm, turning her around. "Are you talking about *Valian* Winchester?"

Violet nodded. "Do you know of the Chancellor?"

"Yeah, but evidently not as much about him as I'd thought." Alyssa digested this new information as they began to walk again, and another question popped into her mind. "So, what about this scepter thing? Is it really as powerful as the king says? I mean, he seems to think he can destroy all of Wysteria with it."

"It is a very powerful artifact, indeed, but one must know how to wield it. The White Queen is hoping that King Aramond hasn't yet discerned how to use it."

Alyssa frowned in the dim light. "She's *hoping*? That doesn't seem like much of a plan. What if he *has* learned how to control it?"

Violet stopped again and turned to her with an inquisitive look. "Did you instruct him on its usage?"

"What? No. I mean, he kept interrogating me about it, but how would I know how it works?"

"Because you are the descendant, of course," the pixie replied as if it all made perfect sense.

Alyssa shook her head. "I'm the what?"

"Kaleb said that you're the descendant of the original Alice. Did you not know this?"

Alyssa pressed her fingers to her eyes and tried not to scream. "I don't know what you're talking about, which is what I've been trying to tell everyone since I got here."

Violet gave her another odd look. "Curiouser and curiouser," she said before turning and continuing on.

It took another twenty minutes or so, but just as Alyssa was starting to think they would never find their way out of the palace, the winding passageway terminated. "Now what?" she asked as she stared at what seemed like a dead end.

Violet placed a hand on the wall, opening another hidden panel that revealed a short flight of stairs leading down to a heavy wooden door. "Now we sneak through the back garden and exit the palace grounds through the chapel gate. We must move quickly, though. The sun has set, but the moon is high and bright tonight, and there will be a sentry at the gate."

Alyssa's pulse began to race, but she nodded. "I can handle moving fast, but what about the sentry? What if he sounds an alarm?"

"I will lead you through the garden and point you to the gate. The guard will stop you there, but no matter what happens, stay calm. All will be well."

Easy for you to say. You can just disappear.

Swallowing back her apprehension, Alyssa nodded and followed Violet down the stairs to the door where the pixie again spread her sparkling dust. With a soft click, the door swung open.

"Stay close behind me now and move as silently as possible."

Stepping out into the cold night air, Alyssa took her first clean, fresh breath in what seemed like months, hoping to finally rid the stench of the dungeon from her nostrils. Snow had blanketed the garden in a layer of white and their footsteps made soft, crunching sounds as they hurried along the path. The garden was lush with trees and bushes, all silhouetted by the bright moonlight. By day, Alyssa thought the garden would probably be quite lovely, but now it just felt eerie and dangerous.

As they came to the edge of the garden, the footpath intersected with a wider lane which ran adjacent to the high palace perimeter wall. Violet stopped and pointed across the expanse. "That structure is the chapel and the gate is just to its right. Do you see it there? Walk directly to it. The guard will stop you there."

"Wait, what? What do you mean the guard will stop *me*? Where are you going to be?" Alyssa asked, her panic rising.

"Though you may not see me, I'll be with you all the way."

"What does that even mean? If I can't see you, how do I know you'll be there?" Alyssa hissed. "And how do I get him to let me through the gate? What if he calls more guards? I won't go back to that dungeon."

The pixie patted her shoulder in a comforting way. "Calm yourself and do not worry, descendant of Alice. All will be well." Then she was gone in a burst of glittering pixie dust, leaving Alyssa alone in the dark.

With Violet's voice ringing in her ears, Alyssa swallowed hard and started toward the gate. As she neared, a guard stepped out of a small hut holding a vicious-looking axe blade on a six-foot pole with a deadly spike situated at its end. "Who are you and what are you doing in the garden at this time of night?" he asked eyeing her suspiciously.

Her heart was pounding so loudly in her ears that she was certain the man could hear it, but she'd come this far and there was no going back now. Clearing her throat, she tried to appear confident and aloof. "My name is Alyssa Montague, and I came outside to get some fresh air and perhaps meditate in the chapel for a bit."

The guard's eyes raked over her, narrowing when he got to the boots on her feet. "You are very strangely dressed. Where did you get those boots?"

"I-I got them from my cousin. He's a palace guard." At this rate, the encounter was not starting out well, which didn't give her much confidence for how it would end. Where the hell was Violet?

"A palace guard, you say? What is his name?"

She watched in horror as he lowered the weapon like a battering ram, the lethal spike at the end glinting in the moonlight and pointing directly at her chest.

"His name?" she squeaked, playing for time. "Why do you need to know his name? They're just boots. I've done nothing wrong."

"I will have his name ... now!"

She froze with terror, but before she could think of an answer or come up with a fictitious name, a sudden gust of sparkling faerie dust blew into the guard's face, seemingly out of thin air. Alyssa watched the dazed look come over him as it had with the guard in the dungeon, and the man's demeanor changed instantly.

In the next moment, Violet shimmered into place beside her.

"Where in God's name were you?" Alyssa asked in a fierce whisper. "I was starting to freak out, and he was just about to skewer me with that deadly-looking spikey thing."

Violet tilted her head in her curious way. "Lesser faeries aren't allowed inside the Red Palace walls without permission, so I needed a distraction to get close enough to enchant him. You did very well." Turning to the guard, Violet gestured toward the entrance. "Please open the gate, kind sir."

"Well, gee thanks. You mean I was the bait," Alyssa grumbled.

The faerie smiled. "Did I not tell you that all would be well?"

The guard let them through the gate without question, and once outside the palace walls, the pixie turned to give him final directions. "Now, lock the gate and return to your hut. You saw no one on this frosty evening."

As Alyssa watched the guard comply with Violet's wishes, she let out a pent-up breath. "You could have at least told me that I was the distraction."

"I thought you were frightened enough as it was. Now, come, we have a fair distance to travel through dangerous territory. We should get started."

Without a backward glance, Alyssa followed Violet into the darkness.

Sixteen

"The recon teams are back from the western border," Alexi said as he entered the briefing chamber. Several soldiers followed the Field Marshal in, grabbing the packs of supplies lined against the wall before hurrying back out the door.

"Our troops are in place along the outlying areas," Alexi continued. "The wards have been repaired...for the moment. But in my opinion they're flimsy, so I wouldn't count on them holding up under a sustained attack."

As Alexi approached, Gray looked up from the map on the briefing room table that he, Valian, and Finvar had been reviewing. Noting his friend's deliberate scrutiny and the lingering concern in his eyes, Gray scowled. "Oracles be praised, Alexi, would you quit looking at me like you expect me to drop at any moment? I may not be the picture of health, but I'm getting there rapidly."

Alexi spread his arms wide. "I didn't say anything," he replied, but there was a touch of guilt on his face.

"No, but you were thinking really loud."

Gray understood Alexi's concern. He'd almost died after being infected with the fae poison and had only been out of bed for less than twenty-four hours. Though he had none of the Elven recuperative powers both Alexi and Valian enjoyed, even he was amazed by how quickly he was recovering. The healers had done a very good job, but he was beginning to wonder if their curative skills were the entire reason for his miraculous recovery. What he'd told Alexi was true. While he may not be operating at a hundred percent yet, it felt like he was getting closer to the mark with every passing moment. Considering the extreme toxicity of the fae poison, it was kind of a marvel that he was still breathing, let alone healing so quickly.

But with bigger issues to worry about, he put his personal thoughts aside and turned back to the map and the coming attack. Kaleb Pilliar had been instrumental in collecting solid intel regarding Aramond's plans. The wood sprite had an extensive network of spies throughout Roseland, and based on the information he'd provided, Gray had stationed the bulk of Wysteria's troops at various points along the border between the kingdoms. But they'd been awaiting word from the field as to what to expect regarding the Red King's army.

"What about Aramond's forces, Alexi? Do we have any idea of his numbers yet?"

"They're still some ways out but approaching fast. By Kaleb's estimate, I'd say we've got an hour, two at the very most." Alexi blew out a breath. "It looks like the king is bringing just about everything he's got, which is considerable."

"We'll be ready for him," Valian replied. "He may have a sizeable force, but we can match his numbers."

A concerned look passed over Alexi's face. "That may be, Val, but a few of Roseland's fae courts have joined him. Evening, Autumn, and Winter, all with significant numbers of their own. And those are only the ones that we know of for certain. There could very well be more. We're gonna have our hands full as it is, but if Aramond uses the scepter, we won't stand a chance. The kingdom will fall."

Valian's head snapped up, and he pinned his cousin with an

icy stare. "This kingdom will never fall, Field Marshal. Not while there's still breath in my body or yours," he said in a severe tone. "Do you understand?"

Alexi took a step back and put up his hands in surrender. "Okay, okay, take it down a notch, will ya? Everyone knows the score here. Both of our clans are in the field right now, ready to fight to the end just as our fathers did in the Great War. All I'm saying is let's just hope the queen is right, and that Aramond doesn't know how to use the scepter. Even then, we know it's only a matter of time before he figures it out and we're all screwed."

Valian continued his stony look, but his tone was a bit more temperate. "Then we simply take the scepter off his hands before he does so."

Gray finally interrupted the argument. "Um, gentlemen, let's try to stay on point here, shall we? Prioritize. We need to get through the coming battle before debating future strategies. So with that in mind, how many of Wysteria's fae courts, other than Finvar's, have agreed to join us, Alexi?"

"It's actually a pretty remarkable turnout, considering how most courts feel about possibly facing their Roseland counterparts on a battlefield. Six of the nine are with us." Alexi grinned and nodded to Finvar on the other side of the table. "In addition to Finvar's Winter Court, we've got Autumn, Spring, Dawn, Daylight—and wait for it—the Twilight Court, if you can believe that."

Gray had a hard time containing his surprise. "Queen Tisharu's brought her warriors?"

Alexi laughed out loud. "In spades. And she's in full friggin' battle gear at the front of the pack. It was quite a spectacle."

"Tisharu can be prickly but is as fierce a warrior as any," Finvar murmured. "And she doesn't like to lose ... anything." The High Lord gave the Chancellor a careful look from beneath his brows and cleared his throat.

Gray studied Valian's face. Considering their history, Tisharu was a touchy subject with his friend, though Valian made no show of it.

Rubbing his chin, Valian studied the map on the table more closely. "It will be interesting to see what happens if her Roseland twin has joined up with Aramond's forces. She and Niall haven't been on the best of terms over the last few years."

Valian may have wanted to ignore Finvar's comment, but Alexi wasn't so inclined to let it go, and needled his cousin a bit. "You should know how that feels, right, Val?" He said with a snicker. "Weren't you and Tisharu ... close at one time as well?"

Valian's stony gaze slowly moved from the map to where his cousin stood smirking. As he regarded him in silence for several tense moments, Alexi's pale face turned a lovely shade of pink, and he quickly looked away.

"What was the word from the other three courts?" Valian finally asked in a flinty tone. "Did they give reason for abstaining?"

Recognizing the jeopardy he'd stepped into with the sensitive topic of Tisharu, Alexi coughed and hurried on. "Juppar is dealing with some internal unrest at the Starlight Court and refused to leave his land unattended until it could be settled. Kellam, on the other hand, said, and I quote, 'I'm not interested in war between the human realms. It isn't Evening Court's problem.'"

Finvar uttered a vulgar phrase and glowered.

Valian raised an eyebrow. "You have something to say on that issue, Finvar?"

"Only that Kellam is an embarrassment to our kind," the High Lord stated with a sneer. "He's lazy and worthless, content to let his court decay while he's waited upon hand and foot. His forces are sloppy and undisciplined. They would be of no use to us, in any case."

"Alrighty then," Alexi said into the uncomfortable silence that followed the Finvar's rant. "Why don't you tell us how you really feel, Fin."

The High Lord turned his fiery gaze to the Field Marshal, and with clipped words, he replied "I believe I just did."

Gray hid his smile but thought it was probably time to move on. "And what about Summer Court? What did Elshandra have to say?"

Alexi made a face. "The illustrious Queen of the Summer Court also declined the invitation, though she didn't give a reason for her refusal."

Finvar surprised them all then—given his previous tirade—by chuckling. "Elshandra is shrewd. I suspect she's biding her time, waiting to see how this all plays out. She's never been one to put all her riches into one pot."

"Shrewd she may be, but is gambling her court on the outcome of this battle the wisest course of action?" Valian asked. "Aramond's mad with grief and fury, has been since he not only lost the Great War but his Red Queen as well. He may blame Queen Beatrice for his hardships, but he won't stop there. He'll destroy the entire kingdom if he can, Summer Court included."

Finvar nodded. "I've heard rumors that the king has promised wealth and prosperity to those who fight beside him ... and destruction to all who oppose him. Her position may be that by doing neither, he would be lenient—should he win, of course."

Alexi scoffed. "Aramond hasn't got a lenient bone in his body. So if that's what she's counting on, she'll be sorely disappointed. And he can't be trusted to hold to his promises, anyway. Everyone —in both realms—knows that his word is rubbish. Elshandra's not stupid. She has to know that."

Gray shrugged and pulled on his gloves. "Regardless, it is what it is. We're as ready as we can be, but this will be no walk in the park. Too many things can go wrong. So, I suggest we all take our positions." He looked around the table at the men who would help him defend their kingdom. "Good luck to you all. May the Oracles bless you with strength and courage."

"Blessed be the Oracles," they all shouted in unison.

As the group started for the door, Alexi suddenly stopped and snapped his fingers. "Oh, I almost forgot. Gray, Old Minerva is in the library with Isabella and the queen. She wants to talk to both you and Val before you go."

"The Witch of the Eastern Glade is here?" Finvar blanched and crossed himself. "I'll be in the field with my warriors, should you need me."

With that the High Lord disappeared out the door and into the chaos of the hallway where servants and soldiers alike were transporting weapons and supplies, preparing for the worst.

Gray tried to ignore the scent of fear in the air as he watched Finvar's progress. "I do believe Minerva gives Finvar the heebie-jeebies."

Valian chuckled. "Do you blame him after their last brush-up?"

"No, of course not. But then again, their altercation was years ago. Besides, his hair has grown back in just fine."

"It seems Finvar has a long memory, if the speed of his departure is any indication," Alexi added.

Gray shook his head. "Come on. We're running out of time. Let's go see what the ancient one wants."

As Alexi headed out to join his battalion, Gray and Valian wove their way through corridors teaming with activity and climbed the stairs to the library. What they found was a surprisingly pleasant tableau awaiting them. When they entered the room, Gryphon was in the process of clearing away the remnants of the refreshments he'd served, and the entire setting seemed almost like an ordinary evening in the palace. By the scene before them, one would never suspect that a raging battle would begin within the next hour or two.

"Here they are at last," Queen Beatrice said and motioned them over. "Come quickly, you two. Minerva would speak to you before you go."

Gray and Valian hurried to join the three women in the sitting area, where the queen was seated with Isabella on her right and Minerva on her left. He and Valian took chairs opposite them.

"What can we do for you, Madam? As you can imagine, we're a bit pressed for time. Aramond will be on our doorstep in short order."

The old woman leaned forward, and winked—her pale, gray eyes sparkling with amusement, "Ah. It's not what you can do for me, young prince, but rather what I can do for you."

"I see. And what would that be?"

Though Old Minerva was diminutive in stature, she was the most powerful sorceress in all of Artemysia. An ancient entity, she was secretive, solitary ... sometimes volatile and unpredictable. She lived in a small cabin in the Eastern Glade, but was given a wide berth by all.

While she could be generous and kind with her extraordinary gifts, she could also be equally terrifying depending on her mercurial moods, and no one dared cross her. To be at odds with Minerva was to court monumental disaster. But if she was here offering her assistance, then Gray was all ears. However, her next comment doused his enthusiasm.

"Do not get your hopes up, as I will not join you in your battle today."

Valian frowned. "Then why have you come down from the Eastern Glade?"

Minerva put up her hand, and the toothy smile she gave him had a crafty edge to it. "While you may be aware that I am no fan of the Red King, I prefer not to involve myself in petty squabbles between the human kingdoms. However, I do come bearing gifts."

Out of the heavy folds of her blood-red robes she pulled two small vials filled with deep blue liquid and placed them on the table between them.

"What is this, Madam?" Gray asked, eyeing the vials with uncertainty.

"Invisible armor, young prince. In these vials, enhancement and protection are woven together into a powerful potion. Drink it and you will be impervious to the fae poisons that nearly took your life so recently. Drink it and your innate powers and abilities will be amplified ten-fold."

Valian eyed the vials as well, and the look on his face conveyed his misgivings.

It did not go unnoticed by the sorceress. "I see the hesitation in your eyes, Chancellor," she murmured. "Do you fear my intentions?"

Valian paused, choosing his words carefully. "I respect your power and wisdom, ancient one. Always."

Minerva cackled and clapped her hands together. "Well spoken, and with the utmost diplomacy. But let me assure you that you have nothing to fear from my assistance. This potion will do exactly what I say it will with no danger to you or the prince."

"Truly, neither Valian nor I wish to offend you, Sorceress. And we do appreciate the gift, but if we take this potion, how long would it last?" Gray asked. "And what ... other effects might we suffer?"

"Do not worry, boy. It will be sufficient to see you through the battle to come. Take it if you wish or leave it be. The choice is yours. It matters not to me."

Valian studied the old woman, a thoughtful look on his face. "Madam, you've stated that you won't fight with us—that you prefer not to involve yourself in our disputes. If that's so, then why offer this benefit in the first place?"

Minerva paused, a shadowy stillness coming over her and radiating into the room. Her words held a dark tone. "The involvement of the scepter alters the situation to a degree. Aramond assumes much, but the artifact is not his to use."

"That may be, but he now has it in his possession," Gray replied. "How can we stop him from using it if he's acquired that knowledge? Will this potion protect us from that?"

"My potion will protect you in battle, but you will not need it to shield you from the scepter." Minerva stood then, and her wheezing cackle filled the room. "Aramond may have the scepter in his possession, child, but he will be unable to use it, no matter how much knowledge he gathers. That is the other reason I came, to impart that information."

Gray and Valian both stood as well.

"But how can you be sure, ancient one?" Valian asked. "We're about to face his forces on the battlefield with or without your potion. Using the scepter, Aramond could conceivably destroy Wysteria and everything in it."

The old woman's eyes glittered dangerously. "Do you doubt my word, Chancellor?" she asked in a voice soft as silk and lined with iron.

"Of course not." Valian lifted his chin but held firm. "But neither do I like surprises."

Minerva nodded slowly, and the crafty smile returned to her face. "Then be of good cheer, boy. When the holy Oracles—in the great wisdom of their trinity—bestowed that powerful relic, they made certain there would only be one to wield the Scepter of Fire, and it is not the Red King."

"Wait, only one? What does that mean?" But before Gray could get an explanation for her cryptic remark, the Witch of the Eastern Glade was gone in a whirl of silver smoke, leaving them all in stunned silence.

"Well, that was sufficiently alarming and intense," Isabella said after a moment.

She'd been silent throughout the entire exchange and her bright green eyes were huge as she crossed to Valian. "She was nice to me, but I have to admit, that old woman is kind of frightening. I don't think I'd want her as an enemy or to meet her in a dark alley."

Gray laughed out loud. "You have no idea what an understatement that is, Isabella. There are stories of her antics that would strike terror in the hearts of even the stoutest of men."

"And I would be one of those," Valian admitted with a smile for Isabella. "You'll be safe here, love. Go with Queen Beatrice and promise me that you'll stay within the palace walls until we return."

"I'll stay here ... as long as *you* promise *me* that you'll return."

The look in Isabella's eyes as she gazed up at Valian made Gray feel like a voyeur on an intimate and private exchange between two people who were much more than friends or acquaintances. Yet he had a hard time looking away. Beyond the affection, he witnessed a growing bond, a trust between them with hope for the future.

Isabella slipped into Valian's arms and hugged him tightly, and then leaning back, gave Valian a brave smile. "Just make sure you return in one piece, mister. Now go kick Aramond's ass."

"We'll do our best." Turning to Gray, Valian cleared his throat when he realized they had an audience. Sadly, the easy smile he'd given Isabella slid from his face, and his look became grim. "I just hope Old Minerva knows what she's talking about with regards to the scepter."

Gray sighed. "Her assurances aside, I guess we'll find out shortly." Picking up one of the vials of the potion the sorceress had left for them, he gave Valian an apprehensive look. "So? What do you think? Do we take her at her word and accept this gift?"

"Minerva may be unwilling to fight, but she's been a good friend to this family and held our secrets for centuries," Queen Beatrice stated with confidence. "We have nothing to fear from her aid, Graydon."

Valian picked up the second vial and held it up to the light. "I suppose we can use all the help we can get."

"That's an understatement," Gray replied with a nervous laugh.

Valian met his hesitant gaze and shrugged. "Doesn't mean I'm not a bit leery, but I'm willing if you are."

They both uncapped their vials, and holding them up in mock salute, downed the contents.

Tossing his empty vial onto the table, Gray crossed to the queen, taking her hands in his. "Don't worry, Mother. We'll hold the border and show Aramond the door."

Queen Beatrice lifted a hand to his face, and her love for him glowed in her eyes. "May the Oracles keep you all safe and bless you with strength and courage, my son."

"Blessed be the Oracles," he and Valian repeated in unison.

Gray leaned down and kissed his mother's cheek before turning to leave. Valian spared one more look toward Isabella, and then followed him out the door to face whatever the fates had in store for them.

Seventeen

"Are you sure you know where we're going? I mean, not that I doubt your navigational skills or anything, but are we even heading in the right direction?" Alyssa asked as she and Violet cleared the tree line of yet another forested region. "We've been walking for what seems like hours. Everything is starting to look the same to me, and we haven't seen a village or another living soul for miles."

Violet's delicate wings fluttered briefly as if yearning to take flight. "We are moving to the northeast, avoiding any commonly used routes, so it will take much longer to reach our destination traveling by foot. This area has little human population."

Alyssa could see why. Here the timber opened up not onto another wide, snow-covered meadow, but to increasingly rocky terrain. In the bright moonlight, she could detect the ground beginning a significant ascent toward the dark shadow of mountains in the distance. The snow was ankle deep at this elevation, but she had a feeling that the higher they climbed, the deeper it would get. And while her fur coat was holding off the bulk of the cold, her feet and legs up to her knees were already freezing.

"Please tell me this path does not have us climbing any

portion of that mountain range, because if that's the case, I can tell you right now, I won't make it."

"We must take an indirect course so as not to be discovered by the king's forces, but we won't go too much higher. We will begin to skirt this hillside up ahead. Once around it, we can descend into Roseland Wood on its northwestern side. Kaleb's cabin is located between the Wood and Wysteria's border very near where the portal you used can be found." The pixie's deep purple eyes glittered in the moonlight as she looked over her shoulder at Alyssa. "However, we must be especially vigilant from here on and move as stealthily as we can. Our path will take us through very hazardous territory before we can get safely through the Wood."

Alyssa frowned. "Define 'very hazardous', please."

Just what she wanted to hear, that they weren't out of jeopardy yet. She'd be damned if she had survived the dungeon and an eminent beheading only to be attacked or eaten by some nightmarish creature that existed in this stupid world. That would piss her right off.

"There are many dangers here," Violet answered, as if reading her mind. "The species that inhabit the northern terrains can be quite perilous, so we must not court unwanted attention."

Alyssa took Violet's arm, stopping her progress and turning her around. "Okay. I think I'm gonna need just a little more information than that. What kind of 'species' are we talking about here? And exactly how perilous? Do you mean like wild animals or something worse?"

"This region is home to a variety of wildlife, yes, some more dangerous than others. But there are also creatures here that are much more frightening than any beast you can imagine."

"For instance?" Alyssa prompted.

"Ogres are some of the worst. Though they are very strong and can crush their victims without difficulty, they tend to be slow-witted and plodding, so easily out-maneuvered. They live in caves at the higher elevations and have a taste for human flesh, which is why we won't venture any higher than needed."

Alyssa shuddered. "Um ... yeah. Obviously you can count me in for avoiding ogres. So, what else?"

"There are a variety of trolls living here in the north." The pixie scanned the area, and Alyssa's pulse picked up speed at the cautious look on her face.

"Trolls? Oh, goodie." she whispered and tried to swallow back a lump of fear. Just the name had all sorts of terrible images swirling around in her head. Alyssa took a deep breath and blew it out slowly. "Just to be clear, I'd rather not be eaten by an ogre or a troll if at all possible."

"No! Of course not. That would be terrible."

"Yeah ... understatement." Alyssa rolled her eyes. "Is that all then? Or are there other terrors I should know about before we encounter them?"

Violet tilted her head as if considering her answer. "Well, there are buggars, equally nasty but not nearly as bad as dunters."

Alyssa threw up her hands. "Okay. English please. What are buggars and dunters, and really, do I want to know?"

"Buggars are quite common and are a shape-shifting goblin of sorts with a nasty disposition, but they can often be reasoned with or bribed with bits of treasure. Unfortunately, dunters are a different story entirely."

"So, dunters are worse than buggars. Is that what you're saying?"

"Oh yes, by far. They are malevolent, murderous, dwarf-like creatures sometimes referred to as Redcaps, for the caps they wear are soaked in the blood of their victims. They move like quicksilver and wield heavy iron pikestaffs." Violet nodded briskly. "Nasty business, and should be avoided at all cost."

"Dear God!" Alyssa's mouth dropped open. She shot a furtive glance around at the surrounding area, searching the shadows for movement as a chill raced down her spine. Her heart seemed to lodge in her throat. "Please tell me that there are no dunters or Redcaps or whatever in this region."

Violet patted her shoulder and smiled. "Take heart, descendant of Alice. While Redcaps are a nomadic lot and can be found in many regions, stumbling upon them is very rare. In fact, I have not seen one in many years."

"For the love of— Then why the hell would you even bring them up?" Alyssa shouted, and then clapped a hand over her mouth when she remembered that they were trying not to attract unwanted attention. Taking a deep breath, she worked to control her mounting terror. "Look, I don't want to hear any more, okay? Let's just get this over with. I'd like to leave this region with its terrors behind as soon as possible. And I definitely don't want to come across any of the nightmares that you've just described along the way."

At Violet's nod, they turned and began to hike up the hillside in silence. Though Alyssa exercised frequently at home and was in pretty good shape, it wasn't long before she'd worked up a sweat despite the icy temperature. So she was relieved when, true to her word, the pixie didn't take them too far up the incline. However, as soon as they started to skirt the butte, a whole new torture commenced. Alyssa had never been one for hiking or rock climbing. The fact that they had to climb over boulders and battle through scrub brush most of the way around the hill was not a welcomed endeavor. The trek was made especially difficult by the boots she'd appropriated from the dungeon guard, which were a few sizes too large.

By the time they began their descent down the far side, Alyssa was out of breath and feeling the strain on muscles she didn't know she had. But the upside was that her initial terror had been mostly forgotten for a time. However, she continued to keep an eye on the passing terrain, her pulse spiking at every unidentified sound.

As they finally came down off the incline and crossed into the shadowy stillness of Roseland Wood, Alyssa's anxiety returned in full force. She'd first stepped foot into this realm somewhere within this forest, but she hadn't been afraid then. At the time she'd been blissfully ignorant of the dangers that lurked here. Now that she was aware, it made the peaceful beauty of the forest that much more eerie and frightening, and it wasn't long before the silence began to wear on her nerves.

"So, where do you live, Violet?" she asked in an effort to steady herself, though she was careful to keep her voice at just above a whisper. "You said your cousin lived on the far side of Wood. Do you have a home here as well?"

"Yes," Violet whispered back. "I live very near my cousin. We are close, as is our little community. We look out for each other."

"That's nice. How much further to the other side of—" Before she could finish her question, a tremendous roar split the night and had her heart pounding double time as terror poured through her. "What in God's name was that?" she whispered.

Violet grabbed her by the arm and tugged her back behind a large fir tree where they huddled in the bushes. "It was a mountain troll. Sometimes they come down into the edge of the Wood at night to hunt. Their eyesight isn't the best, but they have an impressive sense of smell and keen hearing abilities. In any case, stay very still and hope that he is too far away to track our scent."

"Not a problem. I'm so scared, I don't think I could move if I wanted to."

Before long a great thrashing could be heard as the beast moved in their direction. The closer the sound got, the more frightened Alyssa became.

"What are we going to do, Violet? He's getting closer. Can you use your pixie dust to subdue him like you did with the guards at the palace?"

Violet shook her head. "It has no effect on trolls. When I happen to run across one, I usually disappear or wait in a treetop until they pass."

"Well, I can do neither of those things, and I have nothing to defend myself with."

"Do not worry. I won't leave you," Violet said, patting her shoulder again.

"While I do appreciate that, we can't just wait here for him to find us."

Alyssa began to dig through the snow on the ground around them, searching for anything, a sturdy branch, a rock, something she could use as a makeshift weapon. Just when she was starting to despair, her fingers ran across a rough, cylindrical object. With hope in her heart, she pulled it from the snow.

Her find turned out to be a branch of fir close to three feet in length and two or three inches in diameter. Though it seemed sturdy enough, if rotted at its core it would snap like a twig. It definitely wasn't much, but it was better than nothing at all and would give her something to swing and maybe buy her some time, should she need it.

As the thrashing sound grew closer, Alyssa peered through the bushes to see a large shadow come into view on the path just to their east. Although she really hadn't known what to expect, the shape of a tall, muscular man wasn't it. The only thing odd about his silhouette was his malformed head. But when the shadow moved into a patch of moonlight, Alyssa realized that the peculiar shape was formed by curved horns—much like a ram's— on either side of his head.

With a shudder, she turned to the pixie. "We can't stay here, Violet," she whispered. "He's coming in this direction."

Violet hesitated, but finally nodded. "Follow me as silently as you can and stay low behind the bushes."

Hunkering down in an effort to stay concealed, they moved cautiously away from their hiding spot but kept to the cover of foliage as much as possible. Just when Alyssa thought they may escape without notice, another deep howl reverberated through the trees. She and Violet both froze in place.

"I smell you, little vermin," the mountain troll growled. "I smell your fear. Come out, come out wherever you are."

Looking through the bushes, Alyssa saw him lift his short

snout and scent the air. Turning in a wide circle, he came to a stop on the path adjacent to where they were hiding and seemed to stare right at her through the thick shrubbery between them.

"Ah ... there you are." In the next moment, he launched himself at the bushes directly in front of her.

With a scream of horror, Alyssa leapt up and followed Violet at a dead run through the trees. When she heard him hit the ground where they'd been huddling only moments before, she made the mistake of looking back over her shoulder. That quick look was her undoing. The toe of one of her oversized boots snagged on the underbrush, and she went down face first in the snow, her makeshift weapon flying from her grasp.

Panic-stricken, she scrambled to her knees, frantically grabbing for the branch even as she heard the terrifying sound of the troll's approach behind her. Snatching up her club, she jumped to her feet and swung with all her might toward the sound. There was a loud *crack* as her weapon connected with the beast's shoulder and broke in two.

If the encounter hadn't been a matter of her life or death, the surprise on the troll's face might have been comical. Alyssa only faltered for a moment before turning to run, but that brief hesitation cost her dearly. The troll roared again and grabbed the back of her fur coat before she could get far, lifting her completely off her feet.

Though he might eventually rip her to shreds, she damn well wouldn't make it easy for him. Before he could get a sturdier grip, she slipped out of the coat and hit the ground running. Where he may have had her in height and brawn, she was quick and nimble. With terror-fueled adrenaline pumping through her system, she was praying she'd be able to outmaneuver him with speed and agility.

She'd lost sight of Violet, so she was now on her own. The breath burst from her in gasping sobs as she dodged trees and undergrowth, weaving a serpentine path through the forest. Throwing a quick look over her shoulder, her hopes soared when she saw that she'd actually gained some ground. Unfortunately, that hope was dashed just as quickly when she turned back to her path and ran straight into an immovable object.

A scream ripped from her throat when said object snatched her up and encircled her body with hard muscle, holding her securely.

"Ah, there you are. I've been looking everywhere for you, Alyssa Montague," a familiar voice murmured in her ear.

Terror seized her, and she began to struggle in earnest. But in the next instant she was released and tossed to the ground. The sound of steel sliding from a scabbard echoed in the silence, and she looked up to see Niall, High Lord of Roseland's Twilight Court striding away from her.

If the troll had seemed surprised by Alyssa's pitiful attack, he looked truly shocked now to find an armed warrior coming toward him with a lethal-looking sword glinting in the moonlight. In any event, it didn't take long for the beast to decide that she probably wasn't worth possible injury or death. With a final growl, he turned and high-tailed it up onto the hillside through the trees.

With the troll's retreat, Alyssa realized that she now faced a far worse threat, and that realization finally galvanized her into motion. As Niall turned back, she leapt to her feet, racing away in the opposite direction as fast as her oversized boots would carry her. But she should have known better. Plunging out of the trees and onto the trail below, she came to a skidding halt when the High Lord appeared in a flurry of starlight in her path, her fur coat dangling from his hand.

"Don't you touch me, do you hear?" she cried, backing away as he slowly came toward her, a predator stalking his prey.

Niall clucked his tongue, and an easy smile crossed his face. "Now, Alyssa. Is that any way to show your gratitude?" he asked in a congenial tone. "After all, I did just save your life."

"Are you kidding me? You want gratitude after your stunning betrayal?" Anger flared at all she'd been put through because of him, drowning out her fear. "So you saved me from that hideous troll. Big deal. The more pressing question to my mind is why. Planning to take me back to the king, are you? Because I'd rather face a hundred trolls than return to that filthy dungeon."

The smile slipped from the High Lord's face. "You're angry. I can understand that. And I'm sure you're questioning my motives, but trust me, I want nothing more than to help you now."

"I'm sorry. What did you just say? You want me to trust you after what you did?" She shook her head and glared at him. "I should have known better than to trust you in the first place. You knew I was looking for Prince Graydon, but took me to the Red Palace instead. You left me with that monster, and I spent what felt like weeks being held in the most inhumane conditions."

Niall sheathed his sword and put up his hands. "It was an unfortunate situation, for certain, but a necessary one."

Alyssa's mouth dropped open. "*Necessary*? The king was going to *behead* me, you asshat!" she shouted. "He made sure to repeat that threat each time he interrogated me about the use of that stupid scepter."

Niall's look became shuttered, and he took another step toward her. "And did you tell him what he wanted to know?"

Alyssa threw up her hands and uttered a frustrated snarl. "For the love of God! How many times do I have to say it before you people get it? I don't know how to power that piece of junk."

She took a deep breath and eyed the fur coat he held. Now that the adrenaline rush was over, the cold was beginning to register again, and she began to shiver. "It doesn't make any difference, anyway. The king is mounting an attack on Wysteria as we speak. And he took the scepter with him. He's determined to destroy the entire kingdom with it, including those who've refused to fight with him. So, I hope you're happy."

Niall shook his head. "Do not trouble yourself over Wysteria's fate. It will be a good fight, but I'm sure they will repel Roseland's army in the end. The king may have the scepter, but it will do him no good. It won't do what he thinks it will," Niall murmured and held out her fur. "Now, put on your coat. I can hear your teeth chattering from here."

She still didn't trust him, no matter what he said, but she took a tentative step closer and quickly grabbed the fur from him. "So, how do you know the king won't be able to use the scepter?"

"Alyssa—"

"And come to think of it, why aren't you there fighting with him right now?"

Before he could answer her questions, there was a burst of sparkly pixie dust, and Violet appeared at her side.

"Lord Niall," the pixie murmured. She bowed deeply, her translucent wings fluttering madly.

Niall inclined his head. "You've done well, Violet. Thank you."

Alyssa looked back and forth between the two. "Wait—what? Don't tell me you're working for him," she said to Violet. "Did you get me out of that cell just to lead me straight back into the fire?"

"No, no." Violet shook her head violently. "I told you, while faeries sometimes mislead with words, we cannot tell an untruth. My cousin Kaleb did send me on behalf of the White Queen. And Lord Niall is also here to help. I promise this is true."

"Uh-huh." Alyssa gave Niall a skeptical look. "If faeries can't tell an untruth, how do you explain the lies you told me?"

Niall frowned. "I've never told you a lie, Alyssa. What Violet says is true. No faerie can lie, not even High Fae."

"But you knew I wanted to go to the White Palace, and you lied when you said you'd take me there."

Niall wagged a finger at her. "Ah, but you never asked to be taken to the White Palace, did you? You said *a* palace. And I told you exactly where I would take you ... to meet the king. Is that not true?"

Alyssa frowned. "That's just semantics, and you know it."

Niall laughed out loud. "Indeed. But as Violet said, we sometimes mislead with our words. However, if you'll allow me, I *will* take you to Kaleb's cabin to await the end of the battle. And once it's finished, I will personally escort you to the White Palace and present you to Queen Beatrice and the prince. Agreed?"

Alyssa studied the situation from every angle but couldn't quite decide what to do. Should she put her trust in this High Lord who'd betrayed her once before? It certainly didn't seem like the smartest thing to do. A very large, unforgiving part of her wanted to do nothing but scream at him to take his offer and shove it. The thought was extremely satisfying. And yet, what would she do then?

When she continued to stare at him in mute silence, Niall finally held out his arm. "You have a purpose here, Alyssa. Let me help you realize it."

"Yes, yes," Violet implored, her wings buzzing anxiously at her back. "We still have a very long way to go with more dangers to face. I cannot protect you as needed. Please let the High Lord help us."

Well, out of the frying pan and back into the fire, Alyssa thought, coming to a decision. But instead of placing her hand on the arm Niall offered—and without ever taking her eyes from his —she reached out and took hold of Violet's hand instead. It was a deliberate insult, choosing to trust the pixie over him, and for a brief instant she saw surprise alight in the bright green of his eyes. His slow smile spread to a grin, and then his rolling laughter echoed in the clearing. With a slight tip of his head, he winked and slid his offered arm to Violet.

The pixie hesitated only for a moment before placing her free hand on his arm.

And they were gone in a blink.

Eighteen

lexi had been right. The security wards had lasted for all of about thirty minutes before buckling once the attack commenced. Though frustrated, Valian had to admire Aramond's strategy. He'd made his move under the cover of darkness—which was much harder to defend against—targeting the wards with lethal precision until they'd finally collapsed under the strain, allowing Roseland forces to inch their way onto Wysterian land. And once bodies began to merge on the field, it became more and more difficult to tell friend from foe in the darkness. Fortunately, the moon was high and bright, which was in their favor and a factor Aramond couldn't control.

The probability of the wards' early failure had been a topic discussed thoroughly beforehand. The prince had initiated a plan to maneuver the fight back across the border into Roseland the moment they faltered and had implemented a second line of defense to protect Wysteria's interior at all cost. It was a tactic that had proven a bit more difficult to execute, as small groups threaded through the slightest gap in their defenses like strands of silk through the eye of a needle. Valian could only hope that any threat slipping through the front lines would be dealt with harshly between the border and Cheshire Wood by Halifax and that second wall of resistance.

Taking a deep breath of the icy-cold air, Valian surveyed the battlefield as he headed toward the tree line. The fresh snow, which had been immaculate only two hours before, was now muddied and stained dark red and iridescent silver in the moonlight with the blood of mortals and immortals alike. All around him, the sounds of volatile magickal energy, howling war cries, and agonizing screams melded together until they were a cacophony of sound in his head, a white noise, a horrific soundtrack to the death and destruction going on around him.

And he was part of that carnage as he fought with magick and bow, amazed at the power singing through his veins, *his* power but magnified and unlike anything he'd ever experienced. Obviously, Minerva's potion had taken hold in a big, bad way, and he wondered if Gray was experiencing the same thing in this violent melee.

Valian notched and let arrows fly, one after another, faster than his mind knew was possible, one missile sometimes taking out two or three of the enemy at a time. When he ran out of arrows, he drew out not his sword but his Elven fighting daggers and began to dodge and slice, cutting a bloody path as he moved farther and farther into Roseland's territory.

Blocking a lesser fae to his right, he buried one of his knives to the hilt in the faerie's chest before jerking it free, flipping it over in his hand, and launching it at yet another warrior hurtling toward him. The thrown dagger found its mark easily and with incredible force. The charging faerie went down as quickly as the first.

Retrieving his weapon, Valian took out several mortal Roseland soldiers when he rushed past them like a blur on his way into the tree line. Once he crossed into the forest, surprisingly the visibility increased somewhat even with the lack of moonlight. Fires burned here and there, fallout from magickal crossfire, and a few lesser faeries were trying to douse one or two of the blazes before they got out of control.

The last time Valian had seen Alexi was over an hour ago when his cousin had led his battalion of soldiers over the border, disappearing into the darkness. Scanning the forest now, Valian saw no sign of him or his warriors, but as his gaze skimmed the fighting clusters and clashing bodies, he was brought up short when he picked Tisharu out of the free-for-all. The Queen of the Twilight Court was surrounded by at least a dozen enemy soldiers, and it was a magnificent sight to see as she dodged in and out of the trees, parrying and slicing. She was playing with them, using her dark power sparingly and only to open a hole here and there in her combatant's line. And he could actually hear her occasional laughter as she blocked and hacked her way through the throng of soldiers, fading away and back again in the blink of an eye.

Valian shook his head. Tisharu had always been a fierce adversary—quick, deadly, and without mercy. In his opinion, she enjoyed conflict just a little too much for his liking. Regrettably, his brief moment of admiration was cut short by a sting of pain in his left shoulder. He'd let himself be distracted and now, looking down at his shoulder, he was almost surprised to see the hilt of a fae dagger protruding from his arm just below his shoulder armor.

Quickly tracking the dagger's owner, Valian smiled as he slowly pulled the knife from his flesh and felt the warm trickle of blood down his arm. The High Fae warrior grinned back, but his humor was short-lived when Valian was suddenly face to face with the faerie and had him by the throat before he'd even registered the movement.

"You're dead already, elf. You just don't know it yet," the faerie croaked, as he struggled against the hand of iron at his throat.

"You think so?" Valian grinned as he lifted the faerie to his toes. "If you're referring to the fae poison you've probably used on your blade, I have it on good authority that it won't make a dent. But by all means, do have your dagger back." With that, he plunged the knife into the faerie's abdomen right up to the hilt before dropping him to the snowy ground and heading in Tisharu's direction.

Fierce though his former lover may be, Valian figured twelve on one was somewhat lopsided odds, so he thought to even the score for her a bit. But when he saw her stumble and go down backward over a log, watched the warriors she'd been toying with close in, he moved like lightning. His blades were a blur of motion as he spun and sliced his way to get to her. Every soldier dropped in his wake apart from the one standing over her, his sword raised high and poised to plunge into her chest.

Knowing he wouldn't get to her in time, Valian let his daggers fly. Both weapons struck the man mid-back with sickening twin thumps as Tisharu faded in a swirl of smoke only to reappear several yards away. For an instant, the soldier seemed suspended, arms holding the sword high in mid-air, and then he slowly crumpled to the ground.

Tisharu met his gaze over the distance, and after a long moment she gave him an almost imperceptible nod before spinning and running into the trees without a backward glance. Blowing out a breath, Valian watched her disappear into the darkness and then went to retrieve his daggers before heading back the way he'd come.

As the battle raged all around him, he was keenly aware of the possibility that Aramond would use the Scepter of Fire, no matter what the Witch of the Eastern Glade had told them. It was like waiting for the other shoe to drop, and the thought was never far from his mind. The old sorceress had said that the king would be unable to use the scepter against them, that it wasn't Aramond's to wield, but she'd given no evidence as to why, and Valian was still skeptical. To that end, he kept a sharp eye out for the king while continuing to fight, but as time dragged on and he covered more and more ground, he caught no sign of Aramond or the scepter.

A little over an hour later, the sound of a horn could be heard from somewhere deep inside the forest to the south. With the scent of smoke and blood in his nostrils, Valian realized that though the fighting had already begun to thin, with the horn's signal Roseland forces were actively retreating. And Aramond had yet to use the scepter. Or perhaps Old Minerva had been correct after all, and he really couldn't use it. Either way, the fighting seemed to be coming to an end ... for now.

On his way back toward the border, he finally ran across Alexi. His cousin looked like he'd been dragged through the mire with his hair clumped with mud, his face and hands streaked with blood and grime. His right thigh was bleeding and he was limping slightly, but other than that, he seemed to be operating under his own steam, which was a relief to Valian.

"Well, shit! That sucked pretty heavily, but it looks like you're still standing, cousin." Alexi rolled his eyes and wiped some of the blood from his face. "The battalion had significant casualties, but at least Aramond's retreating."

"Yes. His forces seem to be scattering quickly, but they'll be back, so we need to make good use of our reprieve." Valian looked around at the fires still burning in spots, the forest floor strewn with bodies of dead and injured. "We need to collect our people, get them back across the border, and then see how quickly we can get the wards back up and running. Aramond's not going to be satisfied with this little three-hour skirmish."

"Oh yeah, he'll definitely be back." Alexi followed Valian's gaze. "So, do you think Old Minerva was right about him not being able to use the scepter? Or do you think he just hasn't figured it out yet?"

Valian shook his head. "No way to know for sure. The potion she gave us worked exactly as she'd said it would, so at least she spoke the truth in that. But just because Aramond didn't use the scepter this time, doesn't mean he can't or won't the next." Eyeing Alexi's thigh wound, he narrowed his gaze. "Take an arrow to the thigh, did we? Fae or human?"

Alexi laughed. "No big deal. Human, so no poison. Some joker got off a lucky shot while I was distracted with dispatching two lesser fae warriors. Went through the muscle. Broke it off, pulled it out, and kept moving. It is becoming a tad bit sore now, though." Alexi studied Valian's shoulder. "Fae dagger? Looks like it got you right under the shoulder armor. Poisoned?"

Valian gave him a bland look. "If the owner's attitude was any indication, I'd say yes."

"Did he know the poison wouldn't affect you?"

"I believe I mentioned it." Valian smiled. "And then I gave him back his dagger. Now come on, let's gather our people and go home."

THE QUEEN OF WYSTERIA'S TWILIGHT COURT WAS waiting for him in the palace's main vestibule when they got back, though she looked less than pleased to be there.

With her hand on the hilt of the sword at her waist, Tisharu stepped into his path when he approached. "Chancellor, I would have a word before my forces and I return to the Twilight Court."

"Of course," Valian replied.

Alexi shot him a wide-eyed look before giving a brief nod to Tisharu in acknowledgement then heading down the passageway as quickly as he could.

Coward.

Addressing the faerie queen, he gestured toward the busy corridor and the people coming and going all around them. "Let's get out of the way and find a quieter spot, shall we?"

She didn't respond but followed him along the corridor to an alcove at the far end of the passageway. It wasn't much more than a recessed niche with a bench, open to all passing by, but he was pretty sure she wouldn't have consented to a more private area. They hadn't been alone together or had much contact at all since they'd decided to go their separate ways. And though that ending had been a very long time ago, he found that he had to consciously steel himself before he turned to her, which didn't set well with him.

"What can I do for you, Tisharu?" he asked, a bit more tersely than he'd intended.

She crossed her arms over her chest and looked as if she'd smelled something rotten when she said, "You fought well today, Valian."

He knew it was as close to a compliment as he would ever get from her and how much it had cost her to say the words out loud, but he only raised his eyebrows. "As did you, from what I could tell."

Her green eyes glittered like polished gems. Even covered in muck and gore, she was an incredibly beautiful female. "I want you to know that while I didn't need your help in the forest earlier ... I am ... grateful for the assistance you provided."

She watched him closely, and Valian knew better than to show any emotion that could be read as sympathy or in any way suggest that she had been lacking in her performance in the field. So, he gave an indifferent shrug. "I happened to have been there at a time when you looked as if you could use a hand."

Those emerald eyes narrowed, but after a moment she appeared to accept his answer. "Yes, well, as I said, I could have handled the situation with ease." She took a deep breath and seemed to relax a bit. "Aramond's forces were weak, for the most part. Even those few courts that fought beside him showed little enthusiasm for the bout." She curled her lip. "Only Mabry and her Evening Court fought with any valor. The king and his army took a sound beating tonight. That, at least, was enjoyable."

"I took some pleasure in it as well, but we had casualties of our own. Alexi's battalion took a fair hit, and both the Daylight and Spring Courts lost a good number each." Valian gave her a sidelong glance. "Speaking of the courts, I didn't see your twin or any of his warriors tonight. I know you two have been estranged for several years. I did wonder how you would feel about meeting him on the battlefield."

A sly look crossed Tisharu's lovely features, and she looked away. "It is true that Niall and I don't always see eye to eye, but he had … other more pressing plans elsewhere this evening."

"So, you've spoken with him recently?"

The faerie queen glanced back at him, and a smile hovered on her lips. "Several times over the last few days, in fact."

There was something there, Valian could see it, a secret tucked away behind her casual gaze. Though it peaked his curiosity, he knew from experience she would air it only when, or if, it was to her advantage. "Well, I'm glad you've made amends. I know family is important to you."

He watched the sorrow seep into her eyes, the old sorrow for him and those he'd lost, and she unexpectedly reached out to take his hand. "For you as well, I know," she murmured. "Your sisters miss you terribly."

He stared at their entwined fingers and had the oddest sense of *déjà vu*. Clearing his throat, he shook his head and let go of her hand. "Anyway, regardless of our success tonight, Aramond will be back, probably sooner than we think."

Though it sounded strained, she made an effort to laugh. "Surely you're not worried, Valian? If and when the king returns, we'll give him another thrashing, and perhaps next time we'll cut off the head of the serpent for good measure and be done with Aramond for all time."

"That's an exceedingly optimistic thought, as I'm sure you've heard by now that he's in possession of the Scepter of Fire. We were lucky tonight, Tisharu. The king didn't use it. Old Minerva seems to think he can't or doesn't know how, though she wouldn't expound on why she's so certain."

"The ancient witch is very wise, Valian. You should listen to her."

"I agree. But I'd rather not leave it to chance. We need to retrieve the scepter before Aramond figures it out and uses it against us. To that end, the prince wants to meet with the Oracles. If they could at least track it for us, give us an idea of where Aramond's keeping it, perhaps we can recover it before he mounts his next attack. It's a long shot, but one Gray's willing to take."

Looking down the hallway, he caught sight of Isabella making her way down the staircase next to the main entrance, and he couldn't help the grin that crossed his face as he watched her progress. She was obviously looking for someone, and when she spotted him, made a beeline in his direction. But the joy he felt at seeing Isabella was smothered in the next instant, and his attention snapped back to Tisharu when she spoke.

"You can tell Prince Graydon and Queen Beatrice that there is no need to consult with the Oracles or take such drastic actions, Chancellor. It has come to my attention that the Scepter of Fire will be delivered to the White Palace without any effort on your part, probably sooner than you think."

Valian frowned and stepped closer to her. "Where did you hear that? And what do you mean it will be delivered? That seems a ridiculous notion, as I doubt Aramond will suddenly find it in his black heart to just turn it over to us, whether he can wield it or not."

"Mmm, yes. That scenario does seem unlikely," Tisharu replied in a cryptic tone.

"What are you playing at, Tisharu? If you have useful information, then spit it out. I don't have the time or patience required for deciphering your word puzzles."

The faerie queen tilted her head and a teasing look danced in her eyes. "Unfortunately, *mo chroí*, your questions will have to wait," she murmured in her native tongue.

My heart. It had been decades since she'd called him that. Though their time had passed eons ago, it felt a little bittersweet the way she'd said it, with such underlying emotion.

Tisharu glanced over his shoulder, and when he turned to see Isabella approaching, he took a step back as she joined them.

"I've been looking all over for you, Valian," Isabella said, slightly out of breath. "Alexi said you'd be back shortly, but I wanted to see for myself if you were still in one piece."

Tisharu gave Isabella a curious look. "Is this the human you brought back with you from the New York realm, Valian? She's awfully ... petite. But I do like her fiery red curls," she finished, suggestively running a hand over her own glorious red mane.

Isabella narrowed her eyes at the faerie queen. "Why do people keep referring to me that way? I have a name."

Valian swallowed a chuckle. "I'm sorry, Isabella. Let me introduce you to Tisharu—"

"*Queen* Tisharu," the faerie corrected with a superior smirk for Isabella. "Of the Twilight Court."

"It's a pleasure to meet you, *Queen* Tisharu," Isabella replied with a haughty look of her own. "I'm Isabella Christensen ... of the New York Christensens."

Valian choked out a laugh that ended in a cough. He wasn't at all certain that Tisharu knew she was being mocked, but the look on Isabella's face spoke volumes.

His uneasiness deepened when Tisharu turned to him, slipping her arm through his, and gazed at him adoringly. "Why, Valian, she's simply delightful," the faerie queen purred. "But do you think it was wise to bring her here? To a dangerous world where she doesn't belong?"

Isabella's frown deepened as she watched the way Tisharu pressed herself closer to his side. "Wise or not, the choice was mine to make, not Valian's" she said, crossing her arms over her chest like armor.

Valian gently disengaged himself from his former lover's embrace, his eyes never leaving Isabella's face. "And a choice, I thought, bravely made."

"I see." Tisharu threw an uncertain glance at Valian. Did he detect a touch of sadness in her eyes? But in the next moment it was gone, and she looked Isabella up and down before shrugging. "Still, it is unfortunate that your brief visit was marred by this conflict. But then, you were safely tucked away here in the palace, so I'm sure that was a comfort. And no doubt you'll be going back to your own realm soon enough."

Valian could see that Isabella had an unpleasant retort to Tisharu's insinuation brewing, but the faerie queen didn't seem to notice— or chose to ignore it outright.

Drawing back her shoulders, Tisharu was once again the cool, aloof Queen of the Twilight Court. "In any case, my warriors and I have tarried here long enough, and I'm anxious to be home." She turned to Valian and surprised him again by taking his hand once more. "It has been too long. It was good to see you after such an extensive absence, *mo chroí*. I hope to see you again very soon."

Then she spun on her heel and walked away in regal fashion, the people in the hallway scurrying out of her way as she passed.

Valian watched her go, feeling the tension in the air slowly dissolve as he turned to Isabella. "Let me apologize for Tisharu's conduct, love. She can be ... difficult at times."

Isabella made a face. "Is that what you call it? I'd say she was rude and condescending at best."

Valian chuckled at the look on her face. "I suppose you're right. But then again, she's ruled the Twilight Court for over a century, so she's clearly developed some bad habits."

"I'll say. Besides, you don't have to apologize for her behavior. That's all on her. But I can see now why Alexi tried to get me to wait for you in the royal salon. He obviously knew who you were with. Still, she is quite beautiful."

Very dicey territory, Valian thought. "Yes, she is," he said aloud.

"And very tall. Almost Amazonian, one might say. I can see how she would be attractive to a strong male such as yourself."

Valian tilted his head. "Is there a question in there somewhere? Or are you just commenting on Tisharu's attributes?"

She didn't respond right away, but her cheeks grew pink, and she wouldn't quite meet his gaze. Filled with a singular delight, he smiled. "Why Isabella Christensen, are you jealous of Tisharu?"

Her head snapped up at that, and her mouth dropped open. "*What?* No, of course not. Don't be stupid. You seemed close, is all. What do I care if you two are a thing?" She turned and took a few steps before spinning back around. "*Are* you two a thing?"

She *was* simply delightful. Tisharu had at least gotten that much right. Valian took another step closer. "We were a 'thing' once upon a time. But that was a very long time ago, love. Tisharu wanted more than I was willing or capable of giving at the time, so we went our separate ways. It was not an amicable decision by any stretch of the imagination then, but she seems to have mellowed. Today was the first time I've seen her, let alone spoken with her in over a decade."

Isabella shoved her hands in her back pockets and gave him a considering look. "So ... no thing, then?"

"No thing." He closed the distance between them, snatching her up around the waist and hauling her against him. "But I have to say, your jealousy is incredibly arousing."

Her mouth formed a perfect *O*, and heedless of the activity in the passageway or the stares they were certain to garner, he crushed his lips to hers and plundered as he'd wanted to do for days.

After a brief hesitation, her hands slid up his arms and over his shoulders, her fingers diving into his hair at the nape of his neck, pulling him closer. The soft sigh she uttered cut straight through him like a knife through butter, and his heart began to pound in his ears.

When they finally came up for air, they were both a little breathless. Isabella looked a bit dazed and swallowed hard. "Well, that was ... uh ... wow."

Valian grinned. "Indeed, love. Well said. And I would like nothing better than to continue this conversation of sorts, but a busy palace corridor is definitely not the place for it." He slipped a wayward curl behind her ear and traced her lips with a fingertip. "Besides, Tisharu said something odd just before you joined us, something that I think may be important, and I need to discuss it with Gray and the queen."

"Odd how?"

Valian frowned. "She seemed to think that the scepter will be delivered to the palace very soon."

"What the—? Did she say how?"

"No, but I got the feeling that maybe she'd said more than she'd meant to. From the look in her eyes, she definitely knows something else."

"Then what are we waiting for?" Isabella grabbed his hand and began to pull him toward the stairway. "Come on. Let's go tell the royals."

Nineteen

Humpty Dumpty sat on a wall. Humpty Dumpty...

"Had a great fall!" Alyssa awoke with a start, jackknifing out from underneath the thick, down comforter with her heart hammering in her chest like she'd just run a marathon. In an effort to clear the sleep-hazed confusion from her mind, she rubbed her eyes and scanned the room.

That confusion increased when she found that she wasn't in her own bed and nothing in the small room looked in any way familiar. It took her several moments to remember just where she was and that the strange things she'd dreamt while asleep weren't dreams at all but a mish-mash of actual recent events.

Kaleb's cabin.

Her anxiety finally began to recede when she made the connection and everything that had happened over the past few days began to fall into place. Flopping back down on the feather mattress, she flung an arm over her eyes. A vague recollection of arriving at the cabin was there at the back of her mind, but it was mostly a blur. It hadn't taken but an instant for Niall to fade them right to Kaleb's doorstep from the north end of Roseland Wood, but she'd been exhausted from lack of sleep. And at that point, the adrenaline rush she'd been operating on for hours had finally run out.

Moaning, she rolled over and buried her face in the pillow when she remembered just how unsteady she'd been on her feet, *and* that Niall had literally snatched her up into his arms as if she weighed nothing at all and carried her into the cabin. At least the High Lord had kept his word this time and had taken her where she'd wanted to go. But the mental image of him holding her so closely against his broad, muscular chest had her blushing at the memory.

Within minutes of their arrival at his home, Kaleb—bless his little green heart—had brought her a tray of tea, berry scones, and a collection of fruits. Though she'd been apprehensive about eating anything offered by a faerie, she'd been so hungry that she'd wolfed down two of the delicious scones and finished off a small bowl of strawberries before she could stop herself.

The wood sprite had also offered her a hot bath, which had been heaven after days in that squalid dungeon followed by the arduous and terrifying trek after her rescue. Still, she hadn't lingered for long in the small tub for fear that—in her exhaustion—she'd fall asleep and drown. Kaleb had also given her clean, dry clothing in the form of a snug-fitting flannel shirt and a pair of high-water trousers, and though the outfit was ill-fitting, she'd almost wept with joy at finally getting out of her torn and filthy cocktail dress.

By the time she'd eaten and bathed, she'd been dead on her feet, and she'd just about face-planted on the bed after he'd ushered her into the little room. The tall, rail-thin sprite had gently pulled the comforter over her, but she'd been down for the count before he'd even left the room.

Rolling over, Alyssa stared at the wood beams of the low ceiling overhead. She had no idea how long she'd been out, but she, Niall, and Violet had arrived in the middle of the night. Now, soft light poured in through the small window over the dresser, suggesting she'd slept for several hours at the very least, and she wondered what—if anything—of importance had happened while she'd slept. In any case, she was actually feeling quite refreshed and more energized than she had since the morning of her New Year's Eve party, before she'd been thrown into this weird and unimaginable wonderland.

But it was time to find a way home. Tossing back the comforter, she stretched the kinks out of her back and limbs, then scooted off the bed.

Taking a quick tour of the little room, she found her cocktail dress and fluffy fur coat lying across the back of a comfortable-looking arm chair in the corner, and to her surprise, both now looked spotlessly clean. Curious, she picked up the shimmery dress to examine it more closely and was amazed to find that it had also been completely repaired. The boots she'd acquired from the dungeon guard were there on the floor next to the chair and polished to a high, glossy shine. A grin spread across her face as she ran her fingers through her sleep-tousled hair. Grabbing her coat and the boots, she padded barefoot from the room in search of her thoughtful faerie host.

Violet was alone in the living room when Alyssa emerged from the bedroom. The pixie was sitting on the sofa in front of the fire staring toward the window, an open book on her lap. She turned when she heard Alyssa approach. "Oh, you're awake. Did you have a good rest?" she asked with a pleasant smile.

Alyssa nodded. "I'm feeling much better, thank you. What time is it, anyway?"

"Mid-morning." Violet became animated as she gestured toward the window. "And it's snowing again. I just love the snow, don't you? It makes everything look so pretty."

"Sure. I guess. I like the snow just fine when I'm dressed for it." Holding up her skimpy cocktail dress, Alyssa made a face. "Obviously I came unprepared for the weather here."

Violet nodded sagely. "Your dress is quite lovely, though. Very sparkly, indeed. But you'll be much warmer now in the clothes that Kaleb's given you, I'm certain."

"Yeah. It was really kind of him to let me bathe and lend me something more appropriate to wear." Looking around the small cabin, Alyssa frowned. "Are you here by yourself? Where is Kaleb?"

"My cousin and Lord Niall are outside."

Alyssa frowned. "Niall is still here?"

"Yes. He and Kaleb are speaking with Mr. Maddux."

"Who?"

"Duncan Maddux." Violet put her book aside and rose, going to the window. "Evidently, the White Queen sent him to fetch you, but he wasn't happy to find Lord Niall here. I'm afraid they don't like each other very much."

Alyssa rolled her eyes. "Yeah, that's a real shocker. Niall doesn't seem to play very well with others."

Violet turned with a curious look. "I don't understand your meaning. Play what?"

"That was sarcasm, Violet. It's a figure of speech where I come from." With a sigh, Alyssa smiled and shook her head. "Never mind. So, why was Mr. Maddux unhappy to find Niall here, other than he doesn't like the High Lord?"

Violet's iridescent wings fluttered briefly and she whispered as if the three males outside might overhear. "Lord Niall told Duncan that he intended to see you safely to the White Palace as soon as you were awake, as he'd promised you that he would. Duncan did not like that one bit. He insisted that the High Lord's presence was unnecessary, that the queen had sent him to retrieve you, and that he was capable of carrying out the task without assistance. But Lord Niall was unyielding." The pixie shook her head and glanced out the window again. "That's when they began to argue. It was most unpleasant. Kaleb finally suggested that they go outside so as not to wake you with their disagreement."

"I see."

Alyssa joined Violet at the window, and the scene outside immediately peaked her interest. Kaleb stood off to one side looking rather uncomfortable, while Niall, standing tall and regal with arms crossed, glowered down at a short, stocky man with a bulbous nose wearing a pinstriped cutaway suit. The little man—Duncan Maddux, she assumed—gestured wildly toward the cabin in a comical fashion, but the thing that held her attention was the ginormous top hat perched on his head. It was so large that it was like something out of a cartoon, and she shook her head in wonder.

A Mad Hatter if I've ever seen one, she thought.

"Mr. Maddux certainly has an interesting sense of fashion. What's with the enormous top hat?" she asked aloud.

Violet tittered. "Duncan is funny to look at, is he not? He's never without his hat, which makes me smile whenever I see him."

Alyssa watched the diminutive man wave his arms and stomp around in the snow, and couldn't help wondering how he kept the huge hat on his head. "It is unconventional, I'll give him that."

"Oh, he's very eccentric and quite unpredictable. Some even say that he's a bit deranged, because sometimes he makes no sense at all. Still, I find him entertaining."

"Yeah, well, the High Lord doesn't look all that amused. Niall looks like he wants to pummel the little guy, which I'd say he's more than capable of doing." Alyssa pursed her lips. "Mr. Maddux, on the other hand, looks like his head is about to explode." Alyssa shook her head again. "And check out poor Kaleb, caught between the two of them without a clue about what to do. How long have they been out there?"

"Not long. I'd hoped they would resolve the issue peacefully and come back into the house, but it doesn't look promising." Violet tilted her head as she watched the proceedings, her wings doing another quick flutter. "Duncan is a nice man, for a mortal, but he sometimes uses poor judgment when dealing with the fae courts. Lord Niall is a very powerful High Lord and not the most patient of rulers. Given their history, I think Duncan would be wise to use a bit more diplomacy."

Alyssa leaned closer to the window. "What history? Have he and Niall had run-ins before?"

Violet nodded and leaned closer as well. "Many years ago, Duncan asked a favor of the High Lord. Lord Niall granted the favor in exchange for completion of a simple task. And so, the bargain was made. But after Duncan received his favor, he didn't keep to his end of the bargain. The High Lord was very angry, and rightly so."

Outside, it was obvious that Niall was angry now as well. He leaned down and shouted something into Duncan's face. Though Alyssa could hear the tenor of his raised voice, she couldn't make out his words. "What happened then?" she asked Violet.

"Lord Niall made an example of Duncan before the Twilight Court," the pixie answered in a grave tone.

"An example how, exactly?"

A sad look crossed the Violet's face. "He transformed Duncan into a braying donkey. He made him eat hay and dance in the grand hall for hours and hours to the laughter and ridicule of the other lesser faeries in the court. Then, when Duncan's body finally gave out and he could dance no more, the High Lord banned him from the Twilight Court forever."

"That must have been some bargain for Niall to do all that to Duncan."

Violet's eyes went wide and round. "It doesn't matter the size or type of agreement. There is a saying in the fae world. 'A bargain made is a bargain met.' To break an accord is disrespectful, but to disregard a bargain made with a High Lord is very dangerous, indeed. Lord Niall showed great restraint and compassion."

Alyssa frowned. "What he did to Duncan doesn't sound restrained or compassionate."

"Oh, but it was. The High Lord could have enslaved Duncan for a thousand years for his offense and would have been well within his right to do so. Duncan should've known better. He was very lucky. As I said, sometimes the things he says and does make no sense at all." She glanced out the window again. "Still, I did feel badly for him. Lord Niall left him as a donkey for several months as further punishment."

Alyssa blew out a breath and glanced back toward the argument still brewing outside. "Well, I can understand now why there's bad blood between them. But if Duncan is so reckless and irresponsible, then why on earth would the White Queen send him to fetch me? If the High Lord doesn't trust him, why would she?"

Violet nodded. "That is exactly what Lord Niall asked when Duncan arrived. It's what started the argument in the first place."

"Uh, yeah ... about that, I think it's zipped right past the argument stage," Alyssa replied as she watched Niall wave a hand toward the red-faced, little man and lift him a good four feet off the ground. "We better get out there and smooth things over before Duncan gets hurt."

Violet hesitated as she watched Alyssa quickly slip on her boots. "I don't think it would be wise to intervene. Lord Niall would not take kindly to interference."

"I don't really care what *Lord Niall* thinks." Tossing the cocktail dress over a nearby chair, Alyssa pulled on the fur coat. "He obviously needs to get a grip, and it doesn't look like he'll do that without some kind of intervention." She walked to the door and looked back over her shoulder. "Are you coming?"

With another anxious glance out the window, Violet nodded and followed Alyssa out the door.

"What the hell is going on out here?" Alyssa shouted as she crossed the yard to where the three males were congregated. Duncan was screaming as Niall spun him around and around in mid-air to the point that his enormous top hat went flying. And from the look on the squat little man's face, Alyssa thought he might puke with the force of the motion. "Niall, stop that right now and put him down. You're acting like idiots, the both of you, and making poor Kaleb uncomfortable."

The High Lord slowly turned to her with a dangerous, narrow-eyed look, and she thought for a moment that he wouldn't comply. But then a wicked smile spread across his handsome face, and he dropped Duncan into the snow with an unceremonious thud.

"As you wish, sweet Alyssa Montague," he said, striding toward her without a backward glance at Duncan. Taking her face firmly in his hand, he studied her features methodically, before giving a quick nod. "You seem much more rested this afternoon. Did you sleep well?"

Pulling away from him, she forced herself to hold her ground, though memories of the way he'd carried her into the cabin the night before had her instincts screaming for distance. "I am feeling much better, thank you," she replied primly. "Now, answer my question, please. What's all this commotion about?"

Duncan retrieved his top hat and gave the High Lord a wide berth as he came closer, making an awkward bow. "My name is Duncan Maddux, Milady."

Alyssa smiled at the rumpled little man. "It's nice to meet you, Duncan. I'm Alyssa Montague."

"Yes, I know. I've come to take you to the White Palace on behalf of the queen."

"Ah! And there it is. The crux of the commotion," Niall crowed, pointing to a horse-drawn wagon on the path at the edge of the yard. "He's even brought a pitiful cart to squire you there with as little comfort as possible."

Like a tea kettle on the verge of boiling, Duncan's face flushed red with anger. "That's extremely unfair, Lord Niall. You know very well that I can't fade. The cart was the best conveyance that I could find on short notice."

"Mmm, on short notice, you say?" Niall crossed his arms and tapped his lips with a finger. "That brings me back to my original question, doesn't it? Why in the world would Queen Beatrice—a monarch with good sense and unlimited resources—send a lying, ill-prepared little squidge like you on such an important mission with only a horse-drawn farm cart for transportation? It's simply baffling."

Alyssa had to admit, she was wondering the same thing, especially after what Violet had told her about Duncan. It did seem unlikely. "Duncan, I'm afraid that Niall brings up a good point. Did the queen actually send you?"

"Of course not," Niall sneered. "It's a ridiculous notion by any stretch of the imagination."

Alyssa sent him a quelling glance to which he only shrugged. Turning back to Duncan, she spoke in a stern tone. "Duncan, tell me the truth, please. Did the queen send you?"

The little man looked everywhere but directly at her for a moment before his shoulders sagged and he turned his large hat around and around in his hands. "Perhaps she didn't *actually* task me with retrieving you."

"And there you have it," Niall murmured.

Duncan's head snapped up, and he became bizarrely animated. "But with the battle over and the clean-up underway, there was no time or personnel available for the assignment. I'd overheard the prince's concerns and only thought to assist him and the queen by taking on the job myself."

"You thought to assist?" Niall laughed out loud. "Don't be absurd, squidge. You were only seeking to curry favor and to make amends for the bedlam you caused all those years ago ... during the Alice debacle, remember?"

"That mess wasn't my fault! That silly girl brought her troubles upon herself. I only tried to guide her."

"*Her* troubles?" Niall took a menacing step toward Duncan. "Your guidance, such as it was, almost jeopardized the war. If it wouldn't have been for—"

"Wait a minute!" Alyssa put a hand on Niall's chest and stepped between the two. "Duncan, did you just say that the battle is over? And that Wysteria is okay?"

Duncan bobbed his head. "Of course, Milady. Even with the failure of the security wards, Wysteria's forces repelled King Aramond's attack with ease, though it was a heated battle with many casualties on both sides."

Alyssa blinked at the new information and turned to Niall.

"But what about the scepter? The king said that he was going to destroy Wysteria with it. Does this mean he wasn't able to use it?"

Curiously, Niall's look became shuttered. "So it would seem," he murmured.

Duncan cleared his throat. "In any case, the wards are being repaired even as we speak. We should leave for the palace post haste, so as not to be caught outside the perimeter once they're restored."

"Just another reason why *I* will be taking Alyssa to the palace. Traveling in your pathetic wagon would take an eternity, and the wards are certain to be repaired before you even get there," Niall stated.

When Duncan began to grumble, the High Lord silenced him with a look and then glanced down at Alyssa. Her hand was still pressed to his hard chest, and she told herself to move away, but he took hold of her wrist and held her in place for a moment longer before finally letting go. By the time she stepped back, her pulse was galloping, and she struggled to regain her composure. The High Lord only smiled in a knowing way, which irritated her to no end.

"The little squidge is correct on one point," he finally said, as if nothing had passed between them. "We need to leave as soon as possible. With the wards down, I can transport us across the border to within a mile of the palace walls and past any sentries that may have been posted. From there we'll have to travel by foot, as a fade-restricting spell has been imposed at that proximity. However, if security is mended beforehand, it will make our journey a bit more difficult."

Though Niall had betrayed her once before, he'd kept his word in bringing her to Kaleb's cabin. And he had promised to take her to the White Palace. Yet, she wasn't certain it would be wise to be completely alone with this virile, enigmatic warrior, even for a short space of time.

Turning, she motioned to Violet. "Will you go with us?"

Violet looked back and forth between Alyssa and the High Lord. "I will accompany you, yes, if Lord Niall is willing."

"Afraid to be alone with me, darling Alyssa?" Niall asked, as if reading her mind. His wicked grin was back, his sensual tone sending heat to her face and accelerating her pulse again.

She lifted her chin and flipped her hair over her shoulder, trying to look as nonchalant as possible. "Don't flatter yourself, Niall. I'm just not all that sure I can trust you yet, given your past *assistance*."

The High Lord raised an eyebrow. "Have I not given you my word? I will honor it, I assure you. But if you would feel more comfortable with the pixie as chaperone, I have no problem with that arrangement."

She wasn't sure having a chaperone would make that much difference, but it did make her feel better knowing she wouldn't be alone with him. Taking a deep breath, she blew it out slowly and nodded. "Alright then. Give me a minute."

Kaleb had been silent throughout the exchange, standing to the side and puffing on his long, wooden pipe. Alyssa crossed to him and took his hand. "I just wanted to say thank you for your generous hospitality, Kaleb. I am very grateful, especially for the change of clothes."

The wood sprite gave her a toothy grin. "You're very welcome, Miss Alyssa. It was an honor to be of assistance to little Alice's descendant. I hope you will come back and visit sometime."

"I'd like that very much." On impulse, she gave him a hug and then laughed at the surprised look on his face. "Take care of yourself, Kaleb Pilliar."

Walking back to Niall, she nodded. "I'm ready to go whenever you are."

"But what about me?" Duncan cried. "I came all this way."

"You're free to follow in your rickety wagon, squidge," Niall quipped. "If you think you can keep up." Holding an arm out to Alyssa on one side and Violet on the other, he winked. "Ladies, shall we?"

As twice before, the moment she laid her hand on Niall's arm, they disappeared in a burst of starlight, and in an instant materialized in the middle of yet another forest. Alyssa had arrived in this world of magick and fantasy in the dead of night. Her escape from the dungeon had also taken place under the cloak of darkness. Now she looked around this forest with new interest. In the light of day, it took on a whole different aspect and wasn't nearly as eerie or frightening. Of course, having a High Lord to protect you from the things that went bump in the night—or daylight—was a plus.

"So, where have we landed and how far do we have to go to get to the palace?" she asked Niall as they began to walk along a seemingly well-worn path.

"It's a little over a mile from here to the palace gates." The High Lord gesture to the land around them. "This is Tarkington Forest. Once we pass through it, we'll cross Larkspur Meadow. On the far side of the meadow is Cheshire Wood, which borders the palace walls."

"Cheshire Wood?" Alyssa laughed out loud. "As in the Cheshire Cat from the Wonderland tale?"

Niall grinned back at her. "Indeed. Halifax is quite proud of the fact that he made the pages of the book. Not everyone did, you know."

She shook her head. "I still can't get over the fact that a well-known child's story dictated by one of my ancestors is based on a real place. So, there's an actual Cheshire Cat. After meeting Duncan and seeing his hat, he's obviously meant to be the Mad Hatter, that's a no-brainer."

"Though the book calls him The Hatter, little Alice herself added the 'Mad' to it. He hates that part, but it's a perfect correlation," Niall added with a sneer. "The little squidge is off his nut."

"I'm guessing the hookah-smoking Caterpillar is based on Kaleb." She gave him a sidelong glance. "But what about you? Did you make the pages of the book?"

Beside her, Violet had a fretful look on her face, and her iridescent wings began to flutter again, which they seemed to do whenever the pixie was excited or anxious.

When Niall continued to walk in silence, Alyssa stepped in front of him, and walking backward, poked him in the chest. "You did, didn't you? Which character? Tell me."

He stopped abruptly and frowned. "It's ridiculous and based on nothing more than my looks."

Alyssa grinned and stared at his leather breast plate. It was engraved with his Court's crest, which was encircled with the large, ornate shape of a heart. And the answer hit her all at once. "Oh ... my ... God. You're the Knave of Hearts!" Hysterical laughter poured out of her at the thought. This proud, strong warrior had been reduced to a minor character who was accused of stealing tarts. It was too delicious for words.

"The child did have an interesting sense of humor to go with her outlandish imagination," Niall grumbled.

Alyssa turned, and they started walking again, but she couldn't stop laughing every time she thought about it. Niall, however, was not amused.

"It's not that funny," he said in a grumpy voice as they crossed into snow-covered Larkspur Meadow. "She was enamored with my breast plate, which I don't find at all appropriate for a child of her age."

Alyssa laughed again. "Oh, come on. You should be flattered. Like you said, not everyone made the book, right?"

"I would just as soon have been left out of it altogether."

They walked on in silence and Alyssa couldn't help but admire the scenery. Larkspur Meadow looked like a pristine sheet of lumpy white cotton. The only thing to mar the effect was their footprints in the ankle-deep snow. By the time they reached the other side and entered Cheshire Wood, big, fat flakes had begun to fall.

They hadn't gone a hundred yards into the Wood before Niall drew up short and pulled her around behind him. Violet, wings abuzz, moved in next to her at his back.

"What's the matter?" Alyssa asked.

"We have company," Niall replied quietly. "Stay behind me."

Out of the trees up ahead came a few dozen soldiers with arrows and swords drawn. One of them stepped out onto the path in front of them and smiled. "Well, well, the High Lord of Roseland's Twilight Court. You're a long way from home, Lord Niall."

The sound of the voice was somewhat familiar, but Alyssa couldn't quite place it. Peeking around the High Lord's shoulder, she only got a quick glimpse before Niall shoved her back.

"I have a need to speak with the White Queen, Field Marshal. I've brought someone with me that she will want to see."

Field Marshal?

"Alexi?" Alyssa leaned out and stared at the tall man in battle gear. It didn't look like Alexi. This man had long, silver hair ... and pointed ears?

"Alyssa?" The man gaped at her. "Alyssa Montague? Is that you?"

With caution, she stepped out from behind Niall and nodded. "I guess we both look a little different than the last time we met?"

Alexi took a few steps closer, and when Niall tensed, the Field Marshal put up a hand. "Take it easy, Lord Niall. I just wanted to make sure that Alyssa was unharmed. We've been awaiting word from Kaleb Pilliar about her whereabouts for several hours. He was supposed to arrange her rescue while we engaged Aramond in battle here. I was actually on my way to Kaleb's cabin to see what the hold-up was."

Alyssa quickly pulled Violet out from behind the High Lord. "This is Violet, Kaleb's cousin. She broke me out of the dungeon last night. Then Niall got us both to Kaleb's."

Alexi grinned. "I'm glad you're finally here safe and sound, Alyssa. We've all been worried about you. And Isabella has been frantic."

"Oh my God! Izzy's here, too?"

"Yes. She came through the portal with Valian when he

figured out what had happened after you disappeared from the gala." He held out a hand to her. "Come with me, and I'll take you to her."

Isabella was here. Alyssa could hardly believe it or contain the joy of seeing her friend again. She started forward, but she didn't get far before Niall took her arm, stopping her. "Niall?" she asked. "What is it?"

The High Lord didn't answer her, but there was a dangerous look in his eyes as he stared at Alexi. "We'll be happy to go with you to the palace, Field Marshal. In fact, that was our destination. However, I suggest that we follow you. You see, I've promised to take Alyssa directly to the queen, and as I also have an important matter to discuss with Queen Beatrice, I intend to keep that promise."

Niall had spoken in a quiet tone, but his words had been edged with steel. Alyssa realized that this was not a suggestion but proclamation from the High Lord of the Twilight Court, and there would be no discussion or negotiation.

Violet had told her earlier that Niall was a very powerful High Lord. Alyssa wasn't certain just what that meant, but she could tell by Alexi's face that he understood this situation all too well.

After several edgy moments, Alexi finally nodded. "As you wish, High Lord." He made a twirling motion in the air with his finger and the soldiers with him began to move. Alexi started to turn but stopped and glanced back. "As you've seen, the wards are still down, so the borders aren't secure yet. We've had skirmishes break out here and there. I don't suppose I have to tell you to keep a close eye on your back."

Niall's smile was anything but pleasant, and a chill rippled down Alyssa's spine when he spoke. "No. That is something you don't have to worry about, Field Marshal."

And with that, they all began walking toward the palace, and hopefully, Alyssa's way home.

Twenty

Pacing back and forth in the grand salon, Gray checked the hour on the grandfather clock again, noting with irritation that only a handful of minutes had passed since the last time he'd looked. He'd had his doubts right from the start about the plan they'd hatched for Alyssa's rescue from the Red Palace. It had seemed like an impossible mission, but Kaleb Pilliar had insisted it could be done, and that he had just the pixie for the job.

Gray shook his head as he continued to pace. What the hell had he been thinking? He'd left Alyssa's fate in the hands of a sprite and a pixie. And since they'd received no word from the wood sprite regarding the outcome, his fears had mounted to the point that he'd been unwilling to wait a moment longer. He'd sent Alexi and a contingent of soldiers to Kaleb's cabin in hopes that they would find Alyssa safe and sound. But there was still no word, and he was running out of patience in a hurry.

"Graydon, please sit down and try to relax. Alexi has only been gone for a little over two hours," the queen said from her post at the window. "You're wearing a path into that lovely hand-woven carpet, and I'd rather not have to replace it."

"Yeah, and you're making Gryphon nervous," Valian added as

he watched the chamber elf calmly refill the teapot from his seat next to Isabella on the sofa.

Gryphon harrumphed, and with a sour look for Valian's attempt at humor, left the room as silently as he'd entered.

Gray blew out a frustrated breath and sat down in an adjacent wing chair, only to pop back up again a moment later. "I'm telling you, the whole idea was ridiculous in the first place. How could a lone pixie be capable of penetrating the Red Palace's security, let alone freeing Alyssa from a dungeon in the bowels of the damn place? It was a ludicrous plan."

Valian lifted his cup to his lips and glanced at Gray over the rim. "We've been over this numerous times, Gray." Taking a sip, he continued. "Since an all-out assault was impossible—especially with Aramond in possession of the scepter— it was our best and only option at the time. And until we know whether it was successful or not, agonizing over it will do no good. So do as Her Majesty says. Sit down and quit stewing."

In an agitated motion, Gray ran a hand through his hair. It was the not knowing that was driving him crazy, and he took out his frustration on Valian. "That's easy for you to say, Chancellor," he snapped. "You didn't get the descendant into this mess or lose the scepter in the process."

"And neither did you, so do us all a favor and stop playing the martyr," Valian shot back in the same manner. "Kasandra Delacourt is accountable for Alyssa's situation, and Finnious Richter's treasonous act is what led to the loss of the scepter. Those are the facts, Your Highness. So, get a grip."

"Stop it! Both of you," Isabella shouted in frustration. Jumping up from her seat next to Valian, she crossed to Gray and fisted her hands on her hips. "Look, I know you're as worried about Aly's safety as I am, but Valian's right. You didn't send her through that portal. Sure, you could say that if that freak show Kasandra hadn't been at Aly's party and done the deed, maybe none of this would've happened, but who knows for certain? Fate's funny that way, you know?"

"Isabella—" Gray began, but she threw her arms wide and continued her tirade.

"And for that matter, both you and Alexi almost *died* trying to protect that stupid scepter, remember? How on earth could you have possibly known what was waiting for you in that forest? I've heard you have some mad skills, but are you psychic now, too?"

In the wake of her angry rant, she took a deep breath and blew it out in a rush. Putting up a hand, the look in her eyes softened. "Here's the deal. In the end, does it really matter who did what to whom or how this all came about in the first place? What's done is done, right? Now we just have to deal with the situation as it is, because there really is no other choice."

Queen Beatrice cleared her throat and smiled. "And that, gentlemen, is that. Thank you, Isabella. I couldn't have said it better myself."

A blush crept over Isabella's face as she returned to her seat on the sofa next to Valian, and after a moment, Gray began to chuckle. He gave the Chancellor a contrite look. "Well, my friend, I guess that puts us both in our place."

Valian nodded and took Isabella's hand. "I suppose so. And in quite the succinct manner, I'd say."

Gray sighed. "I just wish—" he began, but was interrupted when the double doors of the salon burst open, and Alexi entered with a huge grin on his face. To everyone's surprise and delight, following him into the room was Alyssa Montague, though she looked nothing like she did the last time Gray had seen her.

Instead of the finery she'd been wearing the night of the gala, Alyssa was now dressed in high-water pants and a flannel shirt beneath a long, white fur coat. Her face was bare of any cosmetics, and her light-blonde hair was loose around her shoulders. But the strangest part of her apparel was the over-sized, black military boots on her feet. Despite the odd outfit, Gray couldn't help but beam. He didn't care what she was wearing. He was just thankful that she seemed to be unharmed.

"Aly!" Isabella shouted and ran to embrace her. "Oh, Aly, you're really here." Pulling back, she looked Alyssa over from head to toe. "Are you okay? You're not hurt?"

Alyssa laughed. "I'm fine, Izzy. Well, as fine as one can be after spending several days in a cold, foul-smelling dungeon followed by a terrifying hike through a troll infested forest."

"Oh my God! What do you mean, a troll infested forest? Like, with actual *trolls*?"

"Yes, with actual trolls." Alyssa shuddered. "There was this pixie that came to sneak me out of the palace, but we had a pretty long hike from there. And when we got to the north end of Roseland Wood, we were attacked by one. If Niall hadn't shown up when he did … well, that's a scary story for another time. Anyway, except for a few bumps and bruises, I'm all in one piece and just happy to be here."

"Wait, did you say Niall?" Gray asked with concern. "As in, the High Lord of Roseland's Twilight Court?"

Alyssa nodded. "And he showed up at a very opportune time, let me tell you. Anyway, once he'd dealt with the troll, thankfully, he made quick work of getting us to Kaleb Pilliar's cabin."

Gray shook his head. "Well, in any case, I'm relieved that Alexi found you there safe and sound. We were all pretty worried."

Alyssa looked confused. "But Alexi didn't come to Kaleb's cabin. We met up with him and his soldiers in Cheshire Wood."

"We?" Gray turned to the Field Marshal.

"Yeah, about that." Alexi scratched his head and looked toward the door. "Lord Niall and Kaleb's cousin Violet are actually waiting in the antechamber."

Queen Beatrice stepped away from the window. "The High Lord is here in the palace?"

"Yes, Majesty. It seems that he escorted Alyssa from Roseland Wood. When we found them, he insisted on coming back with us. He wants to speak with you."

"About what?" Gray asked with suspicion.

Alexi shook his head. "Didn't say. But he was pretty adamant."

The queen drew herself up to a regal height and lifted her chin. "Then I suppose we mustn't keep him waiting. Show him in, Field Marshal."

Alexi slipped out of the room and returned a moment later followed by Lord Niall and a tall, thin pixie with pale green skin, deep lavender eyes, and delicate, iridescent wings. A pixie who looked frightened out of her mind, Gray noted.

"Lord Niall." Gray gave the High Lord a nod. "Your presence here is quite unexpected."

Niall pursed his lips. "Yes. It has been a very long time since I've stepped foot in Wysteria, let alone the White Palace."

"I understand you were instrumental in getting Alyssa here unharmed, so for that, I thank you."

The High Lord gave him a stoic look. "It was not done on your behalf, I assure you. I'd been made aware of the planned rescue and the path it would take leading away from the Red Palace, which is quite a hazardous route, as I'm sure you're aware. In an unfortunate turn of events, I was detained with a court matter so arrived at the rendezvous point later than I'd hoped. As it turned out, I was right on time to avert what could have been a tragic situation."

"Nevertheless, we are grateful for your intervention, High Lord." Queen Beatrice came to Gray's side, and in deference, gave a slight nod in Niall's direction.

The High Lord smiled for the first time since arriving and tipped his own head with respect. "There is actually a matter that I wish to discuss with you, Madam. And since I'd given Alyssa my word that I would see her safely to your side, here we are."

Lord Niall glanced around the room as his comment was processed, and a tense silence followed.

After a moment, Isabella filled it with nervous energy. "Oh, I can't tell you how good it is to see you, Aly. We were all so worried. Sounds like you've had a crazy time of it," she gushed and then gestured to Alyssa's clothing. "Nice outfit, by the way. Very chic."

Alyssa laughed again. "Kaleb gave me the clothes when we got to his cabin last night. I can tell you, after several days in that cocktail dress, I was happy to get these. And I scored the stylish boots off a dungeon guard free of charge when Violet rescued me."

As if just remembering the pixie, Alyssa turned and motioned to her. "Come here, Violet. I'd like you to meet Isabella."

The pixie tentatively stepped out from behind Niall with her translucent wings aflutter. But her unusual eyes went wide, and her mouth formed a perfect *O* when in the next moment she found herself enveloped in Isabella's enthusiastic embrace.

"Thank you so much for saving my friend, Violet," Isabella cried with tears in her eyes. "You are incredibly brave."

When Isabella let her go, Violet blinked and then smiled shyly. "You are most welcome." The pixie tilted her head, studying Isabella's red hair. "I like your bright curls very much."

Isabella laughed and swiped at her eyes. "Thanks. And I like your beautiful wings."

Turning to Alyssa, Gray slowly shook his head. "Alyssa, I have no words for how sorry I am for everything you've been put through. On my honor as Prince of this realm, I hope you know that it was never my intention to put you in harm's way."

"Oh, I know. But to tell you the truth, I was angry with you at first, because I thought you and Alexi had stolen an old family treasure. I had no clue what it really was. Of course, Kasandra Delacourt didn't help matters, and that part of this whole thing is still pretty hazy." Alyssa gave him a smile and reached out to take his hand. "Anyway, I get it now. I don't know the entire story of how my family came to be custodians of the scepter, but I only wish you could've been honest with me in the beginning."

"Seriously?" Isabella snickered. "Come on, Aly. I mean, get real. Would you really have believed him if he'd been up front with the full story? I had a hard time with just the small portion that Valian explained to me. And even then, I thought he was delusional until he brought me here and I saw it all for myself."

"Really, Isabella?" Valian raised an eyebrow. "Delusional?"

Isabella waved a hand in the air. "Oh, you know what I mean."

"I don't believe I do, no. You'll have to elaborate later."

Alyssa chuckled. "I suppose you have a point, Izzy. I did think I was dreaming for the longest time after I arrived. I kept waiting to wake up with my alarm blaring."

Isabella turned to Valian and gave him a playful swat. "See?"

Gray watched the way Alyssa bit her lip, the warm look in her eyes as she turned back to him, and thought, *what if?* What if they would've met under different circumstances? He would've liked to have had that chance, but unfortunately, he was afraid the time for 'what ifs' had passed. Perhaps when all was said and done they could start again.

"In any case, you have my deepest apologies," he said. "I only wish we could send you and Isabella home right now, but with the wards down, the outer portals are still compromised. It wouldn't be safe just yet."

"We could take them through the tunnel portal—the way Isabella and I arrived," Valian suggested. "Being located underneath the palace, it's the only portal that's still fairly secure. But we'd need to do it quickly. Aramond and his forces may have been discouraged for a time, but you know he won't wait long to make another assault."

Isabella turned to Valian with wide eyes. "I don't want to go back to New York without you."

"Isabella, it's not safe for you here, love. At least in the New York realm you'll be well out of this madness."

"I don't care." She went to Valian and put a hand to his face. "If you're staying, I'm staying."

Valian tucked a bright, red curl behind her ear. "But think of Alyssa and all that she's been through already. I'm sure she's anxious to go home, to get back to her family. Are you willing to let her go alone? And what about your own family? They must be sick with worry."

Isabella glanced over her shoulder at Alyssa, a stricken look on her face. She was obviously torn between staying in Wysteria with Valian and accompanying her friend back home to their respective families.

"I'm afraid it would be unwise for Alyssa to leave Wysteria at this time," Lord Niall spoke up in a deep voice, and everyone in the room turned to him. "If you intend to use the scepter to rid the entire realm of the Red King for good, you will need her."

Gray frowned. "I would love to use the scepter to do just that, Lord Niall, but that would be difficult, considering Aramond has it in his possession."

The High Lord tilted his head and gave Gray a crafty smile. "Does he, now?"

"You know that he does, Niall," Alyssa replied. "We were both there at the Red Palace when that loathsome man brought it to him."

"Mmm, yes. Finnious Richter did bring the king a scepter. That is true."

"What do you mean 'a scepter'? Are you saying that what he has is not the Scepter of Fire?" Gray asked.

"But I saw it with my own eyes, and I ought to know," Alyssa insisted. "The king brought it right to me. He even made me touch it, remember?"

"I do, yes. And tell us, sweet Alyssa, how did that work out for him?" Niall asked with another sly smile.

Alyssa started to speak, but then blinked several times. Frowning, she shook her head. "It didn't. He kept asking me how to power it, but I couldn't tell him what I didn't know?"

"Exactly."

"For the love of the Oracles, Niall. I know you have a strong sense of theatrics, but let's dispense with the bullshit, shall we? What's this all about?" Valian asked in an irritated tone.

The High Lord's eyes narrowed as he stared at Valian, and

Gray thought he would respond in anger, but after a moment he only grinned and shook his head. "Ah, Valian, there was a time when you enjoyed my bullshit. As I recall, you had a talent for it yourself way back when."

Valian scowled. "That was a very long time ago, and things change. You've obviously got something to say, so why don't you just spit it out before we all die of boredom."

"And what does any of this have to do with the scepter in Aramond's possession?" The queen asked in a royal tone.

When Niall glanced her way, his good humor fled. "That is just the matter that I wished to discuss with you, madam. The Red King has never had custody of the Scepter of Fire. What Finnious Richter brought to him was a replica, one that I hand crafted with magick from memory."

"What?" Alexi blurted. "Are you kidding me? Aramond doesn't have the Scepter of Fire at all? It's just a useless trinket?"

"Indeed. But I do have it on good authority that, for a *useless trinket*, it's an excellent likeness of the original."

Alyssa gasped. "That's the reason you took me to the Red Palace in the first place. You knew who I was from the minute we met. You just wanted me there for authentication."

"Well, I wouldn't say that was the only reason I wanted you."

The wicked smile the High Lord gave Alyssa had Gray wondering exactly what had transpired between them, especially when the wicked smile became an equally wicked grin as Alyssa blushed and rolled her eyes.

Before Gray could speculate further, Niall returned to the subject at hand. "No one in this realm has actually seen the scepter in generations, Alyssa. I needed to be certain that it would pass muster, so to speak. However, I did have a bad moment when Aramond brought it close and made you touch it. I had no way of knowing how much you knew about the scepter, or for that matter, what interaction you'd had with it. Of course, the Red King is a mad fool blinded by his need for power, so in the end all that really mattered was that he *believed* it was the Scepter of Fire."

"Okay, so if all of this is true, where the hell is the real scepter, Niall?" Gray asked. He found the High Lord's story interesting, but was still skeptical of its veracity. The whole thing seemed quite implausible. "Alexi and I took it from Alyssa's townhouse the night of the gala and came straight back through the portal. I had it with me the entire time and it didn't disappear until the attack."

The High Lord grimaced. "I'd been informed of Richter's treachery early on, so I was aware that he'd conspired with the king and Queen Mabry to ambush you and the Field Marshal with intent to steal the scepter. They'd also planned to kill you both in the bargain, by the way."

"No doubt at Richter's suggestion." Alexi made a face. "That treasonous bastard will get his, mark my words."

Niall raised an eyebrow. "Nevertheless, I had a group of my own warriors follow the raiding party. Toward the end of the fight, one of my commanders slipped in and removed the scepter from the field, swapping it for the forgery. The real Scepter of Fire was brought directly to me, while the replica was handed off to Richter, who delivered it to the king with perfect timing."

"So, if your warriors were there the whole time, did it never occur to you to have them step in and help us when the attack began?" Alexi asked in a sardonic tone. "They were just waiting for an opportune time to swipe the scepter for you?"

"As usual, he was playing both sides of the fence, Alexi," Valian said in a cynical tone.

The High Lord turned to Valian and pinned him with a steely glare. "The Twilight Court will always be my first and only priority, Chancellor. I'm certain you understand that very well."

Queen Beatrice stepped forward and cleared her throat. "I suggest we stay on point, gentlemen. And that would be the whereabouts of the real Scepter of Fire. Where is it now, Lord Niall?"

The High Lord's eyes glittered as a brilliant grin spread across his face. "Why, it's right here, madam." He twirled his hand in the air, and amid the twizzle and sparkle he generated, a long, leather bag materialized in a rush of starlight. Plucking the bag from mid-air, he reached inside and pulled the scepter from its confines.

Gray stared at the richly jeweled artifact in Niall's hand with equal measures of awe and skepticism. It did look like the scepter they'd taken from Alyssa's townhouse, but how could they be certain, given the story the High Lord had just told? It was a dicey thing to question a High Lord's word outright, but if Niall had made one copy and given it to Aramond, what was to say he wasn't pulling the same thing here?

Evidently, Valian had no such qualms about questioning Niall's word. "And what proof do we have that this is the real Scepter of Fire and not just another one of your replicas, Niall?"

Surprisingly, the High Lord took no offense at Valian's thinly veiled insinuation, which Gray put down to their long and varied history. And the fact that they had been good friends at one time.

"That is a valid query, Chancellor. Although, I must say it pains me a bit that you would ask." When Valian rolled his eyes, Niall grinned again and turned to Alyssa. "Why don't we let little Alice's descendant answer that question for us?"

Alyssa's eyes went wide. "*Me?*" she squeaked. "But if I couldn't tell the difference between the real scepter and the one Richter gave the king, how can I possibly verify this one?"

Niall crossed to her, his eyes never leaving hers. "Hold out your hands and close your eyes."

"Don't be ridiculous, Niall. How am I supposed to say one way or another with my eyes closed?"

"If I'm correct, you won't need them for verification," Niall murmured, and the smile he gave her was almost tender. "Trust me, darling Alyssa."

She stared up at him for several long moments before huffing out a breath and doing as he'd asked.

Niall placed the scepter into her hands and took a step back.

And a collective gasp echoed throughout the salon, as the moment he placed the artifact into her hands, the Scepter of Fire began to hum and glow with brilliant light.

"Oh, my gosh!" Isabella exclaimed.

"Well, I'll be damned," Alexi murmured. "It's the genuine scepter."

"Seems like old Minerva was right after all," Valian acknowledged. "She did say that there would be only one to wield the Scepter of Fire. It looks like that's Alyssa."

"What?" Alyssa opened her eyes and stared down at the radiant artifact in her hands with open dismay. "No. I can't. I mean, I don't know how to—"

And the scepter's spark of life abruptly died before she could finish her sentence.

Twenty-One

"Wait. What the hell just happened here?" Alexi asked. "Yeah, I don't get it." Isabella frowned. "The scepter was working. We all saw it. The minute he handed it to her it flared right up."

Alyssa looked around the room at the faces staring back at her and wondered what they expected her to say. She'd been so happy and relieved at the prospect of finally going home only a few minutes ago. Now, she felt nothing but the burst of panic flooding her system. She imagined it was like being on stage in front of a full audience without knowing your lines or even which play you were performing.

Studying the now lifeless scepter in her hands, she slowly shook her head. "I I don't know what happened. One minute I could feel its power coming to life, vibrating through me like static electricity. And then it just ... stopped."

"It has been dormant for over a century," Valian speculated. "Perhaps over time its power has been diminished."

Alyssa looked to the High Lord for help, for some small morsel of wisdom that might bring understanding to the situation, and pleaded in a trembling voice, "Niall?"

"Yes, this is an unexpected development. And while you may

have a valid theory, Chancellor, I highly doubt the Oracles would have created such a powerful artifact with an expiration date." He gave Alyssa a speculative look and pursed his lips. "You are the descendant of the original Alice, the one the Oracles chose to originally wield the Scepter of Fire. I have long suspected that you alone would be capable of fueling it now."

"Then what did we just witness?" Valian asked. "The scepter clearly reacted to Alyssa the moment you placed it into her hands. Yet, in the next instant it died."

Niall continued to study Alyssa intently, and her breath hitched as she felt heat rise to her face at his prolonged scrutiny. She was only able to breathe a bit easier when he finally turned back to Valian.

"Unfortunately, I don't have any answers for you, Chancellor," he stated. "I'm afraid that this may be something only the Oracles themselves can untangle."

"Then we meet with them, and the sooner the better," Gray said. "Surely they can give us the answers that we need to finish off the Red King for good."

"In the meantime, Alexi and I will begin preparing our forces for Aramond's next assault," Valian said. "I'm not going into this next battle counting on having the scepter to fall back on. Now that we know Aramond doesn't have a working scepter, either, we need to be ready to fight with conventional warfare."

"Yeah. And kick his bloody ass again, with or without the scepter," Alexi added with a grin.

Valian studied the High Lord through narrowed eyes. "And what about you, Niall? Will Roseland's Twilight Court be joining us this time around? Or do you have something better to do?"

Alyssa could sense Niall turning the angles every which way in his mind as he held Valian's gaze for several long moments. Just when she thought the High Lord wouldn't respond, one of his wicked smiles spread across his handsome face. "It seems my calendar is wide open, so I suppose I could make the time. You know me, old friend. I only gamble when I know the odds." His gaze found Alyssa's again, and the look in his eyes had her pulse rate doubling. "And I must say, I do like these odds ... very much."

ONCE THE REQUEST FOR A MEETING HAD BEEN SENT TO the Oracles, Alexi and Valian had gone out to organize Wysteria's assets for the battle to come. And after a brief nod in her direction and a promise to return soon, Niall had left to collect his own forces. The rest of the group waited on pins and needles for nearly three hours before the Oracles finally replied with their consent. Evidently, the mystical beings weren't always accommodating, and everyone seemed to take their response as an encouraging sign.

The Temple of the Oracles was located several miles south of the White Palace itself, and horses had been saddled to take them there. Alyssa had been none too pleased about that decision since she hadn't ridden a horse in years. Also, with the security of the borders uncertain, a dozen soldiers had been assigned to escort her and Gray to the temple's perimeter wall.

Alyssa's first thought as they approached the shrine was that it seemed more like the entrance to a fortress or prison rather than a holy place. The thick stone walls encircling the temple itself were at least twenty feet high with notched sections every few feet around the top. And the inset of solid wooden gates looked to be the only way inside. She wondered briefly if the wall served to keep people out or the Oracles in.

As they dismounted in ankle-deep snow, the soldiers followed suit and began to set up a small camp off to one side of the path as Alyssa and the prince walked up to the solid iron gates. Her frayed nerves must have been evident, because Gray took her hand and gave it a squeeze.

"Don't be nervous," he said. "The Oracles are incredibly powerful beings, and though they're not always accommodating, they're wise beyond words and usually very gentle."

"Right. Usually very gentle." Alyssa glanced up at the

imposing perimeter wall again and then frowned at him. "Okay, not to critique or anything, but if that was your pep talk, you need to do a little work on it."

Gray chuckled. "Fair enough. How about this—the Oracles exist to protect us, Alyssa, as well as give guidance and support. Really, there's nothing to worry about. I promise."

"This is all just so strange, and it freaks me out. Especially not knowing what to expect." She chewed on her lip and stared at the entrance, her pulse rate jumping a couple levels when the gates began to swing open of their own accord. Swallowing back her apprehension, she glanced over at the prince. "Have you done this before? Met with the Oracles?"

"Absolutely. On many occasions." Gray gave her an easy smile. "Trust me. It'll all work out fine."

With a nod, she followed him through the gates where they found themselves in an enormous garden in full bloom. It was a stunning riot of color with dozens of floral varieties, and the blooms ranged from tiny clusters to some the size of serving platters almost two feet in diameter. And although snow covered the ground outside the temple walls, there was none here. It was like entering another world with a climate all its own.

The temple itself stood on the far side of the garden. Alyssa didn't know what she'd expected—perhaps a grand structure with spires and carvings—but what lay before them was quite different than she had imagined. Its stone exterior was obviously ancient but surprisingly plain, with only leafy, green and red ivy covering a good portion of its walls as adornment. In fact, the only ornate thing about the temple seemed to be the set of massive wooden doors at the entrance, which were carved with numerous and varied mystical symbols.

As she and Gray climbed the steps, the huge doors opened—again as if expecting their arrival. But Alyssa's heart really began to pound in her chest once they crossed the threshold and those colossal doors shut behind them enclosing them in a dim vestibule lit only by fiery torches. To distract herself from her mounting anxiety, she glanced around the large antechamber. Though the outer walls of the temple were austere and unembellished, here was the elaborate stonework she'd been expecting when they'd arrived. Mystical symbols and ancient-looking petroglyphs covered every spare inch of the walls, each more intricate and foreign than anything she'd seen before.

"This is amazing," she said in wonder, as she moved closer to study some of the engravings.

Gray stepped up next to her and nodded. "The Oracles are ancient beings. The temple has stood in this place for thousands of years. A portion of their history is etched on these walls."

"It's incredible. I've never seen anything like this." Alyssa shook her head and ran a finger along one of the engravings. "Kind of makes you feel small and insignificant, doesn't it?"

At that moment, the doors of the inner sanctum swung open and a tall, thin priest dressed in flowing white robes stepped out into the antechamber. "The Oracles with see you now," he murmured, gesturing toward the entrance of the sanctuary.

Swallowing back a rush of fear, Alyssa took Gray's arm and started forward. But the priest put up a hand. "Only the descendant is requested at this time."

Alyssa's breath backed up in her chest as her anxiety grew, and she turned to the prince. "I don't want to go in there alone," she cried. "Can't you come with me?"

Gray gave her a sad look and shook his head. "I'm sorry. Looks like they only want to speak to you for now. I'm afraid that if we want answers, we'll have to abide by their wishes." The prince took her cold hands in his and gave them a quick rub. "But don't worry. It will all work out the way it's supposed to. Just breathe, Alyssa. You've got this. And I'll be right here when you come out, okay?"

Alyssa took a deep breath and let it out slowly. With much trepidation, she finally nodded. Turning, she gathered her courage and walked past the priest through the entrance into the inner sanctum. But when the priest closed the doors behind her, she whirled around and found that he hadn't followed, that she was all alone.

"Come closer, descendant of Alice." The ethereal voice seemed to echo all around her—or maybe it was in her head—and she turned to find three wraithlike beings hovering above the altar at the other end of the chamber.

Alrighty then, she thought. And swallowing hard, she took another deep breath and began walking toward the altar feeling a bit like Dorothy arriving in Oz and about to meet the wizard for the first time. Only in Alyssa's case, there wasn't just one wizard. And there wasn't a wicked witch to deal with but a Red King. She didn't know which scenario was worse.

"She has come with many questions," one of the Oracles said when Alyssa stopped a few feet from the altar.

"And a great many doubts," another added with a skeptical look.

"Y-yes. I do have questions," Alyssa stammered, then blurted out the issue in a rush, "See, the Red King is threatening Wysteria again, and we need to know how to stop him, to get rid of him for good."

There was a short pause and then, *"Mmm, but you have the Scepter of Fire, do you not?"*

"Well, sure, but—"

"Then what more do you need from us? We created the scepter for Alice with just this purpose in mind."

Alyssa nodded and took a step closer to the altar. "Yes, we get that. But the prince needs you to tell him how to use it. If you'll just let him in here, he can—"

"Prince Graydon cannot use the scepter," an Oracle sternly interrupted her, and all three of the spectral beings frowned as one. *"No one can power the scepter but the descendant. You are the great-granddaughter of the great-granddaughter of Alice,"* the being finished, as if it would answer her question.

"I'm the great-granddaughter of the great-granddaughter—"

Alyssa scrubbed her hands over her face. "I don't even know what that means."

"You embody the power of the mystical number of three. In this way, you are connected to our Trinity. Therefore, the scepter can only be wielded by every third generation in the Alice line, as it was created to do."

Alyssa blinked. So, Niall had been right after all, but that didn't solve their immediate problem. "Okay, so if I'm the only one that can use the scepter, tell me how to operate it. Because, I've tried to power it up, and it did come to life for about a millisecond, and then it just died. Does it need to be charged or something? If we bring it to you, can you fix it? Aramond is preparing a second assault, and we need answers fast."

"There is nothing to repair. The scepter … is."

"Then why won't it work?" Alyssa cried. "Tell me what to do. Please."

Again, the Oracles shook their heads as one. *"We are greatly disappointed by your queries. The child Alice understood how to utilize our gift without instruction. It troubles us deeply that—as custodians of the powerful artifact we created for her—its history is unknown to her descendants."*

"I'm sorry, but until recently, I didn't even know what it was. Please don't punish Wysteria for my short-comings or those of my family. So many here have pinned their hopes on me, and I can't let them down. Can't you help me?"

The three mystical beings looked to one another. They appeared to silently communicate, and after a few moments, seemed to come to an agreement. *"You have everything you need to power the scepter, descendant of Alice."*

Alyssa's hopes plummeted. "But I don't know—"

"You are filled with doubts which block your senses. You must find the courage to reach inside yourself and take control of your destiny. We will not intercede in this matter."

"No, wait! There has to be some guidance that you can give me."

"As we decree it, so shall it be."

And with that, the doors to the sanctuary opened behind her and the three Oracles simply vanished before she could utter another word. With a heavy heart, she turned and made her way out of the sanctuary, and could hardly meet the prince's eye when he came to her in the vestibule.

"That was faster than I thought it would be. Did they tell you what was wrong with the scepter?"

Alyssa shook her head and gave him a despondent look. "Evidently, there's nothing wrong with it. And it sounds like Niall had it right, because the Oracles said that I am definitely the only one who can power the scepter."

"Okay, then that's good, right?" he asked. "So how does it work?"

"*That* they wouldn't tell me. All they would say is that I had everything I needed to wield it, which of course is no help at all." She made a face. "Oh yeah, and they also said that they were troubled by the fact that my family had been such poor custodians of such a powerful artifact, that they were disappointed that we'd let its history be lost."

"That's it?" Gray asked with a deflated look. "They didn't say anything else?"

Alyssa opened her mouth to tell him the rest, but then just shook her head. "They said they won't intercede. I'm sorry, Gray."

The prince searched her face as if looking for what she'd held back, but then simply pulled her into his arms and held her close. "It's okay. You tried, and that's all we could've asked for," he murmured in her ear, and her heart nearly broke at the sadness in his voice. But when he leaned back, he gave her an encouraging smile. "Don't look so miserable. It's not your fault, Alyssa. Besides, we may not be able to use the scepter, but at least we now know that Aramond can't either, right?"

She sighed and tried to smile back at him, but knew she fell short of the mark. "But he'll still attack, and you'll have to fight him all over again."

Gray grinned. "And like Alexi said, we'll kick his ass again, with or without the scepter. Now come on, let's get back to the palace and get the party started."

Though she couldn't control the scepter, the prince obviously didn't blame her for the loss of a powerful advantage. Still, the words the Oracles had spoken rang in her ears, and she stewed about it all the way back to the palace.

You are filled with doubts which block your senses ...

Well, duh! She'd never asked to be part of this strange legacy, indeed, never had a choice.

You have everything you need to power the scepter ... No one can power the scepter but the descendant...

The thought of wielding a mystical weapon of mass destruction was completely unthinkable to her. She'd never used a weapon against anything or anybody her entire life, and she didn't want to start now. She was terrified about the battle to come and wanted nothing more than to go home before it started. *And why not?* a voice at the back of her mind whispered. After all, what good was she to Wysteria if she couldn't control the scepter?

You must find the courage to reach inside yourself and take control of your destiny ...

She had no idea what that meant or how to even begin—wasn't sure she wanted to—but she wasn't about to turn tail and run, either. What the hell was she going to do?

Her apprehension kicked into high gear when they got back to the palace and met Alexi, Finvar, Valian, Niall, and his twin, Tisharu preparing to leave the palace to join their troops in the field.

"How'd it go?" Alexi asked. "Do we have the scepter or is this going to be down and dirty?"

Gray shook his head. "The Oracles wouldn't help."

"What? Why not?"

"They told me the scepter's not the problem. Evidently, it's me," Alyssa replied with a quick look to Niall. "And it looks like you were right, Niall. I'm the only one that can power it, but the Oracles wouldn't tell me how. They just gave me some spiel about how I had everything I needed."

The High Lord stared at her with a shuttered expression on his face, but said nothing in return.

Alyssa finally looked away when Alexi's words grabbed her attention. "Well, that's unfortunate, because my scouts returned thirty minutes ago. Looks like we've got about an hour before Aramond's troupes arrive at the border, and we haven't been successful in getting the wards back up. I doubt we'll be able to do that in the next hour. This is gonna get messy."

Alyssa felt like the breath had been sucked out of her lungs. Without the wards, there was every possibility that Roseland's forces could bring the fight across the border into Wysteria, maybe even right up to the palace walls.

"It is what it is. With everything on the line, we go out and fight harder." Though he sounded casual, the look on Gray's face was grim. Holding out his hand palm down, Gray looked around the group. "May the Oracles bless you with strength and courage."

One by one, they all placed a hand over Gray's and shouted, "Oracles be praised!"

"And may you all fight with honor and do your families proud," Finvar said before turning on his heel and striding away.

Tisharu gave her twin a fierce look. "Show no mercy, brother." A slow smile crossed her face as she too walked away. "And don't do anything to embarrass me on the battlefield," she called over her shoulder. Her throaty laughter trailed after her on the light breeze.

Niall shook his head. "I think she actually lives for conflict. I've not seen her so animated in some time."

"She is quite the badass," Alexi agreed with a laugh. "Come on, Val. I'll race you to the front lines."

Valian rolled his eyes and muttered, "Imbecile." But soon they'd said their goodbyes and were gone as well.

And yet Niall remained. "I would have a word with the descendant before joining my warriors in the field," he said with a pointed look.

Gray seemed uneasy, but nodded. "I need to get into my armor," he said with a smile for Alyssa. "Come in when you're ready, and I'll get you situated with the queen and Isabella before I go."

She watched him stride away, and then turned to Niall. "This whole thing is a nightmare. I don't know how you all can be so cavalier about it. You're literally about to go to war."

"As the prince said, it is what it is. We must all follow our destiny."

He studied her face until she grew uncomfortable and threw her hands in the air. "What? You have something else to say, so say it."

"I sensed your doubt earlier, and I see the fear in your eyes now."

"Well, duh. Of course I'm scared," she cried. "The Oracles said my doubts block my senses, and that I should take control of my destiny. But what if I don't want it? I had no choice in any of this."

She walked to the stone railing and looked out toward Cheshire Wood in the distance. "A week ago, I was just an art gallery owner happily living my life with no idea this world even existed. And then everything changed."

"Change is the way of life, Alyssa," Niall murmured, joining her at the railing. "A thousand different events in a constant state of flux."

"Look, obviously I don't want to see Wysteria in ruins, or for you all to have to fight repeatedly, but to be the weapon that destroys countless lives to save a kingdom?" She turned to him and held out a hand. "I don't think I can do that, Niall. That's not a destiny I'm prepared to embrace."

"Then change it," he said abruptly.

"Is that what you do? Mold events to your liking?"

He grinned at her. "Every chance I get."

Alyssa shook her head. "You're always so sure of yourself. Just do me a favor and don't die out there today, okay?"

"Worried for me, darling Alyssa?"

She gave him a sarcastic look. "Don't be stupid."

The High Lord burst into laughter, suddenly grabbing her up against his hard chest. "Such a feisty human you are, Alyssa Montague."

In the next moment, he crushed his lips to hers in a kiss that she felt all the way to her toes. Every doubt, every fear flew from her mind at lightning speed, leaving one thought front and center ... *Niall*.

Then it ended as quickly as it had begun, and she could do nothing but stare at him with her mouth hanging open.

He beamed down at her and winked. "For luck." But then the grin slowly faded from his face. "The Oracles were right, you know. You do have everything you need inside you. Never doubt it. Hold the scepter in your hands, step up to the wall, and change your destiny, descendant of Alice."

Then he set her from him and walked away without a backward glance, leaving her in confusion with the taste of a faerie Lord still on her lips.

Twenty-Two

As it turned out, they'd had a whole lot less time than Gray had hoped. He'd barely joined his crew at the outer mile marker in Tarkington Forest when the first wave hit the border. Though the Wysterian battalions stationed along that line had been ready and waiting, it hadn't taken long for the first swarm of lesser fae to realize that the security wards hadn't been restored. And this time there was no holding them.

Instead of pushing the invading army back into Roseland and fighting them there as they'd done before, large groups of lesser fae began fading right up to the restriction spell's perimeter by the scores. They bypassed the border and Wysteria's front line entirely while the following swells of Roseland's army kept those troops engaged.

Soon the forest was filled with the sounds of war, the dissonance of clashing steel and battle cries ringing through the trees, the dense smoke from brush fires and ozone from spent magick cutting visibility. Gray and his squad fought the incoming enemy throngs beside Finvar and a group of his fae warriors. One of which was in a heated battle with two faeries a few yards away, and as Gray turned to help, a wicked throwing dagger whizzed past his head, missing him by mere inches. He struck down one of the attacking faeries and then spun on his heel, shooting a stream of lethal energy at the dagger's owner, hitting his mark point blank as that warrior exploded into a bloody mist.

Gray lost track of Finvar in the smoke, but as more and more Roseland forces poured into the forest, it became clear that this battle would not be as easily won as the previous bout. Dodging to his left, he cut a bloody swath through a group of soldiers, blocking a barrage of magickal blasts and firing back his own as he continued on.

He located Finvar through the rolling haze a few minutes later. A hundred yards to the north, the High Lord was fighting several combatants at once and looked to be making progress when—to Gray's shock—two lesser fae warriors materialized directly behind him. Somehow they'd managed to bypass the restriction spell and faded *inside* the zone. In the heat of battle, Finvar was unaware of the new danger at his back. Gray tried to shout a warning over the din, but was horrified when the High Lord began to turn and one of the faeries ran him through with a sword. The faerie grinned evilly as he watched Finvar drop to the ground.

"*No!*" Gray roared, throwing out a hand, and with it, a burst of pure, deadly energy. Every enemy soldier within a thirty yard radius shattered, their broken bodies dropping where they stood. Racing to the High Lord's side, Gray dropped down next to him.

Finvar moaned and opened his eyes as Gray gently turned him onto his back. The faerie's sword had pierced the right side of the High Lord's chest, but Gray had no way of discerning what kind of internal damage had been done.

"Graydon—"

"Don't try to talk, Fin. Just lay still." They were out in the open, vulnerable, and an arrow pinged off of Gray's armor as a deadly reminder of that fact. But before he could react or decide the best approach to Finvar's injuries, Old Minerva materialized beside them, protecting them both with a wave of her bony hand.

"Do as you're told, High Lord," the sorceress said. "And let your boy heal your wounds."

"Minerva... please... don't..." Finvar ground out. "Just take him... and go."

"I'll do no such thing," she replied with a disgruntled look.

"She's right, Fin. We're not leaving you."

Minerva gave Finvar a stern look. "He should have been told the truth before now. I'll not let him watch you die in this way."

"Truth?" Gray frowned. "What are you talking about?"

"Minerva, not now. Not... the time. Please," Finvar begged, and then gasped in pain.

After a moment the old sorceress acquiesced with an irritated grunt. "I concede that this is not the appropriate time or place. But it *is* a story for later." She shot a quick look at Gray. "Heal him now and make quick work of it. Yulis, the Red King's sorcerer has found a way to nullify my fade-restriction spell, and you both must return to the palace before it comes under siege."

"But how—" Gray began.

"Do it." Minerva shouted. "*Now!*"

As arrows began pelting the invisible shield Minerva had created, she put her energies into clearing the field around them as Gray placed his hands over Finvar's wound. Slowly, he let the heat of his healing powers build, mending tissue and repairing damage. With a final surge, Finvar gasped and bolted into a sitting position, the color beginning to return to his face.

As Gray helped the High Lord to his feet a moment later, Minerva nodded with satisfaction. "I must go now to deal with Yulis, but be warned, High Lord. There will come a reckoning for you and the queen when this conflict is over," she told Finvar. "Now *go!*"

With a look of resignation, Finvar took Gray's arm and they faded.

WITH THE MAIN CONFLICT TAKING PLACE IN Tarkington Forest, Valian had sent Alexi and several battalions to Larkspur Meadow as a second line of defense, along with hundreds of dwarves from the northern mountain regions. He felt confident that their sheer numbers could stem the flow of any enemy forces breaking through from the front lines.

But as backup, Valian had stationed himself with Halifax in Cheshire Wood, along with Tisharu and her fierce fae warriors. The faerie queen had not been pleased to be so far from the action, and had argued that she and her warriors were needed closer to the front lines. But with the wards still down, they all knew that the battle would more than likely spread in their direction eventually, so she had reluctantly agreed to the arrangement.

However, Valian hadn't realized how quickly they would become embroiled in the conflict, and they were all stunned when lesser fae actually began *fading* into the Wood. He didn't know how they'd bypassed the restriction spell, but it was the least of their worries as they engaged the enemy forces which began to appear at an alarming rate.

Halifax shifted into his leopard form—disappearing here, resurfacing there, and viciously taking out one fae after another with a cat's version of surprise attacks. But Valian soon lost sight of him completely as the Wood continued to fill with combatants and the battle intensified.

For a time Valian simply fought in one place, pivoting and spinning, hacking and slicing as Roseland fae warriors material-ized by the dozens. He recognized many of those from Mabry's Evening Court, as well as Dyagmon's Winter Court by the crests emblazoned on their armor. But soon, mortal soldiers followed on foot, flowing in from Larkspur Meadow in waves.

Out of the corner of his eye, Valian caught movement and whirled in that direction. His dodge was almost too late, narrowly missing a thrusting sword before burying his dagger in the wield-er's abdomen. Retrieving his knife, Valian had just shoved the warrior to the ground when white-hot pain exploded through him, robbing his breath and taking him to his knees.

Looking down at his chest, he found the steel point and first four inches of a long bow arrow protruding from the left side of his upper torso. The arrow must have been fired at a good distance from somewhere inside the Wood behind him, because the velocity of the missile had shot it straight through his armor. He could literally feel the blood draining from his face, and he gasped as he tried and failed to regain his feet.

"Well, well. What do we have here?" a sultry voice asked from behind him. "Is this the great Wysterian Chancellor I see on his knees before me?"

Glancing over his shoulder, Valian found Mabry's lieutenant, Kasandra Delacourt—sword in hand—standing over him with a smug grin on her face.

And he knew he was in deep trouble.

Unable to stand and face her, he could hardly catch his breath, let alone conjure a strong enough stream of magick to take down a High Fae. He'd lost one of his daggers when the arrow struck, but he made an effort to protect himself. Turning, he flung a weak shot of energy at her, but she sidestepped it easily. He tried to raise the one dagger he had left, but his grip had grown weak, and it, too, slipped from his grasp.

Kasandra laughed at his pitiful attempt and then delivered a hard kick to his shoulder, knocking him to the ground. "To think that the White Queen actually put her faith in you, yet neither you nor that pipsqueak of a prince could protect the scepter *or* the descendant. It really is too pathetic."

Heaving a sigh, she walked around him, shaking her head. Then she stopped and hunkered down beside him, wisely taking care not to get within arm's reach. "What happened to you, Valian? You were once a great warrior. I'll admit that I've never liked you much, but at least I had respect for you. Now, you're just another elf about to die by my hand."

His vision blurred as he glared up at her, but she just grinned.

Standing, she twirled the hilt of the sword in her hand. "Any last words, *Chancellor*?"

"Go fuck yourself? " he ground out. "See you in hell? Take your pick."

A hard look came into her eyes, and her grin vanished. "I'm going to enjoy this immensely," she said, giving her sword another quick spin.

Time seemed to shift into slow motion then as Valian braced himself and prayed for a miracle. He thought of Wysteria, his cherished homeland, and the faces of family and friends flashed through his mind like a fragmented slide show. However, his last thoughts were only for Isabella as Kasandra raised her sword high into the air.

But in that last moment, Valian was stunned when the miracle he'd hoped for arrived. The faerie's head was cleaved from her neck with such force that it flew from her body like a shot from a gun, spraying him with blood and gore as it soared over him and into the brush to his right. Like a delayed reaction, the rest of her body dropped to the ground a few feet from him a moment later.

And then Tisharu was kneeling beside him, bloody sword still in her hand. "Hold on, *mo chroí*." she murmured, examining the arrow protruding from his chest. "I'll get us both to the White Palace where the healers will remove this arrow and take care of you."

He was getting light-headed, perhaps from the loss of blood, and his vision was beginning to gray around the edges, but he shook his head. "Leave me and go, Tisharu. With the restriction spell broken, the enemy may fade right up to the palace walls. The queen must be protected at all cost."

"I'll not leave you, Valian, queen or no. But rest easy. I've sent my warriors on ahead, and I know for a fact that several of Wysteria's fae courts are already in place at the palace. They won't allow anything to befall the queen. You have my word."

He heard her as if from a long, deep tunnel and tried to form a reply but found he couldn't quite find his words.

"Stay with me, *a ghrá geal*. I'll take you home..." was the last thing he heard her say before everything went black.

⁂

Alyssa stopped pacing and stared toward the chamber's leaded windows where Isabella had been holding a silent vigil. The terrifying sounds of battle had been steadily growing closer over the last fifteen minutes, and the last explosion sounded like it was just outside the palace wall.

"Wow. That one was really loud," Isabella said. She glanced back at Alyssa with a tense look. "The battle is getting closer."

Alyssa joined her friend at the window and studied the landscape with dismay. Plumes of smoke could be seen rising from Cheshire Wood in the distance, but what had real fear forming in the pit of her stomach was that she could actually see warriors materializing in the open fields between Cheshire Wood and the White Palace's perimeter wall.

"I thought there was a fade-restricting spell in place," she said with eyes wide. "How are they fading so close to the perimeter wall?"

"The Red King's sorcerer somehow found a way to break the spell Old Minerva put in place when the security of the wards was first detected," the queen replied as she stepped in between Alyssa and Isabella at the window. "Gray and Finvar came back from Tarkington Forest briefly with an update. They said that our warriors were taken by surprise, and that Roseland forces were flooding into the kingdom. Hundreds of lesser fae have begun fading closer and closer to the palace."

"Dear God!" Isabella whispered in a frightened voice. "What are we going to do?"

Queen Beatrice gave her a confident look. "We're not going to panic. This chamber is hidden in the north wing and has a complicated protection spell that will keep us perfectly safe. And I trust that Wysteria's army combined with the faerie courts—not to mention the hundreds of goblins and dwarves from the outer regions—will prevail in this fight when all is said and done."

"Yes, but how many will die before it's over?" Isabella asked, then gestured toward the window. "Valian's right out there in Cheshire Wood where it looks like all hell has broken loose. The prince may have come back here briefly, but he's gone out again, right? And who knows where Alexi is? Then there are scores of others, like you said, with families waiting at home for their return." Isabella took a breath and glanced at the queen. "And no offense, Majesty, but if the king's sorcerer could undo the spell that Minerva put in place, what's to say he couldn't undo the protection spell on this room as well?"

The queen ran a hand over Isabella's bright curls and smiled. "You have a valid question, Isabella. But you needn't worry. Though Minerva is the most powerful sorceress in the kingdom, she is not responsible for the hidden chamber's protection spell. That was put into place by the Oracles themselves during the Great War. It was designed to protect me and my son. To enter, you'd have to be with one of us, you could never enter alone. So you see, we've nothing to worry about."

Isabella blew out a breath and nodded. "Good. That's very good. But it still doesn't help those out there fighting, does it? It almost makes me feel guilty, like I'm hiding in here while they're out there in harm's way."

Alyssa stepped away from the window and resumed her pacing, her stomach churning. Isabella had a point, and she felt guilty as well. Just the thought of Gray, Alexi, Valian... Niall out there fighting, possibly dying to protect family and kingdom, made her sick to her stomach. And the enemy may not be able to get into this chamber, but what if they invaded the palace? Gryphon and all the other innocents living here would be at risk.

You do have everything you need inside you. Never doubt it... Niall's parting words to her played over and over in her head. But what did that mean? If she had everything she needed, then why couldn't she make the scepter work? The Oracles had made it clear that she was the problem, that she had doubts that blocked her senses. Well, no kidding. She had more than just doubts. Like no interest whatsoever in destroying the bulk of a kingdom, even an invading one. She didn't want to be anybody's weapon of mass destruction. Could the problem with the scepter be as simple as that?

Hold the scepter in your hands, step up to the wall, and change your destiny...

Was it possible? Could she use the scepter to stop this war without bloodshed, without massacring hundreds, maybe thousands? Could she change her own destiny and maybe that of a kingdom? Glancing over at the queen, watching the worry flit across Isabella's face, Alyssa came to a decision.

"Queen Beatrice, where is the scepter now?"

The queen turned from the window with a curious look. "It's hidden here in this chamber where it's also protected. Why do you ask?"

"Because I think I'm going to need it."

Isabella's eyes went wide with surprise. "Aly, what are you saying? Are you going to try to use it again? I mean, you know what happened before. What makes you think you can power it up now?"

Alyssa shook her head and shrugged. "I don't know, Izzy. Maybe I can't. All I know is that I have to try." She turned to the queen. "Look, I don't know how much stock I put into this destiny thing, and trust me, I really don't want to kill anyone, but I can't stand by and watch the people we all care about get hurt and not lift a finger."

The queen scrutinized Alyssa for several long moments before finally nodding. Crossing to the opposite side of the room, she placed her palm over one of the stones in the wall. After a loud 'click', it smoothly slid out of the wall like a dresser drawer, revealing the secret compartment. Beatrice removed the scepter from a drawstring bag of royal blue velvet, and handed the artifact to Alyssa.

"What else do you need?" the queen asked.

Alyssa looked back and forth between the two women before walking to the window.

Hold the scepter in your hands, step up to the wall, and change your destiny...

Turning back to the queen, she took a deep breath. "I think I need to be out there... on the tower wall as high up as I can get."

Queen Beatrice frowned. "You do realize that we're only protected inside this chamber. If enemy forces have compromised the palace, it could be very dangerous to leave this space."

Alyssa nodded. "I understand. And I don't know why, but I think that's the only way this is going to work."

"Very well." Queen Beatrice lifted the lid on a large chest in the corner, pulling out a couple of razor-sharp fighting daggers and a sword from its depths. "If we're leaving this space, we need to be properly armed. Isabella, you and Alyssa will carry the daggers, and I will use the sword."

"Oh, but don't you think you should stay here, Your Majesty? I don't even know if this is going to work. And what if it doesn't? Then we'd all be in trouble." Alyssa said. "Why don't you just give me directions—the fastest route to the highest point on the rampart?"

The queen drew herself up to full royal height and raised an eyebrow. "We all go, descendant of Alice...or no one goes," she replied in a tone that allowed no argument. "It is, however, your choice."

They had a short stare-down that Queen Beatrice won, hands down. So, Alyssa just took a deep breath and nodded. "Okay, then we all go. Izzy? Are you down with this?"

Isabella looked skeptical but pressed her lips together and nodded as well.

"As you wish," the queen said and handed both her and Isabella each a dagger. "Follow me. There is an unused passageway just at the end of the corridor. It leads to the tower's spiraling stairway that I think will take us to a perfect spot for what you need. Stay close, and do as I say."

When Alyssa and Isabella both agreed, the queen moved to the chamber door and took hold of the handle. There was another light 'click' and she slowly pulled the door open. Taking a quick look both ways in the passage, she turned back and nodded. "Let's go."

What the heck was she gonna do if she couldn't get the scepter to work, Alyssa thought to herself. Would they be able to make it back to the secure chamber?

No turning back now...

With that last thought, she and Isabella followed the White Queen out of the chamber and down the hall.

Twenty-Three

Valian came awake with a start, disorientation fogging his mind and terrible pain radiating through his chest. Struggling to sit up, a gentle hand reached out to stop him, and after a quick scan of the room, he saw with relief that he was in the hospital wing of the White Palace.

"I'm not quite finished here, Chancellor. Please be still and let me complete my work," said the healer standing over him as he eased Valian back down onto the bed.

Valian's breastplate and underlying body armor had been removed and the healer was in the process of closing the oozing wound on the left side of his chest. The long bow arrow had been taken out in two pieces, both of which were on the instrument table beside the bed.

Valian cleared his throat and muscled through his pain. "How long have I been out?"

"I really couldn't say, Chancellor. My apprentice said you were unconscious when Queen Tisharu brought you in, and that was over an hour ago, but I can't speak to anything before that. What I can say is that you were extremely lucky. The projectile entered your back at high velocity and passed straight through both layers of body armor—back to front—doing significant damage along the way, I might add. It did, however, miss your heart—praise the Oracles—albeit by a narrow margin." The healer shook his head as if he was somehow disappointed in Valian. "Had the arrow pierced your chest just an inch or two lower, we wouldn't be having this conversation. Fortunately, with your Elven anatomy and restorative capabilities, your injury has already begun to mend itself."

Valian rubbed his eyes and grunted, taking a breath around the throbbing ache in his upper torso. "Then what did I need you for?" he muttered.

The healer gave him a stoic look before leaning over him and smearing some sort of nasty-smelling ointment over the exit wound on his chest. Valian clinched his jaw in pain as the healer made a twirling motion with his finger, levitating Valian's body and turning him on his side, giving the entry wound on his back the same treatment. He concluded the process with the application of bandages to both wounds. When he'd finished, he lowered Valian back to the bed and wiped his hands, giving Valian another tolerant look. "And to answer your question, which I realize was rhetorical but will address anyway, you needed me to remove the arrow from your chest and make certain it wasn't tainted with fae poison."

Valian was still fairly light-headed but as long as he kept still, the pain from his injury seemed to ebb a bit. He narrowed his eyes at the healer. "And was it?"

"No," the man replied with a smug expression. "Which is one more reason you were lucky. Of course, that and the fact that Queen Tisharu acted so quickly in getting you to the palace."

Valian glanced around the room again. "Speaking of Tisharu, where is she?"

"Evidently she went back to the battle once she was certain you'd recover. I wasn't in the medical wing when she dropped you off, but she assured my apprentice that she would be back to check on you as soon as she could."

Swinging his legs off the bed, Valian planted his boots on the floor and waited for another wave of vertigo to pass before standing under his own steam.

"Wait! What are you doing? You'll have your wounds bleeding again. You're in no shape to—"

Valian silenced the man with a hard look. "What have you done with my armor, healer?"

"Surely you can't be thinking of rejoining the fight, Chancellor. I said your wounds have *just begun* to mend, and any exertion will have consequences. You need rest for your body to finish repairing itself."

"Unfortunately, I have no time for rest or repair. The fade-restriction spell has been broken. It's how Tisharu got me here so quickly." Valian raised a questioning eyebrow. "Now... my armor?"

The healer frowned and pointed to a corner where Valian's damaged breastplate and body armor had been dumped in a heap. "My apprentice did say that the fae queen had *faded* you here, but it seemed so far-fetched that I dismissed it as the boy's over-active imagination," the man said, his tone conveying mild surprise. "Old Minerva is the most powerful sorceress in the entire realm. I know of no other with the skill to undermine her magicks."

"Nevertheless, it seems to have been done, so I would suggest barring the door when I leave. And having a weapon wouldn't hurt, just in case. Now, help me with this," Valian commanded as he struggled to don the body armor.

The healer blanched as he began to assist with the breastplate. "I trust our army to hold the enemy outside the perimeter wall. In any case, no Roseland soldier would be so bold or so foolish as to fade directly into the White Palace."

Before Valian could comment on the absurdity of that statement, there came a loud rumbling from somewhere inside the palace walls, and the color bleached from the healer's face.

"You were saying?" Valian shot back as he stowed his fighting daggers, and with effort, sheathed his sword at his back. He was far from a hundred percent. In truth, he wasn't certain how far he would get once he left the infirmary, but there was simply no other choice. Someone needed to get to the hidden chamber in the north wing and make certain the queen was secure. And as far as he knew, there was no one else to do it.

"No. No, this can't be," the healer stammered, shooting a worried look toward the door as another volley could be heard, nearer still. "What are we to do?"

"If the palace has been invaded, I'd say you'd better be prepared to defend yourself if you want to survive, because the bulk of our troops are still in the field. We're on our own here in the palace with only a skeleton crew until reinforcements arrive… if they arrive."

"B-but I have no weapons other than surgical knives."

Looking down the long row of beds to the other end of the room, Valian nodded in that direction. "Then the best you can do for now is to take your knives and your apprentice and barricade yourselves in the inner chamber along with any others still left in this wing."

Valian headed for the door, but the healer called after him. "Chancellor, wait. Please. Can't you stay, just until help can get here?"

"I'm sorry, but time is crucial, and I have a duty to protect the queen. Her safety is imperative. Go into the back chamber and bar the door. Stay hidden until this is over," he said over his shoulder.

Pulling one of his daggers out of its holster, Valian quietly eased open the door to the hall and took a quick look in both directions. Finding it clear, he slipped from the room and made his way to the medical wing's main corridor. He'd need to go up four levels in order to connect to the north annex. Fading would've been his choice—and easier in his condition—but he wanted to check the main floor for possible intruders, and headed toward the central stairway.

He'd only gone a hundred yards or so when—in a swirl of smoke—four lesser fae warriors materialized in the hallway ahead of him. Normally, he would've cut through them like a knife through butter, but he knew in his present state he would need every advantage he could get. Quickly ducking into a recessed doorway, he'd have to wait for them to pass and try to take them out as quickly as he could.

Barely breathing, he waited and listened. There was the sound of a commotion, but then footsteps continued in his direction. Pulling out his other dagger, he was poised to strike as the footfalls grew closer and closer, nearly to his hiding spot. And just as he was about to leap from the doorway, two familiar faces came into view.

"By the Oracles, Val! Are you trying to give me a heart attack?" Alexi groused when he saw his cousin. He held up his sword. "I could've run you through. There are intruders fading in and out all over the place. Lord Niall and I just took care of four Roseland fae from Mabry's court up the hall."

Valian stepped out of the niche into the corridor and nodded. "I know. I saw them appear and ducked into the doorway before they caught sight of me. I was waiting to catch them off guard. What are you two doing in the hospital wing?"

"When it all started to go sideways out there, we came to protect the queen." Alexi pointed at the hole in Valian's armor where the arrow had struck. "But Tisharu said you'd been substantially injured, and that she'd faded with you from the field to the infirmary. Lord Niall and I were just on our way to check on you and make sure the hospital wing was secure."

"You look like death warmed over, old friend. There's not a whit of color in your face," Niall said. There was a smile on his face, but the shadow of concern darkened his eyes. "From the looks of you, the slightest breeze would topple you. Should you be out of bed?"

"Don't be an idiot, Niall. I took a long bow arrow through the chest only a couple of hours ago." Valian gave a weak laugh, and then leaned against the wall as another dizzy spell came and went. "From what I understand, it barely missed a vital organ or two. So no, I probably shouldn't be up and around, but then, we *are* being invaded. And I'll be damned if I'm going to die in bed." He glanced at Alexi. "But that's beside the point. Right now we need to get to the north wing and make certain the queen is secure."

"Way ahead of you, cousin. Gray and Tisharu faded directly there when we all left the field. Niall and I came looking for you."

Valian nodded and swiped at the sweat pouring down the side of his face. "Then we should follow. With the enemy penetrating the palace walls, who knows what they've found."

"Are you sure you can make it, Val?" Alexi asked with a skeptical look. "All kidding aside, you look pretty bad."

"For the love of the Oracles, Field Marshal," Niall complained. "You should know how hard this one's head is. You're not going to deter him, so don't waste your breath. Take the invalid's other arm and let's go, already."

With Niall on one side of Valian and Alexi on the other, they disappeared in a swirl of smoke and starlight, reappearing in the north annex outside the secret chamber where Tisharu paced the hallway.

"Tisharu, where's Gray?" Valian asked.

Before she could respond, a hidden door opened in the stone wall to their left, and Gray emerged from the secure room in a panic. "It's empty. My mother, Alyssa, and Isabella were all supposed to stay inside until the fighting was done, but they're not here."

"Why would they leave the protected chamber?" Tisharu asked with irritation. "That's just foolish and irresponsible."

Niall narrowed his eyes at his twin and clucked his tongue. "As always, so quick to judge, sister. There may have been a good reason for their departure. Why don't we find out before spouting condemnation?" he suggested.

"And just how do you propose we do that?" Alexi asked. "Are you suddenly psychic now?"

"Perhaps." The High Lord smiled and turned in a slow circle. "Violet?" he called softly.

A moment later, there was a shimmering burst of faerie dust, and the pixie appeared with Gryphon, the queen's chamber elf at her side. "I'm here, High Lord."

"What the—" Alexi began.

"I spoke with Queen Beatrice before leaving to collect my warriors and convinced her to allow Violet to stay here in the palace during the battle," Niall said. "She and Gryphon were tasked with keeping a sharp eye on the chamber... just in case." The High Lord turned to address Violet. "Do you know where the queen has gone, pixie?"

Violet nodded, her wings abuzz with her anxiety. "They emerged from the hidden chamber less than ten minutes ago, High Lord. Gryphon and I heard them talking about heading for the rampart."

"The rampart? Why the hell would they do that?" Valian asked with concern. "With the restriction spell broken they'll be out in the open, vulnerable."

"The descendant had the Scepter of Fire in her hand," Gryphon replied. "It sounded as if she was going to try to use it."

"But I thought she didn't know how to power the scepter," Alexi said.

A thoughtful look stole over Niall's face and he smiled. "Perhaps she's figured it out at last."

"And if she hasn't but intends to try again, she'll need backup to buy her some time," Gray replied.

"Agreed," the High Lord said. "I suggest we go up and give her that time."

With that, the five warriors faded toward the tower wall.

ALYSSA AND ISABELLA FOLLOWED THE QUEEN OUT OF the turret's spiraling staircase and into the room at the top of the tower. With her pulse racing, and a death grip on both the dagger in one hand and the scepter in the other, she looked around the small space with its openings to the ramparts on either side.

Alyssa was reminded of Dorothy's trip to Oz and her failed attempt to escape from the wicked witch's castle. She and her friends had been trapped by the witch and her henchmen in a tower room very much like this one. And though in that story the little girl from Kansas had saved the day, Alyssa knew that should she and her own companions get trapped in this spot, there would be little hope of survival. No amount of water would melt away their enemies with such ease.

Shoving the disturbing thoughts away, she breathed a sigh of relief once she and Isabella followed Queen Beatrice through the archway leading to the massive rampart connecting the north and west towers. However, her relief was short-lived when she stepped out onto the battlement itself. Here, the frigid wind whipped the falling snow into a frenzy of white, cutting to the bone and impairing visibility. As the trio made their way to the center of the rampart, Alyssa stepped up to the wall and looked out toward the fields in the distance and the battle raging there.

To her horror, she saw that the fighting had also spilled over the perimeter wall into the palace keep below, and terror lodged in her throat like an icy stone. Without some sort of miracle, she realized it was entirely possible that they could all perish in this place. Wysteria could be destroyed. She and Isabella would never see home again, and their families would have no idea what had happened to them.

Hold the scepter in your hands, step up to the wall, and change your destiny...

With Niall's words again echoing in her mind, and her heart pounding in her chest, Alyssa dropped the dagger to the stone floor of the rampart. With trembling hands, she held the Scepter of Fire out in front of her and prayed for that miracle.

But even as she began to concentrate on the scepter, fae warriors suddenly began to appear on the battlement around them. Across the way, Isabella and the queen were instantly surrounded and backed against the opposing rampart wall, Queen Beatrice doing everything she could to hold them off. But Alyssa knew the queen's efforts wouldn't be enough to save them, and it wouldn't be long before the monarch was overcome.

Twin blades of guilt and regret sliced through her hope like a sharp knife through tissue paper. This was her fault. She'd put them into this situation, and now they could all die because of her arrogance. She'd talked the queen into leaving the hidden chamber based on an impulse, when in fact, she hadn't even known if she could wield the scepter.

Torn between helping her friends and trying again to power the artifact, she hesitated just a moment too long, and a fae warrior appeared in a whirl of smoke only an arm's length from where she stood. Alyssa screamed as the warrior grabbed her arm, jerking her toward him, and the scepter flew from her grasp, landing with a soft thud in the accumulating snow a few feet away.

"Let go of me, you asshole!" she cried, and the faerie laughed as she struggled against him. But his amusement died in his throat when, on instinct, she spun and kneed him in the groin as hard as she could, twisting out of his grip as he doubled over in pain.

Dropping down to retrieve the dagger at her feet, she stood and whirled with it just in time. The faerie had recovered faster than anticipated, and he lunged at her. But his momentum was to her advantage, and her dagger ended up buried to the hilt in the warrior's abdomen, almost by accident. His shock should've been comical, but as he stumbled and fell forward, he took her down with him, collapsing on top of her.

With her breath coming in gasps, Alyssa saw two other lesser fae moving in her direction—swords in hand—and pinned beneath the fallen warrior, panic overwhelmed her. In her terror, she struggled beneath his dead weight, but he was too heavy for her to move before she would be set upon by the two fae closing in.

But just when Alyssa was sure all was lost, she began to see familiar faces appear. The two fae warriors were almost on her when they were both cut down in mid-stride by Gray and Alexi.

"Are you alright," Gray shouted as he hurried to her side, finally rolling the dead warrior off her and helping her to her feet.

She nodded as she watched Alexi rush into the fray to help Valian, Niall, and Tisharu fight to protect Isabella and the queen and to clear the rampart of the enemy fae. But they weren't out of the woods yet as more fae warriors began to appear, and Gray was forced to turn and wade in as well. Looking back out over the wall, Alyssa knew that she had to do something quickly.

Retrieving the scepter from its snowy resting place, she prayed for help—but from whom she didn't know. The Oracles had told her she had everything she needed to power the scepter, but she still had no clue what that meant. Holding the artifact aloft, she closed her eyes and tried to clear her thoughts, concentrating on the scepter and the power within it.

Precious minutes ticked by, but yet there was nothing, not even a spark, and soon she started to panic all over again. But then it happened. Like a car engine suddenly catching on a frigid winter morning, the scepter roared to life in her hands, and along with it, a soothing, child-like voice filled her head.

Don't be afraid. Center yourself and let go of your doubts. Only in this way can you release the scepter's power and send its light to push back the darkness.

With the voice came a strange tranquility. And as it settled over her, Alyssa's pulse began to slow, her heartbeat began to quiet. She ceased to feel the bitter wind or the snow swirling around her. The sounds of battle vanished, replaced by the quiet hum of power and energy flowing through every fiber of her being. It was as if she'd stepped into another dimension where nothing could touch her, and her fear simply melted away like dew in morning sunlight. She could feel the strength of the scepter unfurling, moving within her, a mystical creature stretching its wings.

And there was dazzling light, as if the sun itself had burst open behind her eyelids.

Yes, feel the light, become the light, the voice in her head whispered. *Guide its power. Remove the threat... become the reckoning...*

In her mind, Alyssa was everywhere at once—in Cheshire Wood, Tarkington Forest, along the border, in fields and glens, in every place where there was conflict. She was without form, both vast and infinitesimal. "I am light," she murmured. "I am reckoning..."

In a final blast of colossal energy, in her mind she saw the light spear out, its brilliant rays searing the enemy combatants where they stood, turning darkness to ash.

And in the next moment, the Scepter of Fire went silent, and Alyssa fainted dead away.

Twenty-Four

Alyssa awoke in stages, slowly regaining her senses and becoming aware of her surroundings. She felt as weak as a newborn, and her mind was so foggy that she had to work at just gathering her thoughts. Her entire body ached like it had been used as a battering ram. Even the act of swallowing hurt. Her mouth and throat were bone-dry, and it was a struggle just to peel back her gummy eyelids. When she finally managed to pry open her eyes, she had to blink several times to clear her vision before focusing on the room around her.

By the look of it, she was obviously in a hospital. But why? Had she been ill or in an accident of some kind? She searched her memory for a clue, but recent events were vague and seemed just out of reach.

"Ah, finally," a nearby voice said. "We were beginning to think you'd sleep your life away."

With effort, Alyssa turned toward the voice and found a man she didn't know standing next to the bed. "Are you a doctor?" she asked in a hoarse voice.

The man's strange golden eyes twinkled, and he smiled in a kindly way, putting the back of his hand to her forehead. "Of sorts. I'm a healer here in the hospital wing of the White Palace."

As he turned to the small side table, Alyssa saw that the healer had pointed ears with countless small hoops and earrings with odd symbols rimming the lobes. Slowly, bits and pieces of memory began to arise. "I'm in Wysteria," she murmured to herself.

"Yes, that's right." The healer said as he lifted a cup containing some sort of dark-blue liquid to her lips. "Now, drink this slowly."

She was so thirsty that she had to force herself not to guzzle the slightly sweet concoction. But it did wonders for her dry, scratchy throat, and within moments, she'd completely drained the cup. "Have I been ill, or was I injured somehow?"

"No. Not at all. But you have been asleep for almost twenty-four hours. How are you feeling?"

"Groggy, confused." Alyssa sighed and closed her eyes. "What happened? I feel like I was hit by a bus."

The healer laughed softly. "I would imagine so, after what you've been through. Your confusion should begin to lift once my potion takes effect. It will help to clear your mind, assist with hydration, and give you a restorative slumber."

Even as he spoke, snippets of events began to flood her mind. She saw a dungeon and a long, scary trek through a troll-infested forest, strange mystical beings hovering over an altar, wind and swirling snow, brilliant light... and fighting. Her eyes flew open. "The war!"

"Yes, I see your memories are already beginning to surface. But ease your mind. All is well."

"So the battle is over?"

"It is, indeed."

"But how—"

"Do not worry. I will have my apprentice fetch Prince Graydon as soon as you wake again. All your questions will be answered in due time."

"No, but wait..." Her eyelids were already getting heavy, and she struggled to focus on him but couldn't hold onto her thoughts.

"Shh... You must rest now and regain your strength, descendant of Alice."

Before she could form another question, her eyelids slipped shut, and she fell asleep.

THE NEXT TIME SHE SURFACED, ALYSSA FELT ALMOST like herself again. Though her muscles were still a bit stiff, her mind was clear again, just as the healer had predicted. Her memories had returned—for the most part—but she was still unclear about how the battle had ended. Her recollections of those last minutes on the rampart were vague and mixed up in her head. Still, she was glad the whole thing was over and hoped all of her friends were well.

Stretching out the kinks in her arms and legs, she was just contemplating getting up to look for something to wear when the door to the chamber flew open. Isabella burst into the room followed by Queen Beatrice, Gray, and Valian.

"Aly! You're finally awake," Isabella gushed as she hurried to Alyssa's bedside. "The healer said you were going to be fine, but when I came in yesterday evening, you were asleep again. How do you feel?"

Alyssa yawned. "The first time I woke up, I felt like I'd gone about twelve rounds with a heavyweight champ. But aside from some stiffness and a few achy muscles, I actually feel pretty good now. What time is it?"

"Just after eleven in the morning. Are you hungry?"

Alyssa's stomach growled and they both laughed. "I guess I could eat."

"I'll make sure the healer brings you something after we talk," Queen Beatrice said. "Can't have you withering away in a hospital bed."

"He told me the war was over but not much else. Is everyone okay?"

"It was touch and go toward the end," Gray replied. "But everyone's fine, thanks to you."

"Thanks to me?" Alyssa frowned. "What do you mean?"

"What, exactly, do you recall, Alyssa?" Valian asked quietly.

"Well, I remember climbing the stairs to the tower room and following Queen Beatrice out onto the rampart." Alyssa bit her lip and thought back for a moment. "The wind... it was raging, blowing the snow sideways. I remember looking down, seeing the fighting in the keep. I had the scepter... and then the fae warriors started appearing. One of them grabbed me and the scepter flew out of my hands. We struggled... and somehow he ended up dead on top of me." She shuddered at the memory and glanced toward the foot of the bed at Gray. "Then Gray was there, and you all showed up as well and there was fighting all around us."

She looked to the queen with regret. "At one point, I saw you and Izzy surrounded by fae warriors, and I-I thought ... Oh, I'm so sorry I talked you into leaving the hidden chamber, Queen Beatrice," she blurted in a rush. "If it wouldn't have been for my stupid idea to try to use the scepter, you would never have been put into such a dangerous situation."

The queen came around the bed to Alyssa's side and took her hand. "You have nothing to be sorry about, my dear. Your *stupid idea* saved us all in the end."

Alyssa blinked. "It did?"

Isabella's mouth dropped open. "Aly, don't you remember using the Scepter of Fire?"

"The scepter? No, I ... did I? I recall looking around and thinking we were all in big trouble, that something needed to be done, and fast. And then I remembered something Niall had said to me earlier—that I should hold the scepter in my hands, step up to the wall, and..."

"And what?" Valian asked when she paused.

Alyssa glanced at him, a vision of standing on the rampart

with the scepter suddenly clear in her mind. "And change my destiny," she whispered.

Valian tilted his head, a curious look in his eyes and a half-smile playing about his lips. "Huh. Who would've thought that Niall would be capable of such sage advice?"

"Valian, don't be unkind," Isabella chastised.

"Who, me?" he replied with a chuckle. "I said it was sage advice, didn't I?"

Alyssa shook her head and continued. "Anyway, I retrieved the scepter and walked to the wall. I closed my eyes and held it high, tried to center my thoughts on it ... but then nothing happened. That's when I started to panic, and I remember thinking that we were all done for, that Wysteria would be destroyed." She gave Isabella a miserable look. "That Izzy and I would never get home, never see our families again."

"Oh, Aly," Isabella said, leaning in for a quick hug. "You must have felt so alone, and so scared. I know *I* was terrified."

Alyssa nodded, overwhelmed with emotion. Then she cleared her throat, and in a flash, the puzzle pieces of those final moments at the wall began to slip into place. "I-I waited for what seemed like an eternity... and then I felt it. Yes. I felt the scepter suddenly come to life in my hands. It was like nothing I've ever experienced. I could actually feel its power shooting through me. And then ... then I heard a voice in my head, and it was like I wasn't there on the rampart any longer but flying out over the kingdom." She pressed her fingers to her eyes briefly. "I can't explain it, but I could *see* the fighting ... literally everywhere. And there was light, brilliant light ... and the voice was saying 'send the light to push back the darkness ... become the light.'"

"Extraordinary," Queen Beatrice murmured.

"I'm guessing that's about the time you lit up like a human candle," Isabella said with a laugh.

Alyssa raised her eyebrows. "What are you talking about?"

"It's true, Alyssa," Gray said. "It was like someone switched on a massive light inside you. You were almost translucent with it.

It was the damnedest thing I've ever seen, and I've seen some pretty weird-ass stuff, believe me."

"I, however, have witnessed the spectacle once before," Queen Beatrice said with a raised eyebrow. "When little Alice wielded the scepter over a century ago."

Valian nodded. "This was the same—the light inside you growing, getting brighter and brighter."

"Yeah, and then it shot out in all directions," Isabella added. "I had to cover my eyes or go blind. I'm not exaggerating, either. I'm surprised you didn't go up in flames."

Alyssa shook her head. "All I remember is feeling the strangest sense of tranquility. I couldn't even hear the battle anymore or feel the wind or the cold. It was like being wrapped in a layer of warmth and serenity." She frowned as she recalled one last thing. "Become the reckoning ..." she murmured.

"What did you say, honey?" Isabella asked.

Alyssa blinked and shook her head again. "It's just the last thing I remember, the voice in my head saying 'become the reckoning.'"

"Well, I'd say that's about what you did," Valian said. "When that last explosion of light winked out, every enemy still fighting was completely gone ... all over the kingdom."

"Really?"

Valian smiled. "Really. You sent the light to push back the darkness, Alyssa. Just like the voice in your head said to do. Leaving nothing left but ash in its place."

"Huh. I guess I'm glad I don't remember that part of it," Alyssa said with a half-hearted laugh. But then another thought came to her. "What about the Red King? Was he... turned to ash as well?"

Gray and Valian exchanged looks before Gray finally gave her an answer. "To be honest, we don't know. Those who were already dead weren't affected by the blast, and Aramond wasn't found among the dead. We really have no way of knowing if he was turned to ash with the rest of his army or not. Alexi took a squad of soldiers out this morning to continue searching the outer areas. But I can tell you that as far as we know, Aramond hasn't been seen since the fighting ended."

Alyssa frowned. "I see."

Gray blew out a breath. "I know that's not the outcome we were all hoping for, but even if he escaped the scepter's power, he has nowhere to go. There's a faction in Roseland that have been waiting for his demise for a very long time. He doesn't dare go back there."

"On a brighter note, Niall did find that little weasel Richter," Isabella explained cheerfully. "Evidently, he'd been tortured and his body dumped on the battlefield outside Tarkington Forest," she added in a conspiratorial, if somewhat gleeful tone.

"For the love of the Oracles, Isabella," Valian exclaimed with an astonished look. "Really?"

"What?"

"Exactly how is that a brighter note?"

Isabella crossed her arms and stuck her nose in the air. "Okay, maybe it was a poor choice of words, but the man was a cretin. Alexi said Richter got no more than he deserved."

Valian rolled his eyes. "Of course he did."

Gray laughed out loud. "Alexi's just pissed that he didn't get to mete out Richter's punishment himself. He's afraid that Niall beat him to it."

"Niall? I thought you said he *found* Richter's body?" Alyssa said with wide eyes.

Gray nodded. "He did, or so he says. Niall also said he didn't know who killed Richter, but Alexi's skeptical."

"And bloodthirsty with a need for vengeance," Valian added.

"Hey, he's your cousin."

"Yes. And my cross to bear."

The queen cleared her throat. "Gentlemen, I think that's quite sufficient. Alyssa has had enough distress over the last few days without adding your morbid foolishness into the mix." She smiled and patted Alyssa hand. "I'm sorry you've had such an ordeal since arriving in our realm, my dear. I hope it hasn't soured you on Artemysia and that you'll come back for a visit now and again."

"I-I would like that very much, Your Majesty." Alyssa squeezed Isabella's hand. "Does this mean that Izzy and I can finally go home?"

"Of course you can. You could leave as soon as tomorrow morning, if you'd like. However, I would suggest staying a day or two to get your equilibrium back." The queen looked around the room. "But I think it's time the rest of us leave—"

"Wait," Isabella cut in. "What about the scepter? If Aly is the only one that can wield it, what will happen to it?"

Queen Beatrice glanced at Gray and then turned to Alyssa. "Though the scepter can only be used in this realm, it cannot remain here. It would not be safe. At present, the threat has been vanquished, but there may come a time when we will need the scepter's power again. But as I'm sure Alyssa has had her fill of it by now, I will speak to the Oracles about sending it to some other realm for its care and safeguarding."

"No!" Alyssa blurted before she could stop herself. She took a calming breath before speaking. "Um... what I mean is, I would be honored to take the scepter back to New York with me." The queen's expression didn't change, but there was a calculating look in her dark, brown eyes, and Alyssa got the feeling she was weighing options in her head. "Look, my family was charged with its care over a century ago. I'll admit that we've certainly dropped the ball over the generations by not passing down its history and significance, but I'm asking for a chance to make that right. If you will allow me to take it home with me, I promise that this time, not only will I guard it well, but its importance will never be forgotten again."

Queen Beatrice glanced at Gray with a speculative look.

"As always, it's your call," he said with a shrug. He gave Alyssa a warm smile and winked. "But I have no problem whatsoever with sending the scepter back with her."

"Please," Alyssa whispered, and then held her breath when the queen turned back to her.

After a long moment, the queen finally nodded. "Very well, descendant of Alice. If you feel that strongly about it, you may take the scepter with you when you go."

Alyssa breathed a sigh of relief. "Thank you, Your Majesty. You won't regret your decision."

"Hey, does this mean that Valian can come back to New York with us?" Isabella asked with a giddy grin.

"Isabella," Valian replied with a warning tone.

But Queen Beatrice chuckled. "Yes, Isabella. The Chancellor and I have already had that discussion. I've agreed that, should Alyssa decide to continue in her role as custodian of the scepter, I will allow him to return to New York in a supervisory capacity."

Isabella bounced up and down on her toes and clapped her hands before practically leaping into Valian's arms.

"However," the queen said in a stern tone, stopping Isabella's jubilation in its tracks. "With the Red King defeated, the two kingdoms will soon be united under my banner. And as Chancellor of Wysteria—and now over all of Artemysia—Valian will be required to come back to this realm much more frequently than in the past. There is much work to be done."

"Can I come with him?" Isabella asked with a hopeful look. When Valian scrubbed his hands over his face, she frowned at him. "Not every time, just once in a while. I do have a business to run in New York, you know."

Alyssa laughed out loud as the queen struggled to maintain a straight face.

"You may come back for a visit any time you wish, Isabella," Queen Beatrice finally said.

"Hold on. Wait just a minute," Alyssa said slowly, as her smile faded to be replaced by a narrow-eyed look aimed at the queen. "If you'd already had that conversation with Valian, then that means you were *expecting* me to take the scepter." Pointing an accusing finger, Alyssa laughed out loud. "You were bluffing with all that stuff about speaking to the Oracles for other options, weren't you?"

The queen drew herself up and her face gave nothing away. "Monarchs never bluff… unless of course they know the odds." Then an impish grin spread across her face that had her warm, brown eyes sparkling. "I had hope, my dear. I always have hope." Looking around the room, the queen nodded. "Now, we all have things to do before lunchtime, so I suggest we get to them. I will have Gryphon gather your belongings and bring you a change of clothes, Alyssa."

When no one made a move, the queen clapped her hands in a brisk fashion. "That would be a royal order, people. Now move."

As her visitors said their goodbyes and filtered toward the door, Gray came to Alyssa's side. He'd always seemed so strong and self-assured, but there was now an uncertainty, a hesitation in the way he reached out and took her hand. "You… you are truly the most beautiful, amazing woman, Alyssa Montague. We are… *I* am so grateful to have met you. Like the queen said, I hope you'll come back and visit. Or at least let me come to New York and perhaps take you to dinner. I'd like to get to know you better, without all the fighting and intrigue to distract us."

Alyssa's breath caught at the intimate look that came into his eyes. She studied his handsome face for a moment before grinning up at him. "I'd like that, Gray. I think I'm going to need some time to digest everything that's happened. My life has changed dramatically in ways I could never have imagined. But I would like that very much."

"That's good. Yes. Excellent." The prince stammered as he beamed back at her. "Well, I guess we'll talk later, then." Leaning down, he tentatively pressed his lips to her forehead before giving her another brilliant grin and walking away.

Alyssa watched him leave the room, and a thought came to her as the queen prepared to follow him. "Queen Beatrice?"

The queen came back to her side. "What is it, my dear?"

"I-I have another small request, if it's not too much trouble."

The queen smoothed Alyssa's hair back off of her face in a motherly gesture. "What is it you need?"

Alyssa fidgeted. She wasn't certain how her request would go over, but she plowed ahead anyway. "I was wondering if it would be possible to speak with Lord Niall in private before heading home."

Queen Beatrice tilted her head and studied Alyssa with a half-smile. "I suppose that could be arranged. I'll send Gryphon in with your clothes directly. Why don't you get dressed and join us in the dining room for lunch, and in the meantime, I'll see about contacting the High Lord." The queen started to turn away, but stopped, a look of concern darkening her eyes. "I don't want you to be disappointed, Alyssa. But you do realize that if Lord Niall refuses the invitation, I cannot compel him to come. He *is* High Lord of the Twilight Court. It will have to be his choice."

Alyssa laughed out loud. "Trust me, I understand that all too well. I've found that Niall is completely unpredictable and only does what he wants to do. The thing is, Niall and I... well, we got off to a really rocky start. After all, he did deliver me right into Aramond's clutches the first time we met." Alyssa's humor faded. "But he also saved my life. And when I was conflicted about all the destiny stuff, about feeling forced to use the scepter as a weapon, he made me see that it was possible to follow my *own* destiny. Without that, I'm not sure this would've turned out as it did. I just want to thank him."

"I'm sure Lord Niall would appreciate the sentiment. Now, I'll see you at lunch." The queen patted her hand and turned away, leaving Alyssa to wonder what Niall's answer would be.

However, as lunchtime came and went, and the day progressed into early evening, there had been no word from the High Lord. Alyssa wasn't all that surprised at his lack of response, but it still stung a bit. And it saddened her that she wouldn't be able to thank him or to see him one last time.

But there wasn't really a moment to ponder Niall's snub, as there was much to discuss before returning to New York. To that end, she and Isabella decided to stay in Wysteria for another couple of days to sort out some very necessary issues. Like the security of the scepter, which was a priority for them all. It was clear that Alyssa couldn't just take it home and put it back into her office curio cabinet. If her present security system had been insufficient to keep Gray and Alexi out, it obviously wouldn't be adequate to house the scepter in any secure way going forward. It was decided that Valian would install a hidden safe that would then be protected by magicks, much like the queen's secure room in the palace. He would also be nearby, providing a second layer of security.

With everything finally settled and the return home scheduled for the following morning, Alyssa could barely contain her excitement. But when she entered her chamber to get ready for bed and saw the steaming cup of hot chocolate that Gryphon had left for her on the nightstand, she realized that leaving this wonderland would also be bittersweet.

Gryphon. Bless his heart.

Most of Alyssa's adventures in Artemysia had taken place in Roseland as she struggled to get to the White Palace. She hadn't spent much time with the royal family, or Alexi and Valian, but over the last couple days found them all to be caring, wonderful people. And Gryphon was no exception. The chamber elf had shown her much kindness and given her laughter and joy with his dry wit. As she lifted the cup of cocoa to her lips, she realized that she was going to miss them all more than they knew, especially Gryphon.

By the time she'd finished the last drop of hot chocolate and climbed into the huge, four-poster bed, visions of home danced in her head as her eyelids grew heavy, and she finally drifted into sleep.

Twenty-Five

Alyssa smiled at Mrs. Davis as she handed over the receipt for the pricy watercolor the woman had just purchased. "Thanks, Gloria. I'll have the painting delivered to the Fifty-Eighth street address by the end of the week."

"Perfect. God, I can't wait to see Alan's face when it's delivered." The woman gave a throaty laugh and pulled on her leather gloves. "I'm telling you, he's going to pop a vein."

Alyssa didn't know if that was a good thing or not, but if Gloria Davis was willing to drop a couple grand on a watercolor for her latest husband—in a very long string of them—who was she to question? "Enjoy."

"Tootle-loo." The socialite gave a wave as she headed for the door where a tall, well-dressed gentleman had just stepped into the gallery. He held the door open for her, and Alyssa shook her head as she watched the woman give him a flirtatious, mega-watt smile before slipping past him toward her waiting car at the curb. It led Alyssa to wonder just how long the latest Mr. Davis would last.

Stretching the stiffness from her limbs, Alyssa stifled a yawn. It had been a really long, really busy day, and she was dog-tired. March had come in with a roar, bringing wind and torrents of rain, and with it, a steady stream of customers. But the weather had mellowed in recent days and it looked like the month would end with a whimper, just in time for Easter. The sky outside was just beginning to be bathed in the colors of approaching twilight as the sun dropped over the horizon, and glancing at her wrist watch, Alyssa heaved a sigh. Another thirty minutes or so and they could close up shop and head home for the evening.

Home.

She still hadn't completely adjusted to the idea of being home, Alyssa mused as she watched her gallery manager, Lenore wander over to the late arrival, engaging him in an animated conversation. Nearly two and a half months had passed since Alyssa had come back through the White Palace's tunnel portal with the Scepter of Fire—accompanied by Isabella and Valian—and returned to New York City.

It had been an unexpectedly emotional farewell. Though she'd been anxious to get home, it had been harder than she'd thought it would be to say goodbye to Gray, Alexi, Queen Beatrice—and especially Gryphon. Her only regret was not being able to speak with Niall before they'd gone. The High Lord hadn't even acknowledged the message the queen had sent to him, which hadn't really surprised Alyssa, but for some reason, she couldn't quite let it go.

But if her exit from Wysteria had been emotional and unsettled, her reentry into New York life had been exhausting and chaotic. To be fair, from their families' point of view, she and Isabella had seemed to vanish from the face of the earth on New Year's Eve, and hadn't resurfaced for a full two weeks. With no word from either of them, naturally, both families had been frantic with worry. Missing person reports had been filed, searches had been made, and the like. And the story she and Isabella had concocted was full of more holes than a slab of Swiss cheese. But fortunately, Valian had been there to lend a hand with memory adjustments here and there to help fill in the voids. In the end, it had been enough to calm the storm and provide acceptable closure for everyone involved.

Everyone, it seemed, with the exception of Alyssa herself.

It wasn't anything too noticeable in the beginning, just a disjointed feeling of being slightly out of step with her life, which she figured was understandable considering everything that had happened to her in Artemysia. But it was as if there was something missing, something intangible yet vital that had been there briefly, but gone again in a wink. She'd thrown herself into her work at the gallery with a vengeance, yet hadn't quite been able to shake the feeling.

She'd tried talking to Isabella about it a couple of times, but her friend's advice had been just to give it some time. However, it was closing in on three months, and she was beginning to wonder if time would solve the problem at all, or if this odd sense of melancholy would dog her for the rest of her days. A reminder of something found and then lost again.

And then there were the dreams.

They'd been practically a nightly occurrence during the first two months she'd been home. Some were detailed snippets of things that had happened or conversations she'd had during her time in that other realm. Others were twisted versions that left her gasping and drenched in sweat in the middle of the night, unable to go back to sleep.

The dreams had seemed to come less and less frequently over the last few weeks, but just when she was beginning to think she may finally be done with them, she'd dreamt of Wysteria again the previous night. She was hoping the lovely dinner she'd shared with Gray here in the city over the weekend had been the catalyst and nothing more.

They'd met several times since she'd been back—always on her turf—going to the theater or having dinner, getting to know each other and catching up on happenings in both their worlds. Gray had causally mentioned the possibility of her visiting Wysteria on a couple of occasions, but only in passing. He never pushed, as if he knew she wasn't prepared to make a commitment for a trip just yet. Smiling to herself, Alyssa pictured the prince's handsome face. He was such a kind, compassionate man. She enjoyed their time together very much, though she couldn't help but wonder how much further their relationship could evolve, given that he was the future king of his realm, and her life was here.

Alyssa sighed as she watched Lenore and her striking customer meander around the galley. As she studied the man, she began to think he had a familiar look about him, though she couldn't remember having seen him in the gallery before. Maybe it was in his stance, so tall and confident. Or the way he crossed his arms as he listened to Lenore explaining about a certain painting or a piece of sculpture. However, he did remind her of someone. She couldn't put her finger on it, but for a moment, the feeling was quite strong. Then they wandered into the next room where the latest collection of blown glass artwork was displayed, and the feeling passed.

Before she could ponder it further, she was distracted by Isabella and Valian coming through the gallery door. Being back in the city, Valian was once again glamoured. And though he was still a very attractive man, oddly enough, Alyssa found that she preferred his true visage to the one he wore here in New York. Isabella didn't seem to mind, though she'd confided to Alyssa weeks ago that she made him remove the glamour whenever they were alone together. The thought made Alyssa grin as they approached the counter.

"Hey, pal," Isabella greeted her. "How's the art business?"

"Booming." Alyssa ran a hand through her hair and laughed. "I'm not kidding. It's been crazy for a Wednesday. We've been swamped all day, and for that matter, most of the month. You'd think the holiday rush hadn't come and gone. It's bizarre. I was just fantasizing about going home, taking a hot bath, and putting my feet up."

"Why don't you come out for dinner with us first?" Isabella

suggested. "Val and I were going to try that new Thai place up on Amsterdam near The Met."

Valian smiled. "It is supposed to be very good. Come and join us for a meal."

"Oh, guys, that's really sweet, but I am seriously bushed, and frankly, a little 'peopled out'. All I really want to do is go home and veg in the peace and quiet."

Isabella stuck out her lip. "Aw, come on, Aly. Just a couple of hours. It's almost closing time. We can wait for you, if you want. Besides, we haven't gotten together for weeks. I miss you."

"I know. I miss you, too, Izzy. We've both been pretty busy." Alyssa shook her head. "But not tonight, okay? I'm so tired I wouldn't be good company, anyway. Rain check?"

Isabella pouted another moment or two before blowing out a breath and nodding. "Alright, alright," she groused. "But soon, yes?"

"Absolutely, bestie."

Isabella glanced at Valian and gave him a nudge.

"Yes, yes, I'm getting there," he said and turned to Alyssa with a tentative look. "Alyssa... I know you had dinner with Gray last weekend, but Isabella and I are going to Wysteria for a few days next week, and were wondering if you'd like to go with us."

Alyssa hesitated briefly. She hadn't left the city since she'd returned from Artemysia, and she did want to return for a visit. Yet something kept holding her back. "You know, it's kind of you to think of me, but—"

"Oh, don't say no again," Isabella whined. "The queen asked about you the last time we were there, and I didn't know what to say to her."

Alyssa frowned. "It's not that I don't want to go back, Izzy. I'm just not sure I'm ready."

"You say that every time we ask. It's been almost three months, Aly. And you haven't left the city in all that time. It's like you keep putting it off. Why?"

"Isabella," Valian murmured. "We talked about this. No badgering, remember?"

Isabella threw her arms in the air. "I know," she exclaimed. "But there are so many changes, and she's missing it all."

"Nevertheless, it's not your decision, love." Turning to Alyssa, Valian gave her an apologetic look. "Should you change your mind, just give us a call. We'd be happy to stop by and collect you on our way."

"Thanks, Valian. I'll keep that in mind."

He winked at her and then eyed Isabella. "In the meantime, I think I'd better get some food into this one, as I do believe she's getting cranky."

"Oh, you're so funny," Isabella said with a roll of her eyes. "Really. You're killing me here."

Alyssa laughed. "You two have a wonderful evening. And Izzy, I promise I'll think about going with you next week. How about that?"

Isabella leaned across the counter and gave Alyssa a quick squeeze. "Give me a call tomorrow. Maybe we can carve out some time for lunch before the weekend, okay?"

"Sounds good."

Alyssa watched them head for the door and gave a wave as they left the gallery. What an unlikely couple they made. Her best friend and the Elven warrior she'd fallen for. Early on, Alyssa had thought it was Alexi that had caught Isabella's interest from their first meeting at the New Year's Eve gala, but at some point during the adventure in Artemysia, Valian seemed to have stolen her heart.

With a shake of her head, she turned as Lenore and her customer came in from the next room. The gallery manager was carrying a stunning, blown glass sculpture. Its swirls of color—midnight blues and deep purples—were shot through with shimmering bursts of silver. It created a sense of nightfall, that sliver of time between sundown and complete darkness, very nearly resembling the sky outside the gallery window now.

"Mr. Fairchild, this is the gallery owner, Alyssa Montague," Lenore said as they approached the counter. "Aly, this is Mr. Fairchild. He's been in town on business and has just chosen this blown glass sculpture to take home with him when he goes."

"It's a pleasure to meet you, Mr. Fairchild." Alyssa again studied the sculpture with its captivating mix of colors before turning to the man with a smile. "You've chosen a lovely piece. I hope you'll be very happy with it."

The man returned her smile with one of his own, his emerald-green eyes sparkling with humor. "I'm certain I will, Ms. Montague. It reminded me of twilight, my favorite time of day. Those moments before darkness falls and the sky is streaked with the deep colors of mystery and intrigue," he replied in a deep, melodic voice. "I'll be sure to put it in a place of honor when I return home."

His poetic words and the tenor of his voice buzzed along Alyssa's skin as he spoke, and the intimate look in his bright, green eyes had that sense of *déjà vu* washing over her again.

"Have you been into the gallery before, Mr. Fairchild?" Alyssa asked in a puzzled tone. "You seem... familiar to me."

The man tilted his head as he studied her face, and the feeling intensified. "Your face is very familiar to me as well," he said after a moment. "But no, I've not been in your gallery before today, but then, I don't get to New York as often as I'd like. Perhaps we met in another lifetime."

When they continued to stare at each other, Lenore's uncomfortable laughter broke the silence. "Well, would you like us to ship this piece for you, Mr. Fairchild? Or shall I wrap it up for you to take now?" she asked.

"I'll take it with me, Lenore. Thank you," he replied without taking his eyes off of Alyssa.

"Alrighty then," Lenore replied hesitantly. "I guess I'll just go package it up and get it ready."

As the gallery manager hurried from the showroom, the awkward silence fell over the room again, and after a moment,

Alyssa cleared her throat. "How would you like to pay for the piece today, Mr. Fairchild?"

The man pulled an elaborately embossed leather wallet from his overcoat breast pocket and removed four crisp one hundred dollar bills, laying them neatly on the counter. "I assume cash is acceptable."

"Of course." Alyssa took her time in making out his receipt, all the while feeling like he was watching her every move. But when she finished and handed it to him with his change, he seemed almost disinterested.

"So, have you been in the city long?" she asked as he pocketed both.

"No. Not long at all," he murmured absently, gazing around the showroom.

While Alyssa observed him, she kept thinking that there was something about him... something a little off. But she couldn't quite get a hold of it. He'd paid for the sculpture in cash and was impeccably dressed, as any prosperous businessman would be. Nothing really out of the ordinary there. He had not one auburn hair out of place, and the smooth skin of his angular face held just the hint of a five o'clock shadow.

Everything about him seemed perfect. And maybe that's the problem, she thought. He seems just a little too perfect. But for some reason, it was the bright, green of his eyes that captivated her, and she couldn't look away. "Lenore said you were here on business. What kind of business are you in?"

Those mesmerizing eyes twinkled with amusement. "Oh, I have great many interests, but with this trip, my business in your fair city is actually more along personal lines."

Alyssa got the feeling he was being intentionally vague, but before she could respond, Lenore returned with his packaged sculpture.

"All set. Enjoy," she said as she handed him the box.

"I will, Lenore. Thank you for your assistance."

When the awkward silence returned, the gallery manager

looked back and forth between them. "Well, have a good trip back to... uh, back home. Yeah. I'm, uh, gonna... I have stuff to do... in the office." With that, Lenore scurried out of the showroom like her feet were on fire.

"It was a pleasure to meet you, Mr. Fairchild," Alyssa said as the man began to back slowly toward the door, his eyes never leaving hers. "Come back and see us the next time you're in town."

"I will, if you will," he murmured with a half-smile as he reached the door.

"I-I beg your pardon?"

Alyssa watched the half-smile morph into a *very* familiar wicked grin, and her heart stuttered in her chest as the glamour he wore disappeared.

"*Niall?*" she whispered.

"It was lovely to see you again, darling Alyssa. Please. Don't be a stranger."

And then he was gone.

Her astonishment held her rooted to the spot for only a couple of seconds before she was sprinting after him. She flew out the door, looking up and down the street in both directions, calling his name.

But he'd vanished.

Alyssa didn't know how long she stood there in the middle of the sidewalk with her pulse racing and her heart beating out of control, staring out at the darkened streets. But when she finally returned to the gallery, all sorts of questions were spinning wildly in her head. She closed and locked the door, then turned and leaned against it in stunned silence.

Niall was in New York City, he'd actually been in her gallery for the last thirty minutes, and though she'd felt the familiarity, she hadn't recognized him because of the glamour he'd worn. But there had been clues. He'd dropped them like breadcrumbs.

It reminded me of twilight, my favorite time of day...

And the name the High Lord of the Twilight Court had

chosen to give to her. Fairchild. Child of Fair... or *fair folk...* His voice, his unique green eyes. How had she not seen it?

He hadn't come to say goodbye to her when she'd left Artemysia, yet he'd obviously sought her out here. Why? And why wait until he was ready to leave the gallery to reveal his identity?

"Hey. Where did this come from?" Lenore had come out of the back and was standing at the counter with a small leather satchel in her hands.

Alyssa walked over and took the bag from Lenore, laying it on the counter and running her fingers over the Twilight Court's crest tooled into the leather flap. Unbuckling the clasps, she lifted the cover and peered into the satchel. Her breath caught in her throat, and her eyes began to fill as she reached inside and pulled out her shimmering, silver cocktail dress. She'd left it at Kaleb's cabin the day Niall and Violet had escorted her to the White Palace. She'd forgotten to retrieve it from the cabin before they'd left.

Niall had brought it back to her.

"Pretty dress," Lenore commented.

"Yes. It is."

"It kinda looks like the one you wore the night of your New Year's Eve party." Lenore picked up the satchel and rummaged around inside. "There's something else in here." Pulling a sealed parchment envelope out of the bag, she turned it over and frowned. "Huh. Fancy. And it's addressed to you, Aly."

Laying her cocktail dress on the counter, Alyssa took the envelope and popped open the seal. With her heart in her throat, she slid the creased letter out of the envelope and unfolded it. Her tears welled and began to roll down her cheeks, and a smile spread across her face as she read the few words written there.

Be fierce, darling Alyssa ... be the warrior I know you to be ...

Mold your own destiny and embrace it without fear ...

~N

Alyssa started to chuckle, and then to laugh as her tears continued to fall. Leave it to Niall to understand exactly what her problem had been since she'd returned home, the fears and doubts that had plagued her day after day.

Like the ordeal with the scepter, she'd been terrified of a destiny not of her own making, a fate she couldn't control. It was the reason she'd been putting off a return to Artemysia. He'd told her to change that destiny, to mold it to her liking, yet after the war had ended and she'd come home, she'd forgotten those words. She supposed that this was his not-so-subtle reminder.

"Aly? What's this all about?" Lenore asked with concern, bringing Alyssa back to the moment. "What's wrong?"

Shaking her head, Alyssa swiped at her tears and gave the woman a quick, joyous hug. "Nothing's wrong, Lenore. Not anymore. But I think I may be taking a few days off next week for a short trip out of town."

"Uh, that's... great," Lenore replied slowly, looking as if she was suddenly a bit concerned for Alyssa's mental state. "I think that may be a really good idea. And speaking of, why don't you go on and head out now? I can close up the gallery, and you look like you need to go home and have a seriously large glass of wine... or maybe even a valium or three."

Alyssa laughed again and felt something loosen inside of her. "Oh, Lenore, you have no idea. But I will take you up on heading home now. I have a phone call to make."

And a destiny to mold to my liking.

About the Author

A native of Oregon, Joni Sauer-Folger spent twenty-two years with an airline traveling and moving around the country before settling down near the beautiful Pacific Ocean with her three very spoiled cats. When she's not spending quality time with the characters she creates, she enjoys gardening, crafting, and working in local theater.

For more information, visit:
www.jonisauerfolger.com

Also by Joni Folger

WRITTEN AS JONI FOLGER

<u>River Bend Vineyard Cozy Mystery series</u>

Grapes of Death

Of Merlot and Murder

Performance of a Deadly Vintage

Champagne Toast, Murder Chaser

<u>Enchanted Affairs Cozy Mystery series</u>

Monkshood, Tea, & Murder

WRITTEN AS J. G. SAUER

<u>Immortal Series</u>

Immortal Reckoning – Novella Prequel

Immortal Obsession

Immortal Savior

Immortal Ascending

<u>Guardian Series:</u>

Tarnished Guardian – Novella Prequel

Search for the Mystic Stone

<u>Looking Glass Series:</u>

New Years Through the Looking Glass

Madness Through the Looking Glass

9 781648 394485